PRAISE FOR *MATEWAN GARDEN CLUB*

"Iris Underwood takes readers on a journey through life in the Appalachians. It's as if you are sitting on the porch with them, listening to their stories, and sharing their struggles. A must read."
—Randy Jorgensen, Page One Corp.

"A wonderfully written story of vivid, endearing characters who depict life in the early 1900s within a small West Virginia coal-mining town—an unforgettable picture of immigrants and refugees building lifelong friendships by trials and triumphs and a brighter future for generations to come."
—Kathi Taylor-Sherrill, director,
Matewan Public Library

"Family. Friends. Faith. Iris Underwood takes her reader on a flower-strewn, multicultural-generational saga through and around the Appalachian town of Matewan. My book club and my garden club will love this book."
—Catherine Baurhenn, Port Sanilac Book Club,
Port Sanilac Garden Club

"In *Matewan Garden Club*, Iris Underwood takes the reader on a meandering journey through some of the most complex and beautiful landscape in the Eastern United States. Built around the central thread of horticulture, the metanarrative is one of growth in, through, and in spite of all of the challenges thrown into the lives of its central characters. It is imaginative, poetic, and symbolic while still being as true to the story as any book dares to get."
—Burton Webb, president,
University of Pikeville

MATEWAN
GARDEN CLUB

IRIS UNDERWOOD

Iris Underwood

BELLE ISLE BOOKS
www.belleislebooks.com

ISBN: 978-1-958754-27-6
Library of Congress Control Number: 2023902389

Cover Illustration by Ruth Forman
Interior Illustrations by Linda Hodge

Designed by Sami Langston
Project managed by Jennifer DeBell

Printed in the United States of America

Published by
Belle Isle Books (an imprint of Brandylane Publishers, Inc.)
5 S. 1st Street
Richmond, Virginia 23219

BELLE ISLE BOOKS
www.belleislebooks.com

belleislebooks.com | brandylanepublishers.com

In memory of Ollie Jane Hunt McCoy Smith

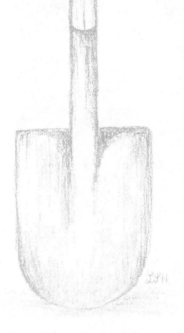

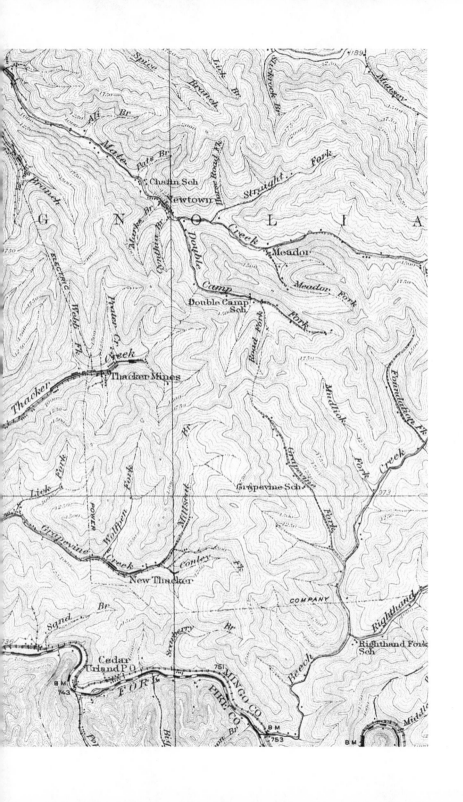

Part One
HENRY
APRIL 1932

Lord knows I've forgiven Pa. Ag'in and ag'in. But I cain't love him.

Granny'd say, "Henry, forgive your Daddy." But she knew I couldn't love him. She's been gone almost three years, the worst on Mommy and me since the mine caved in on Pa nine years ago and made him bedfast. He didn't like Granny washin' him and changin' his bed, but she did it anyway with kindness and patience.

I hated Pa for infectin' Granny with hepatitis. I think he meant to kill her—the only way he'd get her out of this house so's he could lay his hands on 'shine. He didn't care about Granny, and he doesn't care about infectin' Mommy and me neither. Doc Bentley told me what to do with Pa's bandages and beddin' so's I protect myself and mommy.

Pastor Hickman says, "Keep forgiving, Henry. Love will come." Sometimes I see in Mommy's eyes what I think is love for Pa, and cain't believe it. She's never said so, but that must be why she's stayed put by his bedside, takin' his cussin' and threats. He's too feeble to hit her anymore.

I smell Pa's stench and want to hate him, but I promised Granny I wouldn't. "Hate'll kill you like it's killin' your pa," she said.

I study the quilt Granny hung on a clothesline between Pa's bed and mine the day Sheriff Taylor brought Pa and Mommy home from the hospital. Pa's been the same miserable man every day-break since.

When Granny helped Mommy take care of him, Pa didn't dare let a moonshiner crawl through this window with whiskey. They'd face the muzzle of Granny's shotgun, the one she called "Old Faithful." Before the accident, my pa was the first miner in line to cash his paycheck every Friday, so everyone called him Friday. And "Friday" Blankenship couldn't be more hateful. Since Granny died, Pa's swapped everything worth anything for 'shine, and we don't keep one dollar in this place for a moonshiner to steal.

A whiff of Granny's peonies blooming outside the window blows in with the birdsong. It's about the last of April's cooler days, when the redbud blooms, just like the day of Pa's accident.

A sign. Doc Bentley's right. Now that I've graduated from high school, I've got to stand up for Mommy. I'm her only kin who will.

So, it's time for me to be a man. I'm goin' to work full-time for Olaf Semenov at Hunt's Feed & Seed.

Now that high school's behind, Olaf's teachin' me more botany from his five Russian books. He keeps my five notebooks of his lessons locked in his big office safe along with my pocket money, eighteen letters from his grandfather, and hundreds more from Fodor Petrov.

Petrov is one of Olaf's friends from Russia, and he lives outside New York City. Every week Olaf gives me one of Petrov's letters to read aloud. Afterward, I ask questions about it, and he answers. My questions are mostly about Polya Tsvetov, the Semenov family's farm in Russia that Olaf and his mother Natalia ran from. Petrov left Russia three years earlier. He's seventy-eight years old, six years older than Olaf's father would be now. Sometimes Olaf cries when he talks about their farm, Petrov, and his father.

When Olaf and his mother fled Russia, Petrov was the first friend who gave them shelter in this country. Now, his letters to Olaf talk about the latest botanical discoveries and organizations, especially in Appalachia—our place in the world. And heaps of encouragement. *Remember, Olaf,* Petrov ends every letter, *you are never alone.*

Olaf says that although he didn't publish a book on botany, Fodor Petrov's letters are just as valuable for any botanical student. "Ve are never too old to learn," my boss says. Petrov sends Olaf a letter or postcard every week. He is to Olaf what Olaf is to me.

Monday through Saturday, Olaf Semenov opens a book and teaches me about one of his favorite botanists. Yesterday, it was his *Gardener's and Florist's Dictionary* by Philip Miller, an Englishman.

"Many botanists agree that England has contributed more to botanical studies and gardening than any other country in the world," Olaf said.

"More than America?"

He smiled. "Oh, yes. Remember, England is America's mother country. How old is the United States of America?"

"One hundred and fifty-six years."

"And how old is England?"

"Over a thousand years. Guess America's still a baby."

Olaf pointed to the publication date of the book. "Printed in 1724. How many years before our forefathers signed the Constitution of the United States?"

"Sixty-three."

Then Olaf turned the pages to a painted picture of an orange daylily.

"Why, that ole flower grows all along our roads and ditches!" I said.

He beamed and said, "*Hemerocallis fulva,*" in his Russian accent, then shook his head. "There is no such thing as an 'ole' flower, Henry."

"Lord-a-mercy, there's so much to learn about plants."

"You are a good student. You vill learn."

Other than Mrs. Cline in third grade, Olaf's the best teacher I've ever had. No wonder. He graduated from St. Petersburg State University with a degree in agriculture, botany, and horticulture. Olaf is the fifth generation of botanists in the Semenov family.

When Olaf broods about Russia's ruin, he'll say, "I followed my father's footsteps back to my great-great grandfather, all botanists. Then Lenin and his Bolsheviks seized the University where grandfather and father were professors. Grandfather earned the honor of distinguished professor."

I could listen to him talk botany and his family's history all day. As a young woman, his Norwegian mother traveled the world with her sister hunting plants, just like Mommy hunts for ginseng and mushrooms off in these ancient hollers, branches, and forks. Olaf says his father and grandfather "traveled to distant countries to find rare and beneficial plants for health, landscaping, and agriculture."

"Remember, Henry," Olaf says, "there's healing in the leaves, roots, bark, and blooms."

"That's what Mommy says. Is that why you both love plants?"

"One reason. You vill learn the others."

One scorcher of a day in July when nobody was out and about, and I'd finished stockin' merchandise, Olaf appeared with two glasses of cold sweet tea.

"Ve shall cool down vith a spontaneous lesson," Olaf said, wiping his brow with a handkerchief.

The man never wastes a minute.

He held Philip Miller's book and led me to the end of the glass-domed counter by the brass cash register where he keeps his ledger. "Now I introduce you to John Bartram, an American botanist who built the most remarkable gardens outside Philadelphia. Ve shall visit this historic place, Henry."

"What's historic about it?"

"When my great-great grandfather, Peter Semenov, was a young botanist of twenty-eight years, he spoke vith George Vashington and Thomas Jefferson on the summer day in 1787 vhen they all visited Bartram Gardens."

"Your great-great grandfather hunted plants in America?" I'm amazed.

Olaf nodded with a gleam in his eyes under bushy eyebrows. "His interest vas insect fertilization of flowers, as vas Philip Miller's. Father and Grandfather often spoke of this chance meeting vith Mr. Vashington and Mr. Jefferson. Tell me, son, how many years ago vas that meeting?"

This is 1932. "One hundred and forty-five," I respond. Olaf knows I like math and often tests me.

He leaned closer and whispered like we were in church. "Now I hold the book my great-great grandfather held vhen he encountered Mr. Vashington amongst Bartram's collection of lilies."

Olaf opened the front cover of Phillip Miller's book. I recognized a few Russian letters in fine script with ink blotches. I've never seen a person love a book so much, other than Granny and her Bible.

He read his great-great grandfather's words in Russian and transported me to the Old Country. Then he translated: "Mr. Vashington bent his tall frame to touch an orange daylily . . ." he paused. "There is no common flower, young man, no matter vhat the botanists claim."

That's why the best part of my day is when I walk out of this sorry shack and into Hunt's Feed & Seed, Olaf's store. The only wood buildin' on Mate Street that survived the fire of 1910. Mommy was just fourteen years old and says she'll never forget the disaster. "Ashes ever'where," she'll say.

After work yesterday, I told Olaf I needed to buy a hammer to make Mommy a window box, but he knows I bought it to stand up to Pa. Olaf knows I cain't face one more day with Pa wastin' everything we have and riskin' Mommy's health, too. But Olaf says, "Forgive your father." And I do because I love Olaf more than I hate Pa.

I listen for Mommy's footfall. She's been awful quiet since Sunday. While we were in church, our neighbor Miss Daisy saw that weasel Four Fingers slinking around our house again. Like he's done before, Pa must've told him to crawl through this bedroom window. But long on Pa's ways, Mommy knew to hide her pocket money in the outhouse.

We cain't hardly ever leave this house without findin' a mess when we return. Sunday, Four Fingers tore everything to pieces, threw what dishes we'd had out of the cupboard in search of Granny's crystal vase Mommy hid way back. But the bum broke Granny's vase, and now Mommy has nothin' big and beautiful to hold her peonies and gladioli.

Precious things mean nothin' but another drink to Pa. God forgive me, but I hate Four Fingers for breakin' Granny's vase and stealin' what Mommy and I work for. I don't know how she doesn't despise Pa.

Four Fingers even emptied our dresser drawers searchin' for my wages from the seed store. Pa doesn't know Olaf helped me open a bank account when I was thirteen years old to deposit my check. And he holds my tithe and pocket cash in his office safe.

Then I helped Mommy open an account for her garden money. She hides her own tithe and pocket cash behind a loose board in the outhouse. She doubts Four Fingers will look in there. I'm not so sure. Mommy says it's not proper for Olaf to hold her tithe and cash in his safe. Guess she's right.

Cain't think of one thing we have left for my father to swap for 'shine other than Mommy's shovel. And I won't let that happen to "Tall Man" because Grandpa built it with his own hands to dig Granny's gardens. After Grandpa died, Granny gave Tall Man to Mommy because she's more than a head taller than Granny was.

Before his accident, Pa dug up the peonies Mommy brought from Granny's childhood homeplace in Kentucky. Mommy had transplanted them right next to our front steps here in Blackberry City, West Virginia. I was nine years old when Mommy and I came home from helpin' Granny can her garden for a few days at her place in Thacker Holler. Grandpa's shovel lay at the foot of the steps where Pa'd thrown it down. He was low enough to leave Tall Man right there to rust in the rain for everybody in Blackberry City to see.

Mommy went to the outhouse and cried. Like a chestnut thorn, the hurt goes deeper every time I think of Pa's wickedness.

And last Christmas Eve while Mommy and I were in church, Pa traded Spark, my coon dog, for whiskey. She was more than a hound. Spark had "personality," as Olaf says. She was the best ol' dog around Tug Fork on the West Virginia–Kentucky border. We hunted squirrel, coon, and possum with Spark. Olaf cried with me when I told him what Pa did. That time, Olaf didn't say, "Forgive your father, Henry."

But I did anyways, for Granny.

Granny's double wedding band patchwork, her Bible, and her good name are all that remain of my grandmother, Sarah McCoy Hunt. Good thing the family quilts are worthless to moonshiners, otherwise Pa would've pawned them too. More than once I've heard my father boast to Mommy's face that he's had many women and didn't love nary a one. He doesn't love anybody but hisself. I grab the hammer beneath my bed. Like Pastor Hickman said, I cain't wait for Jesus to save Pa. He's right because my father doesn't give a possum's ass about salvation.

Just like it is this April mornin', the redbud bloomed that day I carried Mommy's rusted shovel down from this place named Blackberry City. I walked along the road under the viaduct onto Mate Street, where Antillo Nenni swept the sidewalk before his father's department store. John Nenni, an Italian immigrant, opened his store before the big fire in 1910. John knew my Grandpa and likes to tell how his own father made shoes in Italy before he mended Grandpa's boots—size thirteen!

All Friday Blankenship knows to make is moonshine and misery.

"Hello, Henry!" Antillo hollered from the other side of the street. "What you got there, boy?"

I wondered if he wondered where I was goin' with Mommy's shovel. Like everybody else in Matewan and Blackberry City, he knows Mommy carries her daddy's spade to dig for pay—and folk old enough to know Henry Hunt call his shovel Tall Man, because he stood six foot five and loved to dig gardens when he wasn't loggin'.

There's no nicer people in all Tug Fork than the Nenni family, Antillo and his wife, and his mommy and daddy, John and Hazel, but I was too embarrassed to tell Antillo what happened to Mommy's shovel. So I put my head down and kept walkin'.

I felt bad bein' disrespectful. But if I opened my mouth, I'd start bawlin' my eyes out, right there on Mate Street in front of everybody.

I passed the Matewan Theater, where *The Hunchback of Notre Dame* was still playing. The sad story of poor ole deformed Quasimodo made me shiver. Mommy said I had no business watchin' scary movies.

Miss Sue Ann, the youngest member of our Matewan Garden Club, waved from behind the soda fountain in Leckie's Drugstore as she poured Crazy Ray a cup of coffee. Some folk say Ray's sweet on Sue Ann, but Mommy says Ray doesn't know how to make a good cup of coffee, and Sue Ann does.

I caught Crazy Ray's nod as he looked up from his cup. He boasted bein' the top salesman for Grace Ford Dealership when he was a sixteen-year-old Magnolia High dropout. Mommy said, "Could be, but don't believe everything Ray says, Henry."

I cain't ever walk by Leckie's window without thirstin' for Sue Ann's root beer float in the tall, frosted glass. Sue Ann's famous for the mountain of whipped cream she makes with spoonsful of cream to a peak at the top. Antillo calls Sue Ann's root beer float "The Matterhorn" because it reminds his daddy of the tall mountain on the border of Italy and Switzerland. Olaf said he and his parents skied down the Matterhorn together when he was sixteen years old. Then my boss explained what "skied" meant. It's often impossible to imagine the Semenovs' lives before they fled to America.

I turned my head away as I passed Matewan National Bank up the street from Nenni's Mercantile. Everybody in town knows I'm Friday Blankenship's son, and who Grandpa's shovel belongs to. It got heavier as I passed Missionary Baptist Church. Hoping Pastor Hickman didn't see me, I hurried by and took a deep breath before steppin' up on the large, wooden porch of Hunt's Feed & Seed.

For the first time in my nine years, I opened the right double-door to the high, wooden building. A bell jingled and I walked into the familiar scent that Mommy brings home in seed packages and chicken feed sacks.

Even then, everybody in town knew Olaf and his mother had run away from Bolsheviks and come to America. I didn't know what Bolsheviks were, but by the way Mommy and Granny talked, I knew they were bad, and Olaf and Mrs. Semenov had done something brave and good.

I walked inside and closed the door behind me. I looked up to the man who everybody said always arrived for work in a black suit, starched white shirt, and shiny black shoes, every Monday through Saturday. He stood at the front end of the long, glass-domed counter by the brass cash register. I'd seen Olaf hundreds of times through the large window on the right side of the doors. But I'd never seen him up close in his white collar and black tie.

With one hand on a book set by the cash register, Olaf bowed, waved to me, and said slow and clear, "May I help you, young man? Vhat do ve have here?"

I walked right up to the man who was my only hope for fixin' Mommy's rusted shovel. I barely understood the words Olaf spoke. Some of the boys in my class liked to poke fun at the way he talked, so that helped me guess what he said. Bein' so close to him now, I felt very little holdin' up Tall Man. Olaf's shoulders were broader and he looked younger than he did far away. He reached out a hand and said, still real clear, "May I?"

I nodded to keep that lump in my throat from lettin' loose.

Olaf gripped the long, wooden handle and crossed his eyebrows. He turned the blade side to side and said each word all by itself. "Do-you-know-who-made-this-magnificent-tool?"

From the way he handled the shovel and how his eyes looked at it, I reckoned his fancy word meant he liked Mommy's shovel. "My Grandpa, Henry Hunt."

"He vas a tall man."

How did Olaf know? "Yes, he was, and the best logger on Peter Creek."

"And a fine blacksmith."

When Olaf ran his fingers over the rusted shovel and looked me in the eye, I couldn't help but cry out, "Pa left it in the rain after he dug up Granny's peonies for whiskey. Now hit's ruint!"

Like it was special, Olaf rested the blade on the floor and held the handle with his big hand. He put his other hand on my shoulder and said, with kindness I'd never seen in a man, "Your name, son?"

"Henry Blankenship. My pa's Friday, and Gertie's my mommy. This is her pa's shovel. Mommy calls it 'Tall Man.'"

Olaf stood up straight and ran a hand over the wooden handle. Tall Man fit his body better than Mommy's because he's taller even than Mommy.

"Come vith me."

I followed the owner of Hunt's Feed & Seed through a double doorway tall and wide enough to drive Granny's old wagon through it. Lord have mercy! Feed and fertilizer bags stood stacked taller than me. Tools, from hand trowels to pruning saws, hung in neat rows on one wall. Bull-tongue plows and wooden barrels from small to large, filled with nails of many sizes, sat lined up on the floor. And oh, my goodness! The bags and barrels of seeds and grains lined up in rows on the floor like fat soldiers I'd seen in a cartoon at Matewan Theatre. I'd walked into another world.

A scoop sat in each barrel, and a large scale and another small scale on two tables took up the center of the big room like they were the king and queen of it all. I wanted to touch them, see the dials move, but I did my best to keep my eyes on Olaf.

He stood before three shelves of colorful bottles, cans, and bags in tidy rows. First, he took a tin with a green label off a shelf, then picked up a file from another, and reached for a folded cloth.

"Spar-ing-ly," Olaf said, "pour this oil on this rag and rub the vooden handle until it shines. Then pour more oil on the rag and rub the rust off the blade. Rub and rub and rub until the rust disappears. Then scrape this vhetstone on the blade's edge. Tall Man vill be as new."

I wiped my eyes and nose on my shirtsleeve. "I ain't got no money."

"You vill work for payment." Olaf pulled a hanky from his pocket and reached it to me. "Please, keep it. My father said a boy should never be vithout a handkerchief."

Nine years later, I still see the kindness in Olaf's eyes that day. And I'm never without a handkerchief.

———— ❧ ————

I stare at Granny's quilt hanging between Pa and me and shake with anger over the memory of Tall Man, left in the rain to rust. And the September morning Granny died. The wake in her house. Her funeral, where Pastor Hickman said good and true things about her. Her burial, the saddest day of my life.

Since Granny died, word of Gertie Blankenship diggin' peony and gladioli gardens spread to the bottoms and hollers of Peter Creek. And up and over Big Creek Mountain into Pikeville. Sometimes, Mommy digs the other way down Tug Fork toward Williamson. Folk call Mommy *the woman with a shovel.*

A few days after I carried Tall Man to Olaf, his mother, Mrs. Semenov, asked Mommy to dig her gardens for pay. Mommy said, "Mrs. Semenov said to please plant the 'roots' and 'corms' on the sunny side of the seed store. The woman knows her flowers, Henry."

Then Mrs. Dill, my sweetheart's mother, who's also President of Matewan Garden Club, and Mrs. Cline, my third-grade teacher, also a member of Garden Club, asked Mommy to dig their gardens for pay.

Mommy started walkin' these rocky, windin' mountain paths bloomin' tulip poplars down into Matewan. Then over the Tug into Kentucky's Blackberry Bottom and hollers. She carried Tall Man up Mate Creek's narrow branches in West Virginia to Red Jacket and Little Italy, and downhill to Blackberry City in her blue dress and brown boots. She carried Grandpa's shovel and the cash it earned in her pocket. We thought we were rich back then, and Mommy's never stopped diggin gardens since.

Then Mommy's name traveled up the road seven miles and crossed the Tug River into Freeburn, Kentucky, to Mrs. DeVenny, the wife of the manager of the Portsmouth By-Product Coke Company store and recreation buildin'. Mrs. DeVenny drove to our house in Blackberry City and asked for Mrs. Gertie Blankenship. When Mrs. DeVenny saw Granny's peonies sprouting on our hillside, she asked Mommy to "develop" peony gardens around her house.

"I'll pick you up and drive you home, Mrs. Blankenship," Mrs. DeVenny said.

"Well, that's awful nice," Mommy said to her, "but would you please tell me what the word 'develop' has to do with gardens?" That's one of Mommy's favorite stories from working for folk.

In Freeburn, she saw for herself what the coal company had built for their miners and their families. "A big buildin', Henry, with a soda fountain and pool tables and a dance hall." The buildin' also has a theater, but Nibby shows the latest movies in Matewan, so we don't need to go to Freeburn.

Mommy grows the purdiest gladioli and peony gardens all over the slopes in Blackberry City where we live, on the other side of Matewan's viaduct. Women come to the seed store from as far as the big towns of Williamson, West Virginia, and Pikeville, Kentucky, asking for Gertie Blankenship. I want to say, "That's my mother!" but I don't. It wouldn't be good business, Olaf says.

Right now, Tall Man is all we have left for Friday Blankenship to swap. And only this hammer in my hand can stop a moonshiner from stealing, so Mommy carries Tall Man with her wherever she goes.

"When you was five years old, your Pa moved you from Thacker Holler, where you both was born, to Blackberry City," Granny once said while we was stringin' beans. Mommy and I didn't want to move away from Granny, but Pa said, "You're mine, Gert."

Then his truck quit. He hocked the tires and parts for 'shine. Year after year, his old black Ford rusted on blocks in the front yard while Mommy walked the roads to dig gardens. At last, one day while I was at school and Mommy dug gardens, Pastor Hickman towed the piece of junk away from before our house. Mommy cried with thankfulness.

Often, folk stop on the road and say, "Get in, Gertie!" She swallows her pride and opens their door. "Much obliged," she says. But she never accepts a ride if a woman isn't in the car or truck, even if it's Pastor Hickman. Mommy mostly walks the mountain paths with her shovel, peony roots, and gladioli corms, so folk won't feel sorry for her.

Sometimes in passing a house surrounded by nothin' but dirt, trash, and hills, Mommy digs a small peony or gladiolus garden for no pay. "Nothin' tidies up a place and makes a woman happy like flar'ers," she says. Granny would laugh and say, "Shiners have torn up every holler tryin' to find where your mommy keeps her bees and sang patch. Her daddy taught her well."

I'd laugh with Granny because the 'shiners couldn't get their greedy hands on the most prized medicine in these hills. I've seen for myself that nothin' heals a wound like honey, and makes strong joints and bones like sang. That's why Mommy can dig like a man.

Miss Daisy, our neighbor, thinks it's the funniest thing that the Garden Club women Mommy gardens for don't know she's killed thirteen copperheads and seven rattlesnakes in their very own gardens this spring alone. We cain't help but laugh about it.

"We have our own garden club, don't we, Gertie?" Miss Daisy says.

After Pa dug up Mommy's peonies, she found roots left behind in the leaf mold. She planted them under this window by my bed to bloom on such a bright morning as this.

"The peonies will give us sweet dreams, Henry," she'd promise when I was a boy.

Now those flowers blanket the sunny slope behind our poor old place. But my dreams are rarely sweet unless I'm dreamin' of Granny. Or Annie Dill.

Granny mostly grew dark pink peonies. Some white and light pink. Back then the neighbor boys called me a sissy because I helped Mommy tend her peonies.

"I don't care what the boys say," I told Olaf one day when we had no customers in the store.

"Oh?"

"Uh-huh. Because Annie Dill, you know, the new dentist's daughter, said she likes boys who appreciate flowers. What does appreciate mean, Olaf?"

The man I most admire smiled. "This means Annie likes you."

When Annie heard about me bringing Mommy's peonies back to life with dried chicken manure and well water, she asked me to teach her how to grow peonies. But Mrs. Dill wouldn't have it. That broke my heart.

When I told Granny, she looked up from stringin' beans with her gold tooth glintin' in the daylight. "The woman will come aroun', Henry. I don't know a mother in these here hills who would be-grudge a boy who watches over flar'ers like she does her biscuits."

"Well, Mrs. Dill ain't from these hills. They come from Co-lumbus, Ohio. Annie says she'd never seen a mountain before they moved here this summer. Columbus is flat as a hoecake, and Annie said her mother doesn't bake biscuits."

"Don't you worry none where they come from, Henry, or where you come from neither, for that matter. Let the Lord take care of that. He don't see no boundary lines any more than you and Annie do."

That was almost nine years ago, days before the mine caved in on Pa. I cain't lay here another mornin' and watch sunlight rot Granny's quilt. The forget-me-nots forgot they were blue a long time ago. And the blood's plumb bled out of the bleeding hearts.

It's Pa's fault. The man everybody calls Friday. The town drunk who disappeared every Friday after he cashed his paycheck. Until the earth shook and caved in on him and made him a bedfast cripple.

That day in third grade, we'd said the Pledge of Allegiance to the Flag, recited the Lord's Prayer, and sat down for our gram-mar lesson. Then the school's secretary, Miss Teddy, came into our classroom. She bent down and whispered to Mrs. Cline. Then Miss Teddy left. Mrs. Cline bowed her head, wiped her eyes, and pushed back her chair. Every pair of eyes watched her stand up because every child whose daddy works in the coal mines knows he could get hurt. This school year so far, the mines took three daddies to the hospital. One never came home.

Mrs. Cline walked to my desk and stopped. She reached for my hand. "Henry, please come with me."

Annie and I locked eyes. This time, *my* Pa fell in a mineshaft.

Mrs. Cline led me down the hall. We passed ten classrooms to the principal's office. Miss Teddy sat at her desk and talked on the phone real low. She looked at me like people do when somebody in your family is hurt bad or dies.

"Henry, please wait here for Mr. Clay," Mrs. Cline said, and she let go my hand. I wanted to float up and out of the office like a balloon, down the hall, and home to Mommy. I'd rather she tell me Pa died than Mr. Clay.

Opposite Miss Teddy's desk, the door with PRINCIPAL on it opened and there stood Mr. Clay in his dark suit, white shirt, and tie. A thin, tall man, he squatted down just outside the door and looked me in the eye. I could smell his spicy aftershave and see a fresh razor cut above his upper lip. He bowed his head and took a deep breath. I looked down too and saw Mr. Clay's black, shiny shoes lookin' like he'd just bought them from Nenni's Department Store, or maybe John Nenni shined Mr. Clay's shoes like he did Olaf's and Annie's daddy's and made them look like new.

Even when Pa could walk, he never wore a black suit and black shiny shoes. He wore his mining boots plastered with coal dust and moonshine mud. Even on the kitchen floor Mommy just mopped.

"It's your father, son," Mr. Clay said and stood up.

I thought for sure the mine killed Pa. And if he wasn't dead before they pulled him out, he'd die not long after, like most miners did, or he'd never walk right and work again. I'd rather he died.

"Please come into my office," Mr. Clay said.

I sat in a big chair. Mr. Clay leaned against his desk covered with neat piles of paper.

"I'm sorry, son. Your father's been injured in the mine. Sheriff Taylor's driving your mother to Williamson Hospital where the doctors are taking good care of him."

I wanted to cry because I thought Mommy would never have to clean up after that drunk again. And we'd be rid of moonshiners.

"Your granny's on her way to pick you up and take you to her house."

"I don't have to go back to class?"

"Not today, son."

My father never called me that, and Mr. Clay did three times.

"Pa's not goin' to die?"

"I don't know that, Henry. He's badly injured."

Now I hold the hammer Olaf sold me and trace the rings on Granny's quilt with my eyes. I cain't remember anything else from that day, other than Granny's hugs and prayers for Mommy, Pa, and me. And the chicken and dumplings she cooked for supper that went cold on my plate.

"You'll find your stomach soon enough, honey," Granny said.

I did the next morning when I smelled bacon, fried eggs, biscuits, and chocolate gravy coming from Granny's kitchen. She let me measure the vanilla into a teaspoon and pour it into the bubbling chocolate. My favorite, what Granny called "good medicine."

Every day I hoped Sheriff Taylor would stop by and tell us that my father died in the hospital and that he'd brought Mommy home. When days added up to five, Mrs. Cline dropped off my lessons to Granny's house. "Henry's a good student, and I don't want him to fall behind in his studies so close to the end of the school year."

Granny put her shoulders back and stood real proud. "Hear that, Henry? You're a good student, so git to the kitchen table and finish your lessons before supper. You don't want to fall behind in your studies, do you?"

No, I did not. That meant Annie wouldn't be in my class, and I couldn't have that. Just five days and I already missed her. I couldn't imagine school without Annie's smile and friendship.

Back then, I wished there was at least one man in Granny's house, but Grandpa died before I was born. His picture hung above Granny's bed, and I liked to think the big man called Henry Hunt watched over her while she slept.

"Oh, I don't mind livin' alone, Henry," Granny would say. "I have you for comp'ny when I'm lonely. You're the best bean stringer aroun'."

As a boy, I'd rather sit with Granny on her front porch in Thacker Holler and string beans than run willy-nilly with Fred and Joe Compton, who lived further up the holler. Granny called them Monkey See and Monkey Do. Fred and Joe would walk by and yell, "How's Granny's boy?" She'd look above her glasses and say, "Don't be learnin' their ways, Henry."

"I won't."

Well, last Election Day, Fred and Joe ended up face down on the banks of the Tug, two grown men with bullets in their backs. Sheriff Taylor called it "another unsolved moonshine mystery."

"When your Grandpa was a boy workin' with his daddy—" Granny would begin, takin' up a handful of greasy beans.

"Uh-huh, where'd they work?"

"Loggin' and loadin' timber rafts along Peter Creek headed toward the Tug."

"What'd they do with the timber?"

"Railroad ties. Thousands of 'em. The first time I ever saw Henry Hunt from the banks of Peter Creek, he stood on a loaded raft leanin' on his timber hook like a Viking. It was love at first sight."

"What's a Viking?" I'd ask.

"A sea hero."

"Grandpa was a sea hero?"

She'd smile and look far up the holler where a falling tree took Grandpa from her, Mommy, and me. "He was to me and your mommy."

"Tell me about Grandpa and how you watched him make his shovel handle outa locust wood and forge the blade in his smithy," I'd say, to change the sad subject. She'd sip on her sweet tea to build suspense, and then I'd listen to that tale one more time.

When the sheriff stopped by that day at Granny's house to tell us he took Pa and Mommy home, I pleaded, "Granny, cain't I stay with you and go to school? I'll string your beans."

"No, honey, there ain't no beans to string yet. Go git your clothes from the bedroom. Your mommy's waitin' for you."

"But Pa ain't."

Granny looked to the sheriff. I thought she might change her mind, but she hugged me real tight, wiped a tear, and said, "I'll take you home, honey. I want to see how your pa and mommy are comin' along."

Sheriff Taylor pushed his hat above his forehead and nodded. "Let me know if y'all need anything." Then he left.

I wondered why Granny took her double weddin' ring quilt with us, but I didn't say anything.

Pa was in bed sleepin' when Granny and Mommy hung the clothesline from one wall to the other, then draped her quilt between my bed and Pa's. I'm glad they did because Pa's face looked like Quasimodo's, much worse than when the moonshiners beat him up.

I'd never seen Mommy look so worn out and sad.

Granny kissed Mommy on the cheek. "I'll be by in the mornin'," she said.

I almost cried when Granny left. But for Mommy's sake I didn't.

Mommy slept on the couch that night and has ever since. I figured out Granny hung the quilt between Pa's bed and mine because a boy shouldn't see his daddy when his Mommy and Granny wash his privates and change his bandages and bedding.

At first, the medicine knocked Pa out so much that he had no idea Granny had her hands all over his body. She'd sing real low, "Softly and tenderly Jesus is calling. Calling for you and for me."

One day I overheard Mommy tell Granny in the kitchen, "I'm thankful Olaf took Henry under his wing. The boy's not meant for the mines."

"Olaf's a godsend, Gertie. One I cain't quite figure out. But he sure does love Henry."

I couldn't figure out Olaf, either—or Olaf's mother, who seemed to love me almost as much as Granny did.

One rainy day after school, when I was eleven, I ran into the seed store for work and found Olaf sittin' on a chair by a little table at the end of the glass-domed counter by the brass cash register. He didn't seem to hear the bell as he sat starin' at what looked like a game. Soaked to the bones, I leaned against the door and watched Olaf as the hands on the clock over his office door ticked off twenty minutes.

"Come," Olaf finally said, without lifting his eyes.

While the rain splattered down the large window behind us, I scooted in beside a new seed spreader on the platform of Mrs. Semenov's window display and sat down. Every month, from the day they opened the seed store, Olaf and Mrs. Semenov arrange both windows real handsome-like with brand-new garden and farm merchandise.

I watched Olaf another twenty minutes. I didn't think it was possible for a person to sit that still for that long, except hunters. Olaf taught me how to be still for hours in the mountains, even if it meant lettin' a rattler or copperhead slither over our shotgun and boots.

"Son, have you seen a chessboard?"

"Is that what you're looking at?"

"*Da.*"

In rare moments when Olaf and I work alone, he'll forget himself and say "*da*" instead of "yes."

"No sir. It's a game, ain't it?"

"*Isn't* it."

"Sorry. Isn't it?"

"Reportedly originated in India."

"I just learned in geography class where India is. That's a long way from here."

"People have played this game throughout the vorld for more than a millennium."

"How long's that?"

Olaf still didn't move his eyes off the board. "A thousand years."

If I didn't know better, I'd think Olaf was pullin' my leg. "A thousand years! People play this game even in Russia?"

"Particularly Russia, second to India. My father and mother taught me to play. And I vould like to teach you."

"Is that your father's—what'd you call it?"

"Chessboard. No. Ve left his behind in Russia. Sergei Mekinov gave us this board. He collects them. As boys ve played chess in his home in Saint Petersburg. Mother said you are of age to learn the game."

Olaf moved a piece from one square to another on the board. He pointed to the empty chair across from him. "Today, your vork is your first chess lesson."

"What? Will I have to sit still for forty minutes?"

"More."

"Olaf—"

"I vill pay you for learning chess. My father said, 'your mind must be nimble to do good business.' I pay you only if you apply yourself to develop a keen sense of strategy."

Like I did hunting in the mountains with Mommy, I learned to sit still as a rock. Instead of concentrating on what moved in the trees, on the forest floor, and in the creeks, I fixed my eyes and mind on Olaf's chessmen and listened with both ears, as Granny would say.

With Olaf's chess lessons, and Granny's, Mommy's, and Annie's help, I graduated second in my class last week, April 20, 1932, the first man in Mommy's or Pa's families to graduate from high school.

Well, like Doc Bentley said yesterday when talkin' about standin' up to Pa, "A man's got to decide to do the right thing and do it—no matter the discipline it takes." He said, "You can get all the good advice in the world, Henry, but someday, you've got to face the giant before you and conquer it with what you have in your heart and hand. You've worked hard and graduated from high school with honors . . . now, face your pa."

Now's the time to stand up for Mommy and myself. I know God's hand rests upon my mother's shoulder, but I won't let her clean up after Pa one more time, even if his hepatitis infects me. Never again will a moonshiner steal anything from this house.

Where is Mommy, anyway? Pa's wakin' up, groanin' and coughin' and heavin' his insides out again. If only he would die and get it over with.

"Gert! My cigarettes!"

I grip my hammer, pull back Granny's quilt, and stand between my bed and Pa's. "You know we don't have money for cigarettes. You spent the last of it on whiskey."

Pa coughs in a spasm of laughter. Mommy stands in the doorway holding her tray of clean bandages, soap, salve, and a pan of hot water, a cloth, and a towel. Her mouth parts in a way to say she's expectin' somethin' this morning.

"After I bathe you Pa, I'm goin' to work. You touch or holler at Mommy again and this hammer's coming down on your hands."

I drop the hammer on my bed out of Pa's reach, remove the quilt from the clothesline, and walk out the back door. I shake dust from the quilt real gentle not to break more threads, and then fold it. Granny's dark pink peonies on the hill nod in the breeze, cheerin' me on.

When I return to Pa, Mommy's left everything on his bedside table. I drop Granny's quilt by the hammer, roll up the clothesline, and throw it on my bed.

Forgive your father, Olaf says in my mind.

"All right, Pa, I'm not goin' to be late for work, so roll over and let's get you feelin' better."

"I cain't roll over."

"You're not foolin' me." I pick up the washcloth and soap.

Pa swats at my hand and misses. I cain't remember the last time he touched me.

"You talk proud all you want. It ain't fittin' for a man's son to wash his ass!"

I glance to Mommy in the kitchen doorway. Pa cain't see her smilin' at this showdown. *Forgive your Pa.*

"Now don't talk like that. Mommy's put up with your cussin' and bedsores long enough. And I've had enough of you wastin' everything in this house on liquor—her gardenin' money, too!"

The flabby skin on Pa's yellow, boney face shakes. He's so weak now his threats are pathetic. "You've had enough? And just what you goin' to do about it?"

I drop the soap and cloth on Pa's ribs and grab my hammer. "I'll do what I should've done a long time ago."

Pa sneers. "Just look at you, thinkin' you can whoop . . ."

He grabs at the hammer. I whack his thumbnail with the true force of driving a spike into a railroad tie. Pa's face blanches as he holds his hand. The man's too proud to cry.

"I'll break every bone in your ten fingers if I have to. You're not lifting one more sip of moonshine to your mouth in this house. So, roll over."

Pa grabs the edge of the mattress and strains to turn onto his side. I hold my breath and turn his paralyzed, mangled legs like Doc Bentley said. I cain't remember the last time I touched Pa.

Mommy's old nightgown she's cut into pieces for bandages pulls bloody, pussy skin off what's left of Pa's bottom and hipbones. The reek of urine and waste smarts my eyes and nose. Pa buries his face in the pillow. I fight my tears because he doesn't deserve them.

No wonder that when I was a boy, Mommy wouldn't let me see Pa's legs. I feel guilty for lettin' her suffer this mess and danger for nine years. *Honor Thy father and thy mother, that thy days be long upon the land that the Lord has given thee.* But I cain't feel shame for not honorin' Pa. He hit Mommy one too many times before he couldn't anymore.

I drop the bandages in the washtub at the foot of the bed. "Hold on," I say, and roll up the soiled sheet and pad, then pull them out from under Pa, careful of his bedsores. I drop the bedclothes into the washtub and dab his backside and between his legs with the warm soapy cloth, then a towel, just like Doc Bentley said.

If he hadn't told me Pa's liver is failin', I'd be tempted to let go my anger.

But I remember what Annie said when I confessed my hate for Pa.

"Your mother's right. We must forgive to be forgiven. We must be forgiven to forgive."

Lord have mercy, that's one of a thousand reasons why I love Annie! Like Mommy and Granny, she never lets me off the hook. And I'm a better man for it.

I spread the clean pad and sheet on the mattress and tuck it under Pa's side. "Hold on. Now the salve."

He doesn't utter a sound as I apply the ointment and place clean bandages on his sores. He's got to feel better on a fresh bed. Mommy carries in another clean sheet, pillow slip, towel, razor, and a basin of hot, sudsy water and sets them on the table next to Pa's bed.

"Breakfast directly," she says with a clip in her step.

"Done. Let go, Pa."

He falls back on the bed with a moan. I change his pillow slip, help him sit up, and cover him with the clean sheet.

"You can finish," I say and nod to the wash basin and razor, ashamed I let Mommy lift and carry this load too long.

Outside, I empty the washtub of soiled linens into another tub Mommy's filled with hot water and disinfectant. When I return to the bedroom, she's left my wash basin on a chair and Pa's breakfast tray on his lap. I close the door and clean up for work with Pa's eyes on my back. For the first time I can remember, he's not cussin' over his coffee.

At last, I sit with Mommy for coffee, eggs, sausage gravy, and biscuits. And her blackberry preserves.

"Thanks for helpin'," she says with a twinkle in her eye.

"Thanks for the good grub," I say, and kiss her on the cheek. I'm the only person who Mommy allows to kiss her.

My mother's a purdy, tall woman with tanned skin, sky-blue eyes, and curly strawberry blonde hair. Doc Bentley said she's the fittest woman on Tug Fork. And with that smile she's wearing, she looks as young and beautiful as in her weddin' picture she keeps on the only dresser in this house. I could cry for what she's suffered.

Mommy puts her hand on mine. "Henry, you done good. Real good."

"I should'a stood up to Pa a long time ago."

She shakes her head. "This mornin' was the right time."

We eat in peace. Not a word from Pa, even when I refill his coffee cup. Mommy gives me a peck on the cheek and whispers so Pa cain't hear. "Your father Abraham waits at the seed store. You better get goin'."

"Olaf didn't come from Ur of the Chaldeans, and this isn't Canaan," I whisper back, playing her game. Mommy has never touched a chess piece, but she knows her Bible.

"You're right. But you know what I mean, and if you don't, you will someday."

At exactly 7:55 a.m., I look up to the large sign in black letters that says HUNT'S FEED & SEED. The polished metal reflects the morning sun and reminds me of the first time Olaf spoke his father's name when I was a boy. "Frederick Semenov loved to 'hunt' food and plants." A smaller, wooden sign, Matewan Garden Club, hangs to the left of the double doors.

When the bell rings, Olaf looks up from his ledger at the end of the glass-domed counter. Pleased with myself and Mommy's praise, I nod. "Mornin', Olaf."

"Good morning, Henry." Olaf pauses his pen, removes his new spectacles, and takes a long look at me. "So, you finished your mother's vindow box?"

I take my timecard from its rack on the counter. Olaf lends me the black fountain pen he brought from Russia. I write the date and time.

April 25, 1932, 7:56 a.m.

I return Olaf's pen with utmost self-control and respect. I cain't fool the man who knows me best. "You know how tools are, Olaf. You have to break them in a little bit before fixin' to build somethin'."

Olaf arches his eyebrows. "In vhat manner did you perform this?"

I put my hands on my hips. "Well, it's this way. Mommy needed somethin' fixed that's been broken way too long."

"I see."

"I reckoned you would."

Olaf closes his ledger. "And may I ask what you plan to build with your hammer?"

I scan the insides of the tall building from ceiling to floor and from wall-to-wall. "As you well know, we've run out of storage space, and you need a classroom for the botany school you and Mrs. Semenov are planning."

"Oh, yes. Now I remember," Olaf teases. "Well then, to vork, young man!"

I take the list of deliveries written in Olaf's fine hand and see *Mrs. Margaret Dill* at the top. I look to Olaf who waits in patient expectation of my response to her name.

We both know Annie Dill leaves for Berea College in two days. Matter of fact, everyone in Matewan, Blackberry City, and Thacker Holler knows. They know Annie and me are meant for each other, too. That's why Doc Bentley looked me in the eye yesterday when I picked up Pa's salve at the hospital, catty-corner to the seed store.

"Henry, how're you ever going to provide for Annie if you let your daddy waste everything you own? And how much longer are you going to risk your mother's health and life?"

Doc Bentley isn't the only one watchin' Annie and me, wonderin' what I'll do about Pa. If I'll stand up to him. If I'll go courtin' other girls after Annie leaves for Berea. Why, everybody knows everything about everybody up and down Tug Fork and Peter Creek, beginning with the make and model of what we drive.

Take John and Antillo Nenni, who know Mrs. Dill's dress and shoe size—they wait to see what I'll do because they care about Annie and me and want our happiness. But when Mrs. Dill yearns for the finest and highest fashion, she drives right by Nenni's on Mate Street and heads for Brown's Dress Shop in Williamson.

I know Saul Brown has Mrs. Dill's size six in the color of the season waitin' for her in the back room in a black bag tagged with her name. Annie told me so.

Law! Everybody knows Saul Brown stocks the dress and shoe size of all his customers. They cain't resist Saul Brown's keen eye for style. Whenever Mrs. Dill returns from Williamson, everyone at the United Methodist Church waits for her to step out of Dr. Dill's spit-shined Buick on the following Sunday in her new shoes, dress, and hat—especially those members of the Garden Club.

Within two Sundays—for it takes that long for Saul Brown's special orders to reach Matewan's post office—from Sue Ann to Nellie Nenni and Mrs. Semenov, the oldest members, the ten members look like a bouquet of zinnias when they gather for their monthly meeting.

Sometimes Mrs. Dill chooses a print of many colors like a summer garden of gladioli. One lunchtime at school, Annie showed me a picture of a painting by a French artist named Monet who painted a lady with an umbrella walking beside a gladioli garden. Annie said Mrs. Dill named her many-colored dress after Monet, but you don't pronounce the "t."

"*Monet* in French sounds more like *money* in English," Annie said.

That's good to know. And that means Saul Brown has to find nine of Mrs. Dill's Monet dress similar in style and print for the other ladies. Other times Mrs. Dill buys a new dress, the Garden Club ladies look like pale anemones when Mrs. Dill's dress is a pale pink, lavender, blue, green, or yellow linen, silk, or chiffon. Olaf calls the shade "pastel." I gobble up his fancy words like Mommy's apple pie. I share Olaf's words with Annie when I grab the chance. She pretends she's never heard the words before. I appreciate that.

However, the ladies never appear in Mrs. Dill's color of the season. As a man who takes his business seriously, like Olaf, Saul Brown knows better than to let that happen. As Olaf says, the clothier is an excellent chess player, with a business mind to match.

Truth be told, Saul Brown chooses Mrs. Dill's colors with his developed sense of *haute couture*, as Annie calls it. She said that's the way Saul Brown is with every customer—coal miner's wife or banker's. One of several Jewish merchants in Williamson, he owns the finest women's shop in the booming town. Someday soon for Mother's Day, I'm driving Mommy to Brown's and buyin' her a dress with shoes, gloves, and a hat to match.

Olaf says Saul Brown is of Greek heritage and carries himself accordingly. Maybe that's why I see what Olaf calls "mutual respect" on Saul Brown's face whenever he buys birdseed for his mother's canary.

Dressed in his white shirt and silk tie, dark three-piece suit, and Italian leather shoes, Saul Brown's sincerity and eye for accessories profit his business. Tug Fork and Peter Creek's menfolk admire the way Saul Brown dresses the women they love just like they admire—truth be told—a new car, truck, coon dog, horse, or anything else they treasure.

The second Wednesday night of the month I set up the chairs and lectern and unlock the door of the seed store for Garden Club meetings. And when the ladies of the club gather, Mrs. Dill pretends she doesn't notice the ladies' copycatting.

Working for Olaf, I'm learning what makes men and women happy—and what their differences are, too. Women want to look pretty and keep a nice house. They want their husbands' praise and affection. Men want to be fed and respected, and that means fried pies in their lunch buckets with a thermos of hot coffee. At the supper table, men want hot cornbread with whipped butter and molasses.

Unless you're Italian, like Antillo Nenni. He'll eat anything, "But nothin' makes my mouth water like a slice of Mother's polenta and a plate piled high with her spaghetti," Antillo's always sayin' to his mommy and daddy's customers.

Lately, I've noticed Garden Club ladies never speak about Annie and me when Mrs. Dill and Mrs. Semenov are around. If they did, they'd have to find another president to replace Mrs. Dill, or another location and sponsor for their meetings. And that would mean no streusel, no Bavarian cream, and no küchen from Mrs. Semenov's oven above the seed store. Nothing's worth risking Mrs. Semenov's

Russian pastries and coffee with heavy cream. Plus, nobody brews a cup of good, strong coffee like Mrs. Semenov. Even Mommy. Mrs. Semenov offers me a cup and slice of streusel or küchen when I'm settin' up the meeting.

If Mrs. Dill ever overhears members of Garden Club speak of Annie and me, they'd also have to find another dentist. And what would Matewan look like without handsome and educated Dr. Matthew Dill? Most locals now smile with a mouthful of their own filled and capped teeth, including Mommy and me.

People say Annie and me are Roseanna McCoy and Johnse Hatfield all over again, like we're lovers doomed to repeat that couple's tragic mistake. But they have another thing comin'. Why, we're no Romeo and Juliet. Anyone who steps foot or gasses up within fifty miles of Matewan knows Annie Dill's parents will never allow their daughter to marry a boy from Thacker Holler. It doesn't matter that everyone calls me a gentleman, including the members of Matewan Garden Club. Except Dr. and Mrs. Dill.

Womenfolk stroll into the seed store for a glance at who they call "our local Romeo." They usually buy somethin'. Mostly garden magazines and books, in hopes I touch their hand in a coin exchange. I've heard they go up and down the road braggin' or jokin' about touching Romeo's hand.

As if they've read all of Shakespeare's tragedy and know how it ends! We didn't read it in school, and Annie wouldn't tell me how the play ended, so I asked Olaf to lend me his big Shakespeare book. Mommy crossed her eyebrows when she heard me fussing over readin' it. I whispered to Annie next time she came into the seed store, "I swear, Annie. Those people are plumb crazy to think we'd do somethin' stupid and wrong like that."

Some folk who love to gossip say, "That boy's special." Others laugh.

Olaf knows the rumor riles me because it stirs up the hornet's nest in Mrs. Dill's new hat all over again. He just chuckles and says, "free advertising."

His humor makes this Romeo nonsense worth the hassle. For I love my boss and this business as much as I love my mother and Annie.

Long last, I heave a sigh of submission to Olaf's patient eyes. "Some 'sing on you mind, Henry?"

Why cain't I ever lie to Olaf? "I reckon it's 'Romeo and Juliet' again."

Olaf bows his head and puts his fingertips together. "I have some 'sing to say in reply, but it must wait until ve close. Now, to vork."

I gather Mrs. Dill's nasturtium and iceberg lettuce seeds from the shelves under the glass-domed counter. *Tropaeolum* and *Lactuca sativa var. capitata*. I wonder what's on Olaf's mind. Have I disappointed the man who taught me the botanical names for every seed we sell? The man who saved me from despair and gave me hope and employment when a boy? Or is he broodin' again over Otto, the young farmer he and Mrs. Semenov left behind in Russia? Olaf was Otto's teacher, too. I feel sorry for Otto and hope Olaf and Mrs. Semenov never leave me and this business.

I appreciate Olaf's code of order. *A place for every 'sing, and every 'sing in its place.* Finally, I switch on the light in the cavernous storage room. Whatever Olaf has to say is important, for I see its weight and the excitement in his eyes.

There's the latest trowel Mrs. Dill ordered for Mommy. Six this spring. Five last year. I give the tool's handle a shake. "This won't work with Mommy's large hand, either. If Mrs. Dill ever dug enough holes, she'd know a trowel has to fit a hand like a shoe does a foot."

Olaf and I suspect Mrs. Dill brings Annie along when she shops and picks up deliveries to see if I'll do something improper, such as smile at Annie. Her plan backfires because Annie and I never take her bait.

I hear Mrs. Semenov's footfall upstairs in their apartment, then water running. Next comes the beautiful music she often plays on her phonograph. I wish I could sit and listen for the joyful part that makes me feel like running in the mountains and leapin' over fallen logs.

Sometimes I hear Mrs. Semenov cry, a weeping, moaning sound that brings Granny to mind when she prayed. Is sorrow why

Mrs. Semenov doesn't invite me upstairs? Olaf's never said a word about what happened to his father in Russia. Is sorrow the burden I sometimes see on Olaf's shoulders?

"Someday, son, I vill escort you upstairs," Olaf once said. Is that what he wants to talk to me about?

I check off the trowel, garden gloves, and a bottle of African violet liquid fertilizer for Mrs. Dill's new *Saintpaulia*. I have to admire the woman's choice of flowers. She can tend the African violet herself without getting her hands dirty. If only I could drop a peony root in the bag for Annie. But that's taking Mrs. Dill's bait.

As I fill the last bag stamped with Hunt's Feed & Seed, the part of Mrs. Semenov's music that sends chills up my spine begins. I decide to ask Olaf the name of the song and turn off the light. As I shut the door, the bell jingles.

"Good morning, Miss Daisy," Olaf says.

"Good mornin', y'all." Miss Daisy's green, sprite-like eyes flitter from wall to wall, taking inventory of new items we've stocked since her last visit. She steps closer to the glass-domed counter where Olaf displays ledgers, garden books, and periodicals the likes of *House & Garden* and *Better Homes & Gardens*. Yesterday, I stacked copies of Richardson Wright's brand-new book, *The Story of Gardening*, with a card Olaf inscribed in his beautiful penmanship: *Matewan Garden Club book of the month signed by the author.*

"Miss Daisy," Olaf says, "as you see, Mr. Wright's latest book is available for purchase. He tells the complete history of gardening from antiquity to contemporary times. Please spread the vord that the Williamson Public Library also has a copy."

"I will, Olaf, even though I'm not a member of Garden Club. Henry, please fetch my copy."

You never have to guess what's on Miss Daisy's mind. I retrieve her copy from behind the glass dome. "Here you go."

As Miss Daisy thumbs through the pages, Olaf says, "I also thought you vould like to know Mr. Wright accepted Mother's invitation to speak to her Garden Club next month, a public event."

Miss Daisy's eyes grow large as dahlias. "Oh, Olaf! That's wonderful news! I love his *Gardener's Bed-Book*. There's nothin' like his sometimes-irreverent Connecticut sense of humor, and he knows what he's talkin' about when it comes to gardenin'."

By noon tomorrow, every woman along Tug Fork and Peter Creek will know what's new at Hunt's Feed & Seed, and that Richardson Wright is coming to town next month to speak to our gardeners and readers. I can hear their chatter now.

"Miss Daisy, your delivery is seventh of twelve," I say.

"Well, if y'all don't mind, I'll take it now if it's ready. I came to post a letter and thought I'd like to get those gladioli corms in the ground this mornin'."

Iridaceae of the iris family. "Don't mind one bit, Miss Daisy."

"You're a fine boy, Henry."

"Thank you, ma'am. I'll carry your order to the car."

We turn for the door when the bell rings again.

Mrs. Dill steps inside, all dressed up in a yellow shirtwaist dress, with a look on her face that could kill a copperhead.

Olaf nods. "Good morning, Mrs. Dill."

The strap to Mrs. Dill's purse hangs in the crook of her arm. "Good morning, Olaf. May I speak with you in private?"

Olaf bows.

Mrs. Dill turns to Miss Daisy. "Good day, Miss Daisy."

"Honey, call me Daisy."

Mrs. Dill stiffens and faces Olaf.

"Let's go, Miss Daisy," I say.

"Such a fine boy," she says to Mrs. Dill, and leads me out the door. I place Miss Daisy's order in the back seat of her car. She leans toward me.

"Don't worry none, Henry. We all know what she's up to."

My mind goes wild like a coon dog at chase. "What's she up to, Miss Daisy?"

"Here I come into town to post you a congratulations card, thought I'd pick up my corms, and Mrs. Dill shows up, fit to be tied because you're headed to Berea College, too."

I fall against Miss Daisy's yellow Chevrolet. "Me, headed to Berea College? Why?"

She puts a hand to her mouth. "Lord-a-mercy, your Mommy or Olaf ain't told you?"

I remember Mommy's smile this mornin'. "Told me what?"

Flustered, Miss Daisy looks up and down the street. "You've been accepted to Berea's horticultural program. Didn't you receive your acceptance letter? The entire town's readin' about it this mornin' in the *Matewan Bullet*."

I glance into the seed store and see the back of Mrs. Dill's daffodil yellow dress and hat. A small woman, she stands as if frozen in place. Not one movement from her hat to the sole of her heels. Olaf keeps a hand upon his ledger, calm as ever. Did he mail the application? Who else would've done it?

"No, Miss Daisy, neither Mommy nor Olaf has told me anything about an application for the horticultural program at Berea College. You know I'd never heard of the place until Annie told me about it."

Miss Daisy's eyes widen with delight. "My goodness! Olaf's gone and done somethin' behind your back. Ain't it wonderful? Just look at Mrs. Dill in there, havin' a hissy fit."

"Miss Daisy, pardon me, but this isn't good. Mrs. Dill will yank Annie out of Berea College before she even gets there. I would never do anything like that behind the Dills' back."

Miss Daisy leans her diminutive ninety pounds against the car door. "Mercy, Henry, you might be right!"

I'm about to lose my biscuits and gravy.

Miss Daisy composes herself. "Now wait a minute. Olaf is one smart man. He got his Mommy out of Russia all by hisself. Go flush Mrs. Dill outa there and listen to what Olaf has to say before the place fills with the town congratulatin' you."

I turn to the store as Mrs. Dill exits. She walks by with her jaw set, hat held high, and purse on her arm. She's forgotten her order, and I'm not about to chase her with the bag.

Miss Daisy puts a hand on my shoulder. "Olaf's waitin', boy. I'll find your Mommy and tell her what's happened."

"Thanks, Miss Daisy."

I watch her drive away and recall the trust in Olaf's eyes when he sold me my hammer. Standing up to Pa was easy compared to facing Olaf, the person I respect more than anyone other than Mommy, Doc Bentley, and Pastor Hickman. I open the door and recall Mommy's face with the soap, cloths, and pan of water. She knew something I didn't, and Olaf knows the same thing, and is about to spill the beans. *Phaseolus vulgaris*, I think, with the taste of Mommy's greasy beans in my mouth. I can't help but smile—despite Mrs. Dill.

Olaf stands in the same place as if sprouted from the floor. "Lock the door and turn the sign. Now I say vhat I must."

"But Olaf, you never lock . . ."

Agony pulls on Olaf's face. "You are my employee?"

"Yes, Sir."

I do as Olaf says.

"Follow me."

Olaf leads me through his tidy office, past the familiar desk, telephone, chair, file cabinets, safe, and shelves of books on the wall. He stands before the closed door I've seen a thousand times and pulls a jangle of keys from his right pants pocket. I never knew he kept the door locked. But it makes sense to protect Mrs. Semenov from intruders.

It's so quiet I hear the latch click. Olaf turns the knob and swings open the door to the scent of sauerkraut and sausage. He drops the keys into his pocket. I'm to the side and don't see the stairwell when he searches my eyes. I don't know what he hopes to see, so I smile regardless of the uncertain situation.

"I lead. Hold the rail," Olaf says, and hits a light switch.

I follow him toward the bare light bulb at the top of the long, steep, dimly lit stairwell with narrow tread. Whoever built this building had small feet. I don't, and Olaf's are larger. And Mrs. Semenov's foot is a good size eight or nine.

I count steps, slide my hand up the rail, and worry Mrs. Semenov might trip and fall down this gloomy-as-death-itself shaft. By the twentieth step I decide to talk with Olaf about ordering a window to install midway for the outside wall's southern exposure.

"Stay," he says when we reach the small, dimly lit landing. "I vill inform mother." Olaf disappears through the nearest open doorway.

I remember twenty-five steps total and strain to see and hear what I can inside their apartment. Sunlit redbud branches in a beautiful crystal vase on a table covered with a white linen tablecloth. Two wooden chairs with spindle backs. I hear beautiful music like I hear above the storage room and know I stand on the edge of another world—*The Old Country*, as Olaf calls the home they left behind.

He appears by the white tablecloth, returning through the doorway to stand before me. "Follow me."

I nod and pass through the kitchen into a large room with dark furniture like Granny's—the mahogany and cherry treasures Pa pilfered for whiskey.

Olaf faces his mother and motions me to sit in a large, green upholstered chair across from her. He stands before a matching chair. So, these are the two backbreakers John Nenni's clerk and Crazy Ray carried up the twenty-five steps. And all along I've believed Ray's been tellin' another story.

I sit, and Olaf does too, a large, round table between us. His five Russian botany books sit in a neat stack under the glow of a wide, pleated lampshade atop a tall, crystal lampstand. Like the moon upon the earth, the light magnifies the ancient beauty of the books' gold, orange, red, blue, and green leather spines. It's as if they grew out of the earth.

Of all the young men in Tug Fork, I'm the one Olaf's taught how to pronounce their Russian titles. Sharp and quick, Mommy's words about "my father Abraham" waiting for me comes to mind.

Mrs. Semenov sits in a spindle-back chair that matches those in the kitchen. Erect as a queen, she wears her wavy, salt-and-pepper hair wound around the top of her head, held together with the same three tortoise shell combs she wears for Garden Club. Whenever I see Mrs. Semenov, she's dressed like she's goin' to church. When she gardens or arranges the window displays with Olaf, she wears a full apron over her dress.

My church, Missionary Baptist of Matewan, is two doors down from the seed store, so Mommy and I sometimes see Mrs. Semenov rockin' in one of the comfortable chairs on the store's back porch facin' the Tug, readin' a book. Sometimes she just looks toward the river. Mommy says the Tug is probably the closest thing to one of those breathtaking fiords in Norway, where Mrs. Semenov grew up.

I wait. Bookshelves stand against every wall like the Williamson

Public Library. And there's Sergei Mekinov's chessboard he gave Olaf next to the large blossom of the phonograph. It's remarkable how that curled horn and a needle make such beautiful music from a record. Someday, I'll buy Annie a phonograph and records for our house. And a chessboard, even though her nimble mind wins every game. You have to love a girl who beats you at chess.

Mrs. Semenov waits for my eyes to stop wanderin'.

"Good morning, Henry."

Her voice is rich as cream. Her dress is black with little white flowers. *Why always black and white?*

"Mornin', Mrs. Semenov."

With a lacy hanky between her large, slender hands, she turns to Olaf. She's never without a fancy hanky. I imagine John Brown at the local dry cleaner's launders hundreds of the Semenovs' handkerchiefs in a year.

"Begin," Mrs. Semenov says.

Olaf's eyes turn to me. "Upon consultation vith your mother, Mrs. Semenov, and your high school principal, it vas I who completed your application for the horticultural program vith Berea College." He pauses for my reply.

I smile and nod because I guessed right. But Olaf and Mrs. Semenov look miserable, and only Mrs. Dill's visit could be the cause.

Olaf pulls at his white collar. "I did not inform you because we vanted to surprise you. And upon this acceptance, we vanted to sponsor your expenses, and, upon graduation, ve hoped you would accept the helm of our business."

I slide to the edge of the chair. The lamplight in this window-less room shadows the anguish on Olaf's face, and that gives me more courage to say what's on my mind. "Wait a minute. What do you mean, sponsor my expenses, and accept the helm of your business?"

Olaf holds up a hand. "However, ve overlooked one significant detail. The press and local gossip circulate news at greater speed upon our secluded mountain roads than the trucks of our U.S. Postal Service. Thus, a distraught Mrs. Dill read your name amongst those students accepted to Berea in the Matewan Bullet and valked through our door."

Now it all made sense. "Mrs. Dill has every reason to be distraught if she thought I applied to Berea. I'd never do anything without talking first to Annie's parents," I tell Olaf. "Our future together means too much to us." I rake my hand through my hair. "How'd she figure out it was you who submitted my application?"

"Mrs. Dill is a very astute voman. Annie assured her that you were not responsible for the application, so that left me as the culprit. Mrs. Dill came for my confirmation."

"What did she say?"

"She and Dr. Dill vill remove Annie from enrollment at Berea College if you sign your acceptance letter."

"That's what I just told Miss Daisy."

Olaf bows his head and stifles a sigh. Mrs. Semenov looks to her hands. It breaks my heart to see them dejected.

"Henry," Olaf says, "I apologize for the distress my oversight carries to you—and to Annie, and to her parents. After you and your mother agreed to my legal paternal guardianship, and partnership in Hunt's Feed and Seed, I mailed your application and afterward requested an audience vith the Dills to discuss your future with Annie." He sinks back into his chair. "They declined. I vas a fool to presume the Dills' approval, and a coward to withhold this information from you. Mother and I planned to inform you of the good news today after ve closed the store." He nods for me to speak.

In the nine years I've known Olaf, I've never seen him defeated like this. "Olaf, I accept your apology, although I don't need it or want it. Y'all meant well. And if Annie's the woman I've come to know, she's already done the same."

Olaf wipes his brow with his handkerchief. "T'ank you, Henry." His heavy voice worries me.

Mrs. Semenov does not lift her eyes. "*Da*, t'ank you."

Olaf rises and stands beside his mother, a hand resting on the back of her chair. The phonograph softly plays the music that lifts me higher than my troubles. I hope it does for them, too. I see and feel the strength of their disappointment and wonder again what they've suffered, and why they chose to give Annie and me the work they've built here in Matewan.

No. That's not right. It's the work five Semenov generations built in Russia. Olaf and Mrs. Semenov carried it to Matewan and transplanted it all around this buildin' and town and Tug Fork. That's what they're mournin'. They foresee the end of Frederick Semenov's work when they pass. I see it on their faces and glance to Olaf's five books on the table. Now the Semenovs have rooted them in me and Annie.

Olaf looks to his large hands. "Henry, ve have offended Dr. and Mrs. Dill. As you say, they have reason to be distraught. Ve went behind their backs concerning their daughter's future. It vas not our place. Ve must apologize and hope for reconciliation."

I imagine Olaf at the chessboard and think that's the best move they can make to win the Dills' forgiveness. But reconciliation is another game.

"Excuse me, please," Mrs. Semenov says.

As if the music calls her name, she glides in her long, flowing dress to the phonograph. She lifts the needle and sets it on the rest. Her eyes glisten as she returns to her chair, composing her agony with elegance and serenity. In quiet tension, I notice she holds one hand in the other on her lap. What was it I once overheard Granny say to Mommy? Something about a songbird locked in a cage?

Then reality shakes me like thunder. Annie's parents could leave Matewan and take her with them. It's time to make my move.

I plant my elbows on my knees and let my hands help me talk this through. "Mrs. Semenov, Olaf, I don't see a problem here. I never wanted or planned to go away to college. I won't sign Berea's acceptance letter."

They look to one another in shock before Olaf turns to me. "Please explain."

"Berea is a college that exchanges the student's tuition for a work assignment on campus. Why would I leave my work and education here with you two and waste my time and your money to work for Berea College? Why would I sit in classes I don't need?" I fold my hands and look to Mrs. Semenov, then Olaf. "Do you truly think I need a degree to know how to steer the helm of Hunt's Feed & Seed into the future?"

Mrs. Semenov looks up to Olaf with my question in her hazel

eyes. I give them time to think before I say what's been on my mind a long time.

"Annie and I have it all figured out. You two are the best teachers in Appalachia when it comes to the businesses of agriculture, botany, and horticulture."

Mrs. Semenov allows the promise of a smile. Olaf seems to be mulling over my question.

"Nobody knows livestock feed and care and beekeeping better than the Semenovs. Ever'body in Tug Fork knows that. Why, no business in West Virginia or Kentucky has ever managed twenty greenhouses and fifty beehives as you did in Russia."

Olaf takes a deep breath. "It is true. As our forefathers, mother and I learned much about agriculture and apiculture in the University."

I imagine the chessboard between us and make my next move. "Well, as I reckon it, five generations of University learnin' in Russia and Norway should be enough to teach a first-generation Blankenship botanist from Thacker Holler."

"Henry—" Olaf begins.

"Pardon me, Olaf, please say—do you believe Berea College is goin' to teach me somethin' about this business you two don't know?"

Discreetly, Mrs. Semenov touches Olaf's hand.

Checkmate.

In surrender, Olaf folds his fingers under his black lapels. "So, vhat have you and Annie figured out?"

I sit back in the chair. "Think about it. What do I need to be able to take the helm of this establishment while Annie's away at Berea?"

Olaf unfolds his fingers from his lapel and lifts his eyebrows to my rhetorical question.

"You two, and this place—six days a week, learnin' from one Norwegian and one Russian botanist. The best team in America. And I need Petrov's weekly letter to keep up to date with what's goin' on in the world of botany in these United States."

As if they both need an anchor, Mrs. Semenov takes her son's hand. I plod on.

"You know and love your business, and you've lived here long enough to know the potential within these mountains. You know what Appalachia needs, better than we do."

"Oh?" Olaf says.

"Uh-huh. As your grandfather and father foresaw Russia's fall to Bolshevism, you see what could—and will—happen to Appalachia after the coal companies boom and leave. Like Dr. Dill and Annie say, 'we have to do something about that, now.'"

Olaf lets go of his mother's hand.

"Vhat do you propose, Henry?"

"We have to offer our people what the coal companies cain't."

Olaf studies the framed, floral prints hanging on the wall as he does Sergei's chessboard. "Vhat will we offer them, son?"

I wish Annie and Mommy were here! They both love Olaf as much as I do. And they're much better at what they call "details."

I sit at the edge of the chair. Oh Lord, help me remember what Annie said. "If people understood and valued the business and lifestyle of good husbandry, they'd find meaningful, steadfast, and safe work and recreation within it. This is America's birthright, tested by the conveniences of industrialization. Our forefathers understood we must learn to love our land and what it provides. This is our means to stick it out in hard times, rather than walk away from the ruins we created."

Olaf paces the floor. He stops and surveys the apartment. "Henry, please, are ve to understand you vill forfeit the many benefits of a college education to remain here vith us? You do not vant to share the experience vith Annie?"

Never in a million years could I imagine what Olaf and Mrs. Semenov had in mind all along. Every day I walked into this seed store, Olaf and Mrs. Semenov wanted me to own it. Planned for Annie and me to own it. To raise our children in it. I shake my head in wonder. Mrs. Semenov lifts her eyes to mine while Olaf stands beside her. Now I make my next move.

"I'll say it again. My education is right here in this buildin', spared from the 1910 fire for this very moment. I believe it was saved for my future and education. Matewan's future and prosperity is in this buildin' with you two leadin' the way. I promise, Annie's education in Berea will be more than enough for the two of us."

Then I think of Pa. It's time to tell the people who have given me the most remarkable love and livelihood I could ever imagine about Pa's health. I stand up and look Olaf in the eye. "But most important of all, Doc Bentley says Pa's liver is failin' fast. Even if I wanted to, there's no way I'm leaving Mommy by herself to care for Pa. When he dies, I'll be right here in Blackberry City to hold her."

Out comes Mrs. Semenov's lacy hanky. She and Olaf look to one another, the blush of embarrassment upon their faces.

"Henry," Olaf says, "forgive us for overlooking your responsibility and devotion to your parents."

I know Olaf's loved my mother for a long time, but I've never said a word to a soul, not even Annie, because it's Mommy's and Olaf's business. He's never said or done anything improper, and Mommy'll tell me she's loved Olaf for a long time when she wants to.

Olaf and Mrs. Semenov only want what's best for Annie, me, and Mommy, so I pray for the right words. "You cain't know what goes on inside our home unless we tell you. And Mommy and I want that between God and us."

Olaf looks to his hands again to figure things out. "I honor your wishes, Henry."

Now I study my hands, remember the hammer he sold me. "I knew you would, Olaf."

Mrs. Semenov looks up to her son with admiration. No matter how he tries to hold it back, a glimmer of love flashes from under his bushy eyebrows. Is it for Mrs. Semenov, or Mommy? Or both?

I take a deep breath to summarize my plans. "My education began in this store nine years ago. And my home will always be in Blackberry City, building Annie's house board by board with my hammer while she's away in school. In three years, I'll have a fine, debt-free homeplace for the six children we hope to have." I blush and carry on. "A house with indoor toilets, and an electric range, and a washing machine and clothes dryer, so Annie will have time to propagate plants, write stories, and whatever else her college education dreams up."

They smile and I don't miss a move.

"We love Matewan and aim to learn from you, Mrs. Semenov, and the ladies in Garden Club, too. Don't you see? Hunt's Feed & Seed is the heartbeat of Matewan and Blackberry City! It's the heartbeat of Tug Fork!"

Olaf shakes his head. "The heartbeat of Tug Fork?"

"And beyond. You've seen our customer ledger. Folk come from as far as Louisa and Ashland, Kentucky, and White Sulphur Springs, West Virginia. Even the Greenbrier's spreadin' the word about Hunt's Feed & Seed since our first shipment of magnolia trees three years ago. I want to take Annie some April to see Hunt's Feed & Seed's three hundred bloomin' magnolias praisin' that graceful lady. Annie won't believe the high ceilings and plush carpets in that resort!"

"I remember when you took the Greenbrier call," Olaf chuckles. "I vas trading Mother's küchen for John Brown's dry cleaning delivery."

"See what I mean? Who's goin' to take my place if I go to Berea? Miss Daisy? She's the only person I know of in Matewan or Blackberry City who loves propagating plants and knows how to grow them. Why, the women in Garden Club mostly play with flowers. And Annie and I aim to change that."

Olaf frowns with doubt. Considering the trust these beloved people have invested in Annie and me, I attempt to explain myself like a rational man.

"You don't have to leave this place. Ever. The store and this home belong to you. We need you. Matewan and Tug Fork need you for our transformation. Mommy and I believe God sent you here like he did Abraham to Canaan."

Mrs. Semenov looks up to Olaf, light in her eyes. "The night before ve left Polya Tsvetov, your father said, 'Natalia, as God sent Abraham to Canaan, I send you and our son to America.'"

I know customers must be waitin' at the door, wonderin' what's going on. "Olaf and Mrs. Semenov, you will want for nothing as long as Annie and I live."

Our benefactors seem relieved.

"But first, I'm goin' to forget that sorry bed in Sears and Roebuck catalog and build myself a new bed with my new hammer. I'll order the mattress from John Nenni. Then, I'm goin' to buy a truck from Crazy Ray and drive Mommy to Saul Brown's for a new dress, pair of shoes, hose, and gloves, and hat. Then, I'm goin' to take her to the jeweler's for a necklace and earrings. She said she's too rough on bracelets.

"Then I'm goin' to begin building Annie's house next to Mommy's. When I'm finished, I'm tearing down the old shack. When Annie comes home, I'm goin' to marry her, and keep growing this business with you, Annie, and one day, our children. Maybe one or two of our young'uns will take the helm of this establishment—and Matewan Garden Club, too! Like Granny said, I think Dr. and Mrs. Dill will come around. And I never knew Granny to be wrong."

"Vat about the Garden Club?" Mrs. Semenov asks with a quiver.

I see more clearly what the ladies mean to her and regret what I said about them "playin'" with flowers.

"Annie's sights are on the second Wednesday of every month—a store filled with women and men who plant and grow their own flower gardens, trees, shrubs, and food. She dreams of a garden show she calls the Magnolia Fair, named after the first plant Miss Daisy taught her to propagate. A fair in our O'Brien Park with judges and prizes for livestock, preserves, pies, quilts, flowers, and a reigning queen and court like they do at Berea College."

Mrs. Semenov's eyes shimmer. "Magnolia Fair? In Norway, our botany club sponsored the Purple Heather Fair every summer. My sister and I served on the committee. Astrid is a botanist, too."

I jump up, for there's no sittin' down now. "And here's the best part. Annie wants Garden Club to sell what we grow at a market every weekend during growing season. And I'm goin' to build a greenhouse behind this store where we can experiment with propagation. Miss Daisy's helped Annie propagate hundreds of hibiscus, every color imaginable! Annie knows their botanical names, too. Ever' single one."

Olaf paces the rug and murmurs in Russian to Mrs. Semenov. I cain't help but enjoy this moment as they wrestle to comprehend our expanding vision. He stops at last, his hands behind his back with that dark cloud that tends to settle over his brow when in thought. *Now what's wrong?*

"Henry, have you considered that Annie may not return from Berea College to Matewan? And that Dr. Dill may not grant you Annie's hand?"

So, this is why he's broodin'. "We've talked about this till we've worn ourselves plumb out. We always come back to this. You and Mrs. Semenov have taught us so many lessons. The one we hope never to forget is life doesn't always turn out like we planned. By the grace of God, we make the best of it."

They nod with understanding and compassion. These two people, who have lost more than I'll ever know, are offering Annie and me more than we could ever imagine.

Stunned with the changes in my life within one morning, I watch my words. "Matewan is where Mommy and I belong. Dr. and Mrs. Dill cain't change that. Annie cain't. If she doesn't come back from Berea, it's you, Miss Daisy, and me lookin' to an empty railroad yard someday to build greenhouses and beehives. And listen to this. Mommy's talkin' about us puttin' up a fine recreation buildin' in O'Brien Park like they have in Freeburn. She says Garden Club can use the buildin' for quilt displays durin' the Magnolia Fair, and anything else their pretty heads dream up. She sees it a place to play chess, checkers, rook, and billiards year 'round like Freeburn's buildin'—and a café that sells good, strong Russian coffee, küchen, and baklava."

Mrs. Semenov tries to hide a smile with her hankie. Olaf lifts his eyebrows in doubt. I pick up *The Gardener's and Florist's Dictionary* and hold it up before them. "There's one big difference between Freeburn and Matewan. When Portsmouth By-Product Coke Company and Norfolk and Western Railroad Company pull out, Hunt's Feed & Seed will have a fleet of trucks delivering throughout Appalachia, and up and down the East Coast. We'll be ready to build greenhouses and beehives in the unused part of the rail yard, leavin' enough track for the future."

Mrs. Semenov holds a hand to her throat and speaks like a song. "I am glad . . . your father forgot . . . your mother's shovel . . . in the rain."

My mouth falls open. Suddenly, after nine years, I know I'm lookin' at the woman with the beautiful voice from the phonograph.

I take a deep breath and whistle. "I have one last question, Mrs. Natalia Semenov. What's the name of that music you were playin'?"

She dips her head. I see her three tortoiseshell combs, done perfect as usual. "'Ode to Joy' by Ludwig von Beethoven."

I cain't wait to tell Annie.

PART TWO
ANNIE
APRIL 1935

We carry my suitcases and boxes to Henry's new, used 1932 Chevy truck. I like the dark blue color but know he's gullible to Crazy Ray's sales pitch. All Tug Fork knows his nickname is the only thing Ray's earned honestly in his twenty-eight years living in Matewan. I just hope Henry didn't buy another lemon, an act of charity upon Henry's part because Ray loses more gambling than he earns.

I watch him secure my belongings in the truck's bed with a rope, lean against the passenger door, and cross his arms and ankles. "Fresh off Grace Ford's used car lot for this special occasion. Crazy Ray gave me a good deal."

"As he does everybody." I recall the one and only lemon Father bought from Ray. Some people give and give. Some take and take.

Henry opens my door. It's wonderful to see Mother's picnic basket on the seat, as usual, and smell the onion and celery in Gertie's chicken salad sandwiches.

"Ray's a good guy, Annie. He's had a hard life."

"And you haven't? I don't see you cheating customers." I put the basket on the floorboard and climb up to my seat.

Henry shuts the door and leans through the open window. He's so close I see the bloom in his blue irises, feel the heat of his stale coffee breath. Oh, what love forgives! I know the man I adore is waiting for his customary kiss before we depart campus.

"Honey, Ray didn't have a granny and a mommy to teach him honesty. But he's learnin'."

"Oh?"

He stands and leans an elbow on my door. "You know Olaf's been teachin' Ray to play chess."

"I do."

"Well, Ray caught on pretty quick and tried cheatin' a month ago. Saw it myself."

I'm not surprised. "What did Olaf do?"

"He said, 'Ray, I regret you violated the dignity of the game and must go.'"

"So, where's the evidence Ray's learning the value of honesty?"

Henry grins. "He didn't show up in the store's storage room for his next chess game with Olaf. So, the salesmen at Grace Ford asked me why Ray worked Wednesday night instead of taking his chess lesson with Olaf. Word got back to Ray, so he went to his knees and apologized to Olaf for cheatin'. He asked Olaf to give him another chance to play honest."

"And Olaf did."

"But if Ray cheats again, he's banned forever."

Henry draws his face close to mine. He won't budge without a smooch, which I give because he's earned it and nobody's around. I've kept my promise to Mother and Father to behave like a lady, and I'm not about to break it now.

Henry Blankenship smiles and knocks his knuckles on the truck's hood, gives me a wink through the windshield before he takes the wheel. He looks to me with the innocence of a boy with a new bicycle. "You like her, Annie?"

"She's a beauty."

"You like the color?"

"Reminds me of your eyes."

He glances at himself in the review mirror. "You're not pullin' my leg?"

I roll my eyes. "What's her name?"

"I figured I'd let that happen naturally, like Trouble named herself."

"I'm surprised to hear you speak kindly of that clunker."

Henry sighs. "Yeah, Trouble reminds me of Pa's old, black truck rusting on blocks in front of our house. I'll never drive a Ford again."

I laugh. "That's what you said every time Trouble broke down. And you've kept your word. That's one thing I love about you, Henry Blankenship."

"Well, at least we learned a few things about mechanics to keep 'er on the road back and forth to Berea and Mommy's garden accounts. That pile of junk was paid for, and I've had a house to build. And I wanted you to graduate first in your class—again."

"And I did. For you, Henry. What else could I do with all that time on my hands?"

Henry puts his arm on the back of the seat and faces me. On cue, I trace his strong jawbone with my right index finger, and for the millionth time, cannot believe this man loves me and has built us a house for us to raise our children and grow old in together. I wipe a tear from my eye.

Henry touches my chin. "Now, we both know that had nothin' to do with it. Other than Mommy and Granny, I've never seen such a hard-workin' woman as you. You know you're makin' history?"

The truck emits the scent of the seed store. "Me? Making history?"

He turns the key and declares above the engine's rumble. "I'd better get the first college graduate from Magnolia High School to her party!"

Henry shifts gears, leaves my boarding house, and for the last time weaves through the small campus. Reflections of classrooms, visits to local farms, Boone Tavern Hotel, and the awful encounter with the Highlander drift into my past. I want to tell Henry how miserable I've been these past three years without him, but not yet. I turn back to glimpse the small cluster of vanishing buildings where I studied agriculture, botany, horticulture, literature, and history.

Again, I imagine Matewan—and all that awaits us.

I face Henry and touch his arm, feel his bicep flex as he drives us toward home. "Believe me, I've done nothing worthy of making history. I obeyed my parents and earned a degree in the process. I would've rather been home in Matewan building our business and family together."

Henry shakes his head and smiles. "Well, you're the same 'Honest Annie' I fell in love with, modest as ever. It's behind us now, honey. And I'm one happy man."

"And I'm one happy woman. How's the Semenov's college coming along? You haven't said much about it lately in your letters."

He gives me his side-glance and crooked smile. "So, you want to go back to college already?"

I cuddle his shoulder. "As long as it's located in Matewan, and a certain handsome young gentleman named Henry Blankenship sits by my side."

Henry turns the wheel onto the main road. "You know, Annie, with Petrov's help, Mrs. Semenov and Olaf could've grown a prosperous business and school in Boston. At times I still cain't believe they chose Matewan. Otto would have a better chance of finding Olaf in Boston than in Tug Fork."

"Then who would've helped you fix your Mommy's rusted shovel?"

Henry looks to me with surprise in his eyes. "How'd you know I've been ponderin' that very thing?"

"Because I've been your soulmate since third grade, and there's a lot of time for you to think while driving alone to Berea for one hundred and seventy miles."

"Annie Dill, sometimes I think you're an angel watchin' over me."

"Henry Blankenship, you'll find out just how wrong you are when you marry me."

"All's I can say is God's been very good to me, honey. You came from Columbus and the Semenovs from Russia. Taking you home to Hunt's Feed & Seed makes this the very best day of my life."

"And all's I can say is God's been very good to me. And going home to our store makes this the very best day of *my* life."

Henry takes in a deep breath of April air. "It's been Christmas vacation since you've been home. I cain't wait for you to see our little town again."

"Remember what you told Olaf and Mrs. Semenov that morning when Mother walked into the store in her daffodil yellow dress and hat?"

Henry whistles through his teeth as he downshifts for a stop sign. "Darlin', I said lots of things that mornin', and that was three years ago. I'd appreciate a hint."

It's a challenge for a woman to compete for her man's attention when he's romancing a new truck. I shake my head and laugh, "You stood up and told Olaf and Mrs. Semenov they were the best teachers for you, period."

"Uh-huh. Go on."

"Mother said in a letter that word's spreading about your fine carpentry work."

"Yeah, but I have to turn everybody down so I can finish our kitchen cupboards and help build the business."

"Do you regret losing the work?"

The subject delights Henry like a glass of cold sweet tea. "Not for a second! I enjoy buildin' our house, Annie, and I cain't wait to walk into the store every mornin'. But I don't want to work at pleasin' anyone else after a day's work."

I adore Henry.

"By the way, you won't believe the new beekeeping inventory! People are goin' nuts settin' up hives and buyin' seed for wildflowers and cultivars that attract pollinators. I tell them the mountains provide more than enough nectar and pollen for makin' honey, but they insist on bringin' bees into their little flower gardens. Cain't say I blame them."

"Mother wrote that every Garden Club member has set up a hive."

Henry hits his palm on the steering wheel in confirmation.

"Lord-a-mercy! Sue Ann set one up behind Leckie's where she can keep an eye on it. And Nellie Nenni put her hive behind their store under a canopy so's the coal dust and soot won't fall on it. I didn't think her hive stood a chance with all the engines puffin' out soot day in and day out. But Nellie said her bees are makin' honey! Do you know what Miss Daisy said?"

I do, but I want to hear Henry's interpretation.

"Law! Miss Daisy laughs and says beekeeping's become 'fashionable'!"

I laugh. "Mother said her 'little creatures' gave her something meaningful to care for while I was away."

"I still cain't believe your mother's risking bee stings. I heard her tell Garden Club that a few stings are worth the pain to have her own honey for pastries. The ladies and the Nenni's have gone plumb senseless over her baklava."

"Father has too."

Henry's eyes twinkle. "Well, so has your fiancé."

I kiss him on the cheek. "Well, fiancé, have you heard Mother's concern about beekeeping?"

"What's she worried about?"

"That keeping bees is more a regional fad than a commitment, like the growing number of garden clubs in West Virginia."

"Well, Margaret Dill's usually right, but this time I hope she's not, because Gertie Blankenship can handle only so many hives, and Matewan wouldn't be the same without Garden Club. Mommy's the first beekeeper people ask to take their hives off their hands. She's now up to ten and she started three. She cain't fit one more hive in her mountain hideaway."

"In my three years at Berea, I saw beekeeping come and go. But the cook at Boone Tavern said there's always mountain folk who will keep bees because honey is a part of our folk medicine."

"Mommy uses her honey all the time for healin' scratches and poison ivy blisters on her hands and legs. And nothin' sweetens tea and biscuits like honey."

"Come to think of it, why don't we adopt some bee orphans?"

Henry looks me in the eye for a second and I know he's beat me to it.

"How many?"

"Oh, two for starters. Mommy's teaching me. They're in the backyard of our new house. I built a tall chain-link fence with a gate around them so's shiners won't rob the honey. I'm tryin' to talk Mommy into moving her bees from her hideaway to our backyard. With our house on a rise, we can see the white boxes from the kitchen window. It's a beautiful sight, Annie. I find myself just watching the sunlight on their wings, comin' and a'goin'."

I lift my voice above the truck's drone and punctuate the air with my right index finger like Mrs. Drango did in Chemistry 101. "Add Beekeeping 101 to the Matewan College curriculum!"

Henry throws his head back in laughter and slaps the steering wheel again. "You're too late again, Annie Dill! The Garden Club ladies are itching to teach what they know. In her lesson last month, Mrs. Semenov put the bug in their ears unawares when she said, 'You vomen now know enough about Appalachian botany and apiculture to teach beginners.'"

I'm overjoyed with this news and chuckle at Henry's impersonation of Mrs. Semenov. "Mother wrote in a letter that she thinks our college is a good match for the Williamson Women's Club and the Williamson Wildwood Garden Club—both are growing in numbers."

Henry grins as if he knows something I don't. "Well, a handful of their members have stopped in the store and asked about Mrs. Semenov's classes. And the garden clubs in Pikeville, Prestonsburg, and Paintsville, Kentucky, are not about to be left behind. The distance isn't too far to Matewan. There's Uriah's Hotel in town for students to lodge overnight in icy weather."

The subject provokes an idea. "Well, George Washington, before our babies come along, I guess we could always put up a few students in Mount Blankenship."

Henry blushes as he downshifts for a turn. "Well, Martha Washington, I declare you're right! Matewan better build a few small hotels because garden clubs are springin' up everywhere. The new American Horticulture Society is spreadin' like hog weed, traveling from state to state for conferences. Why not have a conference in Matewan, West Virginia?"

I look to my engagement ring, the tiny diamond, and wonder what it cost Henry. Now's the time to speak my heart. "I'm so glad to hear this. I have all the faith in the world in you and the people in Matewan, but I couldn't have imagined such good news the day my parents drove away from Berea's campus."

Henry's face blanches. He takes his foot of the gas and turns to me. "Annie, what's wrong?"

His face is so strong. Confident. Trustworthy. "I couldn't think for loneliness, Henry. I walked around the town square in the dark. I watched the Tavern's lights go out. And everybody and everything I loved was one hundred and seventy miles away."

"Lord, Annie! You just tellin' me now? I would've come and taken you home and faced the music."

"That's exactly why I didn't tell you. I'd begin a letter and tear it up because the right words just wouldn't come. I was embarrassed, wanted to do what you and my parents wanted me to, and thought I was strong and independent enough to leave everyone behind."

I see hurt in Henry's eyes. "Well, I'm sorry, honey. I wish you would've told me. That's a hard burden to carry alone."

"I didn't want to ruin Christmas and summer breaks with you worrying about me. We always had so much work to do with the business and building the college."

Henry shakes his head. "You're tellin' a story, Annie. When did you ever have trouble findin' the right words?"

I look to the man I love with all my heart. "I'm telling the truth. I was one homesick seventeen-year-old girl, but I had to keep my promise to you and to my parents."

We're on an open stretch, so Henry steers with his left hand and wraps his shifting arm around me. "I'm sorry, darlin'. It hurts me to know how alone you were while I was surrounded by everyone else I love. I'm sorry for bein' such a knucklehead. I would've written you more had I known."

"Written more? You wrote me every day! Remember your 224 letters?"

Henry smiles. "Okay, let it all out. We have a little less than five hours alone in this truck, then it's goodbye Annie for a few days."

"I don't know where to begin."

"At the start, honey."

"You make it sound simple."

"I didn't say it was simple, Annie. Remember how hard it was for you to tell me about the redheaded Highlander?"

A shiver runs through me. I touch my forehead where the brute pushed my head onto the tavern's check-in counter.

"Just tell the truth, sweetheart."

I study Henry's profile and draw strength from it as I have since third grade when he sat two rows to my right in Mrs. Cline's class. "It goes back to Columbus, and it's a long, sad story."

"Okay. I'm in Columbus, and I know a few sad stories myself."

I think of Henry's pa and begin. "I had no family other than Mother and Father. No vacations with cousins, aunts, grandparents to tell my classmates or write about in school. No family Bibles or heirlooms handed down from generation to generation. My parents had no close friends. They didn't take me to Sunday school and church when we lived in Columbus. They never let me out of their sight. They were my world until I met you in third grade."

Henry kisses my ring. "I'm sorry. I cain't imagine what my life would've been like without Granny."

"Mother must've sensed my loneliness. She wrote in a letter that she left her home, gardens, and garden club in Columbus and followed Father because she loves him, and for that I'm most grateful. She said his love opened her eyes to Matewan's virtues."

Henry kisses the top of my head. "One of the most surprising gifts of my life is the friendship that's sprung up between your mother and mine."

"You know I didn't want to leave you after high school graduation."

"Yeah. But you did so your father would grant me your hand."

"I'll never forget your smile when you said, 'Annie, college is a good way to test the waters.'"

"So, tell me about those waters, honey."

"Well, American Literature class, for one. Willa Cather's *My Ántonia*."

"Placed out west, right?"

I nod. "One day, studying for a test, I remembered seeing the title on Mother's bookshelf. She's always reading one of the American or English classics. She loves Charles Dickens. But you know, not once did I touch *My Ántonia* before college."

"Olaf loaned me *A Tale of Two Cities*."

I smile at the image of Henry setting aside his tools and seed orders to read the epic. "Well, what did you think?"

He shifts the gears with gusto. "Lord-a-mercy, I couldn't get past *It was the worst of times, and the best of times, it was the age of wisdom, it was the age of foolishness.* All that goin' back and forth, *the season of Light and the season of Darkness* got me plumb lost. Guess I had buildin' our house on my mind."

I'm impressed with what he remembered, and improvised, but I can't help but grin at Henry's mistake in the opening line.

"Okay, 'fess up, Annie Dill. What'd I say?"

I touch Henry's arm, and I can't help but admire him all the more. "You switched *best* and *worst*."

Henry swipes my hand with a kiss, his nimble mind turning as if he's about to move the Queen on his mind's chessboard. "Well, I reckon it all depended on which side of the guillotine you stood on during France's Reign of Terror. Olaf said his great-great-great grandfather and fellow Scandinavian botanists barely escaped from their last visit to Versailles."

"I'm glad they did."

Henry nods. "And so is Mrs. Semenov. Her great-great grandfather was also one who escaped."

"Not all of them did?"

The glint falls from Henry's eyes. "No, honey."

"Last month, Mrs. Semenov loaned Mother her copies of *The Scarlet Pimpernel*."

"Isn't that a flar'er?"

"Yes, a symbol the author used throughout the series."

Henry slows for a car turning off the road. "Who's the author?"

"Baroness Orczy. Hungarian-born Brit."

Henry shakes his head and speeds up. "There we go again with British writers. So, what's the big deal with the scarlet pimpernel?"

"The hero, that's all."

"Well, I'll be," he says and grips the steering wheel. "A little flar'er. The hero. I can believe that."

"The main character disguises himself with the name 'Scarlet Pimpernel' and helps British and French aristocrats escape the guillotine. Mother's read all five books."

Henry whistles again. "I swear, Annie, your mother must be some reader."

"When she unpacked our household in Matewan, she unwrapped something from a chest of books that resembled Father's diploma in his dental office in the hospital. She called me to her side and whispered, 'Read it, Annie.'"

"Well, what'd it say?"

I inhale the fresh, spring air and surprise myself. "*Ohio State University, Margaret Lynne Lewiston, the Degree of Bachelor of Arts.* Mother looked to me and said, 'Daughter, this is what I want for you.' Then she locked her diploma in the chest. I wondered why she didn't hang it in her library."

"Now that's sad, Annie. Your mother majored in literature?"

I pause, "Yes, but I didn't know it then. She never mentioned *My Ántonia* until I wrote her a letter including one of my many favorite passages in the book."

"What's the story about?"

"An orphaned boy tells his story about his relatives in Blue Ridge, Virginia, sending him to his grandparents in Black Hawk, Nebraska. The story begins on Jim's train ride west where he first sees Ántonia and her family, Ukrainian immigrants who also settle in Black Hawk."

"That's one long train ride for a boy alone," Henry says. "Sounds interesting. Olaf said Ukraine borders Russia and has some of the most fertile farmland in the world. So, what's your favorite passage?"

I laugh. "My mother's greatest nightmare for her daughter."

"Go on."

"Well, I've not recited it lately. The boy Jim tells his story about Ántonia."

"Got it."

"*When I rode over to see her ploughing, she stopped at the end of a row to chat, then gripped her plough-handles, clucked to her team, and waded down the furrow, making me feel that she was now grown up and had no time for me. Grandfather was pleased with Ántonia. When we complained of her, he only smiled and said, 'She'll help some fellow get ahead in this world.'"*

There go Henry's brows again, thinking as he shifts on a curve. "Well, I guess that's a straightforward way to tell your mother that you love growing things and aim to stick it out with me. How'd she take it?"

"A week later, I opened the most beautiful letter. Mother wrote a passage of Jim on his wagon ride across the prairie to his grandparents in Black Hawk. It's Jim thinking."

"I'm followin'."

"*I had never looked up at the sky when there was not a familiar mountain ridge against it. But this was not the dome of heaven, all there was of it. I did not believe that my dead father and mother were watching me from up there; they would still be looking for me at the sheepfold down by the creek, or along the white road that led to the mountain pastures. I had left even their spirits behind me.*"

Henry whispers. "You're right. That's awful sad."

"The saddest thing, Henry, is Mother wrote of her parents who died of the Spanish Flu after they returned from England. I was four years old and had never met my grandparents."

"You didn't know about your grandparents until your mother's letter?"

"No. It broke my heart, but inspired me to write about Appalachians as Willa Cather wrote about prairie pioneers."

"So, you wrote about Matewan."

"Yes, I did. The town's much more than mine wars and the Hatfield-McCoy Feud."

"So, what'd you write about?"

"The Nennis, Olaf, Mrs. Semenov, and your mommy, Gertie Blankenship. My parents. Daisy. Mrs. Cline. Doc Bentley. Pastor Hickman. Garden Club. The college. Even Sue Ann and Crazy Ray."

Henry lifts his eyebrows and clicks his tongue in approval. "Lordy! Your Berea classmates must think Matewan's a goin' place.

You'll soon see how our little town's pullin' itself out of the Depression to throw you a party. I've never seen such excitement. Be prepared, honey. You're a celebrity now."

"Celebrity?"

"Yeah. Your purdy face in your cap and gown with your diploma is in six small-town newspapers and the *Williamson Daily News.* Made the front page of the *Matewan Bullet.* Their new reporter, Punkin' Smith, quoted you about your fingers itchin' to dig, plant, grow, and teach women and men good husbandry along Tug Fork."

I'm concerned about what else Mr. Smith wrote because he asked some personal questions I didn't want to answer in his phone interview. "What else did the article say?"

"Oh, somethin' about when you were a freshman you thought you had to choose either agriculture or literature." We stop at an intersection. Henry wipes his brow with his handkerchief. "I remember you saying this in a letter. I wrote back and asked why you couldn't choose both."

"Because most people don't earn a double major in college for a reason. And most coal miners don't work a second job because going underground takes so much out of a man."

His eyes smart. "So, are you sayin' a double major would've taken too much outa you, and workin' both literature and horticulture wouldn't leave enough of you for raisin' a family?"

I check my watch. Nine o'clock, and the truck's cab is warming up. I inch out of the way of the gearshift and place the picnic basket on the seat between Henry and me. "Yes. And if it came down to one, you know it had to be literature."

Henry turns to my sweaty face. "Because few people write about Appalachia with the affection and respect it deserves."

"No one knows better than locals the work it takes to reverse the damage done by writers and publishers who don't take the time and interest to understand Appalachian history and culture. But the stories and photos sell, and people embrace the stereotype."

"Go on," Henry says.

"Then I read your letter."

"Which one?"

"Where you said I could do both. That you'd be my helpmate."

"So, how can I help?"

I put the basket on the floorboard and slide back to Henry's shoulder. "After I dig and plant all day, I'll need a little library with a typewriter."

Henry's large hands grip the wheel as he grins like a little boy with a lemon sour from Leckie's Drugstore. "My hammer can do that, honey. I cain't wait for you to see our house. You'll love the porch."

"Big enough for six children?"

"And the grandparents and us, of course. Promise you'll sit down and rock with us of an evenin', Annie. After three years without you, I need you by my side a spell after supper."

The sweaty scent of Henry's skin and clothes roots me deeper into our past, present, and future. Dispels my doubt that Matewan will embrace me again. "I promise."

"Oh Annie, I don't want to spoil the surprise. The whole town and Blackberry City are invited to Hunt's Feed & Seed. And the passionflower's vining all over the pergola I built behind the store. Come September, we'll smell the blossoms clear from our porch!"

"*Passiflora incarnate* of the *Passifloraceae* family," I say.

Henry kisses my forehead. "Like I said, just two more weeks for the finishing touches on your kitchen."

"The cabinets or plumbing?"

"Don't you fret, darlin'. You go on and rest a bit and leave the driving and the house to me."

This is our last trip from Berea sitting side by side—best we can with Henry pushing the clutch and shifting all the way home. The partnership worked well these three years. Henry loves to drive, so as usual, he's driving while I sleep off late nights studying and working the check-in desk of Boone Tavern Hotel.

But before we arrive in Matewan, I have to settle one last thing with Henry and myself. "Henry?"

"Yeah."

"I never told Mother and Father I worked the hotel's check-in desk."

His shoulders fall imperceptibly. "What're you afraid of, honey?"

"Their disappointment when I tell them I lied about my college work assignment."

"Lied is a strong word for it."

"Well, at the very least I deceived them, and that's a strong word, too. Don't you think it's only a matter of time before the Highlander incident reaches them in some way, or he shows up in Matewan?"

"Well, I cain't say, Annie. Even if he does, don't you think your parents will believe you and the police report?"

"Yes, but you know my parents didn't want me waiting tables or working the tavern's desk. I let them believe I chose the admissions office for my part-time assignment. If I hadn't worked the desk, the incident wouldn't have happened."

"Hmm, I doubt that, Annie. A man with violence on his mind would follow a defenseless person most anywhere. Man or woman. He could've followed you to the house you boarded in, for instance. It's a good thing you were in the Tavern—in public, and he was drunk enough and loud enough to reach over the check-in counter and assault you. I'm ever grateful the cook heard the Highlander's threats and called the police. The knot on your forehead was enough proof for a criminal offence."

"Henry, my parents don't know any of this. They trusted me to tell the truth. If the Highlander shows up, how do I begin to explain my decisions and the incident?"

Henry smiles. "Don't worry, Annie. Your parents love you and will understand you did nothing to provoke the Highlander's assault. Please rest and leave the past behind."

I lean my head on Henry's shoulder, but there's too much on my mind to rest.

"Talk to me, darlin'."

"Remember the women I met from Georgia's Athens Garden Club?"

"They still plannin' on meetin' with Garden Club this summer?"

"Yes. And so is Elizabeth Martin."

"The founder of the Garden Club of Philadelphia you wrote about?"

"Uh-huh," I mumble, impressed at Henry's sharp memory.

"Mrs. Semenov said she's looking forward to making Mrs. Martin's acquaintance and learning more about the Garden Club of America."

"Have you read Richardson's latest book?" I ask.

"*The Story of Gardening?*"

"Yes."

"Nope. Olaf reads passages when we have a minute. The last piece ended with this statement: 'Gardening is leaping social barriers to become a universal feminine diversion.'"

I've yet to read Wright's book and don't want to respond out of context. However, I find "feminine diversion" misses the mark in observing women's devotion to gardening. I've never considered my mother's gardens or her membership in Garden Club a diversion. Rather, a significant expression of her creative work as a homemaker. Like cooking, gardening is mother's joyful necessity. Yes. That's it. A necessity. And for Olaf, Mrs. Semenov, Henry, and me, and many hill folk up and down these Appalachian creeks, in one means or another, gardening is our livelihood.

Henry kisses my forehead. "Say, what you so quiet about, Annie Dill?"

I admire his strong profile in the backlight of passing roadside. "Did you and Olaf discuss that last passage?"

"Why, if you want to call it that. Olaf closed the book and asked, 'Vat do you think, son?' Well, I said, I don't appreciate someone callin' Mommy's work with her shovel a 'feminine diversion' any more than callin' the labor and skill to build my herbarium a 'feminine diversion.' Why, just by watching Mommy plant their little gardens, women throughout Tug Fork and Peter Creek are learnin' how easy it is to plant and grow peonies and gladiolus. You should see the field Dixie DeBoard up Smith Fork is growin' from the few roots and corms Mommy planted for her five springs ago. Dixie's cuttin' and sellin' her flar'ers from buckets at the end of her runoff! And people are walkin' and drivin' to her field to cut their own peonies and gladiolus! Now, that's good husbandry."

I smile in agreement as Henry stretches his back and shoulders. I love it when he's in the mood to talk about flowers.

"One day while we were stocking inventory, Olaf said that botanists from the world over would send rescued herbariums to Mekinov, each with its own story. Mekinov forwarded several of the herbariums to Olaf, knowing his father's fate. I followed him to his office one day where a large, beautiful book, an herbarium, waited on his desk. He nodded to the white flar'er painted on the book's cover and said, 'This is a German Alpine named Edelweiss, botanical name: *Leontopodium alpinum.*'"

"What a wonderful gift, Henry."

"Annie, I could smell cigar smoke in the cover. And the store was so quiet we could hear the spine crinkle when Olaf opened the book. He turned fifty pages, spoke the common and botanical name of every preserved flar'er, and had me repeat them."

I'm speechless.

"There's more. Olaf said, 'It is customary for every student of botany to create their own herbarium for posterity.' So, Olaf helped me create my own herbarium, and believe it or not, Richardson Wright helped Olaf create his herbarium while he and Mrs. Semenov lived in Boston."

"Did Olaf show you his herbarium?"

He nods. "The artwork is somethin' else. Makes my book look like somethin' from grade school."

"Well, Olaf's had a lot of practice, and he and Richardson are artists. How many specimens have you completed?" I ask.

"None. I just finished the book."

"How many pages did you add for specimens?"

"Olaf suggested fifty to begin with, so I did. Mrs. Semenov's teachin' me to preserve the plants and label them for the sample page. Since I'm better with a hammer than a paintbrush, Mrs. Semenov's helpin' me draw and paint the prints with the proper color of each flar'er. She says herbariums are labors of love to complete over several years, perhaps even a lifetime. That's prob'ly how long it'll take me to complete my book. Did you know Emily Dickinson made her own herbarium? Mrs. Semenov bought me a book of her poetry. It's tough readin' sometimes, but I'm workin' on it."

I'm impressed. "You're reading Emily Dickinson's poetry?"

"Yeah. I remembered her quirky little poems about nature and human nature from English class in school. I can lay down my hammer long enough to read a handful of verses without feelin' guilty. Olaf and Mrs. Semenov want us to take a trip to Emily's house in Amherst, Massachusetts, someday. That means we need someone to mind the store for several days. Cain't see that happening any time soon."

"I'll say it again. I hope someday Olaf and Mrs. Semenov tell us why they chose Matewan for their home and business."

Henry relaxes his shoulders. "Does it really matter?"

"Perhaps not. If it did, wouldn't they tell us?"

Henry nods. "I'm just glad the seed store survived the fire of 1910 so they could choose our home as theirs."

Home. I'm going home.

"Henry."

"Uh-huh."

"I'm glad you put two sinks and toilet stalls in the bathroom."

"That so?"

"My roommate never cleaned up after herself. Do you?"

"Granny and Mommy wouldn't have it any other way."

"Would you have it any other way?"

"Nope. As Mommy and Olaf say, 'a place for everysing, and everysing in its place.'"

I rest my head on Henry's shoulder, close my eyes, and let my mind wander. "I saved my wages for months to buy silk hose, then ruined them with hangnails."

"Did you bring them home for tying up tomatoes?"

I mumble, "Nothing goes to waste. 'A place for everysing, and everysing in its place.'"

"That's my girl."

He drives into the Appalachian foothills, leaving loneliness and the Highlander behind with every turn. I wake as the truck turns off the road and Henry stops by a small, abandoned store with a gas pump. Henry wipes away a tear.

"Your pa?"

He nods.

Henry parks and fixes his baby blues on a rusted sign with faded red letters spelling *Boone's*. I've pitied this forlorn filling station my three years living and learning in Boone County. This is our last opportunity to stop and take a good look. The scene is another business gone by the wayside.

"Before Pa's accident, the few times he sat down for supper with

Mommy and me, he'd talk about the man who built this little place. The owner's pa was a descendant of Daniel Boone, so he thought he could make some money off the local hero's name by sellin' gas and moonshine. But the fool drank what profits he made and ended up dyin' of liver failure, just like my pa."

Henry talks with his eyes fixed on the sign. "I bathed him for three months before his liver finally gave out. I think he couldn't take the July heat. After I stood up to Pa, he never spoke another cross word to Mommy or me. I just wish he would've asked us and Jesus to forgive him. I'm sorry to spoil your special day, Annie, but sometimes regret gets the best of me."

I've observed Henry's battle from that day in third grade when Mrs. Cline stopped at his desk. My first year in Matewan Elementary School, I held my breath when our eyes met because I'd learned that meant it was Henry's father who fell in a mining accident. The whole class knew because people who live in coal towns know mountains sometimes claim men for the paychecks they yield.

Henry didn't come back to class for a week. I clung to my father's side until I heard Henry's pa came home. That's when I knew I loved my father, and he loved me. And when Henry came back to class, I knew I loved him.

But I cannot know his sorrow, the anguish that follows any recollection of his father.

"Henry?"

"Yes, darlin'."

"You've not spoiled my day. I'm your helpmate, remember?"

He pulls me close and kisses my hair. "Makin' me eat my words, aren't you, Annie Dill?"

I nod to the *Boone's* sign. "What does it bring to mind?"

Henry's eyes flash. He pretends a scowl. "I don't know what you're driving at. Remember, I don't have a college education to understand what you writers call *allusions*."

I punch him on the arm. "Think like Emily Dickinson, you might see something in this forsaken place to bring you peace of mind."

Henry wraps both arms around the steering wheel in the

posture of sincere thought, one of his problem-solving poses I've observed when we've met with Olaf and Mrs. Semenov to discuss business—or when he's building something and comes upon a snag.

He turns his head from side to side, opens his door, and walks to the gas pump and touches the nozzle. He aims for the little cinder-block building and tries the dirty doorknob. It opens. He turns and waves me to come. I'm off my seat and by his side in two breaths. We're in third grade again.

We stand inside the door. We look and listen. The only sound comes from what we crunch under our feet. On all manner of scat, Henry walks around upturned display shelves, a trashcan, chairs, moldy maps, and empty Pepsi bottles. On the floor behind a filthy counter to my left, a cash register lies open on its side, the till empty. Of all the glorious things, a *Cercis Canadensis* seedling looks up from the dirt along the wall.

I think of Olaf's beautiful, brass cash register on the polished counter in Hunt's Feed & Seed and feel again the strong pull of pity for this abandoned place. I resist the urge to rescue the little redbud sapling and stand by Henry in the center of the one-room building.

As I've seen him in the seed store, and between the studs in our unfinished house, Henry Blankenship stands in communion with the Almighty. Light beams through the one dusty window upon his shoulders. I see more clearly the burdens they bear.

Here and now, I know God's speaking the "still, small voice of the Comforter" to my beloved. So, I wait, and I trust Him to deliver the man I love from regret.

He falls to his knees in a squall of dust. We cough as I kneel before him. He takes my hands. I know he's praying, between him and God, as he says.

Mice scamper in the walls and on the floor. Cars and trucks pass on the road.

Henry's warm, strong hands hold mine still. With our eyes closed, I wait and listen a long while, and want to rescue the redbud to transplant beside our house. The litter on the floor pains my bare knees until Henry says, "Annie."

We stand to our feet. I dust off my dress. He hands me his hanky. "Your knees, honey."

I wipe scat and rubbish from my shins, shake out the hanky, and fold it. Henry returns it to his back pants pocket.

He looks to the window. "You know, it would take a lot of work, time, and cash to restore this place to serve people again. Just like it's going to take work, time, and cash to build our future. I think I see something to bring peace of mind."

"You do?"

As he does when sizing up a project to count the cost of supplies and labor, Henry surveys the four walls and corners, foundation, and ceiling of the building. A truck with a loud muffler pulls off the road for several seconds, then spins gravel and roars back onto the road. But it doesn't distract Henry.

"Annie, life hasn't turned out as I planned. It's turned out better than I could ever imagine. It's time to leave my disappointments and painful memories of Pa right here in these ruins and walk into our new life together."

I nod. Henry's never said this before, but he's sincere and he makes sense.

"It's time to give back to Olaf and Mrs. Semenov. To Matewan," he says.

He's never said this before either, but from what I've read in his letters, I have a good idea what he means when he returns his eyes to the window, fingers splayed upon his hips. "I see it, honey."

"How to give back?"

He nods, eyes fixed on the grimy, sunlit glass. I'm witnessing the fruition of twelve years under the Semenov's tutelage. I see it growing in the redbud seedling. Like Moses, Henry turns to me with the light of the burning bush on his face.

"We build upon Petrov's letters and the five books Olaf and Mrs. Semenov brought from Russia. We build with the help of Garden Club, our plants, honey, and all you've learned at college. With the help of local newspapers and our college, our work reaches beyond the seed store and Matewan to teach good husbandry throughout Appalachia."

I ask the question he's waiting to hear. "So, where's our work reaching?"

He glances back to the window as if it's whispering the answer.

Then he looks me in the eye. "The railyard—as Olaf envisioned when he and Mrs. Semenov first laid eyes on it. Richardson Wright called it 'prime real estate.' Higher ground for twenty greenhouses and fifty apiaries close to the rails for shipping plants and honey north and south. Close to the Tug for pumping water up to the greenhouses."

He takes my left hand. A ray of light finds the diamond in a spark of confirmation. "You saw it before I did."

Again, I submit my racing heart to our visions. "With my father's help."

He picks up an empty Pepsi bottle and rubs off the grit. "I'm not sayin' it'll happen in our lifetime. But some day that coal yard's goin' to stand empty, waitin' for another industry to employ and prosper Peter Creek, Mate Creek, Matewan, Tug Fork, and greater Appalachia. We have to be ready when that window opens."

Henry closes his eyes and bathes his face in the window's beam of light. I do the same, and thank God we stepped inside this building.

I look at the time. Henry destroys or loses every watch he buys. "So, it's settled? We leave our old burdens here, and carry our visions into Matewan?"

Henry kisses my hand. "What in Heaven's name would I do without you?"

I will do anything this man asks of me, because whatever he asks is entirely worthy of my trust. "And what in Heaven's name would I do without you?" I see longing in his eyes, and know he sees it in mine.

"Well, we'd better get goin'," he says, blushing.

I return a blush and nod.

He leads me to the door where I see the cash register beside the redbud sapling to the right. "Look, Henry."

He stops and spies the sapling. "Well, I'll be. Just look at that little darlin'."

Before I can ask Henry for his pocketknife and hanky, he removes them from his pants' pocket and squats between the counter and wall. He shakes open his hanky and within five seconds extracts the redbud's tiny root ball and wraps it within his hanky. He cuts a piece of a bootlace, ties it around the hanky, and holds the rescued redbud before me.

"For you, Annie, my beloved. Congratulations on your graduation from Berea College. I couldn't be more proud of you. Let's remember this day as we watch this redbud grow with our children. As Petrov said, may we remember we're never alone."

I accept Henry's gift. "How did you know?"

"Your eyes, honey."

What else can I do other than stand on my toes and give Henry a kiss? And I don't care who sees us.

We walk into the fresh, bright April air toward his truck. We pause and admire its rust-free body. "It's a beauty, Henry. And it rides so much smoother than Trouble. What did she cost?"

Henry's eyes linger on his second love. He smiles. "Nothin'."

"Crazy Ray didn't give it to you."

"Nope." He pulls me close to his side, careful of our redbud. "Olaf and Mrs. Semenov bought it for our weddin' present. I was waitin' for the right time to tell you. Listen to this, Annie. In his last letter to Olaf, Petrov included signed and notarized documents that bequeathed the value of his estate to our college."

I know again our benefactors' boundless charity. "I can't wait to show you the articles and my sketches for recycling railroad ties."

He looks to the *Boone* sign. "Olaf says it's a matter of timin' and talkin' with the railroad. Findin' investors. But Annie, I didn't want business, or Pa, or the Highlander to dim the joy of this special day. I just want to love you and celebrate your homecomin'."

I hold Henry's little darlin' before him. "You already have. I want nothing else than to drive into Matewan in enough time to plant your Darlin' in our front yard and make myself presentable."

Henry looks to his truck. "Well, I'm warning you, Annie. I think that little boy will always be a part of me because Pa will always be a part of me."

"And I have a feeling that lonely little girl you fell in love with in third grade will always be a part of me because Father will always be a part of me."

Henry steps back and looks me over head to toe. "Lonely little girl?"

I didn't plan this, but Henry's started something, so here I go. "I cannot remember one time my father hugged me. He never tucked me into bed or bounced me on his knee. I thought something was wrong with me."

Henry shakes his head with a puzzled frown. "You know better now, don't you?"

I nod.

"You know anything about your father's parents?"

"Yes. On my sixth birthday, Mother dressed me in my favorite yellow dress for Father to take me to a dairy. As the children played and licked their ice cream cones, I noticed at least one parent or grandparent watched over them. So, I asked Father about his parents. He said they died when he was a baby."

"That was it?"

"Yes. I was too young then to understand the concept of adoption. Father's never spoken about it. Mother says to be patient, that he'll tell me someday about his train ride from New York City to Columbus."

Henry furrows his brows. "You mean an orphan train?"

"Yes."

"How'd you find out about that?"

"Newspaper articles in Berea's library. I wrote an essay about the orphan trains and my father in my senior English composition class. Afterward, my professor loaned me two books with photos. Henry, the orphan trains were wonderful and miserable. I couldn't sleep for several nights imagining my father traveling alone with hundreds of orphans."

"That's why Jim and Antonia in *My Ántonia* mean a lot to you and your mother?"

"I believe so."

"Before Pa's accident, Mommy read an article in the *Williamson Daily News* about the orphan trains. She cried. I didn't know what an orphan was until then. In Tug Fork and Peter Creek, there's always some kin or neighbor to take in a child abandoned by death or neglect. Your mother never told you about your father's train ride?"

"No. I think she doesn't want to betray his trust. I think he's ashamed."

"After hearing your mother's favorite passage from her book, do you think she might be helping you understand a little about your father's suffering?"

"Yes, and I think she's trying to understand, too."

We stroll through shaded weeds and spring wildflowers to lean against our first wedding gift. We shield our eyes and look high into springtime sky.

"Honey, my father didn't understand what he missed. But these past three years, I think your father's come to know what he's missed."

I kick off my shoes and feel the warm earth under my feet. "You know, I'm beginning to see the reason for Father's obsession for dentistry, his daily routine. Breakfast at 7 a.m., lunch at eleven, and dinner at 5:30 p.m. He smiles when someone calls with an emergency on the weekend. He drops whatever he's doing and takes the call, then phones Lucy with instructions to prep for the patient."

"How does Lucy take it?"

"Oh, she's happy to oblige because she likes the pay. She has no dependents or debts other than paying off her Nenni's and Saul Brown credit."

He grins sideways. "And Henry Blankenship for a home improvement. She came into the store last week and asked me to build her another clothes closet."

I know Henry will never want for work. If Lucy were fifteen years younger, Mother could have grounds for jealousy. As Father does for Mother and me, he supplies Lucy's material needs, too, but Mother and I know Father finds affection difficult to express. "When I asked would he please drive me home today, he said you would prefer the honor."

Henry crosses his ankles and rests an arm on my shoulders.

"Shor' is a purdy day, Annie. Your father knows me better than I thought. I'm more than honored to drive you home."

I'm in the safest place in the entire world, wrapped in Henry's sincere love.

"Annie, Matewan's a different place since you left after Christmas. The friendship between our mothers continues to chip away differences between the women in Blackberry City and Matewan. I see it every Wednesday night when they gather for Garden Club. Cain't believe my eyes."

"I'm very thankful to see and hear of these developing friend-ships, Henry. Do you remember the first week in third grade, when I asked why you call where you live Blackberry City when it isn't a city?"

"Uh-huh. I said I didn't know, and asked why you call the city you came from Columbus when he had nothin' to do with it?"

I laugh into the sweet scent of spring, the season for lovers, and know I'm more helplessly Henry's than ever before.

"Can you tell me why the women in Blackberry City aren't members of Garden Club?"

Henry stands akimbo. "Miss Daisy says the women in Matewan think they're above the women in Blackberry City and won't let them in the club."

I mimic Henry's posture. "Well, Miss Daisy has it backwards. Matewan is along Tug Fork, and Blackberry City's on the other side of the viaduct, high on the mountainside. The women in Blackberry City look down on the women in Matewan."

Henry lassos my waist with his arms. "Annie Dill, if we don't get goin', we won't arrive 'til nightfall after your shindig's begun. And we have Darlin' to plant."

I slip on my shoes, open the door, place Darlin' on the floor-board, and step up onto my seat. A breeze swings the Boone's sign back and forth, screeching its rusty hinges.

Henry sits behind the wheel as we watch the sign swing. "Well, would you listen to that? This old place is sending us off with a song, Annie!" He turns the key and shifts into first gear. "Take us to Mat-ewan, Boone!"

Redbud blooms along the road and up hillsides, stunning us anew with beauty as Henry drives us homeward. He wiggles us through one worn-out town after another, past mouths of hollows and branches where people we'll never know live and die by the sweat of their brow, and rest in peace on hilltops.

Carcasses of every make and model of car and truck that rolls off Detroit's assembly line litter the landscape. I marvel again at Nature's faithfulness to heal man's abuse. Every time we pass this way, the earth's buried more waste. We see pawpaw, redbud, and hickory trees sprouting through broken windows. Hope never fails to inspire us through these dark times of the persistent Depression.

Olaf's right. In a matter of ten years, Flora in all her glory will devour these rusted castaways. But at this very moment, I remember something brand-new: the silk hose Saul Brown promised for my graduation gift. If anybody can track down a pair, it's him.

"Thank God the Depression's burning itself out," Henry says. "Perfect timing, too. Look how everything's greening up real good. And no place is purdier than Matewan."

"I can't wait to see the peonies."

He honks the horn in exclamation. "Garden Club gathered them in vases and put them all over town yesterday evenin'. Folk were joking we should change Matewan's name to 'Peony' for the month of April."

"Must smell wonderful."

Henry looks to the hills. "This is when I miss Granny most."

He stops at the crossroads of Salyersville on the Licking River. "We're halfway. Ready for lunch under our oak in the park?"

"Do we have time?"

"Yeah, the road was good comin' in before and after daybreak. It's dry, and that helps shave off time. Better dusty than muddy. Besides, Mommy's chicken salad sandwiches are too messy to eat in the truck. And this is our last time to visit Frank."

Henry parks along a sidewalk before the post office and takes Mother's basket from the truck. When I was a girl, Mother packed the basket with her ginger cookies and iced tea and took me and my classmate and neighbor, Cammy, to a large park in downtown Columbus. We loved the swings and slides and building tunnels in the big sandbox. I remember Cammy's giggle when Mother opened the lid of the basket for our ginger cookies. After all these years, Mother found Cammy in Columbus and invited her to my party. Like Gertie, Mother thinks of everything.

Henry walks into the park swinging our lunch basket by the handle. The man must be starved. I take in Salyersville for the last time, after three years of driving back and forth to Berea.

The town's turned lush and green since we stopped on our way home for my Christmas break. Frank, the postmaster, insisted we come into the post office and eat our chicken salad sandwiches in the warmth rather than shivering in Henry's truck. In many ways, Salyersville's long-standing postmaster and town philosopher reminds us of Olaf.

Salyersville is about Matewan's size without her caressing mountains. Folk are out and about doing business in the post office, bank, filling station, and a few small stores.

Dr. Benjamin Ford, Dentist, is printed in black letters on a white sign before a small, red brick building next to the white-bricked post office. The bank faces both businesses on the other side of the street. Father speaks highly of Dr. Ford. "Leading the way in Appalachian dentistry," he says.

"And Dr. Matthew Dill, twenty years his junior, is close behind," Mother replies, affectionately.

Still no feed and seed store in town. I feel again the marvelous gift of a promising future swell within my heart. Sadly, Salyersville needs flowers. Just because we're still climbing out of the Depression doesn't mean life has to be drab. Every town, every home, needs color and bloom. Every person can afford a packet of flower seeds. And if they can't, I'll do my best to give them *Zinnia elegans* seeds to plant around their home and locally, or to pot up to sell under Matewan Garden Club's tent at the Magnolia Fair. This is the third year for our Fair, and do the ladies ever have the zinnias, magnolias, hibiscus, rhododendrons, mountain laurel, gladioli, blackberry lilies, and peonies for sale!

Henry sets down Mother's basket under our oak tree set up on a hill. "Come on, Annie!"

"There's not one flower blooming in this town!" I holler, and run up to the tree and the man I love. He sweeps me up in his arms and gives me a twirl. I laugh. It feels good to exercise my legs. That's why I rented a flat on the second story of a boarding house on a hilly street in Berea. And that's one benefit of gardening in Appalachia. There's always a rise to climb. Henry hands me a faded quilt to spread out on the lawn. At least the grass is green.

"So, what you planning to do about it?"

"About what?"

"Salyersville's sorry lack of flowers."

I spread the quilt upon the mowed lawn and am struck by the blanket's faded beauty. "Give away zinnia seeds. Who made this quilt?"

"Why, Granny," Henry says, with his back to me. From the basket, he extracts two canning jars filled with water that were ice when he left home.

I'm near frantic, studying the double-ring wedding band treasure. "Henry, we shouldn't put this on the ground or sit on it. Look, the threads are too fragile. This quilt is valuable, not just because your Granny made it, but because it's her art. This belongs in a glass case displayed in the seed store, out of sunlight, for all Matewan to see but not touch!" I look up to see Henry staring at me, shaking his head, mouth agape, and holding a brand-new thermos. He wipes his eyes.

"What did I say?"

"Lord knows I'm thirsty enough to drink this Lickin' River dry! After drivin' almost five hours to Berea, now halfway to your graduation party, could you please wait until I open this here thermos and take a good, long swig before I answer?"

I blush. He tips the thermos until emptied. Then he digs into the basket and removes another one identical to the first. "For you, Flar'er Girl." He hands the thermos to me. "We're sellin' these like hotcakes beside Mrs. Semenov's streusel and your mother's baklava. Keeps tea chilled real nice—or coffee hot as Hades' hinges. Why, there's nothing wrong, honey. Thirst is prone to make a grown man cry. But truth is, you love my granny's quilt. She hung it between Pa's bed and mine the day Sheriff Taylor brought him home from the hospital. So, Mommy thought it's high time she passed it on to us for our house."

Now I wipe my own eyes, drink half the tea, and realize I need a lady's room.

Henry places our sandwiches on matching plates from Mother's picnic basket.

"Be right back. Flower Girl has to visit Frank first."

Henry waves me on as he chomps into his sandwich.

Frank sits at his desk when I open the door, with its predictable scrape against the concrete floor, his signal a customer's calling. He looks up. "Well, if it ain't Annie Dill! Needin' the facilities?"

I nod and push open the Dutch door at the end of the counter. Frank knows there's no time for small talk.

The post office is larger than Matewan's and serves as Salyersville's unofficial public bathroom. If there's one steadfast complaint I have about Appalachia, it's the filthy lavatories.

When Father first drove Mother and me to Matewan from Columbus, we couldn't find one clean public toilet anywhere until we stopped at Leckie's Drugstore—where we also discovered their root beer float. But this lack confirmed Mother's opinion of mountain people as backward. She's since learned many mountain homes still use outhouses, including Henry's. He'd once said in third grade, "If the outhouse is good enough for my mother and Granny, it's good enough for me." I smile and wash my hands, thankful for Frank, and leave the sink cleaner than I found it, as Mother taught.

Frank stands at the counter sorting papers. "Well, I hear congratulations are in order."

He speaks a mix of expressions gained from serving all manner of passersby and those who live and die in a small community like this one.

"Thank you." I want to tell him I'm so glad to go home, but don't want to sound ungrateful for my education or like a homesick child.

"So, you're on your way home to Matewan?"

"Henry's in the park chowing down his mother's chicken salad sandwich. And I'm aiming for mine."

"Well, I'm goin' to miss you two, Annie."

"And we'll miss you, Frank. Our trips wouldn't have been as pleasant otherwise."

Frank casts a glance to the lavatory door and pushes his glasses up on his forehead. He avoids my eyes. This isn't like him.

"Annie, I've wrestled with myself about tellin' you somethin' if you stopped by."

"What is it, Frank?"

"I don't want to detain you and Henry. Word's got out in all the papers, and ever'body between Berea and Williamson knows you're celebratin' your college graduation tonight. That was a fine piece of journalism about you in the *Salyersville Independent*, by the way. You're a regional celebrity, Annie. So, I'm thinkin' you and Henry would like to know there might be some trouble afoot."

"Is a storm brewing?"

Frank shakes his head. "I think it's a good idea to call Henry inside." Struck with dread, I swing the Dutch door open. I don't want to tell Henry what Frank said. I want to drive away as fast as we can. But Henry opens the door and we're face to face.

"Annie, why do you look like the sky's fallin' in?"

"Frank said there might be trouble afoot."

Henry shuts the door and looks to Frank. "What trouble?"

The Postmaster turns the sign in the window to *CLOSED*. "Y'all step into the storage room." He carries the chair from his desk to inside the small space, out of view from the front window. "Please sit."

I do and Henry stands behind me, his warm hands on my shoulders. "Please get to it, Frank," he says.

"I regret to be the bearer of bad news, but my post requires a report to the sheriff of any violence or violation of goodwill within these premises, which I've done. He suggested I tell y'all the incident if you happened by."

"Go on," Henry says.

I fold my hands on my lap to calm myself.

"A stranger stopped in an hour ago, spreadin' a rumor about seein' Henry Blankenship's empty blue truck outside the old Boone's fillin' station. I didn't like what he said about you, Annie, and told him to get out and keep his gossip to hisself."

"What did he say?" I ask.

Frank looks to his inky hands. "I cain't repeat it. Even in a court of law."

I know Henry's mind is splitting into a million directions trying to figure out who would slander my name. "Did you catch his license plate number? What did he look like?" he asks.

"He walked in when three locals stood in line. He hovered over poor old Joe by the door and opened his foul mouth before we knew what happened. A big guy, his beady eyes and red head taller than the other men, he talked like those young fellers who dress up as Scottish Highlanders and invade Berea every September to throw poles and eat haggis. I reckoned he might've seen you at school, Annie."

What I feared has come upon me.

Henry gently presses his hands on my shoulders. "Go on, Frank."

"He reeked of liquor. Took the four of us to pitch him out the door. He jumped into an old gray truck and turned off the street before we could get his license plate number."

Henry removes his hands. I stand before Frank. "Thank you for caring enough to warn us. We'd rather know if someone's spreading lies about me than not."

Frank's eyes fill with compassion. "Not just you, Annie."

Henry wraps an arm around my waist. "What'd he say?"

Frank shakes his head. "You two go on. I know how to reach you if I need to. Our sheriff's on the case. He said he's had trouble with this Highlander bunch before. And the redhead is the top offender in several small towns. He goes by the name Rusty. I know, not too original, is it? Anyway, our sheriff has talked with your Sheriff Taylor and all those between here and Matewan. They're all watchin' the road. The feller's impossible to miss with his red hair and loud muffler."

I remember the loud muffler and spinning wheels at the filling station. And the look in Henry's eyes says he does too.

Ever the gentleman, Frank picks up a small, slender box from his desk and hands it to me. "Here's a little somethin' for your graduation."

I open the box to a blue Cross fountain pen and run my fingertips over the engraved initials: AMD. Speechless, I look to Frank.

"The newspaper said you want to write about Appalachia, so I found you a real purdy pen."

"It's lovely, Frank. Thank you for everything. You've been so kind these past three years."

He smiles. "I'm goin' to miss you two love birds passin' through ever' now and then, 'specially Christmas time. Gave me somethin' to look forward to. Now, go on to your party."

We walk to the oak and gather the canning jars and remnants of our picnic lunch into Mother's basket. There I find her ginger cookies sealed in tin foil, and tears fall. Henry wraps his arms around me. "Your mother said you might cry over her cookies. Something about your childhood friend Cammy from Columbus. Or is it the Highlander?"

"Both. And Frank's gift."

"He's a good and wise man, Annie. As Granny would say, 'A gift God puts on our path to show us the way to go.'"

I fold his Granny's quilt. Henry takes up the basket. "So, let's go, honey."

We walk to the truck in silence and put the basket and quilt between us on the front seat. Henry reaches his arm around me and searches my eyes. "Don't worry about the Highlander."

The power of his sincerity cannot overcome my dread. "I'll try not to." I see Darlin' wilting on the floorboard. "Is there any tea left?"

"I think in your thermos."

I remove the two from the basket and find a quarter cup left in my thermos.

Darlin' soaks it up into Henry's hanky and fits snuggly into the lid.

He winks. "That should keep her in good shape until we reach the seed store."

I hold Darlin' on my lap because the floorboard is too hot and will dry her out. I roll up the window halfway to reduce the wind. My affection for the redbud doesn't disguise my worry about the Highlander. Henry starts the engine. "Sheriff Taylor's part coon dog. He'll sniff out the Highlander if he gets too close to Matewan."

I want to believe him, but Henry steals too many glances to the review mirror as he drives out of Salyersville and onto the main road. He turns the wheel toward home. I watch the road and wait.

"Nobody gets past Sheriff Taylor, Annie. Even the redheaded Houdini. By now, all Williamson and Matewan are lookin' for a redheaded man named Rusty who drives a truck with a loud muffler."

"That's what worries me. I should've listened to my parents and never worked the check-in desk."

Henry takes my hand between shifting gears. "Remember, we left regrets behind. It'll all work out for our good, Annie." He drives as though he was born behind the wheel of a truck. "Now, get your sandwich and eat. There's nothin' else we can do but keep goin'."

Darlin's small enough to fit into the basket with the lid closed, out of the wind and sun. I'm so hungry I eat my sandwich and all the cookies but the one I offer to Henry.

"Thanks, honey. Now put Granny's quilt against your door and doze for a while."

⁕⁕⁕

Peace fills the cab. I slumber in safety beside this six-foot-two man who loves nothing more than making me smile. I sleep soundly and wake craving a cold glass of sweet tea and a sudsy bath. Henry's pulling off the road onto our favorite lookout.

My good Lord, we're almost home.

It's midday. We're sweaty and gritty, but I've never felt more revived as we stand high above the gorge where Peter Creek, Mate Creek, and several other tributaries converge into Tug Fork.

Side-by-side, we look down upon our beloved Matewan, carved into the mountains by watery fingers coursing the border between Kentucky and West Virginia. There, our folk wait on Mate Street to embrace us, and feed us the Bread of Life no matter where we worship. They wait to shower us with love and mercy and the scent of *Paeonia*. And I've never needed it more than I do now.

Sunlight gleams on the river and the old windows Henry scavenged to assemble his first greenhouse. With the Highlander on the loose, it will be the most difficult thing of my young life to leave Henry's side at tonight's end and return to my childhood bed.

I look up to the vast panorama of overlapping mountains—far as the eye can see, lush green and blue forests nurse hidden farmsteads built on hillsides in winding hollows navigated by mule and horse and wagon in bottoms cradled between creeks, runoffs, and railroad tracks.

Blessed land of redemption and liberty, a refuge for the strong of heart.

Hidden from the eye dwells Red Jacket, named after a Native American chief of the Wolf clan of the Seneca tribe that migrated from New York. A community where Russian and Black immigrants settled with Italians, who claimed a portion of Red Jacket as Little Italy for their home.

"Tug Fork's runnin' high after the rain this week," Henry says. "It's a matter of time before there's floodin'. That'll wash away my silly ole' greenhouse. Just as well. It's served its purpose—full of cuttings, transplants, seedlings, trees, and shrubs, each one waitin' for a safe home."

Home. The word excites every nerve in my body. "We've got to get the eucalyptus and chestnut cuttings to higher ground, too. I called the Civil Corps of Engineers last week. We're not the only mountain town in harm's way. I think we need to do something ourselves."

"Like everybody said, I shouldn't a built the greenhouse so close to the Tug. But it's also close to the store, so that it made it easier for Olaf and me to load orders for deliveries while keeping an eye on the store."

Henry kicks a stone over the edge of the mountain. We listen to it tumble down the hillside. "The greenhouse belongs up in Blackberry City, close to Miss Daisy and our house. We've been lookin' at greenhouse plans Olaf drafted. Did you know his father designed their greenhouses and bee skeps?"

I nod. "Mrs. Semenov mentioned it in one of her Garden Club lectures. Twenty greenhouses and fifty skeps, spread throughout one thousand acres, with one hundred and thirty staff."

He fans his fingers on his hips. "Now Annie, where in Matewan and Blackberry City is there one thousand level acres for twenty greenhouses and fifty beehives in one place?"

I love to play this game. "There isn't. But there's the railroad yard."

Henry takes my hand and fusses with my diamond ring. "As always, it all depends on how our negotiations go with the coal companies and railroad. As long as coal's boomin', they'll refuse the business of shipping plants, honey, and bee equipment throughout Appalachia, the Midwest, and East Coast. Our business is too small to compete with the volume and profit of coal."

"Okay, but don't forget to add garden supplies, tools, and greenhouse kits to our products."

"Greenhouse kits?"

"You think you're the only person who loves building greenhouses? I have several do-it-yourself models in that black box in the bed of your truck."

"Where'd you find them?"

"One of my classes and several garden magazines."

"What else do you have in that black box?"

"You'll find out in two weeks after our wedding."

"That ain't fair."

"That *isn't* fair. Now you know how it feels."

"What else you holdin' out on me?"

"Nothing, other than the owner of The Greenbrier is interested in our vision for the railroad yard, and so is the Vanderbilt family."

"Why the Vanderbilts?"

"They plan to build a greenhouse and conservatory for Smokey Mountain plants on the grounds of the Biltmore Estate."

"How'd the Vanderbilts know about our idea for the rail yard?"

"One night after the family dined in Boone Tavern, they gathered in the lounge. They reserved all the rooms and were the only guests, so the conditions were perfect for eavesdropping. I poured one cup of coffee after another, and we became acquainted."

Henry lifts me off the ground, spins me around, and sets me on my feet.

"Annie Dill, you're full of surprises."

"Didn't you say in a letter something about thirty able-bodied men out of work who know how to use a pick and axe? That might get us started in the right direction."

"Removing railroad ties, for instance, for space to build greenhouses with railroad ties as the foundations?"

"And space and foundations for beehives. We'll figure it out with Olaf's and Mrs. Semenov's help. And Daisy's connections with the railroad, I hope. Mother wrote that Father and Olaf are collaborating on the project."

"Yes, they are."

"When I was a child in elementary school, I remember Father

saying to Mother, "If Matewan's going to thrive into the twenty-first century, the people need to establish an industry other than coal."

Henry plays with my stringy hair. "Annie Dill, will you marry me?"

I swat his hand. "Henry Blankenship, you make me furious when you don't take me seriously. I know you've heard Father's perspective before, but that's not very polite. Do not call me Annie Dill again. And do not ask me to marry you again. After tonight, I'll meet you at the altar in two weeks as I've promised."

The sun on the windows of Henry's greenhouse shines like a beacon. I love and need this land so much I could cry.

"Well, I'm sorry to hear that, honey."

"Oh?"

"Uh-huh, because Garden Club has decorated the church for a double weddin' ceremony at six o'clock this very evenin'."

I turn on my heels. "So, your mother finally accepted Olaf's proposal?"

Henry nods with the same smile when he first told me he loved me. "It's taken her a while to trust him. But if you cain't trust my boss, you cain't trust anyone. I tell you, he's a new man."

"I couldn't be happier for them, and to share our wedding day with Olaf and Gertie. They've waited a long while for true love, just like we have."

"Olaf bought the Chambers place two doors down from the store. It's a little neglected but built upon a good foundation. It's a fine house, and with the attached apartment for Mrs. Semenov, it's perfect for the three of them. Mommy said it's as good a place as any to start a new life with the man she loves."

We cast one last glance down upon Matewan, our small portion of Tug Fork. Henry takes my hand. "Annie, isn't it strange how you wait and wait for something good like this to happen, and when it does, you can hardly believe it?"

"Like your mother and Olaf finding love in each other."

"Last week, after Mommy said yes, I overheard Olaf make reservations on the phone with the Greenbrier Resort. He asked for the honeymoon suite. I thought it was strange because he's always been private with his phone calls."

"You're right. That isn't like Olaf. Did you talk to him about it?"

"Not then. It seemed like he wanted me to hear his call, so I asked Mommy if she and Olaf were going on a honeymoon. She said, 'I don't know what a honeymoon is.' I told Olaf what Mommy said, and he said, 'Mrs. Dill vill know what to do.' And she did. That same day she drove Mommy to Saul Brown's and helped her choose her wedding dress and a 'trousseau worthy of dining in the Greenbrier,' as your mother put it. Come to find out, Saul Brown's kept several dresses aside since their engagement."

"Olaf is quite the tactician. He's putting his best foot forward with your mother—and you."

"I don't know what a 'tactician' is. But I have a feeling I'm putting my worst foot forward."

"Oh?"

"Uh-huh. After our double weddin' reception tonight, we're going to the Blankenship Hotel for our honeymoon."

"What about waiting two weeks for your finishing touches?"

"They're all there, darlin', just waitin' for you."

I refuse to swoon and give Henry that satisfaction. "Then I reckon we'd better drive down the road and make ourselves presentable."

Arm in arm, we walk away from our lookout and toward Boone. "How 'bout a little kiss to hold me over 'til tonight? You know, some juice to keep me goin' through the ceremony and reception," Henry says.

"I love you," I say and close my eyes for his kiss, juice to keep me going, too.

Boone's engine rumbles. We make the first curve when we hear a police siren behind us on a straight stretch of road. Henry lifts his foot off the accelerator and eyes the review mirror.

"What the blazes? It's Sheriff Taylor!"

I spin around, dreading to see the redheaded Highlander in the Sheriff's backseat. Thank God it's empty. Sheriff Taylor pulls us over.

"Well, I never!" Henry says and brings Boone to a stop half off the road and half on the narrow shoulder. This is obviously not one of Henry's surprises.

The sheriff parks his car and strolls up to Henry's window. I've never seen Sheriff Taylor move otherwise and can't imagine him chasing and capturing a felon. He bends his tall frame and there's his hat, the brim pushed above his wet forehead. The man never ages.

"Evenin', y'all. Got Frank's call from Salyersville. Been waitin'. Hope I didn't scare y'all."

Henry and I sit speechless.

"Seein' how all Tug Fork's waitin', thought it'd be proper to escort our celebrity to the seed store."

I swallow. "All of Tug Fork?"

Sheriff Taylor pushes his hat back farther and looks apologetically to me. "Well, that ain't quite true, Annie. Williamson. Peter Creek. They heard about Rusty the Highlander, too."

"Rusty the Highlander?" Henry and I say in unison.

"Uh-huh. Spreadin' like wildfire."

"What's spreadin', Sheriff?" Henry says.

"Sheriff Daly locked him up in Williamson."

"Locked him up?" we say.

"Yep, Sheriff Daly and I waylaid him. Stopped him for speedin'. So drunk he couldn't walk a straight line." He looks to the shoulder, front, and end of Henry's truck. "Right about here, I reckon. Resisted arrest before witnesses. Just takes a few."

Sheriff Taylor stretches his back. Henry and I shake our heads to one another. There's no stopping this wildfire.

"Well," Sheriff Taylor says and knocks his knuckles on Boone's hood like a true Appalachian man. "Let's go."

Henry follows the sheriff down the mountain, along the Tug into Matewan.

I wonder how on earth the Garden Club women are going to feed Tug Fork, Peter Creek, and Williamson. And I see chicken salad, tea, and Darlin' stains on my pink, wrinkled dress. My wind-whipped pin curls gave out before Salyersville. Mother will not be happy with my appearance. There's nothing I can do about it but laugh.

"Atta girl. Put on your happy face."

"It's that or cry. Just look at me, Henry. I'm a mess!"

He smiles and steers Boone with his left hand relaxed over the wheel. Contentment and completion flow from Henry's heart to mine. The strength of his devotion to Matewan and to me catches in my throat. We're almost home. I've made it this far without crying, and will not arrive with red eyes. "If you don't mind, I'd like to hear you tell the story of when I first said I loved you."

I welcome the diversion to indulge the man I love. "Dirt from head to toe, I'd been digging and planting Mother an asparagus patch and walked into the store for zinnia seeds to plant as a border. Olaf discreetly excused himself with paperwork in his office. You leaned over the glass counter with the seed package and whispered, 'Annie Dill, I love you.'"

Henry sighs in feigned ecstasy. "My darlin', dirt is my favorite perfume."

I look to my watch. "Well, I'm sorry to disappoint you, but it's three-thirty, and I'm taking a hot, sudsy bath first chance I get. Then I'll meet you at the altar at six without a speck of dirt on my wedding gown or me. And I'm warning you, Henry Blankenship, you'd better make a fuss over how pretty I look, and how the fragrance of Mother's Tabu sends you to the moon." Henry puts his head back and laughs as he does when surprised by fresh joy. Parked cars appear along the road a quarter of a mile outside of Matewan. "I hope this is the wildfire spreading, and not for my graduation party."

Henry grins. "Hold onto your zinnia seeds, honey! I guarantee you, Matewan has never seen the likes of this. The Depression couldn't defeat Tug Fork, and everybody's makin' the most of these celebrations. You'll see, Annie, even if we don't make it to the altar until midnight, there's nothing more I want in this whole world than to see you walkin' down the aisle in your weddin' dress this evenin'."

"Are you telling me another story?"

Henry's smile is so luscious and sincere I kiss him on the cheek. "Just wait and see, darlin'."

We follow Sheriff Taylor onto Mate Street where a banner proclaiming CONGRATULATIONS ANNIE stretches over the road from Matewan Hospital to the former Chambers place, already under the renovations of Henry's hammer. I can't believe what's happened to Matewan since Christmas vacation. Mate Street sparkles! No coal soot in sight.

"Look at the peonies hanging on every door! Even the post office!"

Folk gather so thick it's like the Magnolia Fair. I could not have imagined this support when I stood forlorn on Berea's campus three years ago. The spirit of our vision blooms like the mountains.

I am one beating heart in this town known as Matewan. This moment could not happen without Mother, Father, Olaf, Mrs. Semenov, Henry, Gertie, Daisy, and Garden Club. Theirs are the invisible names on the banner.

Sheriff Taylor parks before the seed store. Henry parks behind him. Bud O'Brien & the Fleabites stand on the porch playing and singing *For She's a Jolly Good Fellow*. How is it a guitar, banjo, and fiddle make such happy music? Even the whistle of a passing coal train can't drown them out. They don't miss a beat.

Mother and Father stand to the left of the open door. Mrs. Semenov, Gertie, and Olaf stand to the right. The jubilation is deafening.

I admire the beauty and breadth of the plain, boxlike building, adorned by garlands of flowers swaged on the two, large front windows.

Then I see what Henry boasted about—*Matewan College of Agriculture, Botany & Horticulture* painted in black letters on a metal sign matching *Hunt's Feed & Seed,* above.

I turn to Henry, Mr. Tactician himself. "I should've read this in your conniving smile way back on the road."

He speaks into my ear above the cheering crowd and music. "Classes began in January. We've had dickens of a time keepin' it from you. Thirty-two students enrolled, and thirty-two took their final exam last Wednesday night. They all passed. And this is just the half of it, honey."

I can't help but kiss him again. Sheriff Taylor opens my door. "Okay, save that for later. There's a reception waitin'."

Henry takes Mother's picnic basket from the front seat and walks around Boone. He takes my hand. We face the band and our family.

Mother, Mrs. Semenov, and Gertie wipe their eyes with white lacy hankies. Reporters flank the porch with cameras. I smile and they shoot pictures of my tangled hair, wrinkled and soiled dress, and teeth that need a good brushing.

Hand in hand, we walk up two steps. Henry lets go my hand. Father opens his arms and I fall into them. I see hats in the air with an eruption of another shout.

"Congratulations, daughter," Father whispers in my ear. "I love you. Your mother and I were very worried about you and Henry. The entire town was, as you can see." He kisses me on the cheek. Tears blur my sight.

Henry places Mother's picnic basket into Miss Daisy's care and cups a hand to her ear. She takes a peek inside, sees Darlin', and winks to Henry and me. Father nods to Mother. Arm-in-arm, he escorts us through the open double doors into the seed store. Henry follows with Mrs. Semenov on his arm. Olaf and Gertie follow them.

Mother, as the mistress of ceremonies, says, "You may enter," to the reporters. They rush to the tables and punch bowls and Garden Club members, their bulbs flashing nonstop. Daisy holds Mother's basket and attends the door while Bud and the Fleabites sing *Happy Days are Here Again*.

Surrounded by family, I'm stunned at the store's transformation.

I gape at vases of peonies and silver and crystal platters on pedestals laden with pastries displayed on white linen tablecloths. I recognize Mrs. Semenov's streusel, Bavarian cream, küchen, and sochniki amongst the sweets. Mother's ginger cookies and baklava. Hundreds of fried pies are arranged on platters like huge dahlia blooms, as well as Gertie's buttermilk biscuits slathered with whipped butter and blackberry preserves. Stacks of small china plates and cloth napkins wait on each of numerous tables. A feast with not one fork or spoon required.

"Beautiful, isn't it?" Father says.

"But . . . how?" I ask.

"Garden Club rounded up almost every kitchen and dining room table and white tablecloth in Matewan and Blackberry City."

Blinded by flashing camera bulbs, I'm dazed at the sight as I cling to Father's arm. Reporters write names of Garden Club members as Mrs. Cline, Sue Ann, Lucy, Lily, Violet, and Nellie Nenni ladle lemonade and sweet tea from six punch bowls that adorn the emptied and polished glass-domed counter.

I see Mother's footed crystal bowl with cups dangling on glass hooks around the bowl's lip. One October in Boone Tavern, I served spiced cider to the college president's wife and her guests. Her modern metal set lacked the grace and cordiality of cut crystal, milk glass, and Depression ware.

Mrs. Cline approaches with a silver tray bearing cups. "Please help yourself to iced tea or lemonade."

"Thank you," Father says and accepts a cup of tea.

He seems very comfortable in his role as father of the graduate and bride. Did fear for our safety alone encourage this remarkable change?

We smile and pose with Mrs. Cline for reporters and answer their questions.

"Yes, Annie and Henry were students in my third-grade class in 1923," Mrs. Cline replies. "They graduated first and second in the class of 1932."

"Who took first?" the Pikeville reporter asks.

Mrs. Cline slides a glance to me. "Annie."

I'm careful not to gulp the delicious lemonade, and see again the resourcefulness of Garden Club. "Where on earth did you find bushels of lemons?" I ask Mrs. Cline.

"The Greenbrier Hotel, special delivery for the special occasion."

The reporters scribble her reply. We pose before their cameras.

"Annie, I'm very proud of you," Mrs. Cline says. "And I'm glad you're home at last. Matewan isn't the same without you."

I recall her classroom on the day when she stopped at Henry's desk, and a lump swells in my throat. "Thank you, Mrs. Cline, I'm glad to be home."

She steps closer and touches my arm linked with Father's. "Annie, I want you to know my first class in Matewan College opened my eyes to see what Mrs. Semenov calls 'the vonderful vorld of botany.' I've registered for her fall classes on creating an herbarium, and Scandinavian horticulture. Your mother encouraged all Garden Club members to sign up for both classes so we may begin our herbariums and better understand the horticulture of Mrs. Semenov's birthplace."

I grope for a reply when a loud giggle draws our eyes to the doorway, where a tall young woman with blonde hair stands before Daisy. "Annie's right there in the pink dress," Daisy says and nods to me.

The stranger giggles again. Her hat, sleek blouse and skirt, heels, and posture remind me of Katharine Hepburn in the movie *Morning Glory*—but the giggle belongs to Cammy Rouge.

Reporters trip over one another to reach her first. She obliges like a movie star and spells her name.

"C-A-M-I-L-L-E. R-O-U-G-E."

"Your residence, Miss Rouge?" Punkin' Smith of the *Matewan Bullet* asks.

"Columbus, Ohio today. Hollywood, California tomorrow."

Mother, Mrs. Cline, Father, and I exchange glances of mutual surprise as Cammy waits for the reporters to ask another question. I excuse myself from Father's arm.

"Welcome, Cammy," I say with open arms.

She shrinks from my embrace with a feigned cough behind a white-gloved hand, a white handbag on her arm. "It's Camille." She removes her gloves, opens the purse's latch, and withdraws a package of cigarettes and a lighter.

Olaf lets a low gasp from behind us. Henry steps beside me. Mrs. Cline stands on the other side of Mother.

"Camille," I say, "this is an historic, wooden building. Smoking is not allowed. May I offer you lemonade and ginger cookies instead?"

My childhood friend stuffs her gloves, cigarettes, and lighter into her purse and clasps it with a "Humph!" She fans her red fingernails on a slim hip and inspects the room, ceiling to floor, wall to wall, acting her part.

"Anyone know where I can find a gin and tonic?"

The journalists snicker. Write hysterically.

Henry steps forward. "Yes, Ma'am," he says and offers Camille his arm. "Come with me."

The reporters follow her every move, flip pages on their notepads.

Camille's ruby-red lips glide into a wily smile of perfectly aligned teeth. Her hazel eyes scan Henry's physique from head to toe like they're peeling off his clothes. "And who might you be, handsome?"

"The one who knows where you can find your highball."

Camille cleaves to Henry's arm. He addresses Father. "Be right back, Dr. Dill."

Henry escorts Camille through the doorway. She giggles, fawns over his affected interest, and doesn't look back. The reporters stand with mouths agape, their cameras limp appendages in their hands. They've never been so close to Hollywood, and they didn't capture the evidence.

Father's touch on my arm breaks Camille's spell. He draws me closer. "Excuse us, Mrs. Cline," he says, and resumes our stroll around the tables. I admire Garden Club's handiwork. The Greenbrier could do no finer. The swags of ivy vines and redbud branches Camille shunned reach down to us from the ceiling. "Who decorated?" I ask Father.

"Henry and I."

"When?"

"Yesterday," Father said. "I couldn't be happier for you and Henry, Annie. Your mother and I are so very proud of you both."

Mother squeezes my hand, Father's words confirmed in her brown eyes. Is their mutual affection part of the other half Henry said waited for me? This public expression of their love, and the transformation of the seed store, overwhelm Camille's contempt for what I cherish.

Father leads Mother and me into the storage room, cleared of feed and merchandise for more tables laden with white linen, pastries, and peonies. Between the two rooms, there's enough food for every clan in Tug Fork and Peter Creek. More ivy and redbud adorn the ceiling. I spin in disbelief. "Who . . . ?"

"John and Antillo Nenni and their staff helped."

"Helped who?"

"Henry and me."

I look for Henry through the doorway into the store and hear guests entering—laughing and calling names to one another as they fill plates and cups.

"Fresh lemonade? Well, I never!"

"Why, I never see'd such fancy bowls and cups."

"Just look at those piles of fat fried pies!"

"Lord-a-mercy, Mrs. Dill outdid herself with all that baklava."

But I don't see or hear Henry.

Reporters follow us toward the back door. I think of Frank in Salyersville and wish he were here to partake in this comfort and companionship. But how could I have known what awaited us?

I feel Father's gentle love and know why Henry fell to his knees in the ruins of Boone's filling station. The same humility prompted him to escort Camille out of the building.

"Excuse me, Miss Dill," says Punkin' Smith. "A picture of your wedding party standing by that purdy pergola would make a fine cover photo."

Father guides me down four steps to the mouth of the vined tunnel. Henry's voice calls, "Wait for me!"

Father and I turn to see his broad shoulders weaving through guests and tables in the storage room. Father's smile reflects my relief. His touch says he understands what we've been missing.

Amongst gathering crowds of people I do and do not know, Mother takes my left hand and kisses my sweaty, gritty cheek as Henry stands by my side. "You two were made for each other," Mother says, and daubs her eyes with a lacy hanky.

I accept her love and search for words when under the pergola a long table spread with white linen and laden with peonies bring me to tears. Mrs. Semenov steps close to me. She places a folded lacy hanky in my hand, her hazel eyes and touch quick with anticipation.

"Annie," she says, "it is my pleasure and honor to introduce to you a beloved friend who has traveled from Boston to celebrate vith us."

Boston? I stand in disbelief as she turns toward the pergola's side. A tall, slim man with gray hair appears from behind the vines. I gasp. "Sergei Mekinov?" I look to Henry, who has his seventh-heaven glow on his face. So, Mekinov is part of Henry's collusion in his "other half'" of surprises.

Sergei Mekinov greets me politely with his dark eyes. He bows, takes my hand, and kisses it. His demeanor and tailored apparel remind me of Saul Brown. "Congratulations, Annie," he says in a Russian accent.

"Welcome to Matewan," I reply, feeling like a shy schoolgirl. "I am honored, Mr. Mekinov."

"And I am honored to at last meet the young voman whose name fills Olaf's letters with her joy and adventures," Mekinov replies.

A man with dark hair and mustache steps from behind the vines just as Mekinov did.

"Richardson Wright!" I'm amazed to see him. And then his forthright redheaded wife steps into view. "Agnes!"

"None other," they say. Richardson takes my hand for a repeat performance of Mekinov's gallantry.

All the while, Punkin' Smith and the reporters flash pictures of my windblown hair, dirty dress, and incredulous eyes until I'm almost blinded. Punkin', who has clearly been granted first dibs of his subjects by fellow journalists, directs our guests and wedding party to stand before the pergola, blanketed with *Passiflora incarnate* vines.

I gaze beyond the storage room's double doors and into the store. Daisy offers a tray of beverages to Saul Brown. He holds a box under one arm and it looks like the Bear-Brand silk hose. Clothed in Saul Brown's harmonious spring colors, the Garden Club ladies refresh punch bowls and platters. Is there no end to this hospitality?

Henry whispers in my ear. "Antillo escorted Cammy to the Dew Drop Inn."

Bud O'Brien and the Fleabites sing *Have I Told You Lately that I Love You* above the clink of plates and laughter. Henry wraps an arm around me. We pose for what seem to be hundreds of photos and repeatedly spell our names and *Passiflora incarnate* to the press. I have no idea what happens next. But I know one thing—there's no escape for my bath.

Henry outsmarts me again.

Father seats Mother and me side-by-side at the head of the table before the entrance of the pergola. He sits beside her. She's luminous in her pale pink chiffon dress and white pillbox hat and gloves. Although I resemble Willa Cather's travel-worn Ántonia, I feel like Mother's princess.

"Olaf and Henry," Father says, "shall we bring our ladies some refreshments? I promised Pastor Hickman to walk my daughter down the aisle at precisely six o'clock, and Olaf will escort Gertie close behind."

Henry smiles that crooked grin. I'm wrong again. He wants more than anything in this world to see me walk down the aisle in my wedding gown tonight—sooner the better.

Henry seats Mrs. Semenov and Sergei Mekinov on the left side of the table and kisses her hand in the contagious spirit of chivalry. Olaf seats Gertie facing Mrs. Semenov and kisses his beloved's cheek. He kisses Agnes' hand before Richardson seats her.

So much kissing! And it's only begun. I smile and blush at the thought.

Now I understand. Sheriff Taylor waited for Henry and me to inform us of the Highlander's capture, guarding my honor and granting us peace of mind.

And I know my parents and little town rejoice to such extremes because Henry and I arrived unharmed. Henry knows my father understands what he's been missing. Oh, how I wish Frank were here, so I could thank him for his kindness and protection.

Three hundred feet away, guests stroll in and out of Henry's greenhouse along the Tug. Most folk have never seen the likes of it. They inspect Henry's ingenuity that props open the cockeyed, recycled windows forming a large A-shape structure. It's not one you'd find in Richardson Wright's *House & Garden* magazine, but it is no less a marvel to behold for what flourishes within.

And there's Crazy Ray, beside Frank, walking down the greenhouse's middle aisle! They're touching, smelling Daisy's and Henry's botanical offspring right and left. They emerge from the greenhouse, wave to Henry and me, and aim for the pergola.

Henry takes my hand. "Surprised?"

I search Henry's eyes and know this was his and Frank's plan all along. I brush a kiss upon his lips. If I don't speak now, Crazy Ray and Frank will command the conversation, so I seize the opportunity to say what I must before Gertie and Olaf leave for The Greenbrier tomorrow.

I stand before the most significant men and women in my life. "I love you all more than I am able to say." I pause to calm my pounding heart. "Henry claims I'm never at a loss for words. Well, he's wrong for once. I'm overwhelmed with your love. Please accept my gratitude for this remarkable homecoming."

Mother takes my hand. "Daughter, I asked Mrs. Semenov to sing Bach's *Ave Maria* for your double wedding ceremony."

Mrs. Semenov's eyes wait for mine. "I said yes, vith great pleasure."

What would ladies do without their hankies?

Part Three
OLAF
APRIL 15, 1946

In the quiet hour before dawn, Gertie's sifter and Mother's spoon harmonize with birdsong. Biscuits and kasha. My table is of two countries.

I hold Petrov's final letter under lamplight. He concludes as usual, *Olaf, always remember, you are never alone. God will never leave you nor forsake you.*

I consider Petrov's meaning as I recall September 24, 1917. Father speaks to me.

"Son, you must see your mother to safety in America."

Natalia Ingrid Semenov, daughter of a Norwegian mother and a French-Russian father, bears Romanov blood. My mother. She stands erect as she did when she performed in the Mariinsky Theatre. Yet, she has no voice. No gleam in her eye. No rouge on her cheeks or lips. No one would ever recognize her as our homeland's prized soprano. My mother makes this sacrifice to honor Father's request to save our lives from capture and execution.

Grandfather, Father, Mother, and I, wayfaring botanists who travel the world to enrich Russian agricultural knowledge, must submit our work and possessions to Lenin's Bolsheviks. Betrayed by several fellow professors and members of the St. Petersburg Horticultural Society, Father surrenders so Grandfather, Mother, and I may flee.

Father places his wallet in my hand. "Bind it to you. Trust no one else. I have taught you wise business?"

"Yes."

"Your grandfather and I taught you sound husbandry and botany?"

"Yes."

"You know how to hunt for nourishment?"

"Yes."

Father holds before me his knapsack. "Study my books and sow the seeds. Practice and prosper."

I am a man of twenty-two years, a fifth-generation botanist. Now Bolshevism terminates my brief wayfaring studies with Frederick and Ivan Semenov, my father and paternal grandfather. The Bolsheviks aim to take our lives, land, and home.

"Is there nothing we can do to save you, Father? The Bolsheviks will kill you if you surrender!" I plead.

"They have seized the University and will hunt and kill us all if I do not surrender."

God help me! As Nicholas was not prepared to rule our country, I am not prepared for this charge.

Father's colleague, Fodor Petrov, scented the Revolution when it first crept into Russian academia. He would not denounce Christ and escaped to America. Father remained and clung to his hope in Russia's people and his own work. Now the bloodhounds sniff after Mother's Romanov blood. She and Father will not denounce Christ. Grandfather and I will not.

"Grandfather, will they hunt and kill you?"

"No. I take refuge in Norway with your mother's family."

"Cannot we join you?"

Grandfather and Mother look to one another. He places a hand upon my shoulder. "Trust your elders, grandson. America holds your freedom and future."

"How will I find courage?"

"You know the answer."

"Trust in the Lord God Almighty."

Father embraces us. "Forgive them, for they do not know they destroy Russia and themselves."

Grandfather, Mother, and I stand on the veranda of our farmhouse as Father's carriage vanishes down the lane of oaks planted by our forefathers. From afar, our house servants and farmhands watch him leave us. Seven months prior, Professor Frederick Semenov delivered lectures to students in St. Petersburg State University.

"Grandfather, how did this happen?"

"Russia wearies of freedom's cost."

"What is the cost?"

"Forgiveness, and submission to the Cross."

Our staff of one hundred and fifty men and women gather around Grandfather. Otto, the young farmer under my stewardship, looks to me. Abandoned by his father to raid with the revolutionists, Otto sought our refuge at Polya Tsvetov, our family farm since 1759.

Father trusted Otto and assigned him to my tutelage for the past year. I embrace Otto and grieve for our workers, for it is impossible to provide them passage to America. I pray Otto and the others somehow escape to safety. But how? Where?

I thank God for Father's knowledge, love, and provision.

Grandfather raises his voice to the staff we leave behind. "Band together for the good of the land as the Bolsheviks band together to destroy it!"

Night and day for months we dispersed to our staff, local farms, and villages our apiaries and the plants and trees from our greenhouses filled with experimental species from world expeditions, including Norway, where Father met Mother and they fell in love.

Grandfather, Father, and I dispersed most of our livestock, poultry, ploughs, and tools to local farms. The Bolsheviks have no interest in them.

It is the farmhouse they want to occupy and plunder, for silver, gold, and Mother's jewels. If they do not find them, they will pursue us. Mother carries only the tortoiseshell combs she unwrapped the Christmas she wed my father in St. Petersburg's Church of the Resurrection of Jesus Christ.

Mother now hides her combs under a scarf.

Grandfather sweeps his hands before his former charges and the home built with timber and stone from the earth. "Go with God!"

"Where will we work?" cries a farmhand.

"This is our home!" pleads Cook with her kitchen staff.

Dressed in our farm clothing, we turn from their pleas and walk in emptiness and woe. Grandfather knows better than I the reaper's paths within the sea of yellow, purple, white, and blue blossoms—sunflowers, alfalfa, flax, and buckwheat sown to feed and clothe our people. Under Mother's influence, we planted a small field of lavender to dry for culinary and medicinal use. "An experiment," Mother said.

How the children loved the harvests! We also leave an empty drying barn, for the Bolsheviks burn what they find. The staff carried what they could of the last harvest sewn within the lining of their coats.

God have mercy upon me! In all our wayfaring, I have seen no more beautiful place than the Polya Tsvetov fields in bloom. Even Norway's aquamarine fiords and golden, sheer cliffs cannot compare to a sea of blooming sunflowers and flax!

Will the Bolsheviks capture our animals in the pastures where we found them refuge? One winter past in the far pasture, Otto and I rescued an abandoned newborn lamb from death. I feel again the warmth of the parlor's fire when we returned to the chessboard.

"Olaf, I have never helped save a life before tonight," Otto says.

"That is one reason why the Semenovs farm," I reply.

Otto furrows his brow in thought. "Will you not also butcher the lamb?"

"Yes, to feed many people."

Will this boy of fifteen years someday understand Father is our sacrificial lamb? Will Otto follow Father's counsel and seek guidance from Albert, our foreman? Where would I be today if not for Father and Grandfather's steadfast supervision and faith?

"Save what you can of our forefather's library," Father pleaded with Albert and Otto. "Teach sound husbandry every opportunity."

I follow Grandfather and Mother, see in my mind's eye our personal and collected herbariums. His letters from Carl Maximowicz on botanizing Japanese flora, and many others. All left behind.

Russia! You listen to the bewitching voice of Marxism. The rule of ruin! You have lost affection for good husbandry and posterity in our great land of 182 million souls.

Weary of war, you reject the power of the resurrection of Jesus Christ. Submit your liberties to communism's hammer and sickle. Mock a day's labor, the sun upon our back and sheaves in our barn. Lenin's tyranny pounds and pounds. Our nation crumbles.

Father's forethought and preparations with local farmers never fail us along our journey through the countryside. We reach Grandfather's destination outside St. Petersburg unharmed. They expected to see father at their door and grieve his absence. They share their food and shelter. "The window of escape closes upon us."

We cry when Grandfather parts from us. "Who will teach me?" I ask.

Grandfather nods to Father's knapsack. "Those who love plants."

At eighty-five years, Grandfather knows every village and farmstead we have passed through. "Take courage, daughter. Look to your son. You and Olaf will carry on our work."

I do not believe this is possible as Grandfather hoists himself onto the carriage seat. "Natalia, I will look for your letters at your Father's home. I will post my letters to Fodor Petrov's address in New York City."

We watch the carriage carry him away. He turns and waves. "Plant the seeds!" he bellows.

I cling to Father's knapsack as our driver slaps the reins on the horses' backs. We travel by wagon and train to the port of St. Petersburg. In a shelter the night before we board ship, I dream I am pouring cow, goat, and sheep's milk into churns for butter and crocks for cheese. I wake hungry for the joy and plenty of Polya Tsvetov.

Mother's steadfast trust in Father's provisions fortifies me. She bears her sorrow silently. Frederick Semenov married Natalia Romanov for love, not for her gold—gold which the Bolsheviks now possess.

"Mother, they cannot steal your beautiful voice."

Now, her song that cheered and guided me throughout my childhood is silent. No longer may we work and walk the estate that my great-great grandfather named Fields of Flowers.

It is dangerous for Mother to speak or sing while we walk through this valley of the shadow of death. I reply to questions on Mother's behalf. I carry our papers and American currency in Father's wallet tied to my chest under my farmer's tunic.

My costume draws raised eyebrows within St. Petersburg, a reminder of my fifth birthday, when Grandfather drove us in his carriage to Yasnaya Polyana, the beautiful home of Count Lev Nikolayevich Tolstoy. The grumpy old man wore a farmer's tunic and pants and waved his hands excitedly. "My bees have swarmed again!" he complained to Grandfather.

I did not know this gray beard wrote the most beloved literature that bleeds Russia's tragedies. He spoke only of bees to Grandfather, one question and objection after another as I romped on his spacious lawn. That night, I slept by Grandfather's side within Tolstoy's manor.

"Olaf, trust the honeybee, and honor and trust the power of a seed to feed and clothe you," he admonished.

I search for Father's face in the crowded streets and courts of St. Petersburg. It is cruel to think of him as in the past. It is impossible to speak it. I am foolish enough to look for him and Otto as we gather like cattle in stanchions to board our ship. Wherever we walk, from habit Mother seeks his hunting hat with the red feather, for he tended to wander on our journeys.

Father would laugh and say, "This is what a wayfarer is called to do!"

My first departure with my parents from St. Petersburg's port sailed to New York City's harbor. In celebration of my eighteenth birthday, we visited Fodor Petrov in New York City and, together, we toured Bartram Gardens outside of Philadelphia. This departure with Mother will be our last from St. Petersburg. What the Bolsheviks cannot rule, they strive to destroy.

Mother and I do not remain on deck to witness the vanishing point of our beloved Russia. Rather, we descend to the lower decks and find our small cabin with two cots. Amongst throngs of the displaced and huddled, we marvel again at Father's foresight in providing us comfortable accommodations throughout our journey.

Mother closes the cabin door and sighs with relief. Face to face, we sit on our cots. I set Father's knapsack beside me. At last, it is safe for Mother to speak. "Olaf, please open your father's knapsack."

I find the photograph of Father's Russian botanical companions, the one he displayed on his library desk. As if for posterity, Father identified them, left to right: Fodor Petrov, Carl Maximowicz, and Sergei Mekinov. They stand before the St. Petersburg Botanical Garden, founded by Peter the Great in 1714, where the elder Maximowicz much later kept the garden's herbarium.

"Remarkable men," I say.

"Yes," Mother whispers, "and a remarkable garden."

I remove each book from Father's knapsack and lift it before Mother for its unveiling. In respect of our quarter's thin walls, I speak softly. "Bernard McMahon's *American Gardener's Calendar*." She nods. "Phillip Miller's *Gardener's and Florist's Dictionary*." She smiles. "John Bartram's *Travels Through North and South Carolina, Georgia...*" Her hazel eyes brighten. "William Cobbett's *The American Gardner*." She hums.

"Lastly, Dr. Benjamin Smith Barton's *Elements of Botany*."

Mother turns her back to me and appears to remove something from her bodice. She faces me, cleaves her eyes to mine, and places Father's small wayfaring Bible into my hands. I bow my face to the cover and will not submit to tears. The scent of Father's pipe sears the fresh wound of our severing, yet it comforts me.

We hold Father's Bible together. With all tenderness, she looks within my heart as only a mother can do. "With these few books and your father's Bible, you need nothing else to build upon your father's work."

How I have the presence of mind to know Mother waited for this appointed hour and place, I cannot perceive, but I do. "Wherever we traveled, I found Father turning the pages of this epistle. He adored the small wedding photograph he kept within the front cover."

Tears swell within her eyes—the only instance on this journey where Mother releases her sorrow. "Open."

The gentle force of her command grants me power to turn the leather cover to find the miniature portrait of those who gave me life, sustenance, and faith. Above all, love. And for love's sake, I will not weep.

"These now belong to you, Olaf, our 'ancestor's remnant.' Read and prosper as your soul prospers."

I am stunned at the sudden and untimely fulfillment of my name's meaning. Peaceful resolve, however, emanates from Mother as if she anticipated the transfer of Father's Bible and wedding portrait to my hands. And the affirmation of the meaning of my name: ancestor's remnant. I commit myself to honor my forefathers.

"Father often bid me the same instruction in the privacy of our carriage, barns, greenhouses, fields, bee skeps, and library."

Tears trail to Mother's lips. "As your Heavenly Father, your father will never leave you or forsake you, for you are his seed."

The word "seed" commands me to my feet.

"Yes! Father's seeds!" I dig into his knapsack and retrieve one hundred and ten small flora envelopes, some a square inch in size, all labeled in Father's fine hand. We count sixty vegetable and fruit-bearing shrub and tree seed envelopes of the same size. Several envelopes of the Cucurbitaceae family contain only two or three seeds.

"Enough to begin," Mother says, and reclines on her bed.

I recall Mother singing when she decorated the farmhouse inside and out with shellacked gourds. Father would laugh and say, "Natalia, leave a path for our feet, please!" Yet, I do not risk speaking it now.

Having read Father's five books in my university studies, I randomly open *American Gardener's Calendar*. A note written in Father's hand and a photograph of a garden fall from the pages like leaves from a tree onto my lap. Mother sits up and leans toward me as I read.

"After the American Revolution, McMahon's seed store in Philadelphia carried a noble catalogue for lists including a thousand species of herbs, shrubs, and tree seeds—some seeds of American plants for export trade. Others were Asiatic, South Sea Islands seeds. McMahon also dispersed seeds collected by the Lewis and Clark expedition to the Pacific."

"Your father wished McMahon to inspire our new life and work in America, the land of Lewis and Clark."

Indeed. We visited McMahon's store in celebration of my eighteenth birthday. McMahon sold gardening and botanical books and became a Philadelphia rendezvous for gardeners and botanists. Perhaps Father's passion for botany does dwell within me.

America! By his sacrifice, Mother and I escape the snare of the fowler and sail to your shores! The home of Bartram's Gardens.

"Olaf," Father had said upon our tour of the gardens, "we walk where America's Founding Fathers walked with John Bartram during the Continental Congress of 1776."

I take the photograph from my lap into my hand.

"Mother, where was this taken?"

She uprights the image in her slender fingers and puts the other hand to her throat. "This is Father's lavender labyrinth in Borregaard Manor, our small village outside Oslo," she says. Just as she guards her wedding ring within her corset, Mother places the photo under the front cover of *American Gardener's Calendar* with Father's letter.

Each morning before we leave our cabin for breakfast, Mother says, "Olaf, please choose a book for our morning lesson." In the afternoon, if the weather is fair, we walk the upper decks and listen the hours away. We most often hear four syllables, *New York Ci-ty*, in various tongues. Unlike our trip to America four years ago with Father, we watch seven thousand kilometers pass as the passengers on deck decrease in number due to seasickness and flu. Before we retire in the evenings, Mother says, "Olaf, please choose a passage from your father's Bible."

Afterward, I remove from Father's knapsack an envelope he inscribed with my name and underscored, his trademark signature. Mother waits for another reading of Father's instructions once our ferry reaches the harbor of New York City.

"Recite, please," she says. For Father emphasized in his letter I must memorize Petrov's address, the names, numbers, and directions of the route and various means of transportation to his home, and the cost. If Mother and I are separated, we must know the way to Petrov's house as well as we knew each room and piece of furniture in Polya Tsevtov when we walked in the night.

I am not concerned, for Mother is well-traveled. Furthermore, I remember the Grand Central Terminal from four years ago. The buses, horse drawn and electric. The subways and train to Petrov's door.

Yet now we are immigrants fleeing our homeland.

Often, I wake in darkness to weeping and wailing outside the walls of our cabin. I do not know if Mother wakes. She does not speak of the cries. Silently, I pray the Lord's Prayer for the poor souls and the families left behind. Although Father schooled me in the sound fiscal management of our farm and household, I worry how I will accomplish his work with the American currency I carry within his wallet.

At last, an ocean away from Polya Tsvetov, we step upon the soil of Ellis Island with Father's wallet, books, and one hundred and seventy seed packages. Mother shields her eyes and looks up to the Statue of Liberty. Still, she wears the scarf tied under her chin.

Now, as refugees, the lady's lamp held high and the inscription on her tablet speak a different, and darker, meaning than on our visit for my eighteenth birthday. Tyranny invades freedom the world over. Mother and I will never see Russia, and all we loved within her, again. Still, I cling to hope and can't help but look for Father and Otto in the sea of dispossessed.

After waiting hours for one stamp after another upon our papers, we stand amongst thousands of our kind and board a ferry. Again, I look for Father's face as I cling to his knapsack and Mother's arm. We approach the harbor of New York City. I despise the sight of the bridge, barges, and skyscrapers. Each wave the ferry crests relinquishes the last shred of freedom we once lived and lost.

I shake with anger because Father is not with us. How will I fulfill Grandfather's trust in me with only five books, and the seeds in Father's knapsack, when misplaced people surround us, filling this land of liberty with our misery?

The Flatiron Building at the corner of Fifth Avenue fascinated me on our wayfaring expedition. Now it rises ominously above the mass of transportation, horses squealing in protest of honking buses and motorcars. How I loved to groom our mules and horses with Otto! Will nothing remain as God created it in this ever-changing world?

"So many people!" Mother says as we follow the herds from one destination to the next. Step by step, we follow Father's directions, board and disembark busses, recognize landmarks and walk closer to our refuge.

It is dusk when Fodor Petrov opens the door of his colonial red brick home. Father does not stand beside the short, stout man I recall as his senior professor and wayfaring mentor. Mother puts a hanky to her mouth. Petrov draws us to him. We let our tears fall upon his threshold.

Inside his bachelor kitchen, Petrov serves us a repast of cold meats, cheese, fruit, and bread, with endless cups of hot tea and slices of küchen.

"You are revived?" Petrov asks.

"Yes, friend," Mother says.

He places his hands upon my shoulders. "God be with you, Olaf. May you carry on your forefather's work wherever you tread."

The weight of his charge falls heavily upon me as we mourn Father's sacrifice and Russia's demise. The disparity between our want and the prosperity of New York City and comfort of Petrov's home crush my hope with guilt and doubt.

"How will I fulfill my forefathers' work with five books and one hundred and seventy seed packages?"

"As every botanist, alongside those who love plants."

I remember Grandfather's words and want to believe.

Petrov leads Mother and me to separate rooms where hot baths and clean bedclothes await. I appreciate his maid's efficiency. I think of our beloved Cook and choke my tears.

"Please leave your traveling clothes outside your doors for laundering, and your boots for shining. Arise when you are hungry for kasha and coffee," Petrov says.

After a restless night in newfound comfort, I hear Mother's voice at the door. She is transformed by laundered, ironed, and mended traveling clothes that miraculously fit her frame, diminished as it is by grief and the diet of transcontinental travel. Her three tortoise-shell combs secure anew her washed and dried auburn hair. She holds my renewed trousers and shirt, her face beaming. "Someone altered our clothing, Olaf!"

This kind gesture lifts our spirits back into the heights of respectability.

We find Petrov waiting breakfast for us with an assortment of local, national, and international newspapers piled at his end of the long table. It takes great discipline for me to use good manners with the substantial bowl of kasha and pot of hot, strong coffee with cream nearby on the table. Mother, on the other hand, holds her spoon and cup as though she had suffered no lack.

We consume a small platter of streusel before Petrov says, "Would you prefer to rest here several days before I deliver you into Mekinov's hands and a parlor full of guests?"

I look to mother in surprise. She seems familiar with the plan, although Father did not include Mekinov's name in his wallet papers. Then again, Mekinov is in the photograph. Maximowicz was not a possibility for lodging and protection because he deceased years ago.

Mother sits back in her chair and speaks with a tremor. "You are an angel of mercy, Petrov. You know the path of a refugee."

"As does Mekinov," he replies.

I cannot remember when I last heard Father speak of Sergei Mekinov, one of many University professors who fled at the inception of the Marxist uprisings within our universities and cities.

Petrov stands and takes up the newspapers. "It is settled. You will rest here until you wish to leave. Meanwhile, stroll my labyrinth and little herb and flower gardens, and take from the pantry what you please. Mildred, my Irish maid, stocked the shelves for a *komanda* of hungry farmers. She also knows the hunger of a refugee. You will find her delicious soda bread on the second shelf to your right. I shall be in my library should you desire my company before she serves our lunch."

After a month confined to close quarters, Mother opens the kitchen door to November's chill and disappears within a labyrinth covered with withered and tangled wisteria vines. The scene depresses me, for I envision Mother's pergola behind our home. God have mercy upon Mother! She and Cook would cool themselves beneath the leafing vines. How she celebrated their rare spring, blossoming from the iron ribs! She would set up her easel and paint on windless summer days within their shade.

I reach for the door's handle to join her when understanding pierces my heart. I must not cling to Mother as those vines do their structures. Now, she must grieve alone. Dear, dear, Father. You and Grandfather provided for Mother's needs. I must trust you provided for mine.

I aim for Petrov's library, reminiscent of Father's. As the gentleman is engaged with the daily *New York Times*, I remove from a shelf *A History of English Gardening* by George William Johnson. A craving to hear Petrov speak Father's name overwhelms me. Our host glances above his paper to the book in my hand.

"A delightful argument to support gardening as an art. I recommend the sunroom for reading on such a fine, autumn day."

A fine day? I am five thousand miles from home, crestfallen and desperate to hear anyone speak of Father.

"Sir, do you have family?"

The newspaper falls to Petrov's lap. He studies me as though in agony. I have trespassed his privacy and know of nothing else to do to escape further disappointment and embarrassment.

Petrov stands. "Olaf, please forgive me. I forget the pain and confusion of newborn grief. Please, sit down. I will answer your question."

I do as he says.

He rests a hand upon the fireplace mantel and stares into the small fire. "My beloved wife died in childbirth three years after we married. I would have gone mad after losing Victoria and our son had it not been for Carl, Frederick, and Sergei's companionship to fill my emptiness."

At last! Though I'm heartbroken for Petrov's confession, the mention of Father's name releases my floodgates. I sink back into the divan.

"I have no companions to fill my emptiness for Father and the others left behind. And the Bolsheviks have stolen our wealth. How shall we purchase a home and land to continue Father's work?"

"Olaf, be at peace. Your father provided for this day."

I sigh with relief.

"You understand why your grandfather and parents could not disclose this to you?"

I nod, grateful for Petrov's discretion and compassion. Father chose my first mentor in America well. "The risks of disclosing to me their plans and provisions for our escape weighed against us, and all those who assisted Father and Grandfather, too, if the Bolsheviks or sympathizers knew their plans and seized our documents."

I do not want to think it or speak it, yet Petrov inquired, and I owe him the entire truth. "And Father understood the Bolsheviks' bloodthirst for Romanovs. Thus, his surrender to rescue Mother and me."

Petrov gazes into the fire in silence before he turns to me. "You speak of others left. The woman you love, perhaps?"

Again, Petrov's wisdom corrects my acuity. My loss cannot compare to Mother's. "No. And for that I am thankful. Yet, I abandoned Otto, a young farmer orphaned by his father, who followed the Bolsheviks."

"Guilt dogs you?"

"*Da.*"

"Let it go. Pray for Otto. Do your father's work."

"How will I know where to go? What work to do?"

"As my friend Frederick Semenov exemplified: by God's endless mercy. He will guide Natalia. You follow. Our God will meet your needs above what you can ask or think. Look how God has attended to my needs so I may be able to meet yours."

"Yet, you live alone."

Petrov smiles. "You are mistaken, son. You are young. Someday you will know what I mean when I say we are never alone."

I stand, for I want to believe Petrov. He places a hand upon my shoulder and vows, "Until I am unable, wherever God leads you, I will correspond with you regarding your work and family. I will sow Otto's name amongst my fellows and pray he finds his way to you."

I know Petrov will do as he says. "What did you name your son?"

"Frederick Sergei."

Later, Mother, Petrov, and I dine on the maid's Irish version of borsht, schnitzel, and sauerkraut. He invites Mother and me into his library. "Please, sit by the fire." Mother and I look to one another in anticipation.

"Natalia and Olaf, please know you are welcome to remain as my houseguests indefinitely."

With grace and dignity, Mother says, "We are most thankful."

Petrov removes a folded paper from his vest pocket. My heart races. Instinctively, I reach for Mother's hand.

"However, according to Frederick's final letter, he requested Olaf complete his degree in botany from Boston College." Stunned, I turn to Mother, who seems aware of Father's request. My eyes move to Father's letter in Petrov's hand. He continues.

"Whenever you are sufficiently rested, we will board a bus to the New York Central train station for our journey to Boston. There, Sergei Mekinov will await our arrival. Then we will commence fulfilling Frederick's bidding to complete Olaf's education."

Petrov pauses and says discretely, "Meanwhile, if you wish, my maid's mother will sew you both new clothing for your journey. She arrives after lunch today with her measuring tape and bolts of fabric for your selections."

Mother bows her head before she lifts eyes glossed with gratitude. "The same maid's mother who beautifully altered the clothing we wear?"

"*Da*," Petrov says. He pulls a handkerchief from the opposite vest pocket that held Father's letter. He removes his glasses and daubs his eyes. "Pardon me. I am a man who wears his emotions on his shirt sleeves, as Americans say."

Again, I understand why Father and Mother trusted Petrov with our care. I remove my handkerchief and daub my eyes.

Two weeks later, Petrov escorts Mother into the train station. She's dressed in fine wool the color of red wine, the collar and cuffs embellished with Irish lace. I walk beside mother on her left, a new man in a black suit, white shirt, and collar, fit for our journey to Boston. Although more than a head shorter than Mother, Petrov walks as though he is six feet tall.

The train leaves the dark shadows of New York City behind, our new baggage filled with new clothing at our feet, shod in new shoes. We gaze out our windows as in a blurring dream. No, not quite. Without Father, passing through suburban and rural New York State into Massachusetts is one dull scene upon another in an enduring nightmare. Yet, as Petrov says, we are not alone.

Over two hundred miles later, the train stops at the station designated on Petrov's copy of the New York Central map. The door opens. We gather our new belongings and exit. A tall, slender man with thick, dark hair graying at the temples stands dangerously close to the tracks.

"Petrov! Natalia! Olaf!" he hails with a wide, easy smile and keen, dark eyes. So, this is Sergei Mekinov. He bows to Mother and embraces Petrov before he takes possession of mother's arm. At last, he acknowledges me. "Young man, I hope you enjoyed New York City and your train ride."

Mekinov speaks and behaves as if Mother and I are tourists. I nod, disguise my instant distrust with a smile.

We walk with streams of people as Sergei Mekinov guides us through the station to a street where he hires a taxi and says, "505 Grandview Boulevard."

The drive seems longer than the twenty minutes my new watch indicates. I am thankful for the Longines Petrov insisted I would need in the city. I understood his subtle meaning. Mother and I no longer live a pastoral life by the rising and setting of the sun. And my heart aches for it.

As the taxi stops before our destination just outside the cityscape, Sergei Mekinov says, "Welcome to Boston!" I look up to see a beautiful loggia flanks the width of the façade on the third floor.

I will ask Mother the appropriate name to address this wealthy man named Sergei Mekinov—this man my father considered trustworthy, yet who displays inappropriate affection for Mother. When I was a child, Fodor Petrov said, "Son, please use Petrov when speaking with me. Fodor sounds quite decrepit." I have loved him ever since. I am wary of Sergei Mekinov as he leads us into a large parlor where a table is set for tea. He rings a bell. I sense his awkwardness. Yes, he is Petrov's opposite.

"You must be hungry," he says.

"Always, after a long journey," Petrov replies in good humor, as to a trusted, old friend. Mekinov keeps constant watch over Mother and me. He rings the bell and requests a pot of tea to be served immediately.

"Petrov," says Mekinov, "do you plan to join us tomorrow night for Natalia and Olaf's reception with our fellow botanists?" Mother's hands move imperceptibly.

"I would not miss it for the rarest dahlia in the world," says Petrov.

"Grand! You know where to find your room."

After subdued conversation over copious cups of hot tea and fine cold meats, cheeses, breads, and cakes, Mekinov leads us to the third floor where a large, well-appointed room with two beds and a bathroom await us.

I find a wardrobe of handsome clothes and shoes and marvel that Father provided Mekinov with my measurements. Father also advanced funds for Mekinov to prepare a closetful of beautiful dresses, hats, and footwear for Mother. As with our traveling clothes, the new clothing is too large. How could Father foresee the shock of grief, the rigors of reaching St. Petersburg's port, and the demands of transatlantic travel without him?

Mother bows her head before the closet, still as the Greek sculpture that graced the foyer of our farmhouse. I determine to request a tailor for altering our clothes.

We retire without a glimpse of the street from the loggia.

After a restful day at meals and in our room, the evening's guests arrive and enter the large parlor. There, Mekinov introduces Mother and me to his Russian, Irish, and American guests. Botanists, professors, authors, journalists, artists. For hours they tell wayfaring stories and shake from their loss of their friend, companion, and correspondent, Frederick Semenov.

"He stands before God and receives his reward!" they say.

"I would not be a free man today without Frederick's foresight and connections," Mekinov says.

According to Father's request, Mekinov arranges my employment and education. By night I sweep halls and classrooms within Boston College. By day I walk the campus and city looking for Otto. No one resembles a fifteen-year-old boy built like a bull with black hair and blue eyes. I repeatedly inquire about Otto and realize I have become a bore to fellow employees and classmates. And without warning, my heart still leaps upon every dash of red I spy in a crowd.

Our first Christmas Day in America passes quietly with Mekinov, our food prepared by his cook in advance. In his empty kitchen, Mother finds an apron and ingredients to prepare küchen. As she works, she sings *Silent Night* in her native tongue, which draws me to the open door. Mekinov follows. We lean against the wall out of her sight and listen to her last note. We remove our handkerchief from our jacket pocket and wipe our eyes. Mekinov embraces me and whispers, "A blessed Christmas to you, Olaf."

I am surprised by his affection. "And to you, Sir."

By day I improve my English with a tutor and pass my college entrance exam within months. A childless widower, Mekinov looks upon me with a father's pride.

"Congratulations, Olaf!"

We hear nothing of Father's whereabouts from our Russian expatriates and dare hope he escaped and someday will stand before Mekinov's door.

And Mother! Mekinov invites fellow professors, the college's botany club, and Richardson Wright, a board member of New York's Horticultural Society, into our refuge for dinner and concerts. Mother performs reluctantly, for she hears Father's words: "*trust no one.*"

"We will be safe in the mountains," she says when we retire to our room. I understand. Mother is made of Borregaard Manor's fiords and cliffs.

Mekinov does not know Mother's plans. Nor do I tell him during the hours we sit with his chessboard between us. Mother does not say so when we play chess, but she knows Mekinov's plans. He loves her. What man in his right mind would not?

Meanwhile, Richardson Wright, an American eight years my senior, befriends Mother and me. He and Sergei introduce us to members of Boston's Horticultural Society. "You must keep a diary of this adventure and begin an herbarium," Richardson says to Mother and me.

Distracted with work and becoming acquainted with Boston, I am in no disposition to commence the laborious and tedious process of assembling covers and pages for an herbarium.

"This is work for the winter so you may gather the plant material in the spring," Richardson says with authority.

Upon his following visit with Mekinov, Richardson carries materials for the covers, including hardware, to assemble my herbarium. He insists, "Olaf, in April, you and your mother must take the train with my wife and me to our country home in Silver Mine, Connecticut. Although it's still chilly in April, thousands of crocus awaken in the upper gardens."

Mother is charmed by Richardson's personality and passion for botanical history. Truly, who couldn't admire a man much like Frederick Semenov, possessed of multiple gifts—one being hospitality? She agrees to escape the city, Mekinov, and his constant stream of guests. In Silver Mine, we meet Richardson's father, who entertains us with his gift of being able to identify every source of smoke as far as two miles away.

We walk Richardson's meticulous upper rockery and lower border, planted to bloom from the first spring crocus to his pampered Christmas roses, also known as Hellebores. His pigs and his wife's hens amuse Mother and me. We smile at the rooster's crow, cast glances at one another in mutual longing for home.

Mother revives amongst Richardson's gardens and groves. Color returns to her cheeks. Meanwhile, I cut plant specimens from Richardson's gardens and press them with the equipment he provides.

"Ah!" Richardson says, looking over my shoulder, "*Iris pallida*, and native of the Dalmatian coast. Good choice. Some say her scent reminds them of vanilla. What do you say, Olaf?"

I look up to Richardson in disbelief, for Father taught me botany in the same manner.

"Yes, particularly when grown in mass as Father and Albert planted."

"Albert?" Richardson asks.

"Father's foreman."

Richardson bows his head in respect.

Richardson's father sets down his fork at dinner that evening. "Mrs. Semenov, while I stretched these old legs in Dickie's lower garden this morning, I heard you singing in the upper garden."

Mother blushes.

Father Wright, as Richardson names his sire, leans closer to Mother as if in confidence. "I have never heard a more beautiful rendition of 'There's No Place Like Home.'"

"Thank you, Mr. Wright. Do you speak the Norwegian language?"

"Yes."

Richardson lifts his fork. "One of five. It is my pleasure to speak of Father's accomplishments and add amen!"

From that evening forward, Mother and Father Wright speak to each other in Norwegian. She cuts flowers and arranges bouquets with Richardson's wife, Agnes, who engages us in conversation about her favorite annuals, perennials, and nurseries. To Richardson's approval, she adores roses above all he grows in his gardens and meadows. Agnes considers Bartram Gardens an American gem.

"Definitely! All other pale to their history and inventory." Agnes declares.

"I was sorry to read of the sad end of Merriweather Lewis after his famous expedition with William Clark. Did you know they brought the Osage orange tree to us?" Richardson says.

He tells stories about his odd, old gardener. "Always on the hunt for a wife."

"That is good to know," Mother says with a wink. She speaks of Cook, who taught her how to bake pastries in Polya Tsvetov's kitchen. "And Cook never stacked the pots we used. She insisted I wash them as we used them to keep the counter clean for another batch of pastry dough," Mother says.

"And so does my redheaded sister when she cooks!" Richardson declares.

This is Richardson's first mention of a sister.

When we dine *al fresco*, Agnes rings a low-pitched dinner bell, a sound distinctive from birdsong. We listen to Richardson's complaints about his editorial life "pinned behind a desk" in New York City. He derides men who golf and evokes our agreement, for Father held the same sentiment. He would laugh and say, "What adventure is there in traversing mowed lawn with a golf club?"

After dinner, we settle into their morning room. Floral prints adorn every wall, some embroidered with satin ribbon, much like those in Father's library. Richardson rings another brass bell for the cook, who brings a tray bearing Father Wright's favorite port and five glasses. The scene is reminiscent of home.

"This, my dear Olaf," Richardson says, taking up a large, ancient book in his hands, "is a water-color herbarium illustrated by Pierre Joseph Redoute, the Raphael of Flowers."

"One of Frederick's treasures!" Mother says in spontaneous recognition.

It seems Richardson invited Mother and me to Silver Mine for her comfort and my instruction. He and his wife love plants and soon come to love us. Richardson's list of achievements astonishes and embarrasses me. We burn a pile of logs each night discussing his most recent published book, *The Russians*. He signs a copy for Mother and me. I keep it beside Father's Bible on my nightstand. I am thankful Richardson's interpretation of Russia and her history does not include the country's present demise. What have I accomplished in my twenty-four years?

Nothing.

Thankfully, Richardson mentors me in botany as I join him in his gardens at Silver Mine. Mekinov, however, shoves his hands in his pockets and sulks on the Fridays we depart Boston. "I lose my chess partners again!"

Richardson's wife spends hours alone with Mother, reading

newspaper and magazine articles and books illuminating Appalachian botany, culture, and history.

"There are too few publications," Agnes says. "Other than the Hatfield-McCoy Feud, it seems journalists and historians have overlooked the immigrants who settled the Appalachian Mountain range."

Richardson sets before me a small stack of books from his library, all titles inclusive of Appalachian flora, fauna, and biography. "Go at it, man!" Wright says.

This is Mother's notice I am to prepare for our future in Appalachia, a region I know little of, other than stories of Father and Petrov wayfaring the Kentucky-West Virginia border together. I was a child and thought Father would never return.

In the evening, we listen to the classical masters on Father Wright's phonograph. The octogenarian stands and invites Mother to sing. Natalia Ingrid Semenov removes the three combs from her hair and places them on a nearby table, for she cannot sing with bound hair.

She stands, lifts her chin and hand as if she is performing in Mariinsky Theatre.

I do not know how Mother wills her mind to bring forth the words, or her mouth and tongue to form them, or how her lungs obey with breath. Yet, she gives her gift of Father's favorite aria. Our awe attends Mother's flawless voicing of Puccini's score for "Un bel di Vedremo." With lips parted and eyes swollen with sorrow, we cling to her last note from *Madama Butterfly*—her relinquished hope for the "one fine day" Father returns.

Mother takes her combs from the table. "Olaf," she says, and extends her arm to me. I rise and escort her from the morning room. Her body weakens with each stair we climb to her room.

As I observed Father do after Mother's performances, I assist her to her bedside and remove her shoes. When I return with water, I find her asleep. And as Father once did, I leave the water on the bedside table. The next day, as we board the train for Boston, I reject Mother's resignation to Father's death. I must cling to hope, my only force to accomplish his work.

One day during the sweltering heat of July, 1918, while Mekinov and I play chess in his parlor, the radio reports the assassination of Nicholas Romanov. There is no mention of his wife and children. Mother closes her copy of Dostoyevsky's *Diary of a Writer* and holds it to her breast. She rises and leaves us. I follow her the two flights up to her room where she lapses into mourning. She will not leave the house for Silver Mine the following Friday.

Father never appears, despite my hope. I complete my herbarium of dried flowers and watercolors with our host's artistic assistance and Wright's edits when he and his wife dine with us.

Prohibition and the vote for Women's Suffrage dominate the newspapers and radio reports. One fall day, from the third-floor loggia, Mother and I watch women march down the avenue in support of their right to vote.

"No one in Russia may vote," Mother reflects. "Not women, nor men."

I nod, encouraged by her observation. "Mother, our asylum here draws to an end. I would like to resume our visits to Silver Mine with the Wrights."

"And so would I."

On the following Saturday morning in Silver Mine, Richardson invites us to celebrate Christmas Week with them. Father Wright sits across from Mother and winks. Mother hesitates.

"Please, Mrs. Semenov," Agnes says. "We shall skate on the pond."

Mother, an excellent skater, glances to me. I nod. Silver Mine is a more congenial place for Christmas than Boston. Mother rests a hand on the table and addresses the Wrights. "Thank you. We accept your generous invitation."

Richardson wipes his mustache with a napkin. "It is settled then!"

Agnes wags a finger of rebuttal.

"Pardon me, Mrs. Semenov," Richardson says, "not to put you on the spot, dear friend, but may we invite Sergei to join us with this promise: we do not speak of your departure for Appalachia and spoil his holiday? You see, we cannot bear the thought of the good man pacing his mansion alone Christmas Day."

Mother looks to her plate. "And I cannot bear the thought of Frederick's good friend alone Christmas Day."

"Grand!" Richardson says, and rings the bell for dessert.

I feel for Mekinov and Mother. I see their fondness for each other, although Mother's attraction to Mekinov seems too fragile to overcome her grief and devotion to Father. Yet, I remember her song upon our previous visit to Silver Mine.

Months later, on Christmas Day, the Wrights' dinner bell calls us to the dining room. To our utter delight, a centerpiece of sleeping, newborn wirehaired pups in a large, wicker basket decorates the long table.

Candlelight glows on jingle bells strung on red, satin ribbons and tied into a bow around the neck of each puppy. A snow-white flannel blanket lines the basket. Mother and I look to one another in disbelief. Christmas morning of my ninth year, in the same manner, Mother presented Father with five whelps of his beloved wire-haired pointer. God have mercy upon Mekinov and Mother! Father and Polya Tsvetov live everywhere in all seasons.

With Mekinov's guidance and my continuous enrollment, I graduate June 1919 and teach as an assistant professor in botany at Boston College. The Irish students, many immigrant offspring from Ireland's Great Hunger, find me curious. "Bless my soul, lad! With your Russian accent, you couldn't 'av come out'a thin air!" jests a young man from Killarney, County Kerry.

"And bless my soul, lad! You are entirely right!"

I persist in my search for Otto's face on campus and in the city. I reveal nothing to my colleagues of my escape from Russia with Mother. Do nothing to risk her safety and peace of mind.

Meanwhile, I receive Petrov's weekly letters and newspapers reporting Russia's collapse into starvation.

"Praise God your father prepared your way of escape," Petrov writes. "We must watch and defend our American freedoms!"

With our benefactors' tutelage, Mother and I study the Constitution of the United States of America. We declare our Naturalization Oath of Allegiance to the United States on Friday, July 3,

1919. We celebrate Independence Day with the Wrights' houseful of fellow gardeners, authors, botanists, and farmers. We sing "The Star-Spangled Banner" in the parlor. Father Wright's voice sounds above all the others.

I envision our ship, *the huddled masses yearning to breathe free,* and begin to understand the meaning of the Lady's lamp and the words on her tablet. Freedom comes with a cost, as Petrov says. We must be diligent to obtain and sustain freedom from tyranny.

At last, Mother writes a letter of business inquiry using the name Olaf Hunt, in honor of Father's favorite sport. Weeks later, a post arrives from Matewan, West Virginia, regarding the purchase of a building.

"The price is surprisingly affordable, "Mother says. "We will be safe in the mountains."

I understand. The news of the murder of Nicholas Romanov confirmed to mother we must hide from the Bolsheviks. For I am also of Romanov blood. She will do nothing to put my safety and peace of mind at risk. And from what Richardson assures us, Matewan, West Virginia is a place within reach of our New England friends. We may vanish along the banks of Tug Fork.

The business reply includes a photo of the building, a neglected, plain wood box with simple window trim and double door. I make no remark of disapproval. When Mother at last reveals our plans to Mekinov, he takes the photo in hand and cries out, *Ssklochnyy!*

"I did not expect such an ugly, neglected building," she reluctantly admits.

Compared to Russian architecture, it is indeed plain. We decide to devote five years to its business success. If we fail, or if Mother is unhappy, we will run again. "You are always welcome here," says Mekinov.

May 20, 1920. We listen to morning radio with our coffee, the room heavy with unspoken sentiments. An international report of Herbert Hoover's humanitarian efforts to relieve Russia's death toll by starvation is followed by: "Yesterday, in downtown Matewan, West Virginia, a showdown between Baldwin-Felts detectives hired by coal companies and the pro-union mayor and sheriff left eight men dead on Mate Street." Mother and I look to one another. The ugly building we purchased is located on Mate Street.

Mekinov turns off the radio.

"We will go," Mother says.

Mekinov lifts disappointed, dark eyes to us. "You are always welcome here," he repeats.

Upon our last visit together to Silver Mine, listening to Rachmaninoff's *Rhapsody on a Theme of Paganini*, Mekinov says to Mother, "You will not find classical radio or recordings in Appalachia."

"The man's right, Mrs. Semenov," Richardson says and jumps up from his chair. "Follow me!"

He directs us to a resale-antique shop where the proprietor replies to Mekinov's request with the jab of a pencil toward a dusty, mauve piano shawl. Mother lifts the fringe and discovers a phonograph in excellent condition.

"Olaf! Look!" She dances her fingers over the curled bell of the speaker with the first smile I've seen in months. The phonograph is much like Grandfather's.

As parting gifts, Richardson buys the piano shawl, phonograph, and recordings of Bach, Beethoven, Tchaikovsky, and Rachmaninoff.

"Did you know Rachmaninoff stands at six feet six?" Richardson asks.

Mother takes his hand. "Yes, he is a good friend, four inches taller than Frederick and Olaf."

"His performance of *Dance of the Gypsies* in New York City swept us off our feet," Mekinov says. "Promise you will return to Boston so we may hear Rachmaninoff together in the city."

I promise, yet we all doubt Mother will ever return to Boston or New York City for fear of the Bolsheviks.

"I am envious," Richardson says. "How I would love to escape to a little Appalachian town. Imagine the flora! Once you're settled, you must invite us to visit."

Mekinov looks to his hands, and I pity him.

Mother cries in her pillow all the night long.

I wonder if I am wrong, and ask, "Mother, do you cry for Boston and Silver Mine?"

"No. Your father is not with us to see your faith and courage."

I do not confess my doubt and fear. I am twenty-five years old and feel like an old man and a failure. Have I done anything to continue Father's work?

September 5, 1920, I drive our Ford Model T Huckster over the muddy Tug River toward Matewan, West Virginia. Mother holds a handkerchief to her mouth. For hours she has clung to her door handle as I turn the wheel side-to-side to navigate hairpin turns much like those in the Italian Alps. For a wayfarer raised below a sheer cliff of a fiord, Mother did not fare well on that expedition, either.

"I prefer my feet on the ground," she said.

We escape numerous pits in the road as we creep along, stop for cows crossing, waving to the herder, who nods and turns his neck to the passing oddity. I fear we will not reach Matewan without slipping into a ditch on the mountainside or rolling down the hill on a blind curve.

"Board the train in Boston! Connections will take you into Matewan," Richardson had advised. A man opposed to the automobile's disturbance to country living, he suggested we take the train and then purchase our truck in West Virginia.

Yet, Mekinov insisted Mother and I take some furnishings from the room he provided for us. "To help you settle in," he said.

"I am thankful Richardson insisted he put two spare tires in the truck bed," I say, determined to conclude this adventure in good spirits.

"I am thankful it is not raining," Mother replies.

And I am as well, for our truck has no windows. Another reason to travel by train, as most immigrants leaving Grand Central Station for their Promised Land. Yet, I understand. Mother and I run from our enemies, and they may wait at the station.

We cringe at each passing of horse-drawn wagons or motorized vehicles on these impossibly narrow roads. At last, I relax my grip on a straight stretch where a rail yard expands upon acres of flatland below. Thousands of coal cars wait on countless tracks.

"This must be the coal yard Richardson spoke of," I say to Mother. "Prime real estate, he said."

"It is smaller than St. Petersburg's coal yard."

Russia. Always with us.

I drive under a viaduct and veer left onto Mate Street, supposedly named after Mate Creek, one of several mountain streams that flows from Beech Creek Mountain to the muddy Tug River. A long, narrow, business district with buildings on both sides stretches before us. Traffic by foot, buggy, motorcar, and truck promises a prosperous business as coal soot billows above the buildings in the distance.

The *chuga-chuga-chuga-chuga* of a steam engine and blast of a whistle follows. The sounds provoke a mutual smile between Mother and me, in memory of our travels with Father. Our truck shakes as the long train passes out of sight on the other side of Mate Street's two and three-story buildings. I am glad there is no wind to blow the soot through the open windows. The river and railroad tracks border the length of Mate Street. Mountains filled with coal encircle us. Yes, we are safe here, yet I remember Mekinov's offer; I am tempted to turn around, but have no nerve left to face the narrow roads and traffic again. And I have no sense of north, south, east, or west. We are lost in Matewan.

"I see little worthy of Richardson's envy," Mother confesses.

Our New York license plate and truck bed covered with tarp offer a spectacle for the townspeople. They stop before the storefronts on both sides of the street and watch as I drive by the ugly building in the photograph Mother holds. I stop, shift, and turn the truck around before the Matewan Hospital, two buildings down on the other side of the street. I block the two lanes and drip with perspiration.

At last, I park in front of the building we purchased with half the American currency Father provided in his wallet. Thank God Mother deposited more in the Matewan National Bank. Most refugees are not as fortunate.

"Wait here," I say to Mother.

My footfall echoes on the building's wooden porch. I hope Mother does not notice the bullet holes in the façade. The massacre is not four months behind this wounded place. We could find little national news of the showdown. Mother and I hope that is a good sign. Why so much fighting and killing? Wherever we go, fighting and killing.

"Now, peacemakers move to Matewan," Mekinov said as we left our host of three years. I feel no peace of mind and heart when Mother's heel sounds like thunder upon the porch. She stands beside me and scans the building's height and width in silence. I pull the bundle of keys from my pocket and hope they will open the doors.

Here we stand on foreign ground without Grandfather and Father, dispossessed of our work, home, and land that taught our people to feed and clothe themselves. I burn with anger. That the Bolsheviks abuse and ruin these honorable means of sustenance strikes me with hate. That I did not follow Father humiliates me. That I have not hunted with Grandfather and Father for three years, and will never hunt with them again, paralyzes me with grief.

We left our land of milk and honey, overcome by thieves who grab for power and belittle farm labor, to dwell in the pollution of coal soot and warring miners! Father! Is this sooty town and its neglected building my reward for obedience to my elders? What future do Mother and I have in Matewan? Truly, I see nothing in this town anyone could envy.

I turn to Mother to suggest we return to Boston, but she places a hand on mine that holds the keys. Her eyes emit a peace I try to comprehend.

"Open the door, son."

Mother's command echoes from the moment in time she placed Father's Bible in my hands. Rebuked by her resolve, I use the last of my will to unlock the door. Where could we run, otherwise?

"We are never alone," I whisper, taking courage.

Mother holds her handkerchief to her face as we walk on mouse scat. I am relieved to see and hear no evidence of rats. The room is spacious with a ten-foot ceiling. We open interior double doors and discover the wall divides the lower floor into two substantial rooms. The merchandise we have ordered would fit into one corner. I cannot imagine the business we must conduct to fill this enormous building.

I want to sit and cry with my face in my hands, but Mother returns to the room facing Mate Street. I follow, amazed, for she seems reconciled to this repulsive building.

A door stands ajar to a small space that resembles an office. I walk into the room, try another doorknob, and retrieve the keys and unlock a second door to a dark stairwell leading to the upper story.

I find the light switch on the wall and look up to a bare light bulb hanging above a landing. Mother and I look to one another in dread. How will I carry Mekinov's obese green chairs up this stairway?

I grab the rail. My heel hangs over the tread.

"Mother, hold the rail."

For three years, we lived as guests in Mekinov's luxurious Boston townhouse and the Wright's snug country cottage. Now, we walk into a primitive, vacant upper floor, expansive enough for a library and dance floor. Our home. It may be a year or more before we achieve renovations of this deplorable place. I am thankful Grandfather put a hammer in one hand and a saw in the other on my tenth birthday. Left behind in Otto's care.

"The accommodations meet our needs," Mother says, and tries the bathroom toilet's handle. "*Da*," she says when it flushes the water from the rusted bowl and the tank refills it. Richardson's wife had warned us about Appalachian toilets.

Mother turns the sink faucets. "*Da*," she says when both hot and cold water flow. She inspects the claw-foot bathtub, much like ours in Russia. The hot water spigot sputters air. The cold water flows, the drain red with rust.

"I will find the hot water tank tomorrow. Until then, as I did when we camped with Father, I will heat your bath water on the stove."

Mother shakes her head. "You have enough work on your hands."

We step into the sparse kitchen. Two large cupboards hang above a porcelain sink and drain board. Mother does not try the faucets. The electric range is her first concern. Her eyes sparkle when the coils turn red.

"I will serve kasha and coffee in the morning."

We scan the cavernous room that will serve for our parlor, library, and bedrooms until I build walls for two private bedrooms. I lift my eyes to view the height of the ceiling and attempt humor. "More spacious than the ship. First, I will carry up your phonograph."

When I return to the truck, a man with dark hair walks around the truck bed with a young boy and looks under the tarp.

"May I help you?" I ask.

He jumps and spins toward me with an extended hand and smile. "Welcome to Matewan!" he says in an Italian accent. He gives a vigorous handshake. "John Nenni of Nenni's Department Store down d'e street." He looks down to the boy. "And d'is Antillo, my son."

"My name is Olaf Semenov. My mother Natalia waits upstairs."

"We help unload your truck," he says and nods to the building. "D'ose steps kill you if you don' watch your feet."

"I cannot impose."

It is as if John Nenni were deaf. He begins to remove the tarp, uncovering our belongings. I know nothing else to do but assist. He takes two of Sergei's spindle-back chairs.

"Upstairs?" he asks. I nod and follow him post-haste with the other two spindle-back chairs so this merchant will not frighten Mother. I introduce her to Mr. Nenni.

"Welcome to Matewan, Mrs. Semenov."

Mother responds with a peculiar, warm smile, as if to a friend. "Thank you, Mr. Nenni."

"Call me John." I follow John downstairs to the truck where he waves to two men. "What took so long?"

"Customers," one said.

"Take one d'ose green chairs—and watch your feet on d'e stairs."

Another man walks up to the truck as people stop and watch.

"Crazy Ray! Help me w'd d'is table," John Nenni says.

Before Crazy Ray or the boy Antillo have a chance to spy the box containing our crystal lamp and shade, I take it and climb the stairs again. I am glad God gifted me with Father and Mother's long arms and large hands like Sergei Rachmaninoff's. Good for steering a plough. Good for holding awkward boxes. And good for hefting Mekinov's large, rolled rug.

Mother's face says she's relieved to see our lamp in my care. In our third-floor room in Mekinov's house, she spent three Boston winters in the illumination of the shade's pleated, silk cloth. There, she read Appalachian literature, news, and maps.

"Oi!" cries John Nenni, "You pack rocks in d'is box?

"Books."

Our volunteers and I empty the truck within an hour. In another half hour we assemble our two beds and move the bookshelf into place until Mother says "There!"

"Now d'e rug," John Nenni says to his assistants.

"Thank you," I say, "however, the floor needs sweeping and mopping."

John Nenni's eyes dart around the spacious, dingy room. "Where d'e broom, bucket, and mop I see in d'e truck bed?"

I blush. Mr. Nenni misunderstood my meaning. "Please, sir. Mother and I will clean the floor later. We cannot further impose upon your time and employees."

Again, Mr. Nenni dismisses me.

"We roll out rug where you like."

Mother hastens to survey the room and says "There!" once more. Submitting to John Nenni's resolve, she retrieves the broom, bucket, mop, and soap from the kitchen.

Mr. Nenni takes the broom and eyes the rolled rug. "Twenty by fifteen feet?"

Speechless, I nod. He is off by one foot on the shorter ends. I understand why his mercantile thrives in this coal town. No. His business would thrive in Boston. Petrov, Mekinov, and Richardson would befriend him on the spot, as Americans say.

"Crazy Ray," Mr. Nenni says, "fill d'e bucket with sudsy water in d'e bathtub and follow my broom with d'e mop."

While the floor dries, Mr. Nenni, his son, and his men walk around the room and mutter, "Where those Goodfellows once met," and, "Bless their hearts, this place is awful nasty," and, "I remember when it was the Chambers Funeral Home before the fire in 1910."

I am intrigued by their remarks. Goodfellows? Funeral home? Fire? Is mother aware of this building's history?

The moment the floor dries, we roll out the rug before Mekinov's two green chairs with the round table between. I offer cash to our rescuers. Mr. Nenni and his employees throw up their hands and shake their heads.

"Welcome to Matewan!" they say and descend the stairs.

The young man they name Crazy Ray accepts my offer.

"Thank you," Mother and I say. We listen to his feet run down the stairwell.

Mother strolls the gritty, unvarnished wood floor as if she were in our farmhouse in Polya Tsevtov. Still in distain of our situation, I follow her beyond the carpet to the middle of three windows facing Mate Street. We watch John and Antillo Nenni and Crazy Ray on the sidewalk below. They talk, slap their legs and one another on the back. Mr. John Nenni's dark eyes look up to the window. He waves. The men smile and wave. We reciprocate.

"We have just seen many things Richardson could envy," Mother says.

I do not want to agree, but must. "*Da.*"

Astonished, gritty, and exhausted, we observe small crowds gather around John Nenni and Crazy Ray. My anger, hate, and self-loathing refuse to bow to their kindness.

Mother holds a hand to her throat. How does she carry this crushing reality? She will never sing again before an audience in her beloved Norway and Russia. And, God forgive me, I cannot find faith that she will embrace her father or sister again. Or Cook. I am sick with regret for her.

"What would we have done without them?" Mother says.

I resist her sentiment. "Hired passersby, as I intended."

"They served us instead."

Her words pierce my soul, yet I cannot trust what she perceives.

"So, this is Matewan. Our new home," Mother says and turns to me. She studies my eyes as she has all my life. "Your father spoke the truth, Olaf."

I step back in bewilderment. "What do you mean, Mother? Father always spoke the truth."

She allows a sigh I cannot read. "*Da,*" she says and takes my hands in hers.

I sense her joy and relief, and am embarrassed of my bitterness. Her face glows with a peace I cannot comprehend.

"Olaf, your father and Petrov walked the Appalachian Mountains in fall 1909. Petrov's last expedition to America."

Memory quickens to Father's favorite story from the adventure. I was fourteen years old and clung to his side after such a long voyage. "Where Father found a cobbler to repair his boots slashed by blackberry canes."

"*Da.* Along the Mate and Tug Rivers in the town of Matewan, West Virginia, he found Mr. John Nenni."

Stunned by Mother's revelation, with unbound respect I look down to the crowd gathered around John Nenni and his son, Antillo—merchants who have left their establishments at day's end. "Why did you not inform me of this on the ship or during the years in New York City and Boston?"

"I was often tempted, hoping the knowledge would comfort you. Yet, Petrov counseled me to fulfill Frederick's last request if at all possible."

"Last request?"

"The night before we departed Polya Tsevtov, Frederick said, 'Natalia, please test the waters. Confirm Matewan remains the welcoming town Petrov and I found it to be. If not, find a friendly Appalachian town to prosper good husbandry. For I am certain you will find the place God prepares for you.'"

I kiss mother's hands. "Father found this place for us."

She turns and faces our great task awaiting us. "Olaf, who will teach me to wash dishes and clothing?"

Grandfather's answer to my question when we parted in St. Petersburg comes to mind. "*People who love plants,*" I say. "And people who love to wash dishes and clothing, as Cook taught you to love baking pastry."

Mother nods playfully. A strand of hair escapes her combs. "Will I remember my recipes after three years?"

"You must! Your son's health and happiness depend upon your küchen."

Mother smiles. "As Cook, those who love to wash dishes and clothing are extraordinary people."

I speak again by Grandfather's faith. "They will find us as Father found John Nenni and Crazy Ray found us."

Mother's mouth curves into her beautiful smile as she returns the loose strand of hair to the teeth of a comb. I hurt to see gray in her hair. I hurt for her unspeakable losses.

"Olaf, how will we repay them?"

I bend and kiss her forehead. "With your pastries."

Her eyes glisten. "Frederick said the way to man's heart is with good küchen and coffee."

I raise my eyebrows. "Father always spoke the truth."

In the midst of our demanding changes, I watch her graceful figure walk to the phonograph. She removes the recording of *Beethoven's Ninth Symphony* from the well-preserved jacket and places the record on the turntable. She inhales a deep breath of musty, sooty air and rests the needle on the vinyl. On the first note, our hearts soar to Polya Tsvetov, New York City, Boston, and Silver Mine. Now Mother claims this abandoned building with Beethoven's joy in what Father called the ever-turning Wheel of Life.

While she sweeps and mops upstairs, I sweep the lower floor and ponder Mekinov's charity. Did he give us his furnishings to comfort us, or to keep him ever before Mother's eyes?

Or both?

As Father, Petrov, Mekinov, Richardson, and Agnes taught us to give to those in need, now John and Antillo Nenni teach us. I pause to wipe dust from my eyes when a woman opens the door.

"Good evenin'! I'm Miss Daisy."

She appears as a sprite, holding the handle of a large basket in one hand and a thermos jug in the other. Her strength impresses me.

I bow. "Good evening. I am Olaf Semenov. My mother is Mrs. Natalia Semenov. She is upstairs."

"Well, I brought y'all some supper. Where would you like me to put it?"

"Thank you!" Surprised again with this town's generosity, I look for a place to set Miss Daisy's gifts, but there is no clean surface available. "I will carry this upstairs to Mother."

Miss Daisy passes the basket and jug to me. My stomach rumbles at the scent of warm beans, pork, and polenta. Richardson raved about Appalachia's ubiquitous cornpone. "This is very kind of you, Miss Daisy."

"It's the least I could do for our newcomers. Where'd y'all come from?"

"Boston."

"And before Boston?"

I smile at her question and forthrightness. "Russia."

"Did you and your mother know Russian folk settled in Red Jacket when the mines opened years ago? They're still comin' from Grand Central Station in New York City with Italian and Irish folk. I heerd you drove a brand-new truck all the way from New York City."

"Yes." I must tell Richardson about Miss Daisy and Red Jacket.

"Well, all's I can say is you're one courageous man to drive these here mountains. I'm glad you chose Matewan instead of Red Jacket, Olaf Semenov. Now, you go on. Y'all must be starved," Miss Daisy says with compassion.

I carry our dinner upstairs to the kitchen table unawares because Mother's back is to me as she unpacks the lamp and hums "Ode to Joy." I return to the lower floor, hungry as a hunter who returns home without meat in his bag; Miss Daisy has taken possession of my broom.

She waves me away. "I have nothin' else to do, so y'all go on and eat your supper while it's warm. I'll pick up my belongings tomorrow mornin' at ten o'clock and help your mother wash up the kitchen and dishes. Bein' vacant so long, that place up there must be a sight."

Although I bound up the steps two at a time, and although Mother and I have never tasted such delicious bean soup and cornbread, and although Miss Daisy is one of those extraordinary people like Cook, the next morning, I order a bell to install on the store's door for some forewarning.

Miss Daisy and Mother scrub and unpack upstairs as I restore the hot water and work downstairs. The merchandise I have ordered, and the handsome oak counter with a glass dome Richardson discovered in a Connecticut antique shop are due for delivery within the month. After our prolonged occupancy as house guests, it is good to toil again by the sweat of my brow.

And Mother's hands have never seen such work! We learn to

respect what our hands can do with soap, a mop, and bucket of water. Day by day, they transform this filthy, forlorn building into a comfortable home.

Throughout the weeks, people enter the store to welcome us. They approach us in the Matewan Methodist Church, the Matewan National Bank, post office, Leckie's Drugstore, John Brown's Drycleaners, and Nenni's Mercantile.

"Welcome to Matewan! We hear y'all are from Russia." Miss Daisy, Matewan's telegraph.

"What's Russia like?"

"Beautiful, as Appalachia." We become friends.

Mother decorates the porch and windows of the store with varnished gourds, bittersweet, rosehips, and chrysanthemums as she did our farmhouse on Polya Tsvetov. Thanksgiving Day is fitting for our first American holiday to celebrate in Matewan.

We are thankful pilgrims, for Richardson, Agnes, and Father Wright insist on celebrating the meal with us in our unusual home.

"We must see Matewan! We'll take the train and bed down in Uriah's Hotel," Richardson says. "I'm taking the week off. Not much gardening to do the month of November."

Mother and I invite John and Hazel Nenni, Crazy Ray, and Daisy to join us in welcoming our Silver Mine guests when they arrive at the Matewan Depot. When the train screeches to a stop, half the town crowds on the platform for their first look at the famous Richardson Wright, world traveler, and Editor of *House & Garden* magazine.

"Indeed, there is more to envy in Matewan than I imagined!" Richardson says.

"Oh, you no see d-other half, Mr. Richardson!" John Nenni says, waving his hands in exclamation. "You, wife, father, come to my house with Mrs. Semenov and Olaf for T'anksgiving feast. Hazel show you d-other half on our table!" As if the Nenni's had planned to abduct our guests, Hazel Nenni nods vigorously.

And so our visit with Richardson, Agnes, and Father Wright

unfolds, one invitation after another, concluding with one day and evening alone with them in our "Upper Room," as Richardson christened it, "foreseeing our futures."

His eye at last lands on my herbarium, displayed in his honor on an easel I crafted from hickory wood. "Beautiful work, Olaf. You have an excellent hand and eye with a paintbrush and hardware. Have you considered teaching a class for the residents of Matewan?"

Mother has said the same. I suspect they planned this question. At this moment, I crave to speak of guns and hunting. I've not provided one morsel of our food since the day we left Russia. "There is much to build in this business. Where will I find time?"

Richardson smiles, confident and relaxed. How I covet his maturity.

"Olaf, is not teaching others to build an herbarium part of building your business?"

Thunderstruck, I see his meaning. And he, Mother, Agnes, and Father Wright see it on my face. Yet, they are gracious and say nothing.

Mother rises and sets Rachmaninoff's *Rhapsody on a Theme of Paganini* on the turntable. She turns to her guests. "As we concluded our last visit to Silver Mine, so we conclude your first visit to Matewan. May there be many more."

The following morning, half the town gathered at the Matewan Depot to "send off" our three favorite people from Silver Mine, Connecticut. An ache in my chest says I will not see Father Wright again.

The following temperate Saturday after closing the store, Mother and I walk to John Brown's dry-cleaning business on the other side of Mate Street and the railroad tracks.

"Good afternoon," says the Negro proprietor.

"Good afternoon, Mr. Brown," mother says, and places two dresses on the counter. I add two suits and five white shirts and collars.

"Would you please dry clean these garments for us?" I ask.

"Certainly." Mr. Brown examines a dress front and back. "Very fine linen."

Mother nods. She does not say Polya Tsvetov produced a finer linen.

While Mr. Brown follows the same procedure for each garment and writes our ticket, I notice *Uncle Tom's Cabin* on a shelf at the end of the counter. Mekinov, Mother, and I passed the novel around in his parlor one January. Our discussions extended into the night in our attempt to learn the origin and history of slavery in our world and America. In Russia, slavery was named serfdom, which the Semenovs opposed and never practiced.

"Your clothing will be available in two days," Mr. Brown says and hands me the bill, which I pay. "Thank you, Mr. Semenov. Per our agreement, I will exchange the delivery cost of your order for a slice of your küchen, Mrs. Semenov."

Mother smiles. "A generous slice."

Two days later, minutes before I lock the door, Mr. John Brown appears. I would like to ask his thoughts about *Uncle Tom's Cabin*, yet I am occupied with a customer. Mr. Brown hangs our clothing on the office door hook according to my instructions. He finds the small bag of Mother's küchen on the edge of the window display.

"Lovely autumnal arrangement," Mr. Brown says of Mother's gourds.

"Thank you. I will pass on your compliment to her. She is presently working on her Christmas displays."

The following week, the glass-domed counter arrives and escalates into another traffic jam before the store and along Mate Street. Mother descends the stairs to observe John Nenni and Crazy Ray returning to supervise.

They hail a crew of men, including Doc Bentley from the hospital, to unload our behemoth purchases. This activity elicits more volunteers who help carry first the counter and then the glass dome into the building and situate them on the office side. At last, the store is fitted with a service counter and a display case worthy of McMahon's seed store in Philadelphia.

I run to Leckie's and return with cold drinks for the movers and volunteers. The crowd flows in and out of the store as our helping hands squat on the front porch in the shade.

"I never see such a beautiful wood, Olaf," John Nenni says. He lifts his Pepsi bottle, "To Hunt's Feed & Seed!" In unison, Crazy Ray and the men repeat Mr. Nenni's salute. It is the unofficial opening of Hunt's Feed & Seed.

"I wish Petrov, Mekinov, and Richardson were here," I say to Mother.

"I wish Frederick were here."

Yes, Father would praise these people who help us do his work. I am beginning to be thankful blackberry bushes slashed his boots while trekking these mountains.

At day's end, I make a note to price a cold drink cooler similar to Leckie's. I will prepare for the town's next extraordinary act of kindness.

Weeks later, Saul Brown, the Williamson proprietor who Miss Daisy claims is "the most handsomely dressed man I ever see'd," parks his sky-blue Nash touring car before the store.

The bell jingles. A man approaches the counter and extends his hand.

"Welcome to West Virginia. I am Saul Brown, proprietor of Brown's Dress Shop in Williamson."

His voice and manners enhance his appearance. I could covet a seed store in Williamson, the largest town in Tug Fork, with its beautiful War Memorial, theater, library, and a courthouse clad with marble. The most remarkable building in Williamson is their Coal House built of bituminous coal quarried as blocks from the local Winifrede seam—and fashioned as stone. The Indian statue that stands confidently before the house fascinates Mother. "Most imaginative and historic!" she says upon each visit. Yes, I could covet the town, yet what would Mother and I do without John Nenni and Miss Daisy?

"I must see this remarkable oak counter and glass dome for myself," he says. "I hear it came from an antique shop in Connecticut."

I respond that a very good friend, Richardson Wright, sought it out for us.

"A friend with an excellent eye for quality and design, as well as utility. Do you refer to *the* Richardson Wright, may I ask?"

"Indeed, Richardson, editor of *House & Garden* magazine. 'The one and only,' as he would say," I add with a smile.

"I understand from Miss Daisy and other clients that Richardson, his wife, and father paid you a visit for Thanksgiving."

I nod. "Yes, Matewan welcomed them as their own."

"As I would expect," says Mr. Brown. "And I understand you offer a delicious küchen for sale."

"Yes. My mother is an excellent pastry chef."

"So is my mother. She also bakes küchen. Would you please explain the varieties of küchen Mrs. Semenov offers for sale?"

"Certainly," I say, "My favorite is apfelküchen."

This animates Saul Brown's serious demeanor with a declaration. "No! My favorite also!"

"And Mother's butterküchen is delightful with a cup of tea in late afternoon."

Mr. Brown shakes his head. "I cannot believe our similarities, Mr. Semenov."

"Please, use Olaf. Mr. Semenov connotes I am my mother's husband."

Mr. Brown allows a genuine smile of understanding. "And does your mother offer a third variety of küchen?"

"Yes, during peach season, she offers peach küchen."

"Made with sour cream and a touch of cinnamon and cloves?"

"Yes."

"I would like to buy what you have of the apfelküchen and butterküchen."

Word of Mother's küchen travels fast. People come from Red Jacket, Delbarton, hollows and branches along Mate Creek, Peter Creek, and Tug Fork to purchase their slice. These three tributaries flow from Beech Creek to Tug Fork, and eventually into the Big Sandy, the river along the road leading to Pikeville, Kentucky.

The following Monday another stranger walks into the store. We shake hands. "Mr. Semenov?"

"Yes, I am the son of Mrs. Natalia Semenov. You may use my name, Olaf. May I assist you?"

"Yes, Olaf, I am James Record, President of Pikeville College, and very pleased to meet you."

"It is an honor to meet you, Mr. Record."

"I've come to see this glass-domed counter and meet the woman who makes that delicious küchen my wife purchased last week."

"I am sorry to disappoint you, sir. At this moment, Mother is baking küchen for sale tomorrow. We sell küchen on Tuesday and Thursday."

"Then I shall return tomorrow to meet the pastry chef. What do I owe you to hold five slices of apfelküchen and butterküchen?"

For one minute I am tempted to persuade Mother to establish a small bakery in the storage room. Yet, that is not within Father's work. Moreover, Mother and I see the need for a small college in Matewan. Küchen is seed money for our dreams of a college, for knowledge is not as perishable as pastries, especially Mother's, in Matewan.

December 23, 1920, I unlock the door and date my ledger when a tallish woman with blonde hair walks in from fading darkness into the lighted room. She wears a denim skirt, or perhaps a dress. I cannot distinguish with the coat she wears. She carries a remarkable shovel in one hand and stands before the counter. Unruly ringlets circle her face and blue eyes from under the scarf tied beneath her chin. Even now, her skin is tanned. She smells of mountains and honey and cannot be much more than twenty-two years. I am taken with her beautiful countenance, untouched by cosmetics.

"May I help you, ma'am?"

"I heard you carry chicken feed."

"Yes, in twenty-five and fifty-pound bags. We offer bulk delivery, also."

"I'll start with twenty-five pounds to see if they like it."

I write the receipt. "What is your name, please?"

"Gertie Blankenship."

I write. My heart races. The only Blankenship in Matewan is known as Friday. The town drunk. I am elated to see she does not wear a wedding band. "Would you like delivery?"

"Much obliged, but my neighbor Daisy will pick it up."

Interesting. Does she mean *the* Miss Daisy?

I notice her long, slender hands and clipped fingernails when she pays the bill with exact change she gathers from a coat pocket. My mouth parts in respect of a woman confident enough to carry a shovel in public. I watch as she walks into the dawn and lifts her face to the sun.

A yearning to kiss her tanned cheek surprises me. And why not? I have just met the only woman who prefers to carry a shovel rather than a purse into the store, and the most beautiful young woman I have had the pleasure to meet. Two feet from my face! I hope her chickens like my feed and she returns. For I cannot risk a word to Miss Daisy about Gertie Blankenship.

Christmas Day is difficult without Petrov, Mekinov, and the Wrights until we receive their succession of phone calls.

"Thank you for the Christmas card and box of pastries," they say, one after another, and lift our spirits. Since Mother cannot garden, she begins baking streusel to sell.

On January 23, 1921, at 8:05 a.m., Gertie Blankenship returns with her shovel for her second purchase of chicken feed. "Daisy will pick it up," she repeats. I watch her walk out the door. The same desire to kiss her brings a blush to my face. Mother and I discuss Gertie Blankenship, her shovel, chicken feed purchase, and Miss Daisy over dinner.

"Miss Daisy speaks highly of this Gertie Blankenship, and says I am certain to meet this woman who carries a shovel to dig gardens for women," Mother says.

On fair winter Sunday afternoons in 1921, I drive Mother through the small coal camps named Red Jacket and Little Italy where I deliver orders. When we stop in Red Jacket above Mate Creek, children gather around our windows, wide eyes peering into the truck. One Sunday, a little girl with blue eyes speaks a peculiar blend of Appalachian dialect and Russian. Mother and I understand "pretty lady" and smile to one another.

"What is your name?" Mother asks the child in Russian.

Her face glows. "Jeanette," she says, and removes a white handkerchief from her coat pocket to wipe her nose. Mother looks to me and smiles.

Whenever we return to Red Jacket, Mother and I look for Jeanette's blue eyes. And we never fail to find them and her white hand-kerchief amongst the children.

We explore passable hollows, or hollers, as locals pronounce the word, and branches along Mate Creek, Peter Creek, and Tug Fork. Most farmsteads keep a flock of hens, a few roosters, a sow, milk cow, beehives—and a mule for those who still pull a bull-tongue plow.

On sunny, winter days, we find people sitting on the front porches of their homes, mostly small cabins. They often wave. If the drive from the road to the house is not too steep, muddy, or icy, we stop. The hill folk call it a runoff, and I see why. I keep the brakes on our truck well-maintained.

"Oh, you're the Russians who bought the seed store in Mate-wan," they say.

"We heerd about that big glassy counter y'all moved from Con-nec'cut. Have ta' come see it sometime or another'n." They ask, "What's küchen?"

"*Cake*, in Russian," Mother says.

We marvel at the people's resourcefulness. We soon learn these people love their land as Mother and I loved ours. We become part of what they love—strive to be worthy of their affection and loyalty. Women often buy at least one seed packet when they buy Mother's pastries. If they planted every seed, Tug Fork would bloom like Par-adise, and never would one go hungry.

I learn they grow corn on hillsides in summer! I see the evidence in shorn hillsides throughout the mountains. "There's no surer way to grow corn on a hillside than with a mule and a plow," the farmers say.

Farmsteads with enough flatland for cattle produce and sell milk and butter. I add milk bottles and butter molds to our inventory. I am able to price competitively with the coal company stores. We sell out, because people are curious about the Russians and their glassy counter, küchen, and now, streusel. Thankfully, the company stores do not provide küchen or streusel, so the slim profit we make grants Mother joy in her baking.

On lonely, confined winter days and nights when the wind howls and snow blows like we remember in Russia, Mother bakes and slices küchen and streusel. One evening, while the wind rattled the kitchen window, Mother says, "Olaf, I am fifty-one years old, Cook's age when we left Field of Flowers, our beloved Polya Tsevtov."

The people find our accent engaging, as I find theirs. Every day someone says "I've never met a Russian before." I answer their questions and learn their dialect, a mix of Scottish and Irish brogue. Mother plants Father's blackberry lily seeds around our humble sanctuary. She knows to be patient, for the seeds can be "ornery," as Miss Daisy says, and sometimes take two years to sprout.

"That lily will grow anywhere where there is sun," Father would laugh.

The Lord God is good and our doors remain open while miners strive to forget what honor called them to do during the coal wars. They and the townspeople do not speak of the fallen, for the shame of having no other choice but to defend their lives and homes from the oppression of coal companies.

I understand the shame of having no other choice, and I do not speak of Father's sacrifice. Within this common bond, beauty rises from ashes. We prosper.

In February, Mother pots Father's hibiscus, honeysuckle, forsythia, wisteria, and crabapple seeds to grow plants to adorn the building's dowdy figure. "I cannot wait for them to root, sprout, and leaf," she says, and orders mature plants from Bartram's Garden in Philadelphia. Mother cries with joy the March day they arrive, for she sees buds and some blooms.

"Olaf, we must propagate these shrubs and trees to sell. Then Tug Fork will bloom like our Polya Tsvetov."

One Wednesday in April, 1921, Miss Daisy says, "Olaf, since you and your mother love to read, you should take her to the Williamson Public Library and write your application for a library card."

The following day after I close the store, Mother and I walk into the library. She smiles as we approach the circulation desk. Two women stamp the inside of books and stack them in a pile. They both wear nametags. Lily Major stands on the left. Violet Minor on the right.

"May I help y'all?" Lily says.

"Yes, Lily. My name is Natalia Semenov, and I would like to apply for a library card."

"Yes, ma'am," Lily says.

"And I am Olaf Semenov, her son. I also would like to apply for a library card."

"Yes, sir!" Lily says, and removes two forms from a drawer.

Lily and Violet step away from the desk and whisper to one another as we complete our forms. When Mother lifts her tortoise-shell combs, Lily says, "Mrs. Semenov, we've seen you workin' around the seed store diggin' little gardens and cain't wait for them to bloom. You've got us curious about gardenin', as well as many other women who live in Williamson and Matewan."

Violet says, "If we come to your seed store, will you teach us how to plant and grow flowers?"

Mother glances to me. I nod.

"Yes," Mother says.

"Oh, my goodness! Now Matewan Garden Club is official!" Lily says.

I am amused at the speed of the agreement.

Meanwhile, Gertie Blankenship appears with her shovel the first Wednesday of every month to buy twenty-five pounds of chicken feed for Miss Daisy to pick up. Fridays, when the miners come into town to cash their paychecks, I overhear them joke about Friday Blankenship taking first place in line at the bank. I worry about Mrs. Blankenship and suggest to Mother we hire her to help with our expanding gardens.

With her knowing smile, Mother agrees.

In April 1922, I build walls for our separate bedrooms and receive Petrov's newspapers highlighting the nationwide coal and railroad strikes. In the face of America's industrial collapse, Mate Street is eerily quiet and clean. When I finish the walls and install the doors, Mother and Miss Daisy hang wallpaper in our bedrooms. Richardson ships eight framed botanical prints for the walls.

The *Passiflora incarnate* is our favorite.

"Bargains my wife and I couldn't resist," Richardson writes in a note.

I build bookcases for the Russian, American, German, French, and British literature we have acquired and ordered. Petrov ships books including Herbert Hoover's philosophical appeal to the United States of America titled *American Individualism*. I devour the little book and mourn again for Russia.

Postmaster Eli declares, "You Semenovs keep our little post office in business."

Mother and I pray for our country's unrest, and Europe's leanings toward socialism. Where do we run to from America?

"One time or another," Antillo Nenni says one day when he picks up an order for his father, "we've all been immigrants runnin' from oppression, starvation, or the hangman."

I can't help but think of John Brown. "You are a wise, young man," I say.

"Now don't be givin' me the credit, Olaf. It's Papa who said that."

I think of Father. "Nonetheless, you heard it, and for that I am grateful."

Peter Creek and Tug Fork have kept Mate Street's doors open for business through the aftermath of the Massacre with the necessities. Feed. Seed. Pastries.

The following spring of 1923, the bell jingles. I expect Miss Daisy. It is Wednesday, the day she inspects our new inventory and pries for information about the growing Matewan Garden Club.

But no. A small boy, perhaps eight or nine years, stands by the door. A face red with fury, he grips the handle of the magnificent shovel I recognize as the one Mrs. Gertie Blankenship carries. I wave the boy to me.

"May I help you, young man?"

He looks down to the blade and lifts eyes rimmed with tears.

"Pa left Mommy's shovel in the rain after he dug up Granny's peonies for whiskey. Now hit's ruint."

I wince from rumors I have heard about the boy's father, Friday Blankenship—also known as Harold Blankenship to the bankers and others to whom he is indebted. I place a hand upon the boy's shoulder. "What is your name, son?"

The boy wipes his eyes and nose on a sleeve. "Henry Blankenship. My pa's Friday, Gertie's my mommy. This is her Pa's shovel. Mommy calls it Tall Man."

How Henry's tears fall! How the hate in his eyes submits to my aid. I hand him a clean handkerchief from my pocket. "Henry, forgive your father."

I equip him with a bag containing a tin of oil, a rag, and a whetstone, and instructions to repair the shovel. I watch his small frame carry the bag and Tall Man out the door. The child has a long, steep walk up to Blackberry City, and I may do nothing else to help.

Oh, how I loved Father. I could not imagine hating him. What a curse for a child to face each morning.

I worry about Henry throughout the day until the bell jingles late that afternoon. He walks in with a smile and Tall Man.

"Look, Olaf! Mommy's shovel's good as new, just like you said. I'm ready to work and pay off this here rag, oil, and whetstone. But not right now 'cause Miss Daisy picked me up on the road and she's waitin' outside. School's out, so what time do you want me tomorrow mornin'?"

"Eight o'clock."

That moment, a little boy, his mother, and her shovel opened my heart to love—the long and remarkable romance between Olaf Semenov and Gertie Blankenship.

Now, April 15, 1946, over twenty years later, the rising sun upon Matewan concludes another remembrance of our odyssey. And another begins!

I smell Gertie's biscuits and Mother's buckwheat kasha. Soon my wife will open the door to this haven, where we have found love and comfort for ten years, including three dreadful and miraculous years without Henry during the Second World War. He insisted he could not stand by while Ray and other Tug Fork young men sacrificed their lives for freedom from fascism. Ray toured Europe. Henry the Pacific.

Those of us he left behind would have unraveled without the

society of Mother's Garden Club. The community held us together during Henry's absence. With Annie's consultation, before he left for basic training, Mrs. Dill designed a rotating schedule of Henry's business duties and Annie's greenhouse and domestic chores. Garden Club enlisted to help, and members fulfilled their duties every day without fail.

Miss Daisy managed the greenhouse development while Mother and I sustained the store and taught college classes. With Annie's toddler and twin infants in diapers, Mrs. Dill and Rosemary Cline alternated helping with laundry and meals for Annie and her children. Lily, Violet, and the other members volunteered wherever needed.

One winter day, I watched Dr. Dill walk across the street from his dental office in the hospital and into the store. "Olaf, would you consider granting me the empty chair at your chessboard during these long nights?"

"Your fireside or mine?" I asked.

"Yours, under one condition."

"Yes?"

"You call me Matthew."

Upon Matthews's first visit to my chessboard, Gertie asked him to bring Margaret the following week. Margaret brought the Dill's chessboard to team up with Mother. With her tatting in hand, Gertie observed them with interest, Henry's name hovering over us in unspoken prayer. My wife never lost faith in Henry's return. I cannot confess the same.

As Ray has no family, Gertie and I adopted him "by heart," as Ray says. As Father did for Mother and me, I believe Gertie would lay down her life for our family.

Ray arrived home before Henry. We thought Ray was our son knocking and ran to the door. Dear Ray—our surprise came naturally. Sheriff Taylor drove Ray from the Williamson Train Station to our door and waited in his car. What would this little town do without Sheriff Taylor? Gertie and I embraced Ray. She took his duffle bag.

"Come on in. Our home is your home."

Three months later, all the Semenovs, the Dills, and Ray met

Henry at the Williamson train station. He returned home from
Guam with a smile of relief on his face.

Now the rooster announces another birth in Matewan! I am a
grandfather again! Frederick, after Father, and my middle name.
Our fifth grandchild in ten years: Matthew; our inseparable twins,
Natalia and Margaret; Stephen, born the year Henry returned; and
now Frederick.

Our joy is complete, yet Annie and Henry say, "Cheaper by the
half dozen."

I am glad it is not "cheaper by the dozen," as they say. Many
Appalachian wives traditionally bear a dozen children.

Is it I, Olaf Semenov, in the bed where Gertie sleeps? Father
spoke truth. America holds my freedom and future. And the loves
of my life. Petrov spoke truth. We are never alone.

Ah! The scent of Mother's coffee with cream! Gertie stands at
the door and knocks upon another daybreak. Mekinov's last letter
spoke of his ill health, and I must tell Mother and Gertie I plan to
leave tomorrow for Boston.

I sit up and switch on the lamp. "*Da!*"

Ever the quiet spirit, Gertie hands me the cup from Mekinov's
house. His parting gift to me—blue of a hundred different shades,
with as many shades of yellow. His wife, an artist, created the cup
for their twenty-fifth wedding anniversary. Their last. After waiting
fifteen years for her love, I cannot imagine living without Gertie.

"The time has come to return to Boston for a visit. I must keep
my promise to Mekinov." I say.

Gertie's eyes agree. She removes Father's Bible from the bedside
table and opens the cover to Mother and Father's wedding portrait.
As she is prone to do, she studies the photograph without a word.

"I leave tomorrow morning. I know you wish to stay behind to
behold Frederick's newborn face. But would you join me? I dread
the long journey alone."

She sits by my side and turns to the back of Father's Bible where
she touches our wedding portrait and smiles. "Ancient remnant,"
she says barely audible.

My lover's blue eyes provoke me to play with her golden ringlets, tight and moist from the heat and steam of the kitchen. I sip my

coffee and wait for her to speak what roams about her mind.

She closes Father's Bible and returns it to the table. "Why didn't you tell me Mekinov was ill?"

"Mother told you?"

Gertie nods. "She would like to visit Sergie. I'm sure Annie's parents and Garden Club will be more than enough help for Annie and Henry with the children and business."

I set my cup bedside Father's Bible and pull Gertie to my chest. I want to cry with joy. "How I wish we could linger here. As you know, Henry is occupied with Frederick's arrival this morning. Therefore, mine is the pleasure to open the store and greet Matewan's men with their fifth Russian cigar. Mekinov mailed two hundred!"

I see something playful in my wife's smile. "The miners on night and afternoon shifts will be lined up on Mate Street by quarter after eight," she says.

A thought strikes me. I whisper in Gertie's ear, "Come with Mother and me to Boston!"

"Your mother waits for you in the kitchen," Gertie says, smiling, and leaves me.

I abandon my coffee and dress in haste, omitting my collar and tie. With whiskers and hair pointing in every direction, I stand beside Mother at the kitchen sink. She looks upon me with her smile reserved for another great-grandchild.

"Where is your coffee?" she teases.

My heart leaps. "Gertie said you wait for me."

My beautiful mother dries her hands with the dishtowel. "I would be most happy to join you and Gertie to Boston. I owe a debt."

I plow my fingers through my hair in disbelief. "Now I may dine with my two lovely women at The Greenbrier tomorrow!"

"Greenbrier?" they sing together.

"*Da.* Their groundskeeper phoned yesterday for a delivery of magnolias, rhododendrons, hibiscus, and redbuds. Henry, Matthew, and I will load the truck after supper." I raise my eyebrows. "Free advertising all the way to Boston and back with *Hunt's Feed & Seed, Matewan, West Virginia* painted on the truck!"

They push me out of the kitchen, laughing with me.

I retrieve my coffee cup from my bedside and take my place at the table. The ladies talk of dresses and hats as we wash down our biscuits and kasha with coffee.

With haste I brush my teeth, shave, wash, comb my hair, apply my collar and tie so as to unlock the store at 7:45 a.m. I hang Gertie's sign on the front door. *Welcome to Matewan, Frederick Blankenship! 9 lbs. 13 oz.*

I place the wooden boxes of cigars at the end of the domed counter and break each seal. The creamy, wood scent associated with my five grandchildren wafts up to my nose. As Father did for my birth, I slide one cigar into my breast pocket.

Death pierces. Birth heals. I whisper, "Live, Mekinov!"

Matthew, a vision of Henry at age nine, throws open the door. "Grandfather!" he says and runs into my arms.

"Matthew!" I give his head my morning knuckle rub. "You are up early. Did you ride your bike?"

He nods. "I didn't know your middle name is Frederick!"

"Do you know Grandfather Dill's name is Matthew?"

"'Course I do. He tells me almost ever' day. Is Frederick a Russian name?"

"Yes, and no. The Russians borrowed it from Germany."

"How do you borrow a name?"

Matthew, a thousand questions a day. "I use an expression, son."

He shrugs his shoulders—one more childhood mystery to unravel within the course of his life, long after I depart for Glory.

"What does Frederick mean?"

The answer catches in my throat.

Matthew leans into me. "You okay, Grandfather?

I sit on my stool. Matthew sits on my knee. "When I was your age, my father said Frederick means 'peaceful ruler.'"

Matthew's eyes widen. "That's just what Daddy said last night at the supper table before he drove Mommy to the hospital!"

"Oh?"

"Uh-huh. Daddy said Matewan wouldn't be the same without our peaceful ruler. I thought he meant Sheriff Taylor, but never heard anyone call him a ruler. I didn't know what a ruler was—other than Moses, the Pharaoh, and President Truman. But come to think of it, Daddy's right. I never heard you raise your voice once."

I look into the eyes of the next generation and hope to sustain this trust. "Do you know what Matthew means?"

"Yep, Mommy told me."

"I cannot remember," I pretend.

"Gift of God," he says and pulls the cigar from my pocket. "I remember when you gave one of these to all the men when Stephen was born."

"You were six years old. Do you know what Stephen's name means?"

"I forgot," Matthew says and picks at the cigar band.

This lesson of names is overcome by a lesson of premier cigars. "Do not destroy the band, son. It marks the cigar's excellence. You are too young to remember that I gave all the men two cigars when Natalia and Margaret were born."

"When do I get a cigar?"

I chuckle. "When you become a father."

Matthew puts the cigar to his nose. "It stinks."

I return the cigar to my pocket. "That's what your great-grandmother and granny say."

"Women don't smoke cigars, do they?"

"Not usually. All the more for the men."

Matthew slides off my knee. "Grandfather, what does Olaf mean?"

I am not prepared for his question and hide my quivering jaw with a hand.

"Ancient remnant."

Matthew steps back, incredulous. "Lord-a-mercy, Grandfather! You ain't ancient!"

"I am *not* ancient," I correct.

"That's what I just said. And what does 'remnant' mean?"

"A part of something else."

"Like Granny's pieces for her quilts?"

As Annie, the boy is quick-witted. "*Da.*"

I intercept his attempt to molest my cigar.

"Will you take me morel huntin' this Sunday after supper?"

I regret to disappoint my first grandchild. Today is Thursday.

Gertie, Mother, and I leave tomorrow for Boston. Mother and I owe Mekinov a great debt and now we must pay it. "Do you remember Sergei Mekinov?"

"Uh-huh. The man who lives in Boston. You and great-grand-mother lived in his house before you moved here."

"*Da.*"

"Is he comin' to visit? Mommy told Daddy last night that if she has a boy, they'd name him Frederick after great-grandfather. Daddy said he'd be tickled to see Sergei Mekinov lay eyes upon great-grandfather's namesake."

"Oh?"

Matthew nods. "What's a namesake?"

"You are named after Grandfather Dill's first name?"

"Yeah."

"You are his namesake."

"Is it the same as borrowing somebody's name?"

It is time to begin this boy's chess lessons. "Yes, and no. You see, my mother named me after her father."

"The one who lives in Norway?"

I look to my hands. "Now he lives in Heaven with my father and grandfather."

Matthew touches my knee. "That's sad."

"Yes, and no. They lived and died loving their family, country, and plants. And as Olaf Frederick Semenov, the names and love for plants live in me."

Matthew's eyes quicken with understanding. "When I grow up and have a son, I'm going to name him Olaf as your namesake."

"Oh?"

"Shor' am."

"Why?"

"Because you love to hunt, and you're the best hunter around. But don't tell Daddy or Granny I said so. He just never has time for morel huntin' or takin' his shotgun into the mountains." The season of man-to-man secrets with my grandson has begun.

"I promise."

"Say, Grandfather, what does Sergei Mekinov have to do with us huntin' Sunday?"

"Before your grandmother and I left Boston, I promised Sergei I would return."

"And now's the time to keep your promise?"

"*Da.*"

Matthew wraps an arm around my neck. "Is Sergei Mekinov sick?"

Matthew. The eyes, ears, and mouth of the Blankenship household. "Why do you ask?"

"Daddy said somethin' to Mommy about it last night."

"Yes, grandson. That is why your great-grandmother, granny, and I are driving to Boston tomorrow morning."

"Granny's goin' too?"

"*Da.*"

"Well, I'll be. Granny's leavin' West Virginia for the first time in her life, just like Daddy said she would. We'll be readin' that in the *Matewan Bullet*, won't we, Grandfather? And don't worry about the store. Daddy and I'll take care of everything. And Antillo always says to run up and fetch him if we need to."

We stand to the sound of a crowd gathering outside. And there's Antillo in the lead.

"Now, to work young man. Remember, after supper we transfer pots from the greenhouses to the truck. So, please double-check every pot with a green tag. They all go to The Greenbrier tomorrow and must also have a white tag with proper identification."

"Got it, Grandfather! Don't worry. I know my plants and won't make a mistake."

Matthew takes his list of deliveries into the storage room and gathers merchandise. The scene reflects the past and fades when the bell jingles.

"Congratulations, Olaf!" says Antillo, with his son Eddie at his side. The boy's a year younger than Matthew, and no less ambitious. "I foresee little Freddie runnin' this store like Henry and Matthew."

"As I foresee Eddie taking the helm of Nenni's Mercantile in the future," I say.

"Where's Dr. Dill? He's always first in line for his cigar," Antillo says.

Before I consider an answer, the bell jumps again and in comes

Pastor Hickman, Warren O'Brien the barber, and Eli the Postmaster. A line of miners follows behind. And there's Ray holding up the end.

Antillo props open the door. "That bell's goin' to drive me crazy!"

I nod to Antillo, my mind swimming within this pool of merriment.

In ten minutes, half the men in town stand in front of the store smoking Russian cigars. "Congratulations, Olaf!" says Punkin' Smith from the *Matewan Bullet*, leading the other Tug Fork reporters from the *Williamson Daily News*. They drop their cigars in their shirt pockets and commence shooting pictures and collecting anecdotes. Fourth time around for Henry and Annie's baby's birth announcements; they know everybody's name and how to spell them: Matthew, Natalia, Margaret, Stephen. And now Frederik.

Little Man McCoy, Henry's cousin from Peter Creek says, "I remember the day Dr. Dill and his family drove into Matewan. The magnolias was in full bloom."

Noonie O'Brien, Henry and Annie's neighbor, says, "Yeah. Come April, there's no place I'd rather be than in Matewan and Blackberry City."

The more aggressive men elbow their way before the reporters for their name in print.

I hold a handful of cigars for the miners and speak their names, smoke wafting in from the porch. Benny Charles, Corny Priest, and Will Stump, all young miners, sit on the curb before the porch and smoke a salute to Frederick, as if he was born a prince, and Annie and Henry were the matriarch and patriarch of Matewan.

As word travels, people gather on both sides of Mate Street for Annie and Henry to appear at the front entrance to the hospital across the street. I smile and glance at the red brick building in anticipation of beholding my father's namesake. May he indeed become a peaceful ruler. I look for Dr. Dill in the crowd.

Saul Brown strides in, dressed in his white shirt, silk tie, and dark grey three-piece suit—his leather shoes, haircut, and even his smile, impeccable. I am embarrassed, for I dressed in haste.

Mr. Brown shakes my hand. "My sincerest congratulations, Olaf."

"Thank you, sir. Your cigar."

He holds the tobacco to his nose, closes his eyes, and inhales deeply. "Ah, what a remarkable day, Olaf. A child is born, and I hold one of the most exquisite cigars in all the world."

The phone rings. "Pardon me."

"Certainly," Saul Brown says and turns for the door.

"Hunt's Feed & Seed, Olaf speaking."

"Olaf."

The tremor in Mother's voice shakes me. I think of Mekinov. "What is wrong?"

"Is Matthew with you?"

"*Da.*"

"Have him stand in your place. Exit the back door and enter the kitchen without notice if possible. Quickly."

It is the same dreadful feeling as running from the Bolsheviks. I pull my handkerchief from my pocket and wipe my brow and upper lip. Have they found us at last?

I return the receiver and find Nibby Stokes' smiling face and extended hand.

"Congratulations, Olaf!"

"Thank you." I offer him a cigar and ask the same question I do upon every meeting, "What is showing at the theater this week?"

"*State Fair, Son of Lassie,* and *Tarzan.*"

"Good lineup," I say.

Mr. Stokes steps closer and speaks discreetly. "Olaf, you feelin' alright? You're white as a sheet."

"Yes, too much excitement. Please pardon me, Mr. Stokes."

"Sure! Thanks for the cigar."

I nod and find Matthew completing orders in the storage room. "Son, I need you to stand in my place with cigars and the telephone. I will return directly. You know what to say and do?"

He stands tall. "Greet every customer with a smile. Answer the phone with 'Hunt's Feed & Seed, Matthew speaking,' and write a message."

"Correct."

The boy runs to the counter and takes a fistful of cigars. I run to Mother as Miss Daisy's commanding voice enters the store—a small comfort as I flee the storage room. My grandson is in good hands.

I race through the pergola to the door of our house. The blow elbows me in the chest and off the top step as I cling to the door handle. I must save Mother.

No! This is not Russia. This is America. Matewan. It is Father. At last, Mother received word of his execution.

Mother's and Gertie's ashen faces strike me dumb. It is not Father I see on their faces.

I remove my handkerchief again and sit with them at the table, wipe my face, and fold my hands to stay them from gathering Mother and Gertie into my arms for comfort.

Theirs. Mine.

Rather, I must spare my mother and wife the agony of speaking the name of our beloved departed.

Swiftly, piece by piece, my heart thuds with the evidence. Yet, I wring my handkerchief and desperately challenge the truth. "Mekinov has joined Father in Paradise?"

They put their handkerchiefs to their mouths and shake their heads.

I push from the table to run to Henry. My chair falls on its side. The room spins. I fall against the wall. It is Annie. "Dr. Dill did not come for his cigar! Annie does not stand beside Henry and hold Frederick before her beloved Matewan!"

Mother and Gertie stand, lift eyes laden with grief. My knees buckle. They catch me.

Blessed Jesus, Gertie holds me. I cannot lift my head from her shoulder. "And Frederick?"

"Dr. Dill fetched a wet nurse, Sarah, from Red Jacket. Frederick nurses like a calf," Gertie says. My wife's voice and answer calm my wretched soul. I wipe my face again, thankful for Sarah and my grandson's newborn life. We return to our appointed chairs, a small and certain order we may control.

"Olaf, Henry and the Dills need us," Gertie says.

"*Da.*" My son, how is this possible? How will he, we, go forth each morning without Annie? "What took her from us?"

"Cerebral hemorrhage," Gertie whispers.

"When?"

"While we ate breakfast."

"Who is caring for the other children?"

"Rosemary Cline, at Henry and Annie's home."

Our eyes smart at the sharp, cruel force of Henry's desolation.

"Does Mrs. Cline know?"

"Doc Bentley phoned her for Doctor Roy. Henry and the Dills thought it best Rosemary knows," Gertie replies.

"Have you spoken with Henry?"

"No. Doc Bentley said Henry's too broken up to talk on the phone. You know Henry doesn't like talkin' to people he cain't see. That's why he wrote letters to Annie in Berea," Gertie says and wipes her eyes. "Henry asked us to come and help him decide whether to have an autopsy to confirm the cause of death. He wants us to say good-bye to Annie before he leaves her there. He said our Annie flew away like a mourning dove."

I swallow hard and touch the cigar in my pocket. "Are the other Garden Club members aware?"

"Daisy," Gertie says.

"I heard her voice as I left the store. You sent her for Matthew?"

"Yes. She knows why your mother called you here. She's drivin' Matthew home and will stay there with Rosemary and the children and wait for our call."

"Who stands in my place?"

"Antillo Nenni."

I gaze out the kitchen window to the Tug River and thank God my father found this little town. "We must immediately stop the celebration of Frederick's birth."

They nod. Mother takes my hand. "I called Lily and Violet and requested they inform the other Garden Club members. They will meet us in the store. I canceled our reservations with The Greenbrier. The receptionist will inform the groundskeeper of our loss and delay in delivery."

Mother's eyes possess an inscrutable hint of joy. "I spoke briefly with Mekinov. He offered his condolences. He is much recovered, Olaf."

This flicker of good news relieves our suffocating loss for a fleeting second.

"Mekinov asked if he could be of any service. After eighteen years of reading your Henry and Annie stories, he would be honored to attend her funeral. Richardson and Agnes will accompany him on the train."

Again, Mekinov's charity is beyond what I could ever have imagined. I hear the echo of Fodor Petrov's charge to continue Father's work, and I know Annie's vision will ever be woven within it, as Henry's is. Dearest Annie. Father and Petrov welcome you into Heaven's portals. Oh, what pain the separation, the disorder of her youth cut asunder while we live.

I escort Mother and Gertie through Henry's pergola, the scent of cigar smoke invading the vining *Passiflora incarnate*. I recall Annie's smile in her wedding gown and know this parting is for Earth alone. We hear laughter and declarations of "Annie sure grows 'em big," and "Olaf must be bustin' his buttons."

We step up into the storage room, the bags of Matthew's deliveries in tidy rows on the floor as Henry taught.

God have mercy upon us! Matthew and Matewan have lost Annie. My wife and mother turn to me. Merciful Lord, put your words into my mouth.

We pass into the store, Mother and Gertie on each arm. Antillo hands Ray a cigar. So forsaken is our countenance they pause in place.

Lily and Violet arrive and stand beside Nellie Nenni before the oak counter and glass dome with other club members. The delay in Henry and Annie's appearance with Frederick, and the absence of Dr. and Margaret Dill, Mrs. Cline, and Miss Daisy, confirms a tragedy. What agony not knowing if the child or mother, or both, have left us.

"Antillo, would you please ask the men outside to extinguish their cigars and return inside?"

Mother and Gertie support me. Right and left, I smell and taste dread and pity. The lamentation commences. The men, including Mr. Smith with his camera, bow their heads in silence as they enter the room and stand shoulder to shoulder. Ray tears up. He, too, perceives the signs. Those who chew tobacco hold their jaw still. Antillo, the joy quenched in his dark eyes, guards the storage room door. Saul Brown folds his arms as sentinel at the entrance.

I bow my head for I cannot speak her name or look upon the men's faces and sustain my composure. "Beloved Matewan, prepare for a blow. Prepare to support Henry and his five children in the loss of his dear wife and their mother."

The men moan in disbelief. The women make no sound.

I must speak the cause of death. In their quest to put Annie and their minds to rest, our people will seek understanding and consolation in the untimely death of such a strong, young woman. They must know the truth to speak it.

"Doctor Roy reported a cerebral hemorrhage took our flower girl. Now, please excuse us. We must join our family."

Like the Red Sea when Moses lifted his rod, the men part. We walk through the huddle of humanity who permit us to do my father's work where we live and die.

Before I step out the door, I glance back to Antillo and his son Eddie. Antillo nods and makes the sign of the Cross. Eddie follows his father's example. Blessed Jesus, Hunt's Feed & Seed is in good hands. But oh! How will we accomplish our work without Annie?

Frederick. Father's namesake.

Death pierces. Birth heals.

There is no running away. I promised Matthew a hike. Annie left us in morel season.

Part Four

GERTIE
MARCH 23, 1954

Margaret and I carry our buckets to the downhill side of the cemetery's arbor that marks its entrance. *Passiflora incarnate* will cover the arbor's iron rods by April's end. Olaf laughs every time I say Latin names. Sometimes he puts his hands over his ears and plays like it's torture to hear me speak them. And I play right back. "Is somesing ze matter, Mr. Semenov?"

Every Friday morning in March, Margaret and I plant rows of peony roots and blackberry lily rhizomes until our buckets run out. Someday, this whole slope will bloom in peonies and blackberry lilies: *paeonia* and *iris domestica,* as Mrs. Semenov says. What a beautiful sight that will be, regardless of what we name the flar'ers.

The mountain hugs the other side of the runoff, keepin' an eye on Annie, the cemetery, and us. Margaret and I have planted some columbine, larkspur, buttercups, and bird-foot violet in the ditch between the gravel runoff and the mountain. The violets' happy faces are bloomin' under columbine britches from the top of the hill to the bottom.

After a long winter, this blessed place is waking up. Next comes the larkspur and buttercups. The larkspur will bloom her beautiful blue eyes throughout the summer and finally go to sleep late fall. That's when she drops her seeds to bloom a stream of larkspur wherever the wind blows and water flows.

Margaret looks to the left toward Annie's gravestone on the hill's peak. It's the only grave in the entire cemetery, thank God. Henry chose the spot for her grave because it was their lookout over Matewan. Where Henry said they stood the day of our double weddin' ceremony. A night I hope never to forget.

Mrs. Semenov, Olaf, and I have our plots marked with three elderberry bushes goin' downhill from Annie's stone where we can still see Matewan. Margaret and Dr. Dill have beauty bushes marking their plots goin' uphill so's they can look down upon Annie—and also see Matewan. I don't even try to pronounce *Linnaea amabilis*. Next to Annie's stone, there's Henry's forsythia bloomin' on the left side. He said it's his favorite shrub because it cheers him up first thing in the spring.

I cain't believe it's been ten years since Henry and Annie bought this mountaintop and hillside. She said, "It has potential for something beautiful."

Little did we know then that something beautiful would be her grave.

Margaret looks into my eyes like she's readin' my mind. "The day Annie told Matthew and me that she and Henry bought this property, my hands were sticky with honey from making baklava. She said she wanted to develop a park of gardens with benches and birdbaths and fountains and a flower and gift shop! All overlooking Matewan."

"Well, we're workin' on the gardens, aren't we, Margaret?"

"Indeed, we are."

No matter where you step in these highlands, you're walkin' on somebody's stories. That's why Margaret and I visit every Friday mornin'. To walk and talk with Annie alone. Rain or shine. Locals call it "Annie's Hill."

After the harsh and sorrowful years with Harold and my mommy's deaths, this ceremony is a kind of redemption of the word *Friday*. I can think it and say it and awake to it without memory dragging me back to Harold's sickbed, to all the regret and misery from the greatest mistake of my life. It was worth the suffering to have Henry, Annie, and their babies on the other side of it. And Olaf. How he loves our grandchildren. And how they love him.

Margaret pulls on her latest pair of pink garden gloves and drops a kneepad on the earth with a new, shiny trowel in her hand. No matter how I try, I can't get used to wearing gloves and kneeling to work a garden. Like Mommy, I wear my long-sleeved denim dress and work on my feet. And Margaret knows I'm partial to Mommy's old trowel. Fits my hand perfect. Mommy was shorter than me, but her hands were big.

This is the only time I see my friend Margaret Dill dressed in pants (perfectly creased by John Brown's Cleaners and color-coordinated with her blouse, of course). Her hair's "presentable for a house guest," as she says. She calls it a "coiffure."

I could listen to Margaret all day long. She sprinkles our conversations with pleasant surprises, unlike my plain words. But I practice her turns of phrase with Henry and Olaf. And sometimes Mrs. Semenov. I mean Natalia. We laugh at my blunders.

And who would've ever thought I'd write a Russian name on my marriage certificate! But Olaf still calls me Gertie with his accent that's "music to my ears," as Natalia says. Although it's not natural to speak it, Mrs. Semenov insists I call her Natalia. I asked her to be patient with me because I'm likely to say one of her two names at any given time.

"Why did Olaf buy a new Chevy truck?" Margaret asks, breaking my daydream.

Margaret looks over her shoulder for my reply. She's learned I'm slow to speak my mind because my mind's slow to think things out.

"Well," I say, "you know Olaf's a practical man. He couldn't resist the last of Chevy's postwar line of what they call their 'advanced design.' So, he bought the one ton 3800, whatever that is."

"Looks like the bed expands its carrying capacity for heavy deliveries. Matthew said he's learned to appreciate the weight of a root ball and its impact on a truck's shocks."

"Yeah, Olaf coached Matthew to fire all their questions at Ray. 'What about cab room?' Matthew asked. 'Expanded. Look for yourself. More'n enough room for Gertie. And with a streamlined body,' Ray said. 'Engine power?' Matthew asked. 'From a 216.5-inch in-line six-cylinder to a 235.5 cubic-inch straight six with a single-barrel Rochester carburetor,' Ray snapped back. Olaf said Matthew and Ray gave a command performance goin' back and forth about the wheelbase, gross capacity, chassis, and options like a radio, armrests, lockin' gas cap, and stainless-steel hubcaps that caught Matthew's eye. I reckon Olaf never had so much fun in his life buyin' somethin'. He's told it so many times I've learn't it by heart."

"Men and their trucks and cars," Margaret says.

"But you know what Matthew talks about the most?"

"I couldn't begin to guess."

"The mud flaps, heater, fog lamps, foot-operated windshield washer, and rear shock absorber shields. Oh, and the two-tone paint."

Margaret turns and glances uphill to the words *Hunt's Feed & Seed* painted on the side of the truck, the subject of our conversation. She returns to diggin'. "It is quite attractive, Gertie. And there's no question they needed a new truck. However, you know that blue two-tone truck will be the talk of Tug Fork by tomorrow morning. I'm concerned Olaf may have indulged our grandson a bit too much."

Margaret's words burst my bubble, and I'm glad she doesn't look up to see it on my face. She sets a blackberry lily.

"Gertie, I know you and Olaf would do anything for Matthew and all our grandchildren to help them prosper as their souls prosper, and to live in peace with their neighbor. So would Matthew and I."

"So, what's botherin' you, Margaret?"

"Please bear with me as I think this through," she says and moves downhill.

"I'm listenin'."

"We agree your son had the maturity and sense of responsibility of a man at age sixteen?"

"Uh-huh."

"Would you say Matthew possesses that level of maturity?"

The question stings because Matthew isn't as grown up as his daddy was at the same age of eighteen. But I've never met another young man like Henry, other than my daddy and Olaf. "No."

"I perceive Olaf's deference to Matthew's choices for the company's truck is partially due to his trusting relationship with Henry. To my knowledge, Henry has never taken advantage of the Semenov's generosity."

"No, Henry never took advantage of the Semenovs or anyone, and I trust he never would."

Margaret stops but she doesn't turn around. She might be thinkin' about her wrongful judgment of Henry's intentions with Annie, when she thought he had applied to Berea College.

"Gertie, grandparents often hold their grandchildren to more lenient standards than they did their children. Although he's devoted to Olaf and Hunt's Feed & Seed, I'm not convinced Matthew bears the maturity to understand the responsibility of driving an expensive one-ton truck with luxury options. You read the Matewan Bullet and Williamson Daily News. You know the increase each year in automobile-related injuries and deaths on our mountain roads."

Margaret's right. Olaf never gave Henry the choice of which truck to buy. Perhaps he was testing Matthew to see how he would handle that choice. But Olaf didn't say anything about that. He spoke about other reasons for buyin' the truck. Perhaps Margaret knows something about Matthew I don't. Something that's worrying her.

"Margaret, I appreciate you tellin' me what's on your mind."

"Sincerely?"

I nod. "You're right. Olaf never gave Henry the choice of what truck to buy for the store. I'm not sure why he did with Matthew, so I'll ask. All's I know is this world's changin' way too fast, and I cain't keep up with it. Ray says regardless of all the families leavin' Appalachia for work in the cities, the coal business is stirrin' up again."

Margaret leans before the earth again and digs, a small woman on this large hill makin' it beautiful. "Oh?" she says. "Ray's a trustworthy barometer for business climates. Did he offer a reason for his optimism?"

"Olaf said he and Ray have see'd some miners in Matewan and Wim'son who left Tug Fork and Peter Creek with their families as early as last fall. They've come back with brand-new cars for their wives to shop at Nenni's and Brown's. They said the customer service in the big cities didn't come close to what you find here."

Margaret takes three lily rhizomes from her bucket. "Matthew said something about that the other night at dinner. Grandson Matthew dined with us and said he's observed our economy swinging upward. He said Eddie Nenni spoke of increased sales at their counter the past two months. Perhaps those favorable reports influenced Olaf's confidence in the purchase of a new truck instead of used. Furthermore, our grandson repeated what Olaf said to my husband last week."

"What was that?"

"He 'thinks it's time for Dr. Dill to count the cost of building his dental school while there's still flatland left on higher ground.'"

"Well, from what Corny Priest told Olaf, there's somethin' else behind the miners movin' back," I say.

"I imagine it might be the same information Mr. Priest and other miners offered Matthew recently during their dental appointments."

"About the miner's union goin' back on their promises?"

Margaret sets three more rhizomes. She plants in threes and fives. "Specifically, confiscating miners' dues for their own wallets. From what I've read, it's much the same corruption in Detroit with the United Auto Workers' Union leaders."

I place three peony roots in a hole and throw in a handful of compost, return the earth, and tamp it down. "Olaf says it's the greed for power and money that corrupts a good thing. The union's not much better than the companies who forced the miners and their wives to buy everything from their stores that we didn't grow."

"The miners tell Matthew that the union's building no safer mines than the coal companies did," Margaret says and moves her kneepad and bucket downhill.

"That's what Olaf and Henry hear. And that's why some of them with the means think it's high time to start up their own operations. It's the mid 50s, and there's no time to waste with the union's makin' a fuss. Lord have mercy! Henry says the miners deal with one tyrant after another."

Margaret moves downhill again, graceful as a cat. She's still a northerner and moves like lightning. "Matthew hopes the conflict doesn't escalate into another lengthy and devastating coal war. Because of the gunfight in 1920, we came very close to moving from Columbus to Williamson, or Pikeville, Kentucky in 1923."

This is the first Margaret's mentioned our town's massacre in my presence. Like everybody else, we're tryin' to forget it and make the best of a tragic thing, so I hesitate to ask and open an old wound, but it seems timely.

"Margaret?"

She turns to the supplication in my voice. "Yes?"

"Why did you and Dr. Dill choose Matewan?"

Her hands rest at her side. "Because Annie liked the hospital and Leckie's when we visited."

We stand on Annie's Hill in silence and let the dappled light of the peaceful moment melt away our awful history.

Margaret takes a deep breath. "I'm very thankful for our five strong, and loving, and beautiful grandchildren."

"Me, too. So, is Dr. Dill still interested in building a dental school with Matthew?"

"At one time, my husband hoped his namesake would sign on as his business partner to expand the practice and perhaps establish a school . . . but my husband's a pragmatic man. He resolved years ago that his grandson's heart and hands are destined to steer the helm of Hunt's Feed & Seed into the future."

"You're right, Margaret. There's no mistakin' where Matthew's heart is. Let's pray we see some growth in his maturity and sense of responsibility. Like Mommy would say, you can want a mess of greasy beans with all your heart, but it's your hands that plants the seed, picks and strings the beans, puts them in the pot, and into your mouth.

"Matthew told Olaf he wants to help make his mother's vision of the rail yard filled with greenhouses and beehives come true. He believes he's the Semenov's seventh-generation wayfaring botanist in the makin'. I don't know how far he'll take the wayfarin' part. He asked me to take him to my ginseng and bee patch and teach him what I know. The boy says he cain't wait for our trip to Bartram's Gardens next month."

"I've heard! I've not seen my husband this excited since Annie and Henry's wedding. I pity his patients. According to Daisy, that's all he talks about while he has a captive audience in his chair."

"Well, as one of Dr. Dill's captive patients, I know Daisy tells the truth. And we couldn't be happier to listen."

Margaret doesn't skip a beat and keeps diggin' and plantin'. I do too.

"Seems to me," I say, "Stephen's more likely to follow his Grandfather Dill's steps. The youngun's at Dr. Dill's side ever'time I visit of an evenin' at Henry's. What do you think, Margaret?"

"Oh, you know how children change as they grow. Henry said yesterday that Frederick asked if Grandfather Dill loved Stephen more than him. Henry's aware that's typical for a nine-year old boy, but he still wanted us to know what Frederick said. What do you think?"

"Well, I'm not the one to speak to that because I birthed one child who's purdy much an old soul and he's walked the same path all his life."

"—As Annie did." We stretch our backs and exchange a glance of common sorrow; Margaret takes a hanky from her pants' pocket and wipes her eyes. "She couldn't understand why anyone would want to leave these mountains."

"Neither can Henry."

"Oh yes, Henry," Margaret says and puts her hanky back in her pocket. "He's concerned Frederick is growing up too fast. For a nine-year old boy who's happiest with Leckies's lemon sours, bridge mix, and chocolate-covered raisins, Frederick's question caught Henry by surprise. He thinks it's time for my husband to teach Frederick to play chess."

I hold my trowel up like the school's safety guards do their STOP and GO signs. "Well, that's just what Olaf said the other night. He said the boy's smart enough to learn the game."

"I'm very thankful for Olaf's sense of order and propriety. I often remember the evening he came to our door and revealed his part in Henry's acceptance to Berea. Annie told Matthew and me that Henry would not leave Matewan to follow her if she didn't return from college. She vowed Henry could depend upon her. They would mate for life, like mourning doves, and live their days together in Blackberry City and Matewan."

It's a taste of honey every time Margaret tells this story. "Only the War could tear them apart. He just couldn't stay home in his big house with flushin' toilets and claw foot bathtub while other soldiers were dyin' in their own filth for his family's freedom. We all did our part. Our country's liberty and livelihood were at stake."

Margaret's small shoulders heave a sigh. "We all feared Japanese airplanes bombing Matewan, the railyard, and coal seams. I sometimes think of what America would be today if Hitler and Japan had defeated the Allied Forces. A great darkness fills my soul."

"You know, Margaret, I think that's one reason why Henry and Ray won't talk about battle. Henry said his sergeant told his platoon, 'What happened here, stays here.' Henry agrees. He says it's an unthinkable burden for a civilian to carry. I asked him how he carries it. 'With God, family, and Garden Club too,' he said."

Margaret leans back on her heels and thinks a minute. Maybe I'm wearin' off on her. "How do people wake each morning without the comfort of Jesus?" she asks.

"I don't know."

Margaret sets three more lilies. "Henry missed so much with Matthew and the twins during the War. Annie looked forward to his bittersweet furloughs."

I tamp the earth over three more peony roots and take two steps downhill after Margaret. "You mean his three-ring circus!"

Margaret laughs. "I thank God every day Henry made it back home in one piece."

I cain't imagine Margaret's sorrow and hope to God I never do. I rub the pang of guilt from my chest. Henry survived Guam and Annie died after childbirth. Sometimes life don't make sense.

Hard as bedrock. Fragile as frost.

I think out loud like Margaret and I do on Fridays when we plant. "Henry's a little beat up, but with two eyes, ten toes, and ten fingers. And a sound mind, too. He's worked them all puttin' up Annie's greenhouses, raised beds, beehives, and the college buildin'. That shor' was some story Richardson wrote about it all in his magazine last fall."

"And he chose the perfect title, *A Tribute to Matewan, West Virginia.*"

I step closer to Margaret and dig. Her new hot pink gloves seem so happy to be workin' with dirt. "It tickles Olaf ever' time he interviews and hires a young man for the store or for buildin' the school. They don't all stick it out, but Corny Priest, Will Stump, and Benny Charles are learnin' the construction trade and showin' up ever' day with a smile. Just look at Corny, doin' a fine job as Henry's foreman."

"And his wife Jeanette is a sunny addition to Garden Club," Margaret says, and moves her kneepad downhill with her buckets. "She's not met Richardson, and neither have the last five new members. Don't you think it's time we invite him back as a guest speaker?"

"Yes, ma'am! And while he's at it, Richardson can lecture at the college. He can also speak at Pikeville College. Henry says the students love his stories as much as we do. Nobody knows garden history like Richardson Wright. He puts you in the caravan with Lewis and Clark, 'huntin' plants and blazin' the trail in a new frontier."

"I understand Henry's considering Lewis' Osage orange tree for a boundary here in the cemetery. It's an excellent spider repellant," Margaret says.

"Olaf's ears perked up because that makes the Osage orange a marketable product!"

"Which reminds me, isn't it wonderful that Richardson hired Mr. Smith as a freelance writer for *House & Garden*?"

"Well, Henry and Annie spoke to Richardson on Punkin's behalf as far back as their weddin' reception. Punkin' didn't feel qualified to write for a fine magazine the likes of *House & Garden*. Back then he was still wet behind the ears. Henry mailed Richardson the story Punkin' wrote about The Greenbrier supplyin' bushels of lemons to make lemonade for the guests of Matewan's largest weddin' in history. It took a while before Richardson called Punkin'. 'You're hired under several conditions,' Richardson said. 'Read every issue of *House & Garden*, take a crash course in Appalachian botany, show up to every meeting of the Matewan Garden Club, mail me monthly reports with photography of the club's meetings, and construct your herbarium.'"

Margaret laughs. "Mr. Wright is quite the taskmaster!"

"To hear Olaf tell it, Richardson is the most imperfect perfectionist he's had the privilege to meet. He often says he and Natalia wouldn't 've survived the 'confinement of Boston' without their monthly train rides to the Wright's country home. Although I never see'd their place in Connec'cut, I can see his 'Madonna of the Swine' sittin' on his summer dinin' terrace in her blue plaid apron!"

Margaret turns with a smile. "Gertie, that's one of my favorite short pieces in his *Gardener's Bed-Book*. So, this imperfect perfectionist is responsible for our first male Garden Club member?"

"I reckon he is."

Margaret drops a handful of compost on three more rhizomes. "After Mr. Smith interviewed Natalia, Lily, and Violet for the club's history, he showed up for the next meeting. I'm anticipating his upcoming work!"

I nod. "Punkin' cain't resist a good story to save his life, and he knows Garden Club ladies love to tell 'em. And Punkin' shor' eats his fair share of y'all's pastries. Olaf's helpin' Punkin' with his herbarium. They've built the hardcovers, now Punkin' has to harvest his plant specimens. We'll see how that goes. He told Olaf he doesn't like gettin' his hands dirty. Olaf said, 'Do not worry, Mr. Smith, you do not need to uproot the plant, rather snip a specimen with secateurs.' Punkin' asked Olaf 'What are secateurs?' Olaf said, 'Pruners. A pair of sharp scissors will also do.'"

Margaret laughs. "Let's ask Mr. Smith to bring his herbarium in progress to our meetings. We'll help him as we work on ours. We can also suggest where he can find plant specimens to collect. And I have something to tell you, Gertie Semenov."

"I'm all ears," I say, and set three more peony roots.

"Henry and the grandchildren dropped by last Sunday with Annie's herbarium."

I wonder where Margaret's goin' with this, and keep diggin' to keep up with her. "Well?"

"Since Maggie is the firstborn twin and my namesake, Henry asked if I would help her continue Annie's herbarium. He also asked Natalia if she would help Nattie gather materials and begin her namesake's herbarium."

Again, my son's devotion to Annie and their children smarts my eyes.

I stand on this holy ground with a fistful of peony roots and watch Margaret move downhill and set three more blackberry lily rhizomes. The power of God's love and mercy is growin' all over this hill.

"So," Margaret says, "why did Olaf think a new truck a wise investment?"

I surprise myself and switch my mind to the subject in a wink. "Henry heard from Mommy's side that the McCoy boys from the Bottom couldn't make roots in the city. Their wives missed Nenni's, Brown's Dress Shop, and their mommy and daddy too much. So, they've come back, and the Hickman children are on their heels."

"—and Ray's prepared with new inventory."

"Uh-huh. He's gotta compete with the Chevrolet dealership across from the high school. He told Olaf, 'Chevrolet's toughened up their engines and chain drives. Just shove it and let it alone.'"

"That sounds like Ray," Margaret says, but I think she suspects there's more to why Olaf bought a new truck.

I dare tell the truth because Margaret and I promised to do so when Annie left for Berea. No matter how it hurt, we wouldn't waste one more day divided by our differences.

"After Ray took charge the day Annie died and loaded up Olaf's truck with The Greenbrier's order and delivered it, Olaf looks for ways to prosper Ray. And with that kind and helpful deed, it didn't seem right to call him Crazy Ray any longer."

"I think every person in Matewan felt the same," Margaret says and sets her kneepad downhill. I follow.

"Olaf says Ray's chess games and tournaments are payin' off. Ray's usin' his nimble mind to benefit others rather than just hisself. Besides, Ray knows Olaf and Henry have no time for truck repairs."

"One of the consequences of prosperity."

I hear Annie's death gnawin' at Margaret's heart. But her slight shoulders never betray the burdens she carries.

Margaret looks up to the highest point in the cemetery to Annie's gravestone, about fifty paces. It's our "ritual," as Margaret calls it, for when loss overwhelms us.

Patches of sunlight glimmer upon red peony shoots drilled throughout the rocky earth. These pointed clusters surround the mourning dove in flight, etched in Annie's stone. Before it, the redbud's about to burst open above the bench in full sun. That's where Margaret and I sit for my chicken salad sandwiches and her ginger cookies, and the most delicious sweet tea in all Appalachia—Margaret's secret recipe she guards with her very life.

"Breathtaking, isn't it Gertie?"

"Shor' is. It's like Daisy's magnolia seedlings grown up along the road from Annie and Henry's lookout through Matewan, past Thacker Holler, and along Peter Creek all the way to Phelps, Kentucky. Took us seven years, but Annie's magnolias are ever'where Mommy, Daddy, Henry, and I come from."

Margaret and I "have an understanding," as she says. We cry during our garden Fridays if we need to, but we must keep digging and planting to finish in time for her to clean up and put supper on the table at five-thirty. Dr. Matthew Dill has changed in many wonderful ways, but he's still a stickler for supper at five-thirty ever' day. "It aids his digestion," Margaret once said.

I cain't fault the man for that, especially when Margaret cooks delicious and fancy dishes like she does. I'd rush to her table too for French food like Quiche Lorraine, Asparagus à la Polonaise, and Beef Stroganoff, although Olaf said Beef Stroganoff was first a Russian dish before it spread all over the world.

"You know, Margaret," I say, thinkin' aloud, "I'd never tasted asparagus until you brought it to Garden Club."

"Annie grew it in our backyard because it's my favorite spring vegetable."

"Well, now it's *my* favorite spring vegetable. And Garden Club will soon be sellin' it in our market with rhubarb, my second favorite. I've loved asparagus ever since the night you brought it to Garden Club, cooked right in the cheese, eggs, and cream in the first quiche I ever tasted. I thought I'd died and gone to Heaven."

"And I thought I'd died and gone to Heaven when you brought your strawberry rhubarb pie with whipping cream."

When Margaret brings her gourmet dishes to Garden Club, we ask her to teach us how to cook them. "Here's the recipe," she'll say, giving us each an index card written in her "elegant hand," as Mrs. Semenov—I mean, Natalia—says.

Mrs. Margaret Dill may dress like Queen Elizabeth, but she doesn't want anyone fussin' over her. She just plain loves to cook and garden. And so do I. We talk cookin' and gardens all the time. She's "mastered" chocolate gravy and buttermilk biscuits. Dr. Dill loves them.

"Thanks to you, Olaf bought me a first edition of The Gourmet Cookbook."

"What's your favorite recipe?"

"When I unwrapped the book Christmas Day, I took it right to the kitchen and sat down at the table. I found the Beef Stroganoff recipe and wrote my grocery list. Well, no matter how I try, my Beef Stroganoff cain't match yours."

"It might be the cut of beef. Ask for Terrance at the Williamson Piggly Wiggly's meat counter and tell him you're preparing Beef Stroganoff for dinner."

"I've never shopped Piggly Wiggly before," I say.

"I guarantee Terrance will solve your Beef Stroganoff dilemma. But I give you fair warning, though, plan to spend an hour strolling Piggly Wiggly's aisles. At first, you're overwhelmed with items you've never seen before. You're welcome to join me next Thursday, my grocery shopping day."

"You grocery shop every Thursday?" I ask.

"I find it necessary with cooking for Henry and the grandchildren, and my culinary lessons with Maggie and Nattie. I also enjoy the drive into Williamson—and discovering new foods. Maggie and Nattie tag along in the summer."

"They talk about Piggly Wiggly all the time!"

"That's where I found a mix for hollandaise sauce that I thought I'd test with the girls. They were convinced the mix tasted no different than my homemade sauce. One night they prepared the mix for Asparagus à la Polonaise to serve with dinner. Matthew took one mouthful and looked to Maggie and Nattie and said, "Okay, what did you girls do to your grandmother's hollandaise sauce?"

I laugh. "So, what's a mix?"

Margaret tamps the soil over more rhizomes and moves her buckets downhill. We're almost to the end of the slope, and there's no slowin' down at Margaret's back, but there's no way my big bones can keep up with her small bones.

"A mix includes dry ingredients blended and packaged," Margaret says. "You add the wet ingredients and heat to serve. For hollandaise sauce, the manufacturer dehydrates the egg yolks and lemon juice and packages it with spices. You just add water."

I mull that over. "Well, I cain't see me buyin' a mix when there's nothin' more simple than cracking my fresh eggs and dividin' the yolk from the white and squeezin' in lemon juice. That's usually when Natalia talks about Pol'ya Sev'tov and the fields of asparagus the Semenovs grew."

"That must've been beautiful," Margaret says.

"Olaf likes to say, 'In autumn, the asparagus ferns danced in the vind like an undulating prairie.' Even without knowin' what 'undulating' meant, I could see the McCoy Bottom as a prairie of orange berries dancing on asparagus ferns."

"Matthew prefers Asparagus à la Polonaise to other recipes. And I'm glad because it's easy to prepare."

I smile. Margaret and I have one more thing in common. "Olaf's favorite is asparagus soup with morels and ramps. That takes more time, but it's worth it."

"Matthew's anticipating our first platter of ramps sautéed in butter and garlic."

"Natalia dices garlic cloves almost ever' day. Since I didn't grow up with garlic, it's takin' me a while to 'preciate the flavor. But I do love harvestin' wild ramps, which is enough garlic for me."

"You know, Gertie, Natalia might enjoy strolling the aisles of Piggly Wiggly with you."

I imagine that in my mind and it feels right, but Natalia still watches her back whenever we go someplace new. "Well, I'll ask her and see what she says. We enjoy takin' the train together into Williamson to shop at Saul Brown's and findin' another book to check out from the library. We both admire the brick streets and grand buildings. As Henry says, it's good to break out of our shells and try somethin' new ever' once in a while."

At last, we take up empty pails. Just one last row along the runoff and we'll have the slope all planted. About two hundred feet wide by three hundred long, best we can figure.

"Mommy's peonies and the Semenov's blackberry lilies are goin' to be beautiful when they bloom, Margaret."

She looks to Annie's gravestone again and fixes her eyes on it. "After I buttoned Annie's wedding dress, she turned to me and took my hands. 'Mother,' she said, 'Henry first told me he loved me the day I planted your asparagus patch. I walked into Hunt's Feed & Seed, covered in dirt head to toe, to buy zinnia seeds to border the asparagus bed. Olaf walked into his office. Henry leaned over the glass dome and whispered, 'I love you, Annie Dill.'"

"So that's why you grow zinnias around your asparagus?"

"Yes."

"That's somethin' real special to always remember, Margaret. I never see'd such a beautiful bride as Annie. It was like she walked on a cloud in her long white dress and veil. And just think, at the same time you buttoned her dress, Henry was dressin' in our livin' room, and I was dressin' in the bedroom for the same ceremony. I walked out of the bedroom and saw my handsome son fussin' over his bow-tie, sayin' he should'a never let Saul Brown talk him into it. He just couldn't get it right. So, I tied his tie. There we stood alone together for the last time in that miserable little house.

"Henry studied my face real quiet for a minute. 'My goodness, Mommy, your eyes are beautiful in that blue dress! I mean you're always purdy, but right now there's a light comin' from inside your eyes.' I said, 'the same light's comin' from inside your eyes, son. Mrs. Semenov says it's love.'"

"And that's something special to always remember, Gertie, for if anyone knows the depth of marital love, it's Natalia Semenov. I will say it again—I respect that woman more than any other on the face of this earth. And Saul Brown knows your color!"

"I cried for joy when Saul said my dress was 'larkspur blue chiffon.' That's the color I had in mind all along."

"I think Mr. Smith perfectly described your role in the ceremony in his *Bullet* article. 'Within the party of a traditional double-wedding ceremony, the bride, Gertie Lynne Blankenship, provided her groom, Olaf Frederick Semenov, the 'something blue' with her chiffon dress the color of larkspur.'"

I laugh and blush. "I don't think my feet touched the ground all night long."

"And neither did Annie's. Without a doubt, you four made the most handsome and happiest wedding party I've had the pleasure to witness."

"Well, the followin' week, that happy weddin' party tore down that miserable shack to build the new greenhouse. But I told Henry and Olaf, don't you touch my outhouse!"

We pause on the gravel runoff with our empty pails and admire our work, and springtime in all its glory. Red peony shoots and green lily flags poke up all over this rocky hillside just like they've done beginnin' eight years ago. It's a marriage of Mommy's Appalachian peonies and Mrs. Semenov's Russian lilies. A bond between Appalachia and Russia that keeps multiplyin' like these old hills love to do. We walk up the runoff with our trowels and empty buckets toward Olaf's truck.

"Blackberry lilies are the hardiest flowers in my gardens," Margaret says. "I wish they didn't fade within a day. It's a good thing they're prolific bloomers."

"You mean lots of blooms?"

"I'm sorry, Gertie."

"What for? 'Expanding my lexicon,' as Olaf says? You talk natural, and I'll talk natural."

Margaret trips on a rock and her bucket swings, but she doesn't lose her balance.

"You're as surefooted as a billy goat," I say.

"Mother would be glad to know my ballet lessons paid off."

So that's why Margaret's so graceful. "Do you miss your mother?"

We stop about midway the runoff.

"Oh yes, Gertie, terribly. Do you miss your mother?"

"Somethin' terr'ble."

As we walk uphill, Margaret smiles with a sparkle of a tear in her brown eyes. I realize we've said the same thing, but different.

Lord-a-mercy! Margaret's the only woman I know who's learned ballet! That must be why there's no sign of wear on her garden shoes. She's the closest thing to a ballerina I've ever see'd.

I wear my old-faithful laced boots and the same denim dress with a collar and long sleeves. I won't let the sun wrinkle my skin like Mommy did hers. I don't want people at The Greenbrier mistakin' me for Olaf's older sister, especially when we all dine together.

There I go again, thinkin' like Margaret talks.

She takes a fancy garden hat from the truck's dashboard and sets it on her perfect hairdo that never turns frizzy like mine. And I don't see one gray hair.

"Do you like it?" She gives me her beautiful, white-toothed smile, one benefit of bein' married to a dentist.

"Yes, ma'am!"

"Saul Brown ordered it. The air vents prevent your scalp from perspiring. And the chinstrap will keep it put. You won't have to chase this hat into a copperhead's nest when the wind blows."

I take my old straw hat off the seat, return my coffee-stained smile, plop the hat on my head, and tie it under my chin. "Well, nothin' like spoilin' my fun!"

We each take two buckets of irises and two buckets of compost from the truck's bed. Two buckets labeled *blue*, and two *yellow*. When these irises bloom, they'll look like Sergei's favorite colors on the cup he gave Olaf the Christmas they celebrated with the Wrights in Silver Mine. I took the cup to Olaf this mornin', filled with his mother's coffee with cream.

"You know, Margaret, I feel a little guilty out here in spring's sunshine while Garden Club is spring cleanin' Henry's house. Washin' walls and winders. Cookin' suppers for the weekend and freezin' a week's worth."

"From what I hear in our meetings, Friday at Henry's is the highlight of their month. Daisy manages the schedule like a sergeant. There are enough members now for Daisy to assign only one Friday a month. It will be interesting to see if Daisy includes Mr. Smith on the schedule. And if she does, will he follow through?"

I smile at the thought. "Henry looks forward to comin' home to a clean and tidy house and dinner ready. He says he smells vinegar and pot roast when he reaches Darlin' in the front yard. When he rocks on the front porch of an evenin', Darlin's right before his eyes. But tonight, Henry'll have lots of comp'ny to celebrate Stephen's eleventh birthday."

"Matthew and I are looking forward to Daisy's chocolate cake with fudge frosting. He eats the frosting first, then puts ice cream on the cake. He bought enough vanilla ice cream to feed Matewan, Blackberry City, Thacker Hollow, and Peter Creek, too."

"Law! I never suspected it was Dr. Dill who taught the grandchildren to skin Daisy's cake! I couldn't figure out why all of a sudden the grandchildren started to swipe my sea foam frostin' clean off the top of my spice cake. They hover over those delicious frostin' peaks with their dirty fingers just waitin' for me to turn my back. Once I do, they skin my cake plumb naked!"

Margaret laughs. "If only all our problems were as innocent!"

Comin' from a stickler like Margaret, I take her words to heart. I think about us all gatherin' on the wraparound porch Henry built and singin' "Happy Birthday" to Frederick. Daisy'll strum along on her dulcimer with Bud O'Brien and the Flea Bites. All Blackberry City will gather around the porch and sing along for their piece of Daisy's cake with vanilla ice cream.

Margaret takes the large, rolled map of the cemetery from the truck's cab and opens it on the hood. Olaf's fine drafting and sketching shows where and what we've planted with color-coded numbers and names. Like the drawings in Olaf's herbarium and botanical books, his work is fine enough to frame and hang in The Greenbrier.

"Where do you think we should plant these irises?" Margaret asks.

I study the map. There's plenty of lilies, irises, forsythia, elderberry, and beautybushes surrounding Annie's gravesite. But bare spots beside the arbor at the entrance need some color. And all along the mountain where the mown cemetery meets it could use "a succession of color and cascading shape," as Margaret says.

"We could use a few more native plants like the holly, crabapple, laurel, and rhododendron we've planted along the mown edge," I say. "Remind me to ask Olaf to load some shrubs and trees in the truck next Thursday."

"You read my mind. We don't want to plant irises along the mountain until we've filled in first with cascading trees and shrubbery."

I smile. "Do you think we need more magnolias?"

Margaret tilts her head sideways like Annie did when playful. She's smaller than Annie was, but my goodness, she's wiry and mighty as any mountain woman.

"A garden can always use another magnolia or two," she says.

"What about startin' the path Garden Club suggested from the arbor to Annie's gravesite?"

"Good idea. Later we can add the boxwood hedge beside the irises without disturbing the rhizomes." Margaret looks to her watch. "It's eleven o'clock. Let's gather our shovels. We'll break for lunch at noon."

With twine, we measure a curvy lane wide enough for Olaf's truck to pass, and pound stakes into the earth—sixty paces from the arbor to Annie's stone. Then we wrap twine around each stake on both sides of the lane.

Margaret lifts her shovel from the truck's bed. "You dig one side. I'll dig the other."

I hold up Tall Man. "Ready. Set. Go!"

Margaret laughs again. Music to my ears.

Along the twine, we dig a shallow, narrow furrow for the irises on each side and finish just after noon. We pull up the stakes, roll up the twine, and take them both to the truck with our shovels. "We'll plant after lunch," I say.

"Hungry and thirsty?" Margaret asks.

"Yes ma'am!"

Under the complaints of a lusty, hungry jaybird, I carry my picnic basket and Margaret her Thermos jug to the metal bench for two. The redbud's poppin' open before our very eyes. I remove a roll of oilcloth from my picnic basket, unwrap a wet washcloth and wipe my hands "acceptably clean" as Margaret says. We touch Annie's sun-warmed stone. Another ritual.

"Gertie?"

I hear sufferin' inside my friend. "Uh-huh." I take our two glasses out of my picnic basket. I think I know what's comin'. She hasn't mentioned Camille since the first Friday in January.

Margaret pours our sweet tea. We sit on the bench and take a good, long drink. She looks to Annie's soaring dove engraved on the wide and tall gray stone monument. "I received another letter from you-know-who."

The woman never stops tormenting Margaret, playing on my friend's sympathy for her "bad luck in Hollywood." She asks for rent money and another chance with Henry. The girl doesn't understand she never had a chance with my son and never will.

He destroys her letters the second he finds them in his post office box. The last thing Henry needs is the twins finding a letter from Camille. She's tried every trick of a cheat. Disguising her penmanship, addressing a letter to the store and the Dew Drop Inn—even Nenni's. She's made a spectacle of herself time and time again. God have mercy! We've vowed never to speak her name. Henry said the girls must never hear or read the word *Camille* until they've passed through the fire of teenage insanity.

We all have our weaknesses, and Camille is Margaret's. Lord Jesus, help us. I want to feel pity for Camille, but cain't. That's my weakness. Henry's suffered enough, with his father's drunkenness and with losing Annie. Now this woman who's ruining her life with gin wants to ruin his and Annie's children's.

"Where's she livin' now?" I ask.

"As usual, the envelope has no return address. The postmark is Columbus. Perhaps she returned to her parents' home. They're good people, Gertie. They've done all they can to rehabilitate her. I don't know what happened with their only child. Mrs. Rouge and I encouraged our daughter's friendship because they had no siblings. My heart breaks for her parents."

I know Margaret doesn't want the Rouges to sit in a cemetery before their daughter's gravestone. "What did her letter say?"

"The same thing as the last five letters with five different postmarks. She needs money for rent and wants me to persuade Henry to meet with her."

"How can you reply with no return address?"

"She wrote the day, time, and place for Henry to meet her in Columbus."

I control my anger. "She's, what'd you call it before?"

"Irrational."

I nod. "Just because Henry took her by the arm and walked her out of the seed store nineteen years ago, she thinks she has some hold on him. There's no way he's goin' to miss a day's work or a Sunday with his children at the chance she keeps her word. And if she does show up, then what? Henry knows that's just feedin' her folly. His kind deed has backfired on him long enough."

Margaret bows her head. Above the drone of distant traffic and coal trucks below, we listen to chickadees, meadowlarks, wrens, and the song of the white-breasted nuthatch. We calm ourselves and think. Another ritual. We drink another glass of Margaret's sweet tea.

"You're right, Gertie. Her request is absurd. What am I to do?"

"You've shown the letter to Dr. Dill as usual?"

Margaret nods. "He said it's another malicious prank, and I must release her to her own devices. Then he lit a match to the envelope and said, 'Enough, Margaret. Do you think Annie would tolerate this madness? Please, leave Camille in God's hands.'"

My words come with great heaviness. "I believe Dr. Dill's right."

"But Gertie, put yourself in her mother's place."

I take a deep breath of Appalachian spring, rich with the scent of humus, moss, herbs, bark, leaf mold, and Mate Creek. I can taste its goodness, wisdom, and truth.

"Margaret, I pray I never know your grief, but like millions of mothers all over the world, I stood in the Rouges' place for three years while my only child fought in the War. Many sons didn't return.

God's grace was enough then, and it will be enough for Mrs. Rouge if she calls upon His name for help with Camille. I pray she does."

Now Margaret takes a deep breath of the very same mountain medicine. Her delicate features relax. "True. We have no guarantee our children and grandchildren will outlive us. There's always some predator waiting for the wing in flight of its independence."

"That's one reason why I love Olaf. He helped guide my son to forgiveness. Now we guide Henry and Annie's children."

"That's my point, Gertie. Who's going to guide the Rouge's daughter to forgiveness? Annie is a child who honored her mother and father, helped build a beautiful family and prosperous community with the man she loved, then died after childbirth. Then there's the Rouge's rebellious and selfish daughter in Columbus who takes and never gives. What happens to her?"

I gaze into my empty glass. "Sometimes life's impossible to understand and accept. As I see it, from childhood we have a choice to give and receive forgiveness. Ever' time we deny someone forgiveness or reject someone's forgiveness, we harden our heart. The harder our heart, the sicker we become. Like Dr. Dill said, we must release Mrs. Rouge's daughter into God's hands."

Margaret lifts her eyes to the clean, sapphire sky. "That is my only consolation."

"Is it enough?"

Margaret creases her perfectly plucked eyebrows. She tilts her head to the side again. "Yes."

We've worked through another rough spot. I gently change the subject.

"Did Henry tell you the twins found Annie's sketch for her gardens and campgrounds, and another sketch for a bakery and gift shop attached to the college?"

"Maggie and Nattie think our botany college students will keep a bakery in business if they serve my baklava and Natalia's pastries and coffee."

"That so?"

"I informed our granddaughters that it would be *their* pastries and coffee that keep a bakery in business after *they* graduate from Matewan College."

We've talked ourselves dry sittin' in the sun, so Margaret nods to my glass and pours it full again. Then I hold her glass while she fills it.

Margaret and I have talked about putting a fancy outhouse into plans for the cemetery. After all, our bladders aren't getting any younger. But Henry says an outhouse will only attract vandals.

I hand Margaret a napkin and chicken salad sandwich wrapped in waxed paper. "Nattie and Maggie are double trouble, like havin' two Annies in the same family. They want their grandfathers and father to build ever' single thing they dream up. We remind them that their mother helped build her dreams with her own two hands." Margaret grins, her lipstick as perfect as it was when we arrived. How does she do that?

"The girls think their father is eighteen years old like Matthew and can maintain a home, business, and make their dreams come true," Margaret says. Then she piggybacks her glance that says there's more to the story. "They also found Annie's college diaries and papers—and the black box of Henry's Berea letters, under lock and key."

"Uh-oh," I say and take a bite of my sandwich.

"They've asked Henry to drive them to Berea College. They're determined to see Boone Tavern Hotel where the beady-eyed, red-headed Highlander assaulted their mother. And you won't believe this, Gertie. They want to stop in Salyersville to meet Frank."

"He still around?"

"Oh yes. The girls called the post office to confirm it. And they want to see their mother and father's oak in the park where they picnicked."

I let what Margaret said sink in. It's hard to swallow while I fight tears. Those girls are missin' their mommy like I missed my daddy as a teenager.

"Gertie, they were only seven years old when Annie left us. Every year they remember less. Sixteen is a hard age to be without a mother."

I know Margaret's speaking from experience, and it pains me. Even now, with Olaf's love, life is hard without Mommy. I don't know what I would've done without her at age sixteen. I let Harold smooth talk me in a minute of foolish trust that cost Henry and me a lot of misery. I think it might be time for Margaret and me to drive Maggie and Nattie to Berea.

Margaret dabs her mouth with her napkin. "I've talked with Matthew about their request. He suggested we are the more appropriate chaperones for our granddaughters' visit to Berea. What do you think?"

"Well, you read my mind again. I think Dr. Dill's right. Henry would never admit this to his children, or me, but goin' back to Berea is hard on my son. What'd he say to the twins?"

"'Put the brakes on, girls! You're only sixteen. First things first. Fetch Matthew and let's look at your mother's park and campground plans.'"

I repeat what Henry last said. "Well, they cain't agree where to build the park and campground—at the bottom of this cemetery by the runoff closer to the road and business in Matewan, or that purdy flat piece of land up Red Jacket, past the mines and away from traffic, almost two miles from Matewan. What do you and Dr. Dill think?"

"The Red Jacket plot is beautiful and spacious, and the price is reasonable. The Italian and Russian mining camps, and the Negro migrants and their families could use another business to service them and attract residents. However, considering the more distant proximity to Matewan, our twins consider the bottom of Annie's Hill the more desirable and accessible location for the park and campground."

I gaze downhill upon the sprouting hillside and know what our girls are up to.

Margaret sighs. "We've planted an alluring place, Gertie."

I'm glad Olaf and Henry warned me about this, and I hold my peace.

"Maggie and Nattie foresee Annie's Hill being a popular visitor attraction where families might also camp, and a have a mere two-minute drive into Matewan to shop and visit their bakery."

I count the twelve feathers on each of the mourning dove's wings, spread in flight above *Anna Marie Dill Blankenship*. The stonemason did such lovely work. I keep expectin' the dove to fly away. "That's what Henry finds troublesome."

Margaret holds the chilled glass of sweet tea to her face. She's never said her age, but I figure she's six years older than me. Sitting before Annie's grave is the only time I see the pull of despair crease her pearly skin.

We both know Henry will never marry again. I repeat what Henry said the last we met. "Henry doesn't want his wife's grave becomin' pop'lar like Devil Anse Hatfield's. He said Annie never wanted to draw attention to herself, and he'll do what he can to honor that."

Margaret bows her head. "My daughter felt embarrassed when the townspeople celebrated her graduation, her wedding, and her children's births, because she was born an outsider and didn't achieve anything greater than any other mother. She admired the hill folk she visited and interviewed, mothers who grew their own food and raised children without stepping beyond the creek that runs by their homeplace. Some mothers live and die in a hollow entirely content without laying one demand upon anyone. 'These are the women we must praise,' Annie said."

"And she did in her book, *Annie Chapman*," I say with a lump of gratitude stuck in my throat. "Annie wrote about my grandmother as if she was her granddaughter. And from what I hear, plenty who've read the book believe she is."

Margaret closes her eyes and inhales the sweet, mountain air. It's as if she cain't face Annie's gravestone another second. This happens sometimes on Fridays.

"Ah," she says to the mountainside, "Annie's foremost quest—to tell as compelling a story about Appalachia as Willa Cather did for the westward pioneers in *My Ántonia*. How Annie wrote a beautiful biography of a daughter of Scots immigrants while nursing twins and chasing a toddler, I'll never know."

"Maybe Annie could tell about my granny's life so true because that was purdy much her life when she wrote it," I say.

The hill falls so quiet we hear a coal truck downshift around the curve below. "And remember, Margaret, you washed, dried, and folded a lot of diapers while Henry fought in Guam. That's what we women do. We help each other."

Margaret slowly turns her eyes to mine. If I speak out of turn, she could break into pieces. So I wait, and quietly remember helpin' my Granny Chapman with her butter molds. Annie was right. My grandmother asked not one thing of anybody. Rather, she took me into her homeplace when my mother fell ill in wintertime after she lost her second baby. Granny had seven children with one a-sucklin', yet she took me in so I could go to school with her older children. Mommy never spoke of her two babies Daddy buried up Thacker Holler.

Margaret lifts her eyes to the mourning dove. "Annie never could resolve why most of Annie Chapman's children and grand-children left their farms for the city. She wondered, what was this 'better life' they sought, never to return? 'There's abundant beauty and opportunity to grow and prosper in these mountains,' my daughter said time and again."

"Well, like I said, life doesn't make sense sometimes. Here you have Olaf and Natalia who loved their farm and had to run for their lives and leave their land to the Bolsheviks who ruint it and caused many of their people to starve. Then there's my Granny's children, who ever' single one left Chapman Holler on Johns Creek for another place to live and work. Mommy married Daddy, who loved loggin' and Appalachia, so they stayed put. He and Mommy grew a garden and kept livestock just for us.

"There's always goin' to be folk who don't want to work a farm, especially when the automobile makes it so glam'rous and easy to up and leave. Ever'body's diff'ernt in a family. But Annie was right. Look at Olaf, Natalia, Henry, the Nenni's, Ray, Dr. Dill, Doc Bentley, the members of Matewan Garden Club—they're all believers in that beauty and opportunity to grow and prosper in Appalachia. Even in Annie's death, her work prospers. Henry said Annie's books are sellin' real good. *A Closer Look at Appalachian Botany* is almost sellin' more than *Annie Chapman*."

Margaret smiles. "In your list of Appalachian believers, don't forget the woman with a shovel and her beautification projects all along Tug Fork, Mate Creek, and Peter Creek. Gertie, do you ever wonder what happened to the redheaded Highlander?"

I wait a minute because I didn't expect this question. "Well, he does come to mind time to time, but I leave the Highlander in God's hands. He's one example of 'what someone means for evil, God uses for good.' And for that I hope he's turned his life around to God. He has a mother, too."

Margaret looks to me real serious. "Will you forgive me for the years I punished you and Henry with my pride?"

I don't know how to answer. She touches my arm.

"Will you?"

"What are you talkin' about, Margaret? I never see'd any pride in you."

"Then what would you call my belittling attitude and behavior toward you and Henry?"

I look into her brown eyes, hungry for forgiveness and peace of mind. "Well, I reckoned it was your breedin' and common sense tellin' you to protect your daughter."

Margaret shakes her head. "You're much too gracious, Gertie."

"Well, what mother wants her daughter marryin' the son of the town drunk?"

Margaret casts her eyes to her glass of tea like she's guilty. She did what she had to do, and I forgave her long ago. Neither of us could help how we grew up.

"Margaret, I know firsthand what can happen when a man deceives a young woman. And do you think I would'a let Henry marry Annie without makin' a fuss if Dr. Dill had been a drunkard?"

Margaret looks to me real quiet like she does when she's thinking hard.

"Truth is, Mommy warned me about Harold Blankenship's womanizin', but didn't tell me what womanizin' was. Green as could be, I was no diff''ernt than the young and reckless logger who didn't heed Daddy's safety rules while lumberin.' In the blink of an eye, the tree fell on the wisest and most loving person in my and Mommy's life."

Margaret looks down to what she calls a manicure. "I'm sorry you lost your father, Gertie. I did, too. And I've since made my share of mistakes."

"You're kind, Margaret, but Mommy begged me not to go to Freeburn's comp'ny buildin' dance. She knew Harold and his kind hung out there like vultures, waitin' to pluck up girls like me.

"Dark and handsome, with a cigarette drooping from his mouth, he was the first man who smiled at me, other than my daddy. And Daddy was gone. Harold didn't even know how to dance, and he stank of body odor, shine, and nicotine. But he knew what to say. *What about you and me go wadin' in the little creek behind your house?*

"I thought of Daddy and how we walked the mountains and creeks catching crawdads together. Daddy taught me the name of ever' tree, vine, shrub, wildfla'er, herb, and burry. We ate pawpaw right off the tree and blackburries off the canes. We tapped maple trees and made syrup. Oh! How Daddy loved Mommy's flapjacks and his maple syrup!

"But that wasn't what Harold had in mind. And there wasn't a thing I could do to defend myself. But I clawed his face real good."

Margaret sits with the last bites of her sandwich, her eyes filling with tears. She swallows. "I'm so sorry, Gertie."

"And I'm sorry to make you cry, Margaret. I'll stop right now if you want me to. It's just that you asked, and we promised to tell each other the truth, and I believe I can trust you with it."

Margaret whispers, "You can. Please continue."

"Well, before I do, I want you to know I forgave Harold and myself a long time ago because Mommy said I had to, for peace of mind and heart. She said Daddy wouldn't have me beatin' myself up the rest of my life and teachin' my child to be ashamed of hisself when he had nothin' to do with my defiance."

Margaret touches my arm again. "Your mother was a wise and loving woman."

Her praise of my mother lets loose what I've hidden far too long—except with Olaf and Mrs. Semenov, who's like a mother. "Mommy wanted me to finish high school, so I did, just a month before Henry was borned. I named him after Daddy. When Henry learned to walk, Harold came sniffin' around sayin' he'd sobered up and wanted to marry me and take care of his son. Mommy asked me not to, said Henry's a happy baby growin' up with us, please don't spoil it. Well, that was my second mistake. Harold gave us nothin' but misery.

"I failed my mother, my son, and myself many times, tryin' to figure out how to get us out of the mess I'd gotten us into. But Mommy always forgave me and helped best she could. What Harold conceived in lust, Mommy and I reared in love. She taught me to read the Bible to Henry, and to put our trust in Jesus. Henry could recite John 3:16 and 2 Timothy 2:15 by five years old. When Henry went to school, I dug gardens with Daddy's shovel for pay." I pause. "Am I talkin' too much, Margaret?"

"No, please, I've waited a long time to hear your story."

"I hated Harold when he moved us to Blackberry City, closer to moonshiners. Thank God for our neighbor Daisy! She was a young, childless widow woman. I'd never met somebody so nice. One day, she told me she was makin' soup beans and cornbread for the new owners of Matewan's seed store, did I want to come along. I said no. Lord knows I love Daisy, but I had another mess from a moonshiner to clean up. Later, she told me about John and Antillo Nenni and Crazy Ray helpin' Olaf and Mrs. Semenov unload the truck and movin' the furniture upstairs into that abandoned, filthy place."

"Between Daisy and Crazy Ray, the entire town knew about the condition of the Semenov's new home. Matthew and I pitied them," Margaret says.

"Well, Daisy told me how mannerly and handsome both Mrs. Semenov and Olaf were. She also felt sorry for them because they had no idea what they had walked into, so she helped Mrs. Semenov clean their apartment."

"That was very kind of Daisy."

I hear the sincerity in Margaret's voice. "I'd never met a Russian before, although some Russian families settled up Red Jacket for minin' 'bout the time the Italians settled in Matewan and Little Italy. Olaf and Natalia met Jeanette one Sunday when they were makin' deliveries in Red Jacket. I knew someday I'd walk into Hunt's Feed & Seed to order chicken feed and see if my hens liked it. Then I'd meet this Olaf and Mrs. Semenov for myself.

"When I did, Mrs. Semenov wasn't in the store, and I knew Olaf wanted to hold Tall Man. But he didn't ask because he's a gentleman. I walked out thinkin' he might be trustworthy. Then, Harold dug up Mommy's peonies for 'shine and left Tall Man in the rain. Later, Henry told me about walking into Hunt's Feed and Seed with my rusted shovel, cryin' his eyes out. After Henry showed me

Tall Man looking brand-new, I shouted with joy. Just weeks later, the mine caved in on Harold."

My voice caught, awful memories tumblin' over each other. "I think you know the story from here, Margaret."

"I do. Olaf spoke of Henry—and you—often. However, the truth is, my parents instilled in my brother and me their unimpeachable sense of superiority, confirmed by our college education. Thankfully, Matthew mistook my pride for self-confidence."

"You have a brother?"

"Yes. He moved from Columbus to San Francisco before we moved here. He objected vehemently to Matthew's practice in Appalachia. He considered Matthew a fool for wasting his fine mind and practice in a coal town.'"

Her brother's judgment cuts deep, yet carries some truth. "I'm sorry, Margaret. If he knew the beautiful changes your family brought to Matewan and Tug Fork he'd change his mind."

"That's very kind, and I would love to believe so, but as of a week ago, he sustains his claim to disown us."

"What do you mean, disown?"

"One by one, he's returned my fifty-three letters unopened, including Annie's graduation and wedding invitation, and envelope enclosing her funeral card and obituary. I recognize his penmanship, *Return to Sender*, on the envelope. I'm just thankful he doesn't throw them in the trash. I pray one day I'll find a letter in our mailbox with our address written in his hand."

I hold what's left of my sandwich and feel sick to my stomach. "Is he married, have children?"

"Not to my knowledge. He's a professor at the University of California San Francisco School of Dentistry. He met Matthew while they were in dental school in Columbus. They became fast friends and chess partners. Matthew subscribes to several dentistry publications and often finds my brother's byline. We read every article."

"What's a byline?"

"The writer's name, usually placed at the top of the article."

My goodness, everything has a word for it.

"What's your brother's name?"

"Samuel Douglas Lewiston. He's a regular contributor to the *Journal of the American College of Dentists*. His area of specialty is gum disease. He's a brilliant man, Gertie. But like the Tin Man, he needs a heart. He lost his, piece-by-piece, during the week Mother and Father succumbed to the Spanish Flu after they returned from Europe in 1918. All medical decisions and paperwork fell upon Samuel's shoulders. Shortly after he closed our parents' estate, he left for California without a farewell. Thankfully, Matthew remained faithful to his calling to Matewan."

"So, Annie was about four years old when your parents died?"

Margaret nods with a solemn face. I pray Samuel Douglas Lewiston finds his Dorothy to help him find his heart. "Margaret, do you remember some good things about your parents?"

"Oh yes. Mother's ginger cookies, for one. She kept the cookie jar full, as did her mother. When Samuel emptied our parents' house, he left a box on our front porch including the cookie jar. I was so happy he left it, yet devastated that he didn't knock on our door. I washed and dried the jar and placed it on my own kitchen counter. Annie loved the little boy on the lid with a wheelbarrow full of grapes. For some unknown reason she named the boy Wilbur. I presented the cookie jar to Annie when Matthew was born."

"So that's why!"

"Why what?" Margaret asks.

"Why the grandchildren call the cute little boy on the jar 'Wilbur!' The grandchildren are always diggin' into it for your ginger cookies. It's a mir'cle it's not been broke to pieces!"

"The gingerbread tradition comes from my ancestors in Germany, who made gingerbread houses. Mother and I made a house every Christmas."

"That's all the grandchildren talk about when you make them."

"Mother also decorated the tree with real candles like Martin Luther did in the old country. She lit the candles Christmas Eve long enough to sing "Oh Tannenbaum." Then I blew them out. Mother lifted me up to the top of the tree to the biggest candle of them all. I still find myself singing the song when I decorate our Christmas tree."

"'I never heard that song. Will you sing it for me?'"

Margaret laughs and I'm relieved to hear it. "I'm afraid my singing lessons didn't pay off like my ballet lessons."

"Lord-a-mercy, what other lessons did you take?"

"Let's see." Margaret counts on her fingers. "Violin, piano, swimming, tennis, equestrian, culinary, painting, chess. And how can I forget golf?"

"What's eques....?"

"Horseback riding."

"Goodness gracious, Margaret! A little thing like you rode horses?"

"I not only rode horses, I jumped horses."

I shake my head in wonder at what my friend has done with her life.

"Do you still play the violin and piano?"

"On special occasions. Birthdays. Easter. Christmas. Matthew and Annie loved to hear me play songs of the season. Matthew still has a few favorites he requests when he's feeling a little blue. His number one favorite is Chopin's Nocturne No. 2."

I never thought it possible for Dr. Dill to feel blue. "Do you still paint?"

"Not as much as I did before gardening took over my life."

Margaret's stirrin' up my curiosity. "What do you paint?"

"I mostly use watercolors. I painted Annie in honor of her fifth birthday and presented the portrait to Matthew for Father's Day. I spent the winter after she died before the easel painting miniatures of all her birthday photos. I hung them in my library. And of course, I paint zinnias and whatever flower catches my eye. I've painted Annie's rhubarb patch at least a dozen times."

I would love to see those miniatures of Annie in Margaret's library, but have a feeling that would be intruding. "Have you ever considered sellin' some of your paintings at the Magnolia Fair?"

"No. But I will."

Her answer is like a good swig of her iced tea for us both.

"Have you and Dr. Dill golfed the Greenbrier's course?"

"Yes. My parents believed an accomplished woman is the most capable woman, equal to an accomplished man. I believed it too when my golf game surpassed my brother's."

"What about your father? Daughters are often closer to their daddies."

Margaret shakes her head, not one hair out of place. "Father had little time for my brother and me. He was an academic ambassador to Europe and spent months at a time away from home. Mother took responsibility for our education and social development. However, Father invited me to his chessboard when Samuel wasn't available. As a teenager, my brother was a champion tournament player. No matter how many chess lessons I took, I could not compete with him. Father tolerated me as long as I didn't slump in my chair. If I made a good move, he offered a hint of a smile. I lived on those hints."

"Olaf's father and mother taught him to play chess when he was eleven years old. He spent hours at the chessboard with Sergei Mekinov during their three years in Boston."

Margaret looks to Annie's stone. I'm wondering if we've sat here too long, but she keeps talkin'.

"One day, when Annie was in fifth grade, while I washed and she dried dishes, she said Olaf was teaching Henry to play chess. My prejudice convinced me Henry was lying. I wince when I think about it. Thankfully, Annie lived long enough for me to ask her forgiveness. Now, a highlight of my month is playing chess with Henry. We usually have several interruptions by the children, but it's worth it to have one hour face to face with your son. I've learned things about my daughter I never knew before Henry invited me to his chessboard."

I laugh. "Your chess games are one of the highlights of his month, too. That's one good thing that came out of the War. And I've learned things about y'all that I never knew before Olaf invited Dr. Dill to his chessboard. Do you and Rosemary Cline still play chess together, too?"

"Yes, the second and fourth Tuesday night of each month."

"Henry and I didn't know what a chessboard was until one rainy day when Olaf set up Sergei's board in the store. Now that Olaf and Henry are like ships passin' six days a week, Olaf goes up to Henry's ever' Wednesday night to play after the children go to bed. That's the only time my son sits down, other than rockin' for fifteen minutes on the porch after dinner—admirin' Darlin' with the children, tellin' Annie stories and answerin' questions."

"Do the children have a favorite story?"

I smile. "The time she saw Darlin' in the old fillin' station."

Finally, Margaret smiles. "The twins love to say, 'Isn't it romantic, Grandmother, how Daddy uprooted Darlin' and wrapped it in his hanky and cut a piece of his bootlace?'"

"The children cain't believe their daddy cut off his bootlace 'cause he's so fussy about his boots. Since then, he carries extra laces in his shirt pocket."

Margaret throws her sandwich scraps to the birds that sing their little hearts out for us. I do the same. My scraps fall where Margaret's do.

Another ritual.

She says, "Henry and the children measure Darlin's height and width each April. Matthew writes the figures down in his Darlin' notebook."

I look up and touch the redbud bloomin' above us. "That's my favorite part of Darlin's story. She keeps growin'."

"Gertie?"

"Uh-huh."

"Would you consider golf lessons?"

I cain't believe my ears. "Law no! Don't take offense, Margaret, but it seems a waste of time. And after hearin' Richardson's 'point of view,' as Olaf calls it, I had to agree it seems a silly game. I'd rather garden or quilt anytime. Even jumpin' horses makes more sense."

Margaret smiles. "I doubt Richardson has ever given the game a chance. Truly, I think he would find golf's strategy as gratifying as a chess game."

"Well, you know how strategy and *I* get along."

"I've observed your hand-eye coordination over the years and think you'd make a good golfer."

"Well, I declare. I'm fifty-seven years old and never heard of hand-eye coordination. What is it?"

"The involuntary cooperation of your hands with your eyes in movement. See how your bread crust fell in the same place as mine? We use hand-eye coordination unconsciously to cook, quilt, garden, write, draw, or catch a ball, for instance."

"Or to hit a golf ball with a club."

Margaret's face is pleading. "Trust me, Gertie. I think you might surprise yourself and drive the ball accurately and to a good distance. And I think you'd also make a good putter."

"A what?"

"After you hit, or drive, the ball onto the green where the hole is, you tap, or putt, the ball into the hole."

"What's the 'green'?"

"The mown area of the lawn where the hole is. The golfer with the least strokes— including drives and putts—to sink the ball into nine or eighteen holes wins the game."

"Margaret," I almost gasp, "I'm Southern as they come and don't have an athletic bone in my body, and I've never played a sport to win. I shor' don't want to embarrass you or myself tryin' to sink a golf ball into nine or eighteen holes. That sounds like torture!"

Margaret sits on the edge of the bench, her back plumb straight. "Oh, Gertie, I beg to differ. Every joint and muscle in your body is toned by consistent exercise. And I promise to give you several lessons before we play our first game of nine holes. I cannot remember the last time I spent an entire day to play eighteen holes."

"Well, I guess my other concern is I don't know how I feel about keepin' score of strokes. Isn't it like comparin' how many rhizomes and peony roots we plant in the same amount of time and claimin' the one who planted the most the winner?"

Margaret looks real sober. "No. Competition is not our purpose on this hill. Golf, on the other hand, is an old Scottish outdoor sport with rules that have stood the test of time to develop particular skills. Personally, I golf to exercise my body and power of concentration in a peaceful, outdoor environment. I also golf to improve my game and compete against my last score. And for Rosemary's companionship once a month when we golf nine holes in Pikeville. I couldn't tell you her last score."

"Well, it's not my turn to compete, even against myself."

Margaret rests her eyes on the mountainside. It's busy birthing redbud and crabapple blossoms as we speak. "Perhaps it's a matter of understanding the context of the word *compete*. For instance, aren't your efforts to improve your Beef Stroganoff challenging you to learn the means and methods of preparing a better dish?"

I sit back on the bench and study Margaret's question. It seems every Friday I learn something new from her while we companion one another on this blessed hill.

"Yes."

"Then you accept my offer for golf lessons?"

"If you think I have . . ."

"Potential," Margaret says and looks to her watch. "Shall we plan for next Wednesday at eleven o'clock? I'll have us back home by four."

I'm flabbergasted at myself. What am I gettin' into? Olaf won't believe it when I tell him. I want to back out, but cain't. There's something about Margaret that makes me believe she just might be right, and I'll never know if I don't try. "Uh-huh, Wednesday at eleven o'clock."

Margaret jumps up from the bench, rarin' to go. We carry our picnic basket and Thermos to the truck and put them in the cab. The inside smells new, like the season. I remember Margaret's concern about Matthew's maturity and know I'll talk with Olaf about it first chance we're alone.

Margaret and I take up the buckets of irises with *yellow* and *blue* written on them. Both standing on our feet this time, we begin at the arbor on the right side of the path. I straddle the furrow behind Margaret, set three yellow rhizomes between her three blue rhizomes, then cover them with soil. She's moving lickety-split, like a northerner again, without one hair out of place. And I'm moving behind like a southerner again, tryin' to keep up with her.

All at once I see the golfer in her shoulders, the swimmer in her back and arms, and the ballerina in her legs and hands. I raise my voice. "I've been wonderin' and keep forgettin' to ask, where'd you go to college?"

"Ohio State University," she says, and keeps moving.

"Is that where you met Dr. Dill?"

"No. We met in a young professionals' organization soon after I graduated. A new friend invited me to the club's golf outing, and there stood 'Mister Tall, Dark, and Handsome.' My friend, also a schoolteacher, introduced me to Dr. Matthew Dill, a dentist. He wormed his way into our foursome and my heart."

I stop. "Margaret Dill, hold on a minute!"

She slowly turns to me with a blanched face.

"Did I hear you right? Did you say you were a schoolteacher?"

She looks to her pink gloves. "I apologize, Gertie. It was a slip of the tongue."

Margaret avoids looking me in the face as if she's heard some real bad news. I regret I asked the question. "You don't have to talk about it if you don't want to."

"Thank you."

I don't want to say the wrong thing, so I just nod and set three more rhizomes in the furrow. It's taken a while for me to see the reason behind it, but Margaret's rule for planting uneven numbers is beginning to bloom up here on this hill. As Margaret says, "*It pleases the eye in balance and harmony.*"

Now I pray for harmony as we finish the right side of the path and start on the other side without one word. I feel awful for Margaret. She won't turn and meet my eyes. Dear Lord Jesus, what's botherin' her? I never see'd her drag her feet like she is now. Something's broke inside her.

We're halfway to the arbor when Margaret turns around and stands aside the furrow. She's about twenty feet away. Her eyes and face burn with something I cain't place. I lift my chin to the side, puzzled, afraid she's going to shatter and fall into a heap. I never see'd Margaret like this, even when Annie died. Oh Lord, help Margaret and me. What's happenin'? Is she sick?

"Gertie, a secret consumes like cancer."

Her words push me back like a blast of hot wind. My mind races to figure out what she means. I heard of cancer, but not one person on Tug Fork's ever died of it that I know of. Black lung, yes. Margaret steps toward me. What does a secret have to do with being a schoolteacher? This time, I'm on the other side of hearin' something tragic.

She stands before me. "Please, let's sit down."

"Our bench?"

She nods.

We walk side-by-side in silence and sit down before Annie's stone again.

Margaret closes her eyes. Her breathing slows down.

"Gertie, I believe this is also the time and place for me to speak of my greatest mistake." She opens her eyes and looks to me. "Are you able to receive a shock?"

My heart thunders in my ears like when Henry called from the hospital the morning Annie died. My Lord, what Margaret's goin' to say is about Annie. "If you can trust me with your greatest mistake, I can hear it."

She pulls off her gloves that smell like Jergens Lotion. She wraps her slender, silky fingers around my calloused, dirty hands. I see and feel her pain and peace, the holy place a mother finds in delivery of a healthy child, the surrender of the child in matrimony, and God forbid, death.

"As you assured me, I understand we live the life God gives us. All is forgiven."

I bow my head and nod.

"In Columbus, 1913, not two months into my first semester teaching high school American literature and composition classes, I fell into my principal's snare."

She pauses long enough for me to absorb her words. Margaret, an accomplished college graduate, fell into a man's snare? I remember Harold's snare, and I don't want to hear what Margaret's about to say. But she listened to me, and I owe her mercy.

"A new friend, the female teacher who invited me to the golf outing, warned me about Mr. Randall's clever ploys, and to never allow myself to be alone with him. This friend's fiancé taught in another Ohio school district and had heard rumors of Mr. Randall's sexual advances from teachers there. Matthew, my fiancé, also warned me never to be alone with my principal. I believed myself capable of recognizing his schemes. I had traveled alone without incident when I lived with my parents in Europe for two years. Cavalier, I underestimated the cunning and physical strength of a criminal mind on the scent of a woman."

"What does *cavalier* mean?"

"Careless and overconfident."

"Oh."

"As Harold planned his attack upon you, so did Mr. Randall plan his attack upon me. A fall Monday before school dismissal, his secretary sent a note to my room requesting an appointment at four o'clock in his office to discuss a phone call from a parent. With the school vacated of teaching staff and custodians at that time on Mondays, I suspected he meant me harm. I returned the note to the secretary declining the meeting under the pretense I had an appointment immediately after school. I requested the name of the student and parent and the phone number to call from home."

"How was that cavalier, Margaret?"

"You don't deny a criminal his victim without certain means of escape for the victim."

I shiver. "What do you mean?"

"As long as I remained in his building, I remained Mr. Randall's prey."

I feel sick to my stomach. "Margaret, what did this man do to you?"

"I gathered my books, papers for grading, purse, and locked my desk. When the secretary didn't return with the note, I knew to flee immediately. Mr. Randall hid outside my classroom, located at the end of a long, empty hall. He moved swiftly and held me from behind."

"Margaret, how on earth did such a sparrow like you survive?"

"An unsuspecting victim is doubly vulnerable, so I owe my life to a fellow teacher. I smelled ether before he pressed the cloth over my face and dragged me into my classroom and closed the door. What he didn't consider were my swimming lessons. I held my breath, feigned unconsciousness, and submitted to his brutal rape."

"For the love of Jesus, Margaret, how did you escape?"

"I heard his belt buckle rattle, footsteps walk out of my classroom, and the door close. To confirm he'd left, I moaned to provoke a response. Nothing. I risked opening an eye. He had left my room. I removed an earring and slid it under my bookshelf for evidence, and pulled on my clothes, but couldn't find my shoes. I grabbed my purse and forced myself through the open window. My classroom clock said four seventeen. Thank God my room was on the first floor."

I'd never heard such a horrible thing. "Where did you go?"

"The gas station across the street. The attendant called the police. Minutes later, several police cars surrounded the school as another police car pulled into the gas station with an ambulance close behind."

"Did the police call Matthew?"

"Yes. He met the ambulance at the hospital. Unbeknownst to me, I bruised and lacerated my face and entire body in my escape through the window. Matthew and the nursing staff covered the bathroom mirror so I couldn't see the grotesque swelling."

"So, the police caught Mr. Randall in the school?"

"Yes, the Columbus police department had put him under surveillance when my fellow teacher reported his inappropriate behavior. The police soon discovered similar reports against Mr. Randall filed in other Ohio precincts. They suspected he was the elusive ether mass-murderer they'd been following for several years."

"Several years? How'd they finally capture him?"

"The sergeant called in two adjacent departments for assistance to guard all the building's exits, including the janitor's door that led to the roof. Three officers found him in the gym teacher's office, hiding in the locker. He held a bottle of ether and a lighter, ready to set himself afire."

I take in a deep breath as I imagine such an evil thing. "So, he came from behind and used ether on all the women?"

"Yes, as evidence and testimonies proved in the trial. My blood tests revealed a low level of ether had induced a state of semi-consciousness that distorted my state of mind during his attack. Thank God the anesthesia dispelled enough to permit consciousness and my escape before the principal returned to my room. That's the only reason I escaped death."

"Where did you live when this happened?"

"In a flat within the school's neighborhood. I walked to work. The investigation proved the principal had stalked me from my first day of work."

"Matthew didn't take you back to your flat, did he?"

"No. I had no family or a close friend in the area, so the doctor on the case recommended Matthew take me to his home to convalesce with the assistance of a day-nurse. Matthew attended to his more critical patients while I healed from internal injuries from the principal's beating, and from pressing myself through the open window. The window's lock snagged my hair and uprooted a patch at the back of my neck. The forensics report said it would have been impossible for my body to escape through the window without breaking it, yet the gas station attendant testified he saw me struggle through the window at four seventeen."

I dared ask, "Did your brother call or write?"

Margaret wipes her eyes. "No. I hadn't heard from him since he left our parents' home in Paris. Oh, about three years before. When the doctor said I was well enough, Matthew and I married. He remained by my side throughout the criminal investigation, trial, and sentencing."

"Did you tell your parents?"

"We had no choice. I immediately changed my address and phone number. Day-by-day, month-by-month, the press swept Ohio and four other states where evidence of Mr. Randall's victims unfolded. My parents couldn't bear the exposure and chose to live abroad during the ordeal."

"I'm sorry, Margaret. Yet, I'm so glad you took swimming lessons and were tiny enough to crawl through the window."

"Gertie, one of the investigators said they discovered I am one of only five women, out of nineteen known victims, who survived to testify in court. In our testimonies we mentioned we couldn't find our shoes at the crime scene before we escaped. This became an obsession with the detectives. They renamed the case to The Ether and Missing Shoes Murders."

"That makes my skin crawl, Margaret. Did the detectives find the shoes?"

"Eventually. They found twenty-five pairs, including my navy blue pumps."

"Lord have mercy on the six women who haven't been found. Where did the detectives find the shoes?"

"Ironically, in two lockers in the boy's locker room in the high school where I taught. The police didn't think to search the lockers until the trial had progressed into its second year, with victim testimonies of missing shoes. When the prosecuting attorney asked the criminal why he kept his victim's shoes, he said they were his 'trophies.'"

"Oh Margaret, the man was deranged."

"His crimes within five schools were so heinous that the districts bulldozed the buildings. He was found guilty upon fourteen counts of murder and nineteen counts of rape. The judge pronounced the death sentence."

I'm so thankful Margaret was one of the five I want to hug her, but now is not the time.

"During my pregnancy, Matthew and I decided it was in our family's best interest not to inform the child, my parents, or anyone else of the biological father. I believe we did the right thing."

Oh, Heavens yes, they did the right thing. "Margaret, was Mr. Randall married?"

"No," she almost whispers, and looks into my eyes as if she can read my mind.

"Did he have children?"

Her eyes glisten like the dew on peony petals. "I know of just one: a girl named Annie."

"What happened to the teacher who warned you about Mr. Randall?"

"After I had recovered from the trial, I attempted to find her. She also testified during the trial. A fellow member of the Young Professionals said she had left the school district with no forwarding address."

"I cain't imagine havin' to leave my home. That must've been a hard thing for her to do."

I look to my hand in Margaret's and cannot believe what I've just heard, yet know it must be true. "I don't know how you, Matthew, and Annie ended up here in Matewan, but I'm so glad you did."

"When Annie's second year in school concluded, Matthew and I decided it was best to leave Columbus with all its reminders of my deceased parents, my brother, Matthew's foster families, the principal, and the trial."

Margaret pauses as if to gain her strength. *Oh Lord, forgive me. If only I had eyes to see through her pretty clothes into her broken heart all these years. No wonder she couldn't trust Henry with Annie. How could she risk her daughter's life and future with any young man?*

"I wasn't thrilled about Matthew's calling to Appalachia, but I understood it, and hoped Matewan would be a good place for a fresh start. The day he drove us onto Mate Street, he pointed to the red brick building with the *Matewan Hospital* sign. Annie said, 'Father, I like the tall steps on both sides going up to the hospital's front door, don't you?' She sat between us, and Matthew looked down to her affectionately. 'Yes, I do,' he said. We stopped at Leckie's Drugs and discovered their soda fountain and root beer float. Annie looked up to Matthew again and said, 'Father, I like Matewan.'"

I smile. "That sounds like somethin' Annie would say."

Margaret's eyes swell with tears, but she's smiling. "Gertie, when Matthew called Matewan Elementary School to make an appointment with the principal and Annie's third-grade teacher, he asked the secretary the name of Annie's teacher. 'Mrs. Rosemary Cline,' she said."

I nod.

"Gertie, it was the same Mrs. Rosemary Cline who warned me about our principal's advances in Columbus. The same Rosemary who reported him to the police and testified what she witnessed. Our Rosemary who left Columbus for Matewan, West Virginia to teach third grade."

I'm dizzy with surprises. "The same Mrs. Rosemary Cline who invited you to Matewan Garden Club when you first moved to Matewan!"

"And who later asked if I would accept her nomination for president of the club."

I remember what Daddy would say when puzzlin' out what he called the "condition of the human heart." "Only the Good Lord knows what people carry inside. Be careful, Gertie. It could be good or evil. Keep close to the Lord and listen to His voice."

Margaret dabs her eyes with a hanky. We sit in silence while a robin sings some sense and peace into our souls.

"Margaret, did the criminal leave any family?"

"No. The investigation tracked his name and birth to one of New York City's orphanages, and subsequently his name to an orphan train. Matthew struggled with the news for months. Annie's father could have been a passenger on Matthew's train. That was another reason for leaving Columbus."

"Dr. Dill sure had a hard life, goin' from one foster home to another. Then the woman he loves is almost taken from him. Then he loses Annie. Is that why he's merciful to us hill folk?"

"I believe so. Just like our beloved Doc Bentley. Matthew said the doctor came from poverty in Illinois near Abraham Lincoln's home."

"How will Dr. Dill take to you tellin' me about all this?"

The sun glints on her snow-white teeth. "Every Friday in March after we plant this slope, when Matthew and I later sit at dinner together he asks, 'Did you tell Gertie our secret today?' When I serve Matthew Asparagus à la Polonaise tonight, I can at last say, 'Gertie knows.'"

I stand to my feet and reach to the redbud branches to touch somethin' beautiful, pure, and trustworthy. Redbuds cannot lie, or cheat, or steal, or kill.

Margaret looks to her watch. "Two-thirty. Plenty time."

We straddle the furrow and finish setting in the irises. Then we empty the compost buckets and tamp the soil. In the sweet company of Appalachia's leafing season, the shady spots in the cemetery make the sunny spots shine all the brighter.

We're climbin' into Olaf's truck when we hear a car drivin' up the gravel runoff. We turn around to see Dr. Dill's shiny new red Buick comin' up the hill. We look to each other expecting bad news because Dr. Dill never interrupts our cemetery ceremonies.

In the next second we see people shoulder to shoulder in the front seat like biscuits baked in a pan.

"Isn't that Sergei Mekinov sitting next to Olaf in the front seat with Matthew?" Margaret asks.

"I declare!" I clap my hands and Margaret and I hug each other like we're schoolgirls. "The man's eighty-four years old! I bet Ray's brought Sergei from Boston to celebrate his namesake's birthday! I heerd Olaf and Ray whisperin' about it when they last played chess, but Olaf never said a thing about it to me!"

We slide off our seat and wait by the truck. "Looks like the back seat's full, too. What's going on?" Margaret says.

"Land sakes! Looks like party!"

Dr. Dill parks behind Olaf's truck. All four doors of his Road-master fly open. First, we see Sergei Mekinov at the left and Dr. Dill at the right front doors, then Mrs. Semenov and Agnes Wright at the back doors. Then we see Olaf from the front seat, and Richardson Wright from the back seat. Everybody's smiling like they do with a plate of Daisy's chocolate cake.

Margaret and I shake our heads in speechless happiness.

Olaf walks to my side and kisses my cheek. "Ve must talk vith Mother about Sergei," he whispers in my ear. Sergei looks real frail.

Dr. Dill herds our New York and Connec'cut visitors before us. Sergei and Richardson take turns kissin' my hand and Margaret's. Agnes gives us a hug. We all look to Dr. Dill to explain how all this gladness came about.

"Ray, Olaf, and I've been planning this surprise celebration for nine years! With every delay due to business, college, children, or weather, Ray and I determined Sergei Mekinov must celebrate Freddie's birthday with us some spring. But one detail after another wouldn't fall into place. Two days ago everything lined up. Ray left for New York City before dawn, and not an hour ago delivered the botanist Sergei Stepan Mekinov to the Semenovs' doorstep."

Dr. Dill lifts Margaret and gives her a spin. Her hat goes flyin'. "Isn't it wonderful?" All Margaret and I can do is laugh.

"Furthermore . . ." Dr. Dill says as he puts Margaret on her feet.

"Yes?" Margaret and I both say.

"Do you remember hearing Olaf talk about Otto—Olaf's protégé from Polya Tsvetov? All these years later Otto read a tribute to Fodor Petrov in the *Boston Globe*. The story included Sergei's name and connections with Boston College. Without further delay, Otto tracked down Sergei and knocked on his door."

Sergei nods. "I am a little frazzled from the hairpin turns. However, there is no more capable chauffeur than Ray. He knows his mountain roads!"

Dr. Dill laughs. "Once Sergei recovered from shock, Otto drove him from Boston to New York City, where they abducted the Wrights for Freddie's birthday party!"

Richardson and Agnes bow like actors on a stage. "Ray jumped at the chance to drive his new Chevy Bel Air convertible in New York City traffic!" Richardson says. "However, we will board the train for our return!"

"At this very moment, Ray's introducing Otto to a Leckie's root beer float," Dr. Dill says.

After all these years waiting for Otto to show up, I cain't believe what Dr. Dill's saying. "Are you sure it's Otto?"

Dr. Dill looks to Olaf and Natalia. "It is Otto," Natalia says.

"All one hundred and eighty pounds of muscle!" Olaf adds.

Other than the night of Annie's graduation party and our weddin' ceremony, I never see'd such joy.

"Furthermore," Dr. Dill repeats, his fingers folded under his lapels like Olaf does. He nods to my husband. Just what could be the icing on this cake?

Olaf folds his fingers under his lapels and straddles his feet like he's some actor playing his part. "We've all been invited to tour Bartram Gardens in celebration of Stephen and Sergei's birthday!"

"When?" Margaret asks Olaf.

I bet she's thinking about what to pack.

"We depart tomorrow morning at ten o'clock," he replies.

I'm thinking we won't be back by next Wednesday for my first golf lesson, and I'm a little sorry about it.

"When do we return?" Margaret asks.

"Tuesday. Richardson has meetings Thursday in New York City."

Margaret gives me one of her purdy, white smiles. I throw her a smile back with my good hand-eye coordination. It lands right where I want it.

Sergei nods to the lone gravestone in the cemetery. "It has been nine years since I valked Annie's Hill vith you."

Dr. Dill and Margaret lead us on the curvy path. She leans to his ear and whispers. I think I know what she's sayin'. Both now gray-headed, Agnes takes her husband's arm as they follow the Dills.

Sergei and Natalia follow the Wrights. Sergei cups a hand to Natalia's ear. I wonder what all this whisperin's about when Olaf pulls me close and says, real low, "Otto vants to vork for Hunt's Feed & Seed."

"What did you say?"

"*Da.*"

"Does Henry know?"

Olaf nods.

"What did he say?"

"Yes."

"Where is our boy?"

Before Olaf can answer, we turn to the sound of Henry's truck roarin' up the runoff too fast. "Wait for me!" he hollers out the window, stops behind Dr. Dill's car, and throws his door open. I like to tease Henry that his children should put *Wait for me!* on his tombstone.

Side-by-side, Olaf, Henry, and I follow Sergei and Mrs. Semenov.

"Well," Henry says, "how do you like Beast?"

"Beast?" I ask.

"Hunt's Feed & Seed's new delivery truck!"

We stop and turn toward the three automobiles parked in a line. Dr. Dill's sedan shines like a ruby, and our new, one-ton delivery truck is indeed beastly. "I reckon you're right."

Henry wraps an arm around my waist and whispers. "Sergei asked Grandmother for her hand again."

"What'd she say?"

Henry looks to Olaf and gives him a wink. "*Da.*"

Well, this must be why Olaf needs to talk with Natalia and me. Guess I'll soon be the only Mrs. Semenov in Matewan. That should make it easier to remember to call her Natalia.

And Dr. Dill just might have to wait for his Asparagus à la Polonaise tonight. Either that or be happy skinning a double portion of Freddie's birthday cake.

PART FIVE
NATALIA
SEPTEMBER 8, 1959

Sergei assists me into my woven linen coat, the color of golden chrysanthemums. I gather my notebook and platter of küchen from the table by the front door. Sergei leans into my lips and lingers. It is the same whenever I leave him alone in the house, which is seldom.

"At my age, it may be my last kiss," Sergei jests.

I play along. "At our age, it may be *our* last kiss."

"No, Natalia," he says with adoring eyes. "You are immortal."

I brush Sergei's cheek with my fingertips. God have mercy upon us. We lost our soulmates. Our homes. Our country. Yet, we've found some comfort with each other.

"Do not wish that upon me," I say.

Sergei shuffles his feet. "You must go?"

As always, I look into Sergei's dim, gray eyes and think of Frederick. Does Sergei see Khristina's brown eyes? "*Da.*"

I cannot expect Sergei to comprehend the gift Lily and Violet granted me the day I applied for my library card. He yawns when I describe their development of the botanical section within the Williamson Public Library. He does not know Lily from Violet. How would I have overcome despair thirty-eight years ago without their vivacious minds and their friendship—their desire to form a garden club!

Sixty-five years from the day Father introduced Astrid and me to Russia's three foremost botanists, Frederick Semenov remains my only true love.

That fateful traipse along the cliffs of Norway's Aurlandsfjord, when Fodor Petrov encouraged Father to accept Frederick's request for my hand. Ever watchful of his daughters, Father trusted Frederick's gentle, strong spirit. Strikingly handsome then, Sergei Mekinov thought Frederick's rugged features no match for my affection.

Poor Sergei. He sees only physical beauty.

He tires and sits in his chair by the fireplace. No, Sergei cannot understand Frederick's hold upon me.

Yet, I wed this man who provided my son and me refuge for three years—the man who introduced us to Richardson and Agnes Wright. Dear Richardson. He knows Russia's history as if he were a Russ—and embraced us accordingly.

Our monthly escapes to Silver Mine, away from Sergei's chessboard, soirees, and marriage proposals, saved me from tedium. As my blessed Savior comforted me in Fodor Petrov's labyrinth and gardens outside New York City, so I poured forth my grief in Richardson's apple orchard. There, I resolved to leave Frederick in our Father's hands and sang my release that evening. Dear Father Wright, thank you for your request to sing "Un bel di."

"Send Freddie over, please," Sergei says now, and nods to the chessmen, his ever-present companions.

"If he has finished his lessons. School has resumed."

"Darling, I will supervise Freddie's lesson before we play. The boy works every day after school and Saturdays. Dr. Dill and I have a spare two years with him before Ray sells him a truck. Then we will lose Freddie to Hunt's Feed and Seed deliveries just as we lost Stephen two years ago to his first truck."

Sergei cannot embrace Matewan's people easily. Our lives are occupied with much labor and little leisure. Yet, according to Henry's direction, Freddie obliges Sergei on Wednesday nights with the promise the game will sharpen his nimble mind. Of all Henry and Annie's children, Freddie thinks more than feels. Olaf considers this a consequence of Annie's death after Freddie's birth. At the appointed time, my son will tell our youngest grandson of Henry's love that quickened his heart of stone to feel again after leaving his own father behind in Russia.

"Do Otto and Olaf play chess with Henry tonight?" Sergei asks.

"*Da*," I answer the third time today. "They discuss Henry and Olaf's trip to Washington D.C. next week."

"Matthew and Otto will manage business for Henry and Olaf?"

It is interesting what Sergei forgets and remembers. "*Da*." I lift my coat sleeve from my watch. Five o'clock. I allow time for this gentle farewell, and my own private musings. "Remember the kielbasa and sauerkraut on the stove. And Charles Priest may appear with Freddie for chess tonight."

Sergei rests his head on the back of the chair, one of the pair Olaf and I brought from our room in Sergei's Boston townhouse to this little town. Each month, when I leave for Garden Club, Sergei sinks deeper into the reupholstered cushions. Doctor Bentley claims this is common for a ninety-two-year-old. I pray to take my last breath while pruning *Passiflora incarnate* vines from Henry's arbor.

"A good chess player, Charles," Sergei says. "Yet, he must practice discipline with his school lessons." He raises his eyebrows. "Ray still honeymoons?"

"He said not to expect him for two weeks."

"Touring New England with a stop in Silver Mine, I understand."

We discussed this at lunch. "Violet was thrilled to receive Agnes's invitation to walk Richardson's gardens. Now I must go."

Sergei sighs. "I will never forget the day Ray drove us from Silver Mine to Matewan for Freddie's birthday party. The man knows these mountain roads!"

I turn to the mirror by the door. A wayward strand falls from the combs Frederick gifted to me upon our first Yuletide as man and wife. We admired the chiaroscuro of the moonlit, virgin snow upon Polya Tsvetov. I believed we would grow old together within Mother Russia's arms, unaware that the light of that blessed night foretold the dark journey to America without him. Now, in my final years, I fulfill Frederick's request to care for Sergei. Light casts shadows, always.

"Ode to Joy" sings in my reverie as I open the door and step onto our porch. The lowing sun blazes upon the leaves of redbuds, crabapples, and forsythia along Mate Street. *Clematis occidentalis* climbs between the two windows Henry installed on the south side of the store to allow light upon the stairwell. One of countless considerate projects Henry wrought with his hammer.

I lift my face to the conclusion of another blooming season, the vines withering against the golden paint of the building's façade. The scene sweeps me away to Norway. Astrid, Father, and I walk the forest with our notepads and pens to record names of flitting songbirds. We mimic them, play hide-and-find behind fallen *Picea abies, Pinus syl vestris,* and *Betula pendula.* The Norway spruce, Scots pine, and birch root the passion for botany deep within my sister and me. Father points to fallen logs with rotted bellies sprouting trees and shrubs.

"Earth wastes nothing," he says.

A beeping horn calls me from my reverie. Antillo waves and smiles from behind the steering wheel of his black Buick sedan. What a pleasure to greet his friendly eyes throughout the years. He serves whomever he meets quickly and promptly. I watch Antillo turn toward the railroad tracks toward their home.

Antillo, ever present in my life, and now his son Eddie.

Yes, as Frederick promised the night before we parted, John Nenni embraced us as fellow immigrants. Family. We prosper as they prosper as Matewan prospers. The Wheel of Life spins before me, around me, through me. I hear Frederick's voice. "Remember always, Natalia, *For of him, and through him, and to him, are all things. To whom be glory forever.*" Romans 11:36, Frederick's most favored scripture.

Unlike the measured farewell of the fading sun on the horizon at Polya Tsvetov, darkness whelms the mountains and Matewan by stealth. Lights flicker above Mate Street's doors as automobiles aim for home "up and down the river," as Appalachians say.

Charles Priest exits Dr. Dill's office door, adjacent to the hospital's entrance. Elevated above the sidewalks and traffic, the boy sees me and waves. I nod and marvel again at Dr. Dill's courage, conducting business within the building where his only child perished.

"Charles, please stop in tonight for a game of chess if you would like."

"I'll tell Mommy you asked and see if she'll let me tag along with her tonight."

He races down the steps facing upriver, mounts Blue Lightin', his Schwinn Hornet, navigates Mate Street, and pedals rapidly. At age fourteen, Charles and Freddie are temporarily safe from Ray's influence to abandon their bicycles for their first used Chevy trucks.

Charles turns into the parking lot of Grace Ford Dealership and disappears. He is the size Otto was when we left him in Russia. Charles and Freddie declare they have been best friends from first grade.

Freddie said, "Ever' boy who lives in Blackberry City has his shortcut home. I know Charles' and he knows mine."

"Are they not the same shortcut? You both live in Blackberry City," I once asked Freddie.

"Why, no! Ever' boy has his own!"

Olaf, Henry, Dr. Dill, and Sergei claim Freddie and Charles are like iron sharpening iron. Every Wednesday night, Dr. Dill and Sergei groom the boys with junior chess tournaments in mind.

"One night a week at the board will not prepare Freddie and Charles for competition. We must play twice a week at the very least," Sergei declares one night over Gertie's tender pot roast.

Olaf agrees, albeit with a side-glance to me in concern of Sergei's health. The two debate how to accomplish multiple, weekly practices. Sergei, an elderly nobleman of ease, cannot understand Olaf's lack of it. He shakes his head at Olaf's affection for and dedication to his father's work.

"Hire more hands!" Sergei commands.

I step up onto the porch of Hunt's Feed & Seed and recall our last evening together in the privacy of the patio at Polya Tsvetov. September 23, 1917. An infamous day, I sit with my husband and father-in-law—fourth and fifth generation Frederick Semenov, respectively.

The older Frederick wipes his brow, the atmosphere dark with disclosure. "My beloved children, we cannot postpone our escape and surrender of Polya Tsvetov any longer. We have distributed the harvest and farm equipment. Natalia, as you know, your family awaits me in Norway."

Frederick and his father exchange a swift glance. I dare speak. "For which I am grateful. I understand my Romanov blood and our wealth hasten Lenin's henchmen to our blessed Field of Flowers."

My father-in-law stands and paces the length of the vining arbor sheltering us.

He returns to sit before me. "My dear Natalia, this uprising would ruin our land if you were born of peasants. Be at peace, and please know your father and I will comfort one another in his home. There, we will grieve for our children."

"And please know, Father, your son and I will comfort one another and your grandson in America."

My father-in-law removes a post from his vest pocket. "From Fodor," he says.

My eyes leap toward the letter. My husband's do not.

"The postmaster concealed the envelope for me the moment it arrived," he says and offers the unsealed letter to me. "Your arrangements are in order, Natalia. Fodor has held Sergei to his word to give you and Olaf refuge in Boston. This . . ."

I push back my chair and stand. "*My* arrangements? Give Olaf and *me* refuge? What is this nonsense?"

My husband slowly rises. "Natalia, please. The violence in St. Petersburg spreads throughout Russia. Bolsheviks arrest thousands daily. I must divert them from your departure with Olaf."

I shake in disbelief of betrayal. "How long have you two been plotting to leave Olaf and me in the care of the most self-centered man I have ever had the displeasure to know? Why have you not consulted me?"

Furious, I turn from the men who determine my fate, and my son's, the sound of gravel grinding under my heels.

"Natalia, please listen," my Frederick pleads.

"I would rather face death than live in Sergei's presence without you. How could you disrespect my love, our love, our holy vow to one another, and cast me into the hands of a man who is incapable of comprehending and honoring your part in his and Khristina's safe passage to America?"

My husband speaks as though rehearsed. "Because I vowed to love, honor, and protect you to my last breath."

I understand his meaning and rage against it. "You choose to surrender your last breath to the Bolsheviks rather than attempt escape with your wife and son? If they capture us, we die together!"

Frederick's broad shoulders remain steadfast, his eyes moist with compassion and sorrow. "Darling, consider the Bolsheviks use all manner of torture, humiliation, and execution amongst their many weapons of warfare."

"You attempt to frighten me so I will agree to save my own life, and our son's, at the expense of yours!"

My husband speaks evenly. "I will do all within my power to prevent you and our son from falling into Bolshevik hands."

Desperate, I appeal to my husband. "Have you considered my vow to love, honor, and protect you to my last breath?"

Again, Frederick speaks as though I prompt him. "Yes. And I believe your escape with Olaf in this dark time will fulfill your vow—in America." Frederick stands before me, close enough that I feel his breath upon my face, and speaks with calm assurance. "Bone of my bone, flesh of my flesh, you and Olaf must continue our work in America. Our lives extend beyond our mortal bodies. I will always be with you."

I hold my stomach with one hand and grasp a rib of the arbor with the other. "And you ask me to sever your bone and flesh from me?"

He touches my lips with the pulse of his anguish. "There is a place in America, Natalia, where the people will embrace you and Olaf and help carry your burdens."

"How do you know this place and people?" I cry.

Frederick takes my hands in his and kisses them. "Remember my letter naming John Nenni, the cobbler who immigrated to Appalachia from Italy in 1888? One of 200,000 who sailed to America that year?"

"*Da*," I say, causing a fissure in my argument. "He repaired your boots when you hiked the Appalachian Mountains. Olaf cherished that letter. Your discoveries. He thought you would never return to Polya Tsvetov. I feared you would not. We clung to you when you returned. Now you ask us to live without you! What I feared then now comes upon me!"

Frederick speaks as a gentle stream from a cleft in a rock. "Yes, my love. I ask our son to live his life, to continue our work. I ask you to live your life, to continue our work."

I pull my hands from Frederick's. "How will we possibly live our lives in peace and accomplish your work when chained to Sergei—who seeks the glory of botany yet eschews the work?"

Frederick and his father hold one another's thoughts in the scented air between them. I see grief and courage battle within their eyes and collapse in my chair. They sit before me, a breeze waving the leaves and purple blossoms cheerfully, unaware of our doom and exodus tomorrow. What will happen to this sacred place? Cook? Our staff?

The love of my life reaches for my hands. A ray of sunlight gleams from my gold wedding band. "Natalia, I know Sergei. He will ask you to marry him, yet he loves his luxuries and will not leave them for Appalachia. All I ask is this promise."

"*Da?*"

"Please care for my friend in his old age. Do not let him die alone. Please bury him on my behalf with an admirable tombstone."

I understand Frederick's reasoning and swallow the difficult truth. My husband will die alone, buried in a mass, unknown grave without a marker.

There is no other choice before me. "Where is this place in Appalachia?"

"The state of West Virginia, along a river named Tug Fork that borders the state of Kentucky."

"My father often spoke of this ancient mountain range. He praised the delicious fruit of its pawpaw tree. Do my father and sister agree with your plan, and this Tug Fork?"

Frederick removes an envelope from his vest pocket. "This confirms so," he says and places a letter in my hand.

I touch my father's beautiful calligraphy. "I may never see him and Astrid again."

As he has for twenty-four years, the love of my life winds the wayward strand of my hair around his index finger and releases it. "Please, Natalia, find solace in this. If all goes as planned, your father and sister will not suffer the grief of your deaths by revolutionists. You may someday be united."

I want to believe him, yet sense a witness of the finality of separation within the eyes of the two men who love me and my child, and my father and sister. "The cobbler's shop was along Tug Fork?"

"*Da*, in a coal town named after Mate Creek."

Persuaded by my lover's gentleness, honesty, and wisdom, I wonder how Olaf and I will survive without him. Where will I sing? To whom will I sing?

"Mate Creek," I say. "An ironic, bitter word, Frederick."

He looks into my eyes with perfect longing, surrender, and patience, as if we had eternity to stand together within Polya Tsvetov's safety. His sacrificial love for Olaf and me, and his faith in us, draws the town's name to my lips.

"Matewan," I say aloud, and the bittersweet word shakes me. I find myself standing before the door of Hunt's Feed & Seed, the building Frederick appointed to perpetuate his work. The only wood building to survive Matewan's fire of 1910. What other community would have embraced my son and me in this ugly building and sooty town?

The door to Hunt's Feed & Seed jingle opens to Henry's broad shoulders and smile.

"Grandmother!" he says and closes the door behind him. "I hoped you'd show up early."

His blue eyes and dark, graying hair, his kiss upon my cheek, all speak of how and why Olaf and I survived without Frederick. Where my voice found an audience. "I thought you would be busy preparing for your meeting with Olaf tonight."

"I was, but Matthew called me to the office to help him iron out a few things. I saw you standin' out here and wanted to tell you how lovely you look tonight. Is that a new coat from Saul Brown's?"

"*Da.*"

"Well, I might hang around long enough for the fashion show I'm expectin' in this purdy weather. There's a lot of buzz around town about tonight's meetin' and the new window displays."

Henry looks to my platter and licks his lips. He nods to the windows, both furnished and arranged with new, identical plant material. "What do you think of Maggie and Nattie's designs? They said they asked you for ideas."

We step closer to better view details in the display to the right. Henry's greenhouse zinnias border the four sides of the display platform. "Yes, a crisp, confident, and colorful fence," I say at first sight. "There's nothing more bright and cheerful in and around Matewan than your zinnias. Perfect for September's Flower of the Month."

"What do you think of the flowering chrysanthemums and garden gloves and trowels on the ladder's steps?" Henry asks, the typical proud father.

"Very clever to utilize the vertical space to draw the eye upward to the redbud. Well done."

Henry's mouth slides into his crooked grin. "Annie's beloved *Cercis Canadensis*, ready for fall plantin'."

Yes, Henry has also survived without the love of his life. No. Henry thrives. And truly, Olaf and I thrive. "The redbud tree returns another September," I say.

"We can count on Annie's tribute to Darlin'. What do you think of the bird's foot violets, columbine, and larkspur hilled around the redbud's root ball?"

I tap my fingertips on my chin in absolute joy and examine the tree from top to bottom. "Margaret and Gertie's favorites."

"Uh-huh," Henry says. "Offspring from the runoff on Annie's Hill."

"Are those Christmas lights strung around the redbud's branches and trunk?"

"Yep. The girls' idea. The cords are attached to a timer. Since Nattie and Michael live above the store now, she wanted to light up the windows at night. She thinks it makes the place more cheerful and likes the light upon the porch."

"I will take notice tonight."

"And look at those herbariums," Henry says, pointing to both windows. At midpoint and front stands the Herbarium of the Month, labeled and open upon an easel—one herbarium in each window to sustain the twin effect of the two large, glass windows.

"Mr. Smith and Rosemary Cline created two entirely different styles," I observe.

Henry nods his head. "Garden Club never fails to hit the nail on the head with its choice for herbarium of the month."

"And you made the easels."

"Easy as spittin' compared to heavy construction."

I laugh. "Maggie's idea to introduce passersby to Garden Club's collection is proving fruitful. The group reviewed six new applications for membership last month."

"That's what Matthew said. And sales for herbarium supplies are up twenty percent. Maggie loves thumbin' through catalogues and orderin' paper samples, stencils, cords, watercolor supplies, and new, improved glues. Says it helps her relax."

This mild night, I am drawn again to the bullet holes in the building's façade. I recall the day Olaf and I first stopped before the store, months after the Massacre. I touch the gouges once again, now freshly painted in memory to those who fell. "You were a boy when the showdown happened?"

"Uh-huh, almost six years old. We hadn't lived in Blackberry City too long. Pa was away bingin' again, so Mommy and I hid under the bed when the detectives drove through and shot up Miss Daisy's house and others. Like ever'body else, Mommy and Miss

Daisy won't talk about it, so that's all I know." Henry scans the building. "Say, do you like the old girl's facelift?"

"*Da*. I'm particularly fond of the honey color. Olaf said Matthew suggested it."

"He did. And I wish I would've kept record of the compliments we've received since. Just as many men as women. Can you believe it?"

"If you say it, Henry, it is safe to believe."

He wraps his free arm around my waist and kisses me on the cheek again.

"That's what Annie would say."

I return Henry's kiss. "I am glad Otto painted the lion's share, as you say."

"Sure lifted a load off'a me and Matthew. With him managing the store and deliveries, I'm thankful Otto showed up in Matewan when he did, raring to go and make up for lost time. We couldn't keep up with the expandin' business demands and trainin' new labor."

"*Da*. Otto and the young men he trained increased enrollment at the college and sales."

"You know somethin', Grandmother?"

I cling to this merciful moment as Henry holds my waist. "Yes, Grandson?"

"Nothin' makes me happier than hearin' Olaf tell of the moment he laid eyes on Otto the night of Freddie's eleventh birthday party."

In similar joyful reverie, I look to the windows on the second floor where Olaf and I stood for the first time on September 5, 1920. Thirty-nine years ago.

This night, I see, hear, touch, smell, and taste an abundance of things in Matewan Richardson Wright could envy. I wish Annie knew it was Frederick who chose Matewan for our home. She left us before she could inherit the helm and history of Hunt's Feed & Seed with Henry.

My mouth parts at the building's transformation. As Polya Tsvetov was beautiful because her people were beautiful, Hunt's Feed & Seed is beautiful because Matewan's people are beautiful.

Under the roof's peak, an exterior light shines in the dusk upon "Phillips Flower Shop," the latest addition to this expanding, family business. I look to Henry, who waits for my response.

"Is that your buttons I hear burstin' under that beautiful coat, Grandmother?"

I laugh and lean my head on Henry's shoulder.

"So, what do you think of Nattie's newborn enterprise as the bride of Michael Phillips, both proud graduates of Matewan College of Agriculture, Botany, and Horticulture?"

"Not too shabby," I say, testing the appropriate use of Matthew's and Eddie's latest expression.

Henry throws his head back and laughs in approval. "Just like their mother before them, nothin' Nattie and Maggie do is half-baked. After she sold her share of the bakery to Maggie, Nattie put half the money in the bank and invested the other into developing her dream of a flower shop."

"I see Stephen and Freddie leaving the elevator with arms full of deliveries every business day from open to close."

"That's right, givin' the seed store stiff competition! Nattie's throwin' together arrangements for every occasion you can imagine along these here creeks. She's 'strikin' the iron while it's hot,' as Olaf said. There are no guarantees in today's business world—unless you're a Nenni or a Brown."

"Even *their* business has a lifespan, Grandson."

He looks up to the Phillips Flower Shop sign with his serious brow. "Thanks for remindin' me. Life's flyin' by so fast I cain't catch its tail. I was so proud when Nattie handed Olaf and me her business proposal."

"*Da.* You and Olaf stood at the end of the glass-domed counter like trees planted by still waters."

"Well, that sounds downright biblical!"

I smile.

"Like I said, I cain't think of a better use for the store's second floor than Nattie's home and flower shop. Lord knows there's all the space she'll ever need up there. Olaf hired Otto and Corny Priest to install the commercial lift."

Little does Nattie know what hardship, sadness, and joy resided within the walls of that upper room. What would I have done without John Nennie, Ray, Daisy, Henry? Beethoven, Bach, Tchaikovsky, Rachmaninoff? Garden Club? They all saved me from despair while traversing that treacherous stairwell until Henry installed the windows.

"Grandmother," Henry whispers.

"*Da?*" I whisper.

"I need to tell you somethin' right now while I have the chance." I touch Henry's arm. "What is it, Grandson?"

He looks up to the windows. "In the mornin', while I filled delivery bags as a boy, sometimes I heard you singing 'Ode to Joy.' I heard you cry."

I blush. "I did not know and am glad you speak this now."

"I wanted to help you but didn't know how."

"You did help me."

"I did?"

"*Da.* You grafted your heart to Olaf's heart. To mine. To our work of good husbandry. You helped us to graft our hearts to you, Gertie, Annie, and Matewan. You became Olaf's son and my grandson. Annie became family. Gertie became Olaf's wife and my daughter-in-law. You and Annie gave me five great-grandchildren."

Henry pulls his handkerchief from his pocket and dries his eyes. "Grandmother?"

"*Da.*"

"Do you still cry for Grandfather Frederick?"

"Whenever I am alone. Do you still cry for Annie?"

"Whenever I am alone."

We inhale Appalachia's autumn air. Praise be to God! Those three, grimy upper windows still shine with prosperity.

"Grandmother," Henry says.

"*Da?*"

"Petrov was right. We are never alone. Great-grandfather Frederick and Annie *are* always with us."

I nod, for words fail me.

"And I think Olaf's right."

"Oh?" I manage to mutter.

"You should write the story of your escape from Russia, and

how you grew Hunt's Feed & Seed and the college. Olaf says, 'We owe it to John and Antillo Nenni, and to Matewan Garden Club.'"

"As I say to Olaf, I shall leave our story to Mr. Smith and Maggie, our writers in residence."

Henry smiles. "Maggie's readin' my Berea letters to Annie again."

"Oh?"

"Last month, I walked into Annie's office that Maggie's claimed as her own. She was playin' the phonograph I bought Annie for our first Christmas as man and wife. And guess what Maggie was playin', Grandmother?"

"I could not guess."

"Beethoven's *Ode to Joy*. She opened two composition books she's filled with notes, lines, and arrows pointin' here and there on almost ever' page. Few days later, I poked my head into the room. Maggie was peckin' away on Annie's old typewriter, books in stacks ever'where. I asked what she was up to. She smiled like Annie and said, 'Writing a steamy, sexy, love story.'" Henry waits for my reply.

"Oh?" I do not break Maggie's confidence and speak of her visit concerning this.

"Well," Henry says, "what I've read so far is about a girl who moves from Columbus to Appalachia and falls in love with its Appalachian, Italian, and Russian people and the land itself."

"That's what Gertie said of what she has read. And Maggie's making good progress since Otto took management of the bakery."

Henry's eyes gleam. "Otto said your Cook taught him how to bake pastries and manage a kitchen."

Memory stings yet brings peace. "Yes. Cook instructed many of our men to bake, and for farmers who did not know how to forage prairies and forests, she taught them to identify wild edible herbs and roots."

"Like Mommy and Olaf taught me, there's no reason to go hungry in these mountains. Cook's lessons and Olaf's business plan built the bakery's success. And Maggie's thrilled. When she suggested I learn to bake and cook some of my favorite dishes, I asked if she was plannin' on leavin' me."

"And her reply?"

"'Daddy, I'm never leaving.' Then I asked what about when she marries and has my grandbabies. She said, 'We'll live together in this big house. Like Mother, I'm never leaving these hills and our people. Or Darlin'.'"

"Good evenin'," says a voice we know and love. We face Daisy's green eyes.

"Good evening," I say.

"How y'all doin', Miss Daisy?" Henry asks.

"Well, I saw y'all lookin' up at Nattie and Michael's sign and thought you might be thinkin' about their new business."

"That and Maggie's bakery and the book she's workin' on," Henry says.

Daisy steps back and surveys the building top to bottom, side to side. "And just look at this buildin'! I never see'd such fine winder displays. Mind, no offense to your lovely, shellacked gourds and bittersweet vines, Natalia."

"No offense taken, Daisy. I used what we had."

"And look what you've done to this old place! Crabapple trees. Forsythia. Mountain laurel and rhododendron."

I follow Daisy's pointed finger. "And do not forget your magnolias, Daisy."

Punctual as always, Margaret joins us on the porch holding a large platter of baklava. Her bright, brown eyes smile under the brim of a new hat the color of her sheath—incredibly, the crystalline blue of Norway's fjords, Astrid's favorite color.

"Good evening, ladies and gentleman," Margaret says.

"Hello Mrs. Dill. I'll take Grandmother's küchen and notebook inside and be right back for your baklava, if you'd like."

"Yes, thank you, Henry."

I notice the blue of Margaret's ensemble is also very close to the hue of Gertie's wedding dress. What did Saul Brown name the blue . . . ? "Good evening, Margaret. That shade of blue becomes you."

"Thank you."

"And thank you for the baklava." I will be the first to take my share.

"My pleasure," Margaret says.

Daisy nods. "Good evenin', Margaret. Uh-huh, that blue is you, all right. We're admirin' your granddaughters' work."

"They surprise me every month with new ideas," Margaret replies playfully. "I think this is the seventh month now. They won't reveal their details because they say it 'influences the effects of their planning and execution.'"

Daisy and I smile and step aside the left window. Henry returns for Margaret's baklava as her hat turns down to Rosemary's herbarium splayed open to *Delphinium,* common name larkspur on the right, and *Alchemilla mollis,* common name Lady's mantle, on the left.

"Lovely balance. Two of my favorite flowers. . . It is amazing the colors Henry and Daisy force to grow in a greenhouse. The blue larkspur reminds me of Gertie's wedding dress," Margaret says.

Yes, larkspur! Indeed, blue leads the evening and season. Margaret's eyes travel down to the border of zinnias framing bird's foot violet beneath the britches of orange columbine and tall, slender stems abundant with dark blue larkspur blossoms. Then her hat turns up to the redbud branches tipped in fuchsia. We stand around Margaret in silence.

Henry reappears long enough for one last kiss on my cheek. "Gotta get back to put my papers in order before Olaf arrives. Some reports say there's no danger in usin' railroad ties for greenhouse and beehive foundations. Others say the creosote chemical is harmful. Regardless, we're thinkin' why not buy what land left in O'Brien Park and build the greenhouses and beehives near the college? Like Dr. Dill said a long time ago, if we don't buy it, someone else will. I'll be kickin' myself if that happens."

I steal another glance of Henry's handsome, strong face.

"Your notebook's on the lectern. Freddie's settin' up like a real pro," Henry says.

"Thank you," I say.

"Been wantin' to do this for ole time's sake, Grandmother. Glad Matthew called me down."

Eddie Nenni drives by, honks and waves. We wave. "Another Nenni following his father's footsteps," Henry says. "Shor am glad John left Italy, landed here, and found Hazel in Williamson. They've been helpin' Matewan prosper for three generations."

I nod. Henry turns and enters the store to exit the back door. Gertie, Margaret, and I have noted a link between Olaf and Henry's long-term negotiations with the railroad and the graying of their hair. I, for one, agree with Henry and Olaf's interest in building greenhouses and beehives in O'Brien Park. Olaf built several greenhouse and hive foundations on Polya Tsevtov, without a single railroad tie. On occasion, even though it may be painful, we must release one vision to receive another.

————— ⇒•⇒ —————

Lily parks her yellow Ford Crestliner Tudor before the store. The women call it Lily's canary. She steps up beside Margaret. "Would you look at those zinnias and redbuds? A tribute to Annie if ever I saw it." She turns to me. "Mrs. Mekinov, has Henry seen these windows yet?"

"You just missed him. He is occupied with preparations for Washington D.C."

"When they leavin'?" Lily asks.

"Next Tuesday."

"Well, it's the railroad's loss if they won't co-operate with Olaf and Henry," Lily says. "Ever'body knows there's no better location for y'all's greenhouses and beehives than O'Brien Park. I cain't wait to get my fingernails dirty in one of those greenhouses! Now, bees— that's another story."

Daisy sighs. "Well, I sure wasn't much help with the negotiations. It's been so long since I've had anything to do with the railroad."

Daisy Deboard. Matewan's mystery. She cares for everybody's sorrows, yet never speaks of her own—the loss of her young husband in a railroad accident.

"Have you heard from Ray's lovebird?" Daisy asks Lily, changing the subject.

"No, and I'm not expectin' to. After hearin' about Bartram Gardens and Silver Mine in Garden Club, Violet's so excited about visitin' the places, she's beside herself. Ever'one at the Williamson Library's askin' about her and Ray. I shor' do miss my sidekick. I'm still gettin' over the shock of those two old independent spirits decidin' to tie the knot."

Rosemary joins Margaret before the window at the left, in quiet adoration of the twins' arrangement. "Beautiful composition of the natural and handmade," Rosemary says to Margaret.

Nellie Nenni, Lucy, Sue Ann, and the other Garden Club veterans, save Gertie, gather around Lily and inquire about Ray and Violet's honeymoon touring The Greenbrier and then New England.

"Their weddin' and visit to Philadelphia's Liberty Bell are the talk of Tug Fork, Williamson, and Pikeville. Who doesn't know Ray?" Lily says.

Three newer, young members—Sissy Fowler, Jeanette Priest, and Kathi Chambers—stand before the window displaying Mr. Smith's herbarium.

I observe this spontaneous prelude to our monthly meeting with utmost joy. Another generation of botanists rises from Russia's ashes and Appalachia's coal dust.

The light above the new Phillips Flower Shop sign catches Lily's eye. She places both hands on willowy hips, her red manicure fanned upon a straight, navy-blue skirt. Her pose is reminiscent of Camille's in the seed store twenty-four years ago. I shudder. Although Mrs. Rouge phoned Margaret three years past with the tragic news, the force of Camille's ceaseless threats and her death still flushes through me. I smile. These ladies, my extended family, miss nothing.

"Watch out West Virginia and Kentucky, here come Michael and Nattie Phillips! You are about to be beautified inside and out!" Lily decrees.

Daisy leans toward Rosemary, Margaret, and me. "Have you ever see'd another place so loved?" she whispers.

Her words echo the sentiment Frederick whispered when we stood before Polya Tsvetov's beloved staff, hours before we abandoned our land.

"No," I say.

"No, I have not," Margaret says.

Rosemary, the quiet soul, takes Daisy's hand. "No, Daisy, I have not. And thank you for asking."

"Where's Gertie? Has she seen the twins' windows?" Daisy asks.

"She is with Olaf on deliveries and will return for the meeting," I say.

"And look at Punkin's herbarium," Daisy says. "How clever to use the flar'er of the Osage orange for his herbarium. Where on earth did he find it?"

"Richardson mailed the specimen from Connecticut. *Maclura pomifera* grows abundantly in Silver Mine," I say.

Lily sings, "It pays to have connections in Connecticut."

We laugh as Mr. Smith rounds the south side of the store.

"We're admirin' your Osage orange blossom," Daisy says.

Mr. Smith observes his book and grins. "Couldn't have done it without Olaf and Richardson's help."

"All of us needed help," Lucy says.

It is five-forty. "Excuse me, please. I must brew our coffee. We begin promptly at six o'clock."

I grasp the door handle. *Open*, memory speaks from September 5, 1920. I feel my hand upon Olaf's. The bell jingles and Freddie runs to me. "Your coffee pots are ready. Daddy put your pastries where you always do. Sure was surprised to see him. Matthew's still in the office callin' in orders."

"Thank you, grandson."

"I'm almost finished settin' up. You said twenty-five chairs with stapled materials at each chair, right?"

"*Da.*"

"Cain't keep Great-grandfather Sergei waitin'!"

"No, you cannot." I watch my growing grandson return to his task. The bell rings. Margaret walks up to me and leans closely, her cheeks blushed with joy, and whispers under her hat's brim. "May I ask a favor?"

"*Da.*"

"Tonight, in the privacy of your home, please tell Gertie I received a letter today from my brother. She will understand my meaning and may share it with you."

Margaret opens the door and walks into our flock of gardeners before I can reply. I turn as Freddie places the last two materials on one of three tables and hang my coat on the hook outside the office door, where I hear Matthew's melodic voice inside. He also thrives on his work.

"Matthew's tryin' to finish so's he won't bother y'all," Freddie says, opens the storage room door, and hits the switch like Olaf, Henry, and Matthew do.

I walk to my great-grandson's side and place a hand upon his strong, lean shoulder. My eyes widen as I scan two rows of bags, counting thirty. "What an abundance of merchandise, young man! No wonder Matthew is still calling in orders."

The boy takes my praise in stride. "Stephen helped."

"You two make a good team. Where is Stephen?"

"Makin' deliveries up Red Jacket."

"With his truck?"

"Uh-huh. Matthew needs his truck after work to check on somethin' for Daddy since he's too busy with gettin' ready for Washington D.C. And Grandfather Olaf and Granny took Beast to Freeburn with a truckload. Granny said she'd be back for Garden Club."

"Thank you. That is a lot to remember."

"Daddy says it's a good thing I have a sharp mem'ry 'cause his is wearin' out like Great-grandfather Sergei's."

"Oh?"

"That's why I like to play chess with 'em. He says it keeps his mind nimble. Is that why Dr. Dill comes to play chess with Great-grandfather Sergei?"

"They have been playing chess together for five years, since Sergei moved here from New York."

"I remember that. It was Stephen's eleventh birthday. I never saw so many people in Blackberry City in my life. I felt sorry for Miss Daisy when she ran out of chocolate cake. She like to cried."

I remember the embarrassing incident and cast a glance to the clock above the office door. "Have you completed the deliveries for today?"

"Yep."

We turn to the ringing bell. Gertie walks in.

"Granny," Freddie says, "I forgot my lessons at the house, and you know Daddy's rule about playin' chess on Wednesday night. So, I'm goin' to take my shortcut home to do my lessons and eat supper. Stephen'll drive me to your house for chess and pick me up."

"Well, why don't you go on over next-door and have wieners and kraut and küchen with Grandfather Olaf and Sergei? Olaf'll drive you and your bike home to do your lesson and play chess with him, your daddy, and Otto."

"What about Charles?" Freddie asks. "He said his mommy might bring him when she comes to the meetin' so's he can play chess."

"We'll have to let Charles and his mommy figure that out, won't we?"

Freddie shrugs his shoulders. "I reckon."

He centers the lectern before the tables. I see Olaf's painting on the shelf inside and feel a rush of gratitude for my son.

Freddie turns to Gertie and me with a gleam in his blue eyes. "He is your replica, Gertie." We watch Freddie exit the storage room door. I am glad Gertie directed him to our house. He should not be riding his bike to Blackberry City after nightfall.

Gertie shakes her head. "The boy avoids Garden Club tellin' him how much he's grown."

"That is why I followed Father's footsteps in the sometimes-solitary science of botany. Thankfully, height is an asset in opera."

"I always look forward to you reading us your letters from Astrid, especially when she writes about the places where you sang together," Gertie says.

I smile, and do not tell Gertie some days I live for those letters.

Gertie and I observe the gathering outside on the porch. I consult my watch. 5:55. The September air is too sumptuous to surrender a minute to the scent of feed sacks and fertilizer. We watch the women gather around Mr. Smith—Matewan's risen star—a voice of humor, purpose, and history. A man who attempts to shed his ridiculous nickname. However, Appalachians do not let these "pet" names die easily.

Gertie and I set up the cream, sugar, cups, plates, and napkins aside the pastries.

With the scent of strong coffee wafting through the store, I pray God's grace upon my lecture for the evening. My flower fades, and there is much to share with these people who love botany and Appalachia; in a quiet second, we hear Matthew's muffled laugh. We smile to one another.

———— ✠ ————

The bell jingles. Two by two, the ladies and Mr. Smith pour their coffee and fill their plates. I take my baklava and cup, observe the group select their pastries as Jeanette Priest, the blue-eyed girl from Red Jacket, stands before me, one of our new members.

"Thank you for invitin' Charles to play chess tonight with Freddie, Dr. Dill, and Mr. Mekinov. I'm sorry, but my boy didn't finish his lessons in time, so he's home with his daddy, broodin'."

"You are most welcome, Jeanette. I think my great-grandson might be brooding with his daddy tonight, too."

I, Natalia Aaberg Semenov, walk to the lectern and stand behind it as the members seat themselves. No one seems to notice a difference in the Butterküchen they consume. As is their habit, they anticipate my every move, the newer members more so. By design, I have no new members to introduce tonight. I take my notes from my notebook—my cue for Daisy, our President, to call our meeting to order.

As the clock above the office door is to my back, I remove my Swiss Welta watch from my wrist and place it beside my notebook. While Daisy conducts attendance, I enjoy her humorous pronunciation of names uncommon to her Appalachian ear and tongue. I think of Gertie and Olaf and their playfulness with one another's articulations, and with mine. A household would be dull without differences and idiosyncrasies. Predictably, Nattie and Maggie slip through the open storage room door five minutes after six. Daisy calls their names.

"Present," they reply in unison.

They find their reserved seats nearest the storage room door and throw me a kiss with Annie's sparkle in their brown eyes. How perfectly inherited. Matthew, Stephen, and Freddie's eyes glint Henry's blue. I sip my coffee to steady my heart, for my cup runneth over. Frederick's work continues to unfold before us.

Yes, we have lost much. Yes, our loving Lord returns more than a double portion.

John Nenni befriended Frederick and repaired his hiking boots while Frederick was wayfaring along Mate Creek. The tree of John's kindness shelters us. The gospel of Jesus Christ cannot be destroyed.

I hear the office door open and close. All eyes before me follow Matthew's presence to my side. He kisses my forehead and flashes his easy smile to the members gathered around three tables Freddie shaped like the letter U. Several of the younger women, including one married, all but swoon.

At age twenty-three, Matthew is one of many eligible bachelors in Matewan. And five young eligible bachelorettes from Tug Fork and the city of Williamson sit before me.

However, three of these infatuated faces will disappear within three months, because they have not successfully impaled Matthew with a marriage proposal. Not to worry. New membership applicants now stand at eleven. Three new members wait for induction next month, one under twenty-five years old.

Matthew. Spice of my life.

The ladies' eyes follow Matthew as he hugs his sisters and closes the storage room door. At the click of the latch, the women turn to me. Tonight, it is Sissy Fowler who blushes with desire. Unwed, thankfully. This is her sixth meeting, so perhaps she may be a "sticker," as Matthew says.

I constrain a smile. If I stand behind this lectern long enough, I will witness similar behavior in response to Stephen's and Freddie's blue eyes.

What marvelous amusement!

Mr. Smith, master of observation, writes in his notebook. Everything is grist for his mill. My Frederick would have found Mr. Smith most engaging, although he would not have borne Mr. Smith's nickname. How "Punkin'," at his age, does not interfere with his professional success is beyond my understanding. Regardless, I pray for a man with Mr. Smith's characteristics for Maggie's mate. I must admit the endearment given him suits his humble personality.

Mr. Smith also possesses a brilliant, creative mind, one that obviously does not depend upon marriage to fulfill his life with purpose and happiness. Yet, I could be reading him entirely wrong. I miss the mark on occasion.

Every notebook lies open with a No. 2 pencil hovering over a blank page. Both notebook and pencil bear the green stamp *Matewan Garden Club*. Matthew's idea.

I sip my coffee again, forget my great-grandsons, and remember Russia.

Russian sage, specifically. *Perovskia atriplicifolia*. And lavender. *Lavandula angustifolia*.

I open my notebook and there is my beloved Norwegian script. My mother's native tongue. French and Russian, my second and third language concurrently, as Father learned from his French mother and Russian father. English my fourth. What delight, wayfaring with English and American botanists and speaking their often-crude vocabulary! Yet, I will never forgive the English alphabet for forcing the impossible W upon my Norwegian tongue.

Although I love Frederick and Polya Tsvetov with all my heart, and I am thankful the Russian alphabet is void of the W, I will never make friends with Russia's harsh Slavic tones.

"Natalia, it is a small price to pay for such a remarkable man," Father would say of Frederick. How we loved to stand and talk amidst our blooming field of *Lavandula angustifolia* and *Lavandula X intermedia* in a gentle breeze!

I hope the members before me have read the materials I mailed them three weeks ago. They may be entirely lost and wearied otherwise, with the additional pages my grandson distributed.

"No matter," Olaf said when I expressed my concern this morning over kasha and biscuits. "You have your veterans, the heart of Matewan Garden Club."

They wait before me, all but Violet. Next month, for our October meeting, she will speak to these ladies and Mr. Smith of her discoveries and adventures within Bartram Gardens and Richardson's Silver Mine.

"Tonight," I say, and sweep my eyes left to right. Mr. Smith and Lily exchange a subtle smile across the two facing tables. I control a flush of joy and hope I missed the mark again. They make a remarkable match.

"In this fall season, according to your materials," I continue, "we discuss the differences and similarities between Russian sage and lavender. In botanical terms, *Perovskia atriplicifolia* and *Lavandula angustifolia*, respectively."

I expect some spontaneous expressions of angst toward Appalachia's humidity and acidic soil, two main opponents to growing healthy lavender in our mountainous climate. To my surprise, no one speaks or raises a hand. All eyes and pencils wait. All plates are empty, save Mr. Smith's nibbled küchen. For some reason, he never plates Margaret's baklava.

"By means of introduction, let us clarify which botanical characteristics *Perovskia atriplicifolia* and *Lavandula angustifolia* share. Who would like to begin with the first likeness listed in your materials?"

"I'd be happy to," says Lucy, Dr. Dill's assistant. "To supplement your excellent materials, Lily and Violet found two wonderful books with information about both plants."

I nod in anticipation. Lucy's consistent participation in our group indicates she reads my materials and they have whetted her appetite for more knowledge.

"Well," Lucy says, "they're both of the *Labiatae*—also known as *Lamiaceae* family. Pardon my Latin, Mrs. Mekinov."

We all smile. "Remember our agreement. You forgive my English. I forgive your Latin. And what is the common name for the *Labiatae* or *Lamiaceae* family?"

"Mint."

"Thank you, Lucy."

"Welcome. I have a question, Mrs. Mekinov."

Every successful group needs what Americans call "the ice breaker," and Lucy often obliges, as Appalachians say. "Yes."

"Since I began studyin' with y'all in Garden Club and at the college, it seems like scientists and horticultural societies like to change the botanical family of flar'ers. For instance, the *Labiatae* family later became known at the *Lamiaceae* family. Why's that? Isn't that akin to changin' my family name?" Lucy asks.

I suppress a smile and address the membership. "Who would like to answer Lucy's question?"

Daisy does not dither. "I would."

Gertie and I glance to one another. On several occasions within, and outside, our meetings, Daisy has enjoyed discussing her harmless and generally correct hypothesis about the subject. The woman who propagated magnolia trees and planted them along the road from Annie and Henry's lookout on the outskirts of Williamson, West Virginia, to Phelps, Kentucky, learned some significant lessons about human behavior amongst Appalachia's horticultural, commercial, and governmental authorities.

"First off, when it comes to plant cultivation, it ain't as simple as human reproduction. At least in this time of human history, far as I know, people ain't cultivatin' and harvestin' babies, and Heaven help us when somebody decides to and makes money off'n it."

Jeannette and the younger women seem shocked. Daisy is not deterred.

"Botanists who devote their lives to creatin' and classifyin' new cultivars sometimes get a little full of themselves with what ends up bloomin' in their pots. Botanists like to name new plants after the feller who created the cultivar or another botanist who wrote a book about growin' fruit trees, like William Forsyth. That purdy forsythia shrub outside the door was named in his honor, and he had nothin' to do with the shrub."

Mr. Smith writes something down, but his eyes stay on Daisy.

Daisy presses onward. "There can be a lot of money in the hardiness and popularity of a new tree, shrub, and flar'er. Ever' since explorers robbed pyramids in Egypt lookin' for a plant's oil that promised to grant eternal beauty and life, people've been stealin' plants for medicine like they do *sang* in these mountains."

Daisy takes a breath. "Punkin'."

He stops his pencil. "Yes?"

"If you haven't already, get your hands on Richardson Wright's *The Story of Gardening* and read it cover to cover. Hit's right over there with Richardson's other books under the glass dome. Sometimes the readin' is dry as chewin' on a cotton ball, but there ain't no more trustworthy authority on the subject that I know of, other than Natalia and Olaf."

Mr. Smith nods and writes. "Thank you, Miss Daisy. That's very helpful."

She continues. "Back to answering your question, Lucy. Some horticultural societies feel like they have to leave some kind of legacy to the botanical world, and one of those ways is to work on changin' the family of the blackberry lily from Liliaceae to the Iridaceae family. It'll take decades of scientific research to prove the Blackberry lily is an iris, but they'll do it and change the name someday."

Jeanette raises her hand.

"Yes," I say.

"How can they get away with changing a lily to an iris? I learned in Botany 100 that botanical societies have rules about such important things," Jeanette says.

Daisy looks to me. I nod her forward.

"Well, they bend the rules as scientists and botanists learn more about the structure, shape, and number of plant parts through molecular discoveries. For instance, since they see the spike of the blackberry lily is more like an iris, and the root is more like a rhizome, they keep workin' on findin' more evidence to change the family name. In other words, the nomenclature, as botanists say."

Daisy led our discussion to my next point. "Thank you, Daisy. Now, who would like to elaborate on the structure, shape, and number of plant parts of the *Labiatae* family, also the *Lamiaceae* family?"

Kathi Chambers, who seems to be one of our new "stickers," and the librarian of our local bookmobile at Warm Hollow, lifts a hand. She's a quiet, pleasant woman who associates with Lucy, Lily, and Violet, before and after our meetings. If memory serves me correctly, she completed Botany 100.

"Mrs. Mekinov, no matter how hard I try, I cain't pronounce Latin names. And I don't want to embarrass myself. So do you mind if for now I say 'mint family' instead of the botanical names?"

"Please do."

"Well, what strikes me most about the mint family is the square stem. I didn't notice it until I read your materials. Then I cut some of my Kentucky Colonel mint that's sproutin' real purdy. My Russian sage is about bloomed out. And since lavender isn't native to our mountains, I've never handled it. I heard The Greenbrier grows lavender plants around their golf course. Is that true?"

I wish Olaf and Henry were here. "Yes, Kathi. To grace visitors with its fragrant, relaxing oil, The Greenbrier's groundskeeper planted a border of lavender in full sun along one edge of the golf course. For the plants to thrive, his staff dug a trench and amended the soil with gravel and sand before they planted."

Kathi brightens. "That's because lavender's a Mediterranean plant and needs full sun and well-drained soil. And I like what you said in your materials about lavender not likin' wet feet. I'll remember that because I don't either."

The members agree congenially.

"Thank you. Any other observations you would like to share?"

"Well, I've seen pictures of lavender fields in long rows. The stems are straight with one bloom on the end, unlike Russian sage. Have you ever seen lavender bloomin' at The Greenbrier?"

"Yes. However, according to the groundskeeper's plan, I scented the beautiful, blue border before I saw it." I keep to my notes and do not yet mention Polya Tsvetov's lavender labyrinth or field. I will ride this pleasant wave to its end. "Do you have further physical characteristics of the mint family to cite?"

Kathi nods. "I've also noticed many plants of the mint family have blue flowers. I was surprised to read you can eat the flowers of Russian sage and lavender."

Dear Kathi, does she read my mind? "Yes, many countries along the Mediterranean—France and Bulgaria for example—dry lavender flowers for culinary use, and extract oil from fresh lavender for perfumery and medicinal purposes."

Maggie smiles. She is determined to build a "Mediterranean oasis" on the Blankenship homestead to grow enough lavender to harvest for culinary uses and fragrance. But I must "keep it under wraps for now."

"However," I say, "as the French and English have used the herb in soap making for centuries, some people associate lavender's scent with soap. In reference to your materials at the top of page two, who would like to comment on the Latin root of lavender?"

Maggie signals me.

"Yes."

She looks across the room to Margaret and Gertie, who sit beside each other. Maggie's and Nattie's collaborators, the grandmothers wait in expectation. As it was with Annie, we never know what will proceed from the twins' fount of knowledge and imagination.

"First," Maggie says, "I appreciate the fact that I can pronounce *'lavare.'*"

We enjoy another round of laughter.

"Second, as you see on page three, *lavare*'s meaning 'to wash' describes the cleansing, antiseptic property of lavender oil. Third, our Celtic folklore of *Les Lavenders*, the night washerwomen who used lavender to cleanse grave clothing by moonlight, speaks of the ancient utility of the herb that grows wild on Mediterranean cliffs. Lavender must have aeration to thrive."

"Thank you, Maggie. Do you have anything else to contribute?" I ask.

"Not at the moment, but I have a family question."

I plant my feet, for Maggie's queries often lead me onto uncharted paths. Yet, I am a wayfarer at heart, and it now beats eagerly. "Yes?"

"Did your mother grow lavender?"

Frederick! Maggie opens the door to my sorrow.

"No. My Norwegian mother left this good earth after she delivered Astrid, before my third birthday. Father, of French-Russian heritage, held the trowel in our household. Father planted one hundred lavender shrubs with other culinary and medicinal herbs in a sunny labyrinth. Please find a drawing of his labyrinth on page four."

The sound of turning pages indicates my race is nearly run for this meeting. Exclamations of wonder echo in the room as each member finds their copy of Olaf's rendering of my father's labyrinth.

Nellie Nenni lifts her copy to me, her hair now as gray as mine.

"Mrs. Mekinov, did Olaf draw d'is?"

Why do I almost slip and say *da*?

"It is a black and white copy of his sketch of the original. Olaf hand-painted the colors on each of your copies."

I consult my watch. Six forty-five. All is well. There is ample time for questions and answers and more coffee and pastries. Nellie raises her hand. I nod.

"Mrs. Semenov, I remember d'is beautiful color in Positano. I was just a child."

"The Positano on the Amalfi Coast?"

Nellie holds her hands to her large breast. "You know my birthplace?"

"Yes, the hillside town where Frederick and I honeymooned during lavender season. The only harvest my father-in-law permitted us to leave in his hands during our marriage. A kind concession on our behalf."

Eyes follow as I reach below the lectern and remove Olaf's watercolor of Father's labyrinth. I hold it before them. Now, all the women hold their hands to their chest. Mr. Smith puts his left hand to his mouth.

"Is that lavender blooming in a labyrinth?" they ask in chorus.

"Yes. *Lavandula angustifolia*, Hidcote variety. You will find numerous cultivars listed in your materials, page four."

Since the night of Annie's graduation party, I've never seen Mr. Smith write so intently. He stops abruptly and lifts his pencil to me.

"Yes."

"Mrs. Semenov, may I take photos of Olaf's painting at the conclusion of the meeting?"

"Certainly."

"I've never seen such a dark blue. Darker than larkspur." Lucy says.

"Hidcote's corollas are the darkest blue of the English varieties," I say.

"Corollas?" Jeanette asks.

"Petals. You will find the plant parts identified on page five of your materials."

Jeanette blushes, for her question indicates she did not prepare for the meeting.

Members compare their copies that Olaf painted to his original watercolor, attempting to absorb their likeness and differences. I did not anticipate this artistic scrutiny.

"Now I know why our water-color prints in our herbariums are so important," Lily says.

Again, my family of gardeners humbles me with their interest and respect. Now I understand why I want to say *"da."*

The twins look across the space between the facing tables to Margaret.

"Grandmother Margaret, are the labyrinths identical?" Nattie asks.

Margaret turns her hat toward me. Rosemary sits to her right. Gertie to her left. Their eyes wait for my answer.

No. For some reason I cannot comprehend, they hunger for my answer.

I see again the tangible, unbreakable bond between these three women, one born from mutual tragedy and loss. No. Annie's death is not the bond. It is something dark and unspeakable. Yet, it dwells in the light of holiness.

As I placed my hand upon Olaf's when he needed strength to open the door of this store upon our arrival, I feel Frederick's hand upon mine. *Open*, he says.

"Yes, your copy is identical to Olaf's watercolor."

"It's beautiful," Jeanette says. "I've never heard of a labyrinth before—or seen a painting of one."

The veterans offer Jeanette a smile of understanding. They responded in awe when Richardson presented them a painting of an English boxwood labyrinth several years ago. A boxwood labyrinth, however, pales to a blooming lavender labyrinth.

I step back from the lectern and open my heart to my secret past. "My husband so adored Father's labyrinth upon his wayfaring visit with Fodor Petrov and Sergei that he photographed it. Frederick preserved the photograph in one of his five Russian botany books of which you are all familiar. In consideration of my preparation for this meeting, Olaf surprised me with the sketch and watercolor of Father's labyrinth. Does it not better illustrate the beauty of color within a blooming lavender labyrinth than a black and white photograph?"

They all offer enthusiastic assent.

I return Olaf's painting to the lectern and step back again to pace myself, as if wayfaring a steep mountain.

"The harvest from Father's lavender labyrinth fulfilled his culinary desires for thirty years, replacing the expired plants with those he propagated. However, Astrid considered lavender's flavor soapy and could not tolerate it in our pastries."

"Pastries?" Rosemary asks.

This stirs another discussion amongst the members as they examine their plates. Margaret Dill raises her eyebrows below her hat's brim and waves a hand like a ballerina. "As in, Butterküchen?"

The members look to me dumbstruck. Mr. Smith lifts his pencil to his chin, then up in inquiry.

"Yes."

"Is it lavender I taste in your küchen?"

"Yes, finely ground, and just a trace."

The members look to their plates again for a speck of evidence. Rosemary nods to me. "Yes. That exquisite taste is lavender."

Rosemary, another mystery. An exquisite mystery.

"Specifically, *Lavandula X intermedia*, a hybrid of the English and French varieties. Please raise your hand if you tasted lavender in your küchen."

All but Nattie raise their hands; she is not fond of küchen. She takes a double portion of her Grandmother Dill's baklava instead.

"Thank you," I say. "If you consider the lavender an enhancement, please raise your hand."

All but Mr. Smith respond. He lifts his pencil again.

"Yes."

"Please don't take offense, Mrs. Mekinov. I'm what the culinary crowd dubs a 'plain palate' and don't adapt well to dietary changes. I prefer your küchen without lavender and life without nuts. I eat to live, an occupational hazard, my fellows say. Always on the run to the next story."

I smile. "Perhaps that will change as you discover the benefits of growing your own herbs and using them in your cooking and baking. For instance, lavender and lemon make an excellent pair, particularly delicious in iced tea."

Gertie turns to Margaret, who returns a knowing smile. At last, Gertie knows the secret ingredient in Margaret's iced tea.

"Now," I say and proceed with our materials, "who would like to comment on the subshrub classification of *Lavandula angustifolia*?"

Amused, Margaret dips the brim of her hat.

I nod and the unruly stand falls from my combs and brushes my cheek. *Yes, Frederick, I go forth.*

Margaret begins, a glow upon her face. "Until I read your materials, I had never heard the term 'subshrub.' I couldn't find the definition in the gardening books I consulted in the library."

Unanimously, the members nod.

Margaret adds, "So thank you for your thorough materials and bibliography of books and scholarly papers discussing the subshrub."

"You are welcome. Would you please share your observations concerning subshrubs?"

The brim of Margaret's hat dips again. "Unlike perennials such as peony, lupine, and chrysanthemum, subshrubs grow in small, woody shrubs. The branches of Russian sage and lavender must be pruned in the spring to produce healthy shrubs and blooms in the summer. My Russian sage appears to be a looser shrub than the more compact, round lavender shrubs I've seen on The Greenbrier grounds."

"Thank you, Margaret." I address the membership. "Any further questions or observations about pruning lavender?"

Maggie lifts a hand, mischief in her eyes. "Did you help prune your father's lavender labyrinth?"

"Yes. When we were children, Father presented my sister Astrid and me with our own secateurs, our initials engraved on the blade of each pair so we could not claim the other's if we lost or damaged ours. We pruned in spring and in summer harvested with a hand scythe under Father's supervision. We sang *There Lives a Baker*, and *Baa Baa Little Lamb* as we wound our way through the labyrinth. For every bundle we harvested, Father baked us a dozen butter drop cookies with a trace of lavender and lemon. The size of a walnut, the cookie melted in our mouths."

"You loved your father's lavender labyrinth?" Maggie asks.

I hold onto the lectern. "As you love Darlin'."

The room falls silent. Sympathetic eyes glance to Margaret. Maggie persists. "Did your father teach you to bake pastries?"

"No. It was Cook, in Polya Tsvetov's kitchen. She lured me to her stove and counter while she cooked and baked. We sang together as I learned recipes and techniques with flour, butter, sugar, cream, and spices. Cook used lavender in many pastries and savory recipes."

"Savory?" Maggie asks. She writes in her notebook.

"Yes. In France, perhaps for centuries, families have blended dehydrated lavender with other herbs native to their region. They name the blend *Herbs de Provence*. Cook blended her own *Herbs de Provence* from those she grew in her kitchen garden."

Maggie and Nattie whisper with one another while Lily raises her red manicure.

"Yes, Lily."

"Mrs. Mekinov, are you sayin' you grew lavender in Russia?"

I choke and tear, pull my hanky from my sleeve. *You are never alone.* Fodor's promise echoes in memory.

"I'm sorry, Mrs. Mekinov," Lily says. "You don't have to talk about it if it's too hurtful."

"Thank you, Lily. You are very kind. Yes, the Semenovs grew a small field of five thousand plants on Polya Tsvetov."

The members gasp at the thought of thousands.

"The equivalent of three acres," I say. "Frederick also used Father's labyrinth design for Cook's herb garden outside her kitchen door. She and I observed the four seasons change upon the labyrinth."

Mr. Smith sits with his mouth parted. Maggie and Nattie wipe tears from their eyes with their napkins. Although they have Darlin' for a lasting lesson on the value of carrying a handkerchief, my great-granddaughters have yet to practice the discipline.

Mr. Smith leans forward as if to console me.

I open my hand in permission and rest it upon the lectern.

"Mrs. Mekinov, please pardon me for askin' this selfish question, and don't reply if I'm out of line. Was the labyrinth and your lavender field of three acres in bloom when you and Olaf left Polya Tsvetov?" Mr. Smith correctly pronounces Polya Tsvetov as *Pōl'-ē-ă S'ĕ-vă-tō* in Russian and provokes an imperceptible swoon. I plant my feet again and return to that day.

"No, Mr. Smith. My father-in-law, Olaf, and I fled September 24, 1917, along paths in blooming buckwheat, flax, sunflower, and alfalfa fields. Lavender blooms in June, July, and August, depending upon varieties of *Lavandula angustifolia* and *Lavandula X intermedia,* and climate of region."

Mr. Smith glances down to his plate before he speaks. "Mrs. Mekinov, I'm wondering how you harvested three acres of lavender, and how you used it."

Memory carries me to Polya Tsvetov's lavender fields. "As Astrid and I harvested Father's lavender, our farmhands harvested the stems with a hand scythe to the rhythm of Russian lavender songs."

Mr. Smith shakes his head in wonder. "How many harvesters did you employ?"

"As the harvest must be swift when the corollas open, thirty reapers divided the three acres to complete the harvest in one day. Our children ran harvest baskets from the field to a drying barn. Page six of your handout illustrates bundled and bound lavender stems hung on wire lines attached to the inside walls of our low, lavender barn, the walls and roof constructed for aeration much like tobacco barns."

I give the members time to find page six of the papers Frederick placed on their tables. I behold their incredulous response. "For each basket the children delivered to the barn, they received one lavender lemon butter drop cookie."

Wonder washes away formality like the tide does the seashore.

Jeanette, the girl from Red Jacket with blue, inquisitive eyes, now says, "What fortunate children."

"Indeed, sometimes I hear their songs and laughter in my dreams," I say.

Jeanette lifts a hanky with an embroidered edge. "Mrs. Mekinov, on summer days, Babushka says she dreams about the children singing and laughing during harvest."

"It was my pleasure to observe one generation of basket runners grow into harvesters to beget another generation of runners. Cook and I baked thousands of lavender lemon butter drop cookies during harvests."

"How else did you use your harvest?" Lucy asks.

"What Cook did not use in her cooking and baking, we sold to bakeries and other culinary markets. We also placed small lavender pillows throughout the farmhouse and housing for our farmhands for fumigation and as an insect repellant. A tithe of our harvest went to the farm and household staff for Christmas presents."

Maggie holds up page six of her materials, "Great-grandmother, I cain't imagine a barn full of hanging lavender bundles! The fragrance must've been heavenly. And how clever to use clothesline props to support the long, heavy lines."

"*Da*," I slip at last. "The west wind carried the scent to the farmhouse and road. The second-generation Frederick Semenov fashioned the lavender poles from young birch wood."

At last, Mr. Smith drops his pencil on the table and leans back in his chair. He rakes his fingers through his hair in a manner unlike him. "I'm sorry, Mrs. Mekinov. A man should be stronger than this. But when I saw Olaf's watercolor of your father's lavender labyrinth, it quickened something tangible of what you and Olaf left behind in Russia."

As I inhale slowly, Mr. Smith waits amidst fellow members for my word to tread further. "Would you like to speak what that something tangible is, Mr. Smith?"

His countenance tenderness, he plants his elbows on the table and folds his hands. "If you are able to hear it."

I touch the face of my watch, a gift from Frederick on our first wedding anniversary, and see the gleam of a tear in Margaret's eyes. Her darkest pain touches mine. I wish Olaf were here to witness this birth of light and liberty. "I am able."

Mr. Smith reaches to touch me with breath as Michelangelo's finger of God ever reaches for Adam's.

"Mrs. Mekinov, I understand Olaf's painting is a mere representation of the real thing, and cain't bear to think of you and Olaf leaving the true, living and breathing beauty, everything you loved and owned, behind, to live the balance of your life here in Matewan."

I hold onto the lectern and permit his words to wash through me.

"Then you spoke of generations of farmhands and their children. They also lost Polya Tsvetov?"

It is as if I dream. "Yes."

"Dare I speak of this ruin of Russia as a people and country without tearing out your heart?"

I lift my fingers from the podium and grant permission.

"After all these years writing about you, Hunt's Feed & Seed, and Garden Club, I'm sorry I'm just now seeing a glimpse of what you left behind. Please forgive my ignorance of the depth of your loss. Appalachia's history may be riddled with bullets, but it's my home. I cain't imagine being forced to run away from the people and land I love to save my own life."

Mr. Smith rubs what Americans call his five o'clock shadow and places both elbows on the table. In that moment, the man's forty-some years seem to seize his countenance with a dark revelation.

"Yes, Mr. Smith?" I say, inviting him to continue.

"Mrs. Semenov, I've studied history from ancient times and write about the human predicament almost every day. And I cain't understand how a few men in Russia, or any country, can turn a nation inside out and destroy the freedom of millions of their own people. My heart breaks for you and Olaf and for John and Hazel Nenni and Nellie Nenni. And Jeanette's sweet, old babushka. I'm sorry I've never put myself in your place."

My legs shake, yet they hold. Frederick, did you foresee this moment? As if we are alone, I see only Mr. Smith's face, overcome with compassion, and regret. I partake in another fulfillment of Frederick's sacrifice. I think of Henry's words, spoken twenty-seven years ago in our upper room.

"Mr. Smith, thank you for your confession and compassion. Please, you cannot know my history if I do not reveal it to you, as I cannot know your history if you do not reveal it to me."

Mr. Smith's face blanches. "Pardon me again, Mrs. Mekinov. I've waited a long time to hear your history, and love to hear you tell it. You already know mine. An open book."

Mr. Smith recedes into a bright tunnel. "The depth of our loss? Frederick Semenov. The love of our lives. And yes, our freedom to love and live in our land. The joy of sowing and reaping. Feeding and employing the needy. The loss of our freedom to worship our God, Creator of Heaven and Earth. The loss of Russia—her soul, mind, spirit. Future." Mr. Smith draws out of me what Matewan and Tug Fork have sown within my mind, soul, and spirit.

I speak to his voice, for I no longer see Mr. Smith's face. "Olaf and I are not alone. We, with Sergei, are but three of many Russians and Germans in this region who fled Bolshevism. Consider that Jeanette's babushka is not alone. Red Jacket, home of Russian refugees and their offspring, and Little Italy, another camp settled by Italian refugees, as well as freed slaves from the South. Remember, our John Nenni, a prosperous cobbler, and his wife Hazel, an accomplished seamstress, left their mercantile behind in Positano, as did Nellie's parents.

"They left their family, sailed to America, boarded the train in New York City's Grand Central Station with thousands of fellow Italians, and at last disembarked in Matewan or Williamson. Many Italian stonemasons settled their families in Williamson, produced bricks and paved the city's streets with their hands." I bow my head, for I have no strength for another word.

I hear Mr. Smith's voice. "People seeking freedom of religion, speech, land ownership, enterprise, and self-representation—faith and ideals upon which our Founding Fathers built our Constitution of the United States."

I revive, lift my eyes to see Mr. Smith's face in a tunnel of light. "Remarkable self-government, one to guard with our lives, as our soldiers have in times past—back to the Revolutionary War."

Mr. Smith furrows his brows.

"Was not the village of Red Jacket named after a chief of the Seneca Tribe in New York? So called because the chief wore the English red jacket during the Revolutionary War?"

"Yes," he says.

"I understand that after the war, the Seneca chief ceded a portion of his tribe's land in New York to descendants of England's refugees."

Mr. Smith nods in agreement. "That is my understanding."

"Mr. Smith, are not Matewan and her surrounding mountains also inhabited by ancestors of American Natives?"

"Yes. A handful," Mr. Smith again nods.

"Is not Appalachia where Scots-Irish farmers settled when they fled England's oppression and starvation?"

He says, "Yes, I am a Scots-Irish descendant."

"And the freed slaves who settled in Red Jacket after the Civil

War; were not these people descendants of African tribes captured by their kings and chiefs who sold them into bondage?"

"Yes. That is what history records."

"Beware, Mr. Smith. Freedom to sow and reap our own food, freedom of speech and press, freedom to hunt our own food and defend our home, are fragile liberties, often spoiled by enemies within our own boundaries, or surrendered to an enemy without. If America falls to the ploys of tyranny, where do we run?"

Mr. Smith's face turns grave as he lifts his pencil toward the storage room door.

The light within the tunnel expands and fills the room. Maggie and Nattie stand with Henry who holds my yellow coat by the open storage room door. He walks to me without his smile.

I turn to Gertie who stands to my left, for how long I do not know. The lights Maggie and Nattie wound around the redbud trees within the display windows now sparkle, circling the branches. I smile in admiration of the beautiful sight.

"Grandmother," Henry says tenderly. I turn to him. He holds up my coat, and I know Sergei has left us. I slip my arms into the sleeves.

I turn to my fellow gardeners. "Excuse us, please."

Gertie loops an arm around one elbow. Henry does the other and whispers in my ear, "We will never forget what you just said."

We pass through the storage room doorway, by Freddie's tidy rows of bags, and between tall rows of merchandise. Maggie and Nattie follow behind. We step down into the night. The newborn scent of *Passiflora incarnate* bathes my face.

ACKNOWLEDGMENTS

The story of Matewan Garden Club began the night of February 21, 1949, when my father assisted my mother up the steps of Matewan Hospital and into the hands of Dr. Roy, who promptly assisted in my birth. My father returned the following day and drove my mother and me home to McCoy Bottom, along Peter Creek, Kentucky. My family's stories began even before that eventful night and have never ceased, for by birthright, Appalachian folk tell stories. As third, fourth, and fifth generation Scots-Irish-German immigrants, we're still telling stories, some with enough colorful truth to survive time.

Upon this tradition, I submitted my first essay to *The Oxford Leader* in Oxford, Michigan. Brad Kadrich, the editor, trusted me with feature stories. *Sherman Publications*, the small, family-owned newspaper, offered me freelance opportunities within Oakland and Macomb Counties. I sowed seed north to Lapeer County and proposed feature stories to Catherine Minolli, editor of Randy Jorgensen's *Tri-City Times*. To date, his paper has published over four hundred of my weekly columns.

Meanwhile, I produced my first piece of fiction and read excerpts to Leaps, my Monday night writing group. Bolstered by their encouragement, I self-published and launched *The Mantle* in July 2018. A year later, I submitted the first chapter of my second novel, *Matewan Garden Club*, to the group.

During Michigan's shutdown of 2020-2021, Leaps persevered through the development of *Matewan Garden Club*. Jack Ferguson, Mary Merlo, and Christian Belz printed, critiqued, and returned their copies of my work-in-progress.

Many thanks to Kathi Taylor-Sherrill, director of the Matewan Public Library, Stephen Fullen, Paul Phillips, and Wilson "Willo" Chafin for their time and personal stories about Matewan's varied and rich history.

ACKNOWLEDGMENTS

I am grateful to Debra Darvick, Richard Rothrock, and Maureen McGerty for their expert edits to prepare the manuscript for submission to my eventual publisher, Brandylane Publishers, Inc.

My praises to Ruth Forman for her beautiful botanical watercolor for the book cover and Linda Hodge for her intricate interior drawings. Appreciation to Alan Coffey, surveyor of Williamson, West Virginia, for providing the map of Tug Fork dated 1926. Cover to cover, the art portrays the spirit of Matewan's story.

In conclusion, I extend gratitude to Robert Pruett, President and Publisher of Brandylane Publishers, Inc., for his trust in *Matewan Garden Club*. I'm ever grateful for Jenny DeBell, my project manager. She's held my feet to the fire of historical accuracy, and zapped every last dangling modifier. I admire Jenny's devotion to good literature and her faithfulness and talent to hear and fortify the heartbeat of my story.

ABOUT THE AUTHOR

Kentucky-born Iris Lee Underwood is a Michigan-based journalist, poet, and author, past president of Detroit Working Writers, and former writer in residence at the Troy Public Library. She writes an award-winning weekly column, "Honest Living," for *Tri-City Times* (Imlay City), and her bylines have appeared in *MacGuffin, Farming Magazine, Michigan Gardener, edibleWOW, Michigan History*, and many metro Detroit and Kentucky-area newspapers. Iris has published three books: *Encouraging Words for All Seasons* (2001), *Growing Lavender and Other Poems* (2007), and *The Mantle* (2018), her first award-winning novel.

Iris enjoys advocating for wholesome husbandry and encouraging people to write their own story and leave their own legacy. She lives in north Oakland County with her husband, two cats, hens, and honeybees.